PRAISE FOR CAROL MASON

'Poignant, emotional, and breathtaking . . . In *The Shadow Between Us*, Olivia is running from something we've all feared and hope to never face. Carol Mason's effortless storytelling and exquisite writing will keep you turning the pages until the book's stunning and surprising ending. Bring tissues!'

Kerry Lonsdale, Amazon Charts and *Wall Street Journal* bestselling author

'Acutely observed, emotionally honest, utterly brilliant writing, with a shocker of a twist that took my breath away.'

Melissa Hill, bestselling author

'A beautifully written story of how we connect with each other in terrible crisis, told with wit and humanity – and one hell of a final twist. I loved it.'

Louise Candlish, author of *Sunday Times* bestseller *Our House*

'A skillful, compassionate journey into the aftereffects of trauma, *The Shadow Between Us* deftly explores what happens when we hold tight to the secrets we keep, and they hold tight to us too.'

Amy Hatvany, bestselling author

'A haunting, heartfelt exploration of guilt and hidden turmoil, of running away, of turning back to face the shadows. I loved it.'

Charity Norman, bestselling author of *See You in September*

'I read *The Shadow Between Us* in two sittings. Carol Mason has created a fast-paced novel. At its centre is a woman whose heart has been broken. She is on the run from herself. Carol takes us on an emotional journey which keeps us gripped right to the very last twist, which hit me in the solar plexus. I had not seen it coming.'

Carol Drinkwater, bestselling author and actress

'This book is a haunting exploration of the corrosive power of grief and the redemption to be found in understanding each other and ourselves.'

Caroline Bond, author of *The Second Child*

'Full of realistic emotional twists. The characters' reactions to the challenges they face are frank and unmelodramatic; there is a refreshing honesty about the numbness that comes from discovering an infidelity, and the shame that comes with perpetrating one. Equally affecting are the counterpoised sources of sadness in Jill's life. Her marriage has faltered because she and her husband can't have children and yet she must be a mother to her own parents in their old age; it's a poignant combination.'

Telegraph, UK

'A sweet, sad tale of love, loss, and the crazy way the world works to reclaim love again.'

Cosmopolitan, Australia

'What really goes on behind closed doors. Carol Mason unlocks life behind a marriage in this strong debut.'

Heat, UK

'Mason's writing is absorbing. While reading a spicy bit about Leigh's affair while taking the bus to work, I rode past my stop.'

Rebecca Wigod, *Vancouver Sun*

'This poignant novel deals with honesty, forgiveness, love and the realities of modern-day marriage.'

Notebook, Australia

'There is a fresh and vital edge to this superior debut novel. Mason has much to say about relationships. Her women have resonant characters and recognisable jobs, which give depth to their messy lives. A bittersweet narrative and ambiguous outcomes make this much grittier and more substantial than standard chick-lit fare.'

Financial Times, UK

'It's got the raw realism of someone writing about a world she knows. A grand little book for the festive fireside.'

Irish Evening Herald

little
white
secrets

OTHER TITLES BY CAROL MASON

little white secrets

CAROL MASON

LAKE UNION
PUBLISHING

Text copyright © 2020 by Carol Mason
All rights reserved.

No part of this book may be reproduced, or stored in a retrieval system, or transmitted in any form or by any means, electronic, mechanical, photocopying, recording, or otherwise, without express written permission of the publisher.

Published by Lake Union Publishing, Seattle

www.apub.com

Amazon, the Amazon logo, and Lake Union Publishing are trademarks of Amazon.com, Inc., or its affiliates.

ISBN-13: 9781542004978
ISBN-10: 1542004977

Cover design by Rose Cooper

Printed in the United States of America

For Tony, again

PROLOGUE

'Zara?' I shout, as I stare at my face in the mirror at the bottom of the stairs. 'They'll be arriving any second. Can you get yourself down here, please?'

I've put too much black liner on my lower lids. It's somehow knocked the balance of my features off, making me appear a little harrowed and hard.

'Mum?' I glance over my shoulder and see Daniel's look of horror. 'You're not seriously thinking of wearing that dress?'

As soon as my jaw drops, he says, 'Kidding!' Then he pointedly gives me the once-over. 'You know, you actually look really amazing! You should glam up more often. Green goes great with your eyes.'

'Don't sound so surprised!' We're not really a family that's prone to doling out compliments, so I wonder if this means I'm a bit over the top for a Saturday morning in West Yorkshire. But I bought this frock especially for today, so I'm wearing it come hell or high water.

Suddenly Eric appears behind me, his big, warm hand alighting on my hip. 'Someone didn't get the memo.'

I gaze at our reflections in the glass. Coincidentally, he's wearing his emerald-green polo shirt.

Daniel splutters a laugh. 'That's hilarious. You look like those sad old couples who sit on a bench in the town centre in their matching outfits, having tea and a toasted teacake.'

I turn to say 'thanks a lot!', but Eric pops a kiss on my half-open mouth, and I smell the peppermint on his breath.

'Well, one of us is going to have to change.' I dig in my make-up bag for my lipstick.

'Go on then,' Eric says. 'You've almost got time.' He nudges my elbow right as I'm applying the brick-red colour.

I stare at the blood-like slash across my cheek. Fabulous.

The journalist, Leslie, is all smiles when I open the door. 'Hiya! Ooh, that's a lovely dress!' So it's official: I really do look ridiculous. She surprises me by giving me an enormous hug, like we're old friends, which calms my nerves a little.

'What about me?' Eric throws his arms wide. 'Don't I get one?' And I can't help but think, *You're in a very good mood suddenly, aren't you?*

For a moment she gawps at me, mock-aghast. 'Well! He isn't forward, is he? Much!' Then, chuckling, she goes over to our dining table and takes off her coat, quite at home. 'This is Darren, by the way.' She indicates the young lad carrying the camera equipment. Darren pulls a grin.

Eric pumps his hand. 'Hello there, Daz. All right?'

Daz? Oh dear.

I was going to suggest we go into the sitting room but Leslie is already setting up camp at the table. I've no idea where they're going to want to photograph us, so I've made sure everywhere is neat and tidy. As Leslie coos about our beautiful Georgian home, and stares out of the patio doors at the rolling greenery of the lower Wharfe Valley beyond our fence, I spot a stray glass hiding behind a neat stack of cookbooks. It definitely wasn't there earlier. I nab it and discreetly pop it into the sink.

Zara appears at the bottom of the stairs.

'Aha!' Leslie turns and spots her. 'Zara Rossi. Sister of the superstar!'

I place an arm around my daughter's shoulders, giving her an encouraging little squeeze. 'If she gets sick of hearing this, she never lets on!' I say. Fortunately Zara smirks.

'So come on then, what's it like having a famous big brother?' Leslie asks.

Zara's ears turn red. 'It's OK.' We wait for her to say more but she just stares at her feet like she wants the ground to open up and swallow her.

'Do you play tennis as well?'

Zara barely manages to shake her head because then Daniel appears, and Leslie swiftly redirects her interest. 'Hell-ooo! Daniel! It's so fantastic to meet you! Winter Cup winner, 2018! How's it feel?' She wraps him in a hug, too.

'Good, thank you!' My son gives her one of his radiant smiles when she releases him. 'It was a terrific result for the team.'

'And not too shabby a personal one either!' Leslie seems charmed by his modesty. Daniel's easy charisma always brings out the best in people. It probably helps that he's a handsome lad – fine-featured, with big brown eyes, flawless olive skin and thick, dark hair – the image of my father in the very first military photo we have of him, when he was around the same age.

'Well, a lot of people have supported me to make this happen – my family, my teachers. It was a victory for them as much as for me.' He flicks his thatch of glossy fringe from his face, then stuffs his hands into his jeans pockets, loosely crossing his right foot in front of his left, like a model.

Leslie gives me a look that says, *Aw!* And while I hate being one of these gloating mothers, I can't help but quietly burst with pride.

Next, we all take a seat around the table. I pat the chair for Zara to sit beside me. Daniel and Eric sit opposite, and Leslie pulls her notepad from a brown suede bag. 'I thought I'd ask a few general questions first – get a bit of a feel for you as a family . . . Emily . . . why don't you start by telling me how you and this one met?' She flicks her head in the direction of Eric.

I smile at the chummy way she refers to my husband. 'Well, it was at Durham Uni,' I tell her, wishing there was some extraordinary story to share, rather than just a garden variety one. 'I was in my final year, studying English Lit, and *this one* was in his last year of Engineering. We met at a concert, much like everybody did back then.'

'She was the first girl I ever kissed.' Eric performs a little prim and proper jiggle.

Leslie beams like she's just loving this. 'Yes! I really, really believe that! So, first love for you too, was it Emily?'

'Nah!' Eric says. 'My wife's been around the block more times than a Royal Mail postie.'

'Terrific!' Leslie catches my slightly aghast face, and tries to stifle a laugh. 'Now, moving on . . . I know we chatted about this on the phone, Emily, but can you just tell me from your perspective as Daniel's mum how championship tennis has made Daniel who he is today?'

I take a big breath, relieved to be on to something else. 'Well, it's hard to know where to start.' I try to remember what I read about speaking in quotable sound bites. 'Over the years, Daniel has had to be a very single-minded, committed individual who keeps a number of balls in the air – pardon the pun. I'd say he's had to learn about balance before most kids could even spell the word. He never wanted his academic life to suffer because of his sport, so that's been a challenge. But one he's met gracefully. Plus he's still managed to keep a set of really good friends around him. I think these skills will serve him well for life.'

Leslie nods, scribbles away, then looks purposefully at Eric, a residual glimmer of humour in her eyes. 'And from a father's perspective?'

Eric glances around, looking bemused. 'Who? Me?'

There's another rumble of amusement, slightly more anaemic than before, and a part of me withers. Then he gets to his feet, stands behind Daniel and clamps his big hands on Daniel's broad shoulders. 'I certainly don't say it often enough but I could not be more proud of my son. Daniel might have been born dangerously premature but he certainly arrived in this world like he was meant to be here.'

Our son hates any mention of the prem baby thing so he sits there grimacing with an expression that says, *F$%k, Dad! Must you?*

'He took to something he liked, and he gave it his all. And he did it for the love of the sport, rather than from the competition aspect – which is always the best reason to do anything, right?' He glances at Darren, who has glazed over, then at me, for approval.

I pull a taut smile.

Then I realise that Zara is sitting rather stiffly, staring into her lap. Eric must notice too, because he says, 'And my daughter . . . I'm immensely proud of Zara as well, in ways she'll never know. Daniel's schedule – especially since he began travelling all over the country and training in Europe – has demanded a lot from us as a family. Airport runs . . .' He seems to be searching for more examples, and failing. 'It has sometimes taken us – well, mainly

Em – away from other aspects of family life . . . But Zara has tolerated it all gracefully. She has never once resented him like some little sisters would.'

'No tennis aspirations yourself, we've established? Right, Zara?' Leslie's pen is poised. 'What about other sports? Are you athletic like your brother? Any cool hobbies?'

Zara, who has acquired a noticeable amount of puppy fat these last couple of years, hardly looks like she hurls herself at sports. I glance at her sideways. The long, mousy hair, always a little lank these days from the flux of teenage hormones. Her poor ear sticking out. It's beet red now. I clasp her clammy hand under the table.

'Zara used to take dancing lessons, and she loves to cook,' I pipe up, hoping Leslie won't want details. The reality is, I've had conversations that have gone on longer than Zara ever stuck at dance lessons. Or gymnastics. Or all the other things we've encouraged her to try.

I needn't worry, though. Leslie says, 'Excellent . . . One last question, Daniel . . . What's the hardest thing about spending all this time training abroad?'

'Definitely having to do my own food shopping and laundry,' Daniel says, without missing a beat.

Everybody laughs except Zara, who mutters, 'God, this is excruciating,' under her breath. I'm glad I seem to be the only one who has heard it.

Outside – because it's a deceptively sunny day for February – there's a bit of fuss about how to arrange us. Standing on the rockery. Sitting on the rockery. The kids in front. The kids bookending us. Leslie moves us around like chess pieces as I try not to shiver too obviously. Eric makes more inane comments. Leslie chuckles. Darren clicks away.

'What do you think of this?' Darren finally shows me one or two. Aside from the fact that my dress is clearly an over-the-top disaster, and Eric's face is a little telltale red, I don't like the way Daniel has been positioned. In an attempt to have him appear more up front and centre, his right shoulder is edging Zara out, forcing her to appear like some sort of sad apparition immediately behind him. But if I draw attention to it, it's going to make Zara squirm even more than she's already squirming.

'Lovely.' I stare at this slightly slanted version of our reality. 'Just perfect.'

ONE

August 2018
Six Months Later

The knock is so quiet I barely hear it. Even Otis, our lazy lurcher, doesn't stir from his cinnamon-bun position under the dining table.

I finish putting a dish of lasagne into the oven and quickly set it at 190°. Through the textured glass pane of the front door I can see two reflections, one slightly taller than the other. Door-to-door callers are rare down here. Our street is largely obscured from the main road by trees, and there are only four houses on it anyway – the Bennings first, who can't bring themselves to speak to anyone, not even the kids, then there's ours, my friend Charlotte's, then the new guy who just moved in nearest to the common. No one really knows we are here other than locals who use the lane as a shortcut to get on to the green.

I rub my hands on a tea towel and trot down the hall, hearing the nimble tap of Otis's nails on the wood floor as he follows. When I open up, a woman and a girl are standing on the top step. Rain pelts the hoods of their matching bottle-green parkas.

'We're collecting for victims of domestic abuse,' the woman says, without any preamble or friendliness. She is carrying what looks like a church collection basket, and it's empty. In the cast of the single light above our door, her face is almost bleached of all colour, except for the glacial blue of her eyes.

It's been a depressingly dark day and is practically dusk already – odd, considering it's barely the end of August. The trees that border the common sway, their leaves rustling like a secret conversation.

'I'm sorry, I don't have any change,' I tell her. 'I just used my last to buy a lottery ticket.' Eric always has some on his desk but I don't feel like going to get it.

She fixes me with those eyes that have a slight downwards turn at the outer edges, making her look a little mournful. 'That's fine,' she says, pushing some blonde hair back off her face with the flat of her hand. 'We take notes.' Her expression has a hint of challenge to it.

Otis nudges the girl's leg and she dangles her fingertips just shy of his head, in half-hearted acknowledgement.

'I don't have any notes,' I tell her, thinking, *That's a bit cheeky!* Then again, she is collecting for a women's shelter; perhaps it's good she's pushy. 'I don't actually carry much cash on me these days. I'm sorry.'

She can't be much older than me, but there is a haggard, hard-lived quality to her face, or perhaps it's the harsh light. *You look a bit abused yourself,* I think, recognising it's probably not the kindest thought I've ever had. But there's something about the way she studies me that makes me feel a little cornered, so I find myself saying, 'Actually, I just gave money to the Salvation Army a few days ago. And my husband's company regularly donates to the United Way.'

Well, Eric's former company used to, and I haven't crossed paths with the Salvation Army since their kettle campaign last Christmas.

The girl sidles up to her mother, because, now that she's given him a smidgen of encouragement, Otis won't leave her alone.

'Bethany loves dogs,' the woman says.

At the mention of her name, this Bethany sends me a bored, vaguely insolent smile. I notice she's quite an exquisite thing. Her eyes are the same lovely colour as her mother's, only hers are a perfectly drawn almond shape, and she has flawless, fair skin with high cheekbones. She's a good head and shoulders taller than her mother too, with the raw materials of a runway model. It's a shame about the long dyed-black hair, though. It makes her look hard. I don't think she can be much older than Zara – perhaps fifteen? – but she seems way less innocent.

'Hiya,' she says, and then I realise she isn't speaking to me. My daughter is suddenly standing behind me like a reluctant hockey player waiting to be picked for a team. The girls eye one another with a certain tribal recognition.

'Hiya,' Zara replies, equally lukewarm.

The staring business continues, then Bethany says, 'Aw, look! A kitten!' It's a little put on; she doesn't sound like the brightest girl in the world.

I feel the cat's tail sweep across the top of my slippers, and I scoop her up. 'She's not allowed out. Hasn't had all her jabs yet.'

The girl reaches out a hand. 'Awww . . . She's gorgeous.' Her fingers graze mine. The hand is corpse-cold, the nails bitten to stumps. I can't help but notice the smell of stale perfume from her coat sleeve, and all the cheap silver rings: *knuckledusters*, my dad would call them. 'What's her name?' she asks, then cluck-clucks her tongue affectionately at the cat.

I experience another flurry of impatience, then feel bad about it. They're door-to-door collecting for a charity, in the rain, for heaven's sake! It's more than I'm doing for the good of humanity. 'Juniper,' I tell her. 'My daughter named her.' At the reference to Zara, the two girls size each other up again.

'Lucky kitty, living in such a big house,' the mother says, and I can't help but think she sounds a little disdainful. She gazes past my head into our living room with a certain disenchanted curiosity.

'I should get back inside,' I say. 'I have something ready to come out of the oven.'

'Of course.' She looks at me again, an unreadable expression on her face, and offers a slightly tart, 'Sorry we inconvenienced you.'

'I'm sorry I couldn't help this time,' I say, feeling like a cad.

They turn to leave. The girl almost forgets there's a step down and stumbles. She says, 'Huuurr!' and wobbles exaggeratedly like a tightrope walker. I watch them head down our path to an old car. It's odd that they aren't going next door to the Bennings'. Or to Charlotte's. You'd think they would have started at one end and worked their way to the other. I stand there until they drive off, keeping watch until they get to the corner, then turn right on to Church Bank. In the background, the trees are loose silhouettes in the changing light.

'Do you know her?' I ask Zara, when I go back inside. The house is cosy and just starting to smell of cooking, and I'm suddenly struck by how we might not be a perfect family but we're a lot better off than some people, and I'm reminded, once again, to be grateful. Zara shrugs her hair off her shoulder then slaps her homework on to the dining table while I dip into the fridge for some white wine. Lately I need a couple of these before I can sleep at night; it's the only thing that calms my racing mind and stops the melancholy from breaking through. My contact with the cold bottle makes me think about the rings and the cold hand.

'Zara . . . I've just asked you . . . do you know her?' I stop what I'm doing and stare at her.

'Who?' she asks, not bothering to look up.

That girl, I want to say. But I suppose I have my answer.

TWO

My mobile rings as I'm picking up all the knickers from Zara's bedroom floor.

'Darling, do you think Zara might babysit for me on Saturday night?' My friend Charlotte never bothers with fluff like hellos and how are yous. 'Lavinia's come down with another cold so I don't want her minding the boys or it'll go round the house like wildfire!'

Damn. I knew this was going to come up. 'Oh, Sharls . . .' I'd intended to be better prepared. 'To be honest, I think she's still a bit young, you know . . . to be looking after three five-year-olds.'

There's a loaded pause. 'But you let her before.'

'I know,' I say, carefully. 'But that was only because you were in a bind.' When Lavinia had some mysterious rash and Charlotte was worried it was a flesh-eating disease. 'I wasn't really thinking it'd be a regular thing.'

Charlotte's triplets may exhibit enhanced learning and development, as she likes to tell everybody, from all that baby music she played them when they were in the womb, but they wreak all sorts of havoc the instant her back is turned. Zara would fare better in the Serengeti being chased by leopards.

'Sorry, Em. I didn't realise it was a big issue or I wouldn't have asked.'

Damn. The muscles of my windpipe constrict. These past four months since my mother died, I can't much be bothered with any sort of drama and confrontation. I just get the urge to flee and hide under a rock. 'It's not a big issue at all.' I try to keep my tone cheerful. 'It's just that, you know, Zara's quite young for her age. I'm just not sure she's ready for it. I mean, I wouldn't have wanted that responsibility at her age, would you?'

'I'd have probably just loved the money!' Charlotte says, tartly. 'But that's fine. Not to worry. I'll find somebody else.'

I haven't told her that, a week or two after the babysitting episode, Zara admitted little Jake had bitten her. She still had a faint teeth-mark impression on her forearm. 'Thanks for thinking of her,' I say. I have learned over the years that sometimes you're better off gracefully exiting certain conversations with Charlotte, rather than digging your heels in. But when she doesn't immediately respond, I feel the need to make amends. 'Look, if you want, I could probably do it for you next time – if Lavinia can't, for whatever reason.'

Eric's going to kill me. *Who gives a toss if Charlotte wants a night off? Let her deal with who's going to look after her three savages! It was her idea to have so bloody many of them in the first place!* Eric seems to forget that Charlotte only ever wanted one baby. Her triplets came about after several failed IVF treatments.

'But that won't help me for Saturday night, will it?' she says, and then there's a loaded pause. 'Hang on, you two are still coming, aren't you?'

Yikes. I don't know why I told her we would, when I knew there wasn't a cat in hell's chance that we were ever attending another of her house parties, after what happened at the last one. 'Oh, gosh, I'm sorry. I meant to tell you. It's Daniel's sixteenth on Saturday so we're taking him out for Thai food. So that's another reason why Zara wouldn't be able to babysit, aside from her being too young . . . Plus Eric's had a long week. I think we're just going to lay low. We could use a bit of time together.'

'You can spend time together! At our house! You can come over after your Thai food . . . Surely Daniel's got his own plans for later, anyway?'

I hate feeling I'm being told what to do, even though it's well-meaning. Charlotte loves her big gatherings. And while I love my friends, I can't say I always feel the same about their mates. Charlotte's aren't the friendliest. *Stiffs*, as Eric calls them, not a sense of humour between them. I'm pretty sure they see us as the peasants next door. Especially after last time. Good grief! It's a miracle she even wants us to come again.

'Look, I am sorry. Really. I know we're becoming the couple who always cancels—'

'"Becoming"?'

There is a note of affection in her tone. I wish I could smile. But somehow it's like we've picked the scab off an old wound. 'Eric's not having a very easy time, what with his job and working away from home . . . He's hardly rung me and when he does he's grumpy and impatient.' Not that that's anything new. Sometimes I don't quite know what happened to him – if it's just the result of life, and carries a certain inevitability, or if Eric being any other way was actually the anomaly. Maybe I married a figment of my own imagination. 'I think he's really burning out.'

'Burning out?' Charlotte scoffs. 'He's only forty-four!'

I try not to let my annoyance show. I can't really expect her to relate. When you're a top barrister and you're married to a Japanese car company executive, you're probably not in a position to comment on our situation. But I have learned that no good ever comes of comparing your life to that of your financially better-off friends. The fact is, Charlotte can't possibly know what it's like when your husband is forced to take a job in London after a chronic spell of unemployment, and for the last six months you've only seen him on weekends. It's changed the very nature of our free time together – our entire marriage in fact. Friday night, he's just flown in so he's tired. Saturday, he's catching up on some chores around the house. By Sunday he's gearing up to go back to London again. I bite the inside of my cheek and perch on the end of Zara's bed, not sure why this conversation has me a little wrung out.

'We miss you!' she says, as though she knows. 'Garth and I were just saying we never see you as a couple any more . . . You really need to get him to leave that place and come home.'

'We miss you too . . . Quick coffee tomorrow?'

'Can't. Got to take Charlie for his allergy tests and then I've got a trial. Next week, maybe? If I survive court, that is.'

'OK.' Usually, no matter what's going on, we always find time to get together for our 'meet and bleat', as we fondly term it. I wonder if she's still peeved about the party. 'Sorry again about Saturday,' I tell her.

'You're forgiven,' she says, then adds, '*this* time!'

'Mum?' Daniel's voice penetrates the fug. 'You didn't forget?'

Somehow I went from sitting on the bed to zonking out.

'Have you been snoozing like a senior citizen again?'

Busted! I spring to my feet, nearly sending Juniper airborne from her curled-up position on my chest. 'No, of course not. I'm on my way!' They say normal people tell a white lie three times a day. Lately, I feel like I'm exceeding my limit.

I barrel down the stairs, seeing stars. Where did I put my keys? I've been misplacing things a lot lately. I joke about early dementia, but sometimes it doesn't feel funny.

'Never mind. I'll just take the bus.' I can hear his disappointment.

Normally Daniel bikes to tennis from school, but his derailleur is broken and we're waiting for Eric to look at it this weekend.

'I'll be there in ten minutes!' I say. 'Stay put.'

As I start up the car engine I am aware of a debilitating tiredness – the kind I felt the day I learned my mother had died and has never left me. Lately I'm always running after life as though it's ten minutes ahead of me. I don't know where the balance went. I glance in my rear-view mirror and happen to see a man going into the new neighbour's house. Charlotte said something about him being a doctor, and his wife dying. And then she added, 'And let me tell you, I'd let him listen to my chest any day of the week!' This man is bald and overweight so I doubt it's him.

Daniel lopes across the almost-empty parking lot – his jaunty, straight-backed run that reminds me of Basil Fawlty. At the entrance to the tennis centre, he turns and waves. I hold up a hand.

Lately I find myself watching my kids as though we are rapidly becoming Venn diagrams that will no longer overlap. Just yesterday, Daniel was on the phone with Apple, politely telling the technical support person that their instructions hadn't solved the problem with his new iPhone. I was so impressed with how he walked that fine line between frustrated and irritated. Who was this clever, well-spoken, almost-sixteen-year-old? Only last week I came across the sterling-silver St Christopher pendant Eric's mother bought Daniel for his fifth birthday. He didn't want to wear it; jewellery belonged on girls. But even back then he had a sentimental streak about gifts. He put it in a little envelope and wrote *Daniel's necklace* on it and gave it to me to keep in my top drawer along with some other precious pieces – my mother's rose gold locket, a pearl necklace and earring set from my wedding – plus the tiny blue card Eric's mother had given me of the Motorist's Prayer. Coming across it after all these years swept me back with such profound nostalgia. How has time gone so quickly? I'd give anything just to return to those days when they were little again, and to keep us all there, to preserve *then*, so we'd eternally have *now* to look forward to.

I realise I'm still sitting here staring into the space where Daniel no longer is, my hand frozen in a wave. I must look half deranged. I put the car in reverse and pull out of the parking space, unsure why I have this unsettling feeling in my bones . . . what could have possibly put it there.

Good heavens, snap out of it! I think. I bet I have a face like a fiddle, as my mother used to say. Though it took me a long time to realise that wasn't a good thing. I always thought fiddles were rather lovely instruments.

THREE

Eric is home. As is usual every Friday evening, I picked him up at Leeds airport a couple of hours ago.

'What d'you mean you said we wouldn't go?'

I watch his hand stroking my bare feet that I've rested in his lap. The big knuckles. The middle one with its cute single freckle. 'I thought I was doing you a favour.'

'Favour?'

'I thought you were exhausted.'

He looks a little perplexed. 'We can probably still go. If you ring her. Be nice to do a bit of socialising for a change, wouldn't it? See faces other than our own? Shake the tree, so to speak?'

'What's wrong with my face or our tree?'

'Nothing.' He pulls his eyes away from the TV and finally, properly, looks at me. 'It's beautiful. Especially when it's smiling.'

'I really don't feel like going,' I say, slightly taken aback by a compliment coming out of Eric's mouth.

I feel him study my profile as I look away. 'OK. Fine. Then say so. But don't make me the reason.'

His attention goes back to the TV and I watch him secretly out of the corner of my eye. The hair, not quite red, not quite sand, shorn to the point that you wouldn't really know its true colour, or that it was naturally very thick. The reddish beard shot through with grey. Last year he did Movember and decided he liked facial hair because it hides what he thinks is his weak chin. Zara said he looked like the kind of serial rapist that the FBI go looking for in the mountains of Salt Lake City. Clearly it didn't dissuade him.

It occurred to me, when Charlotte sent me the video, that I should let Eric see it too, but then for some reason I decided against it. I wasn't at all happy she'd chosen to show it to me. Up until then I'd rather imagined that Eric's little white secret had been kept within our own four walls.

It was taken a few weeks ago at their house. A gathering to celebrate their tenth wedding anniversary. There was one fellow who seemed intent on taking videos of everything with his phone. When she sent it to me I remember thinking, *Hmm . . . What makes her think I care to see this? A camera panning a room? Various group-ings of people engaged in boring conversation?* But then the camera focused on Eric.

'I love my food,' he was saying to a rather stiff couple of book-ish types, who looked cornered. 'Basically, if there's an avocado in it, I'll eat it.' He swayed a little, clutching his whisky glass high up by his chest. 'I bloody love avocados! Do you? I bet you don't love them as much as me. I love them so much I could marry them.'

The stiffs couldn't bring themselves to look amused even out of charity, as though Eric's inanity might be catching. On he prattled about avocados . . .

'Ugh!' I groaned, and switched it off.

'No!' Charlotte said when I rang her and she was done laugh-ing. 'That's not the best part! Didn't you see the rest?'

The 'rest', it turned out, was Eric even more hammered, loom-ing over a startled, fair-haired young woman. 'I'm a weak man. A bad person. No, you don't understand . . . I mean a *bad* person.

I've done things . . .' Hiccup. 'Things I'm not proud of . . .' He was hanging on to his whisky glass for dear life, talking off to the side of her head like he was losing focus, clearly oblivious to the iPhone camera that was trained on him. 'Where is my wife, anyway?' He turned and scanned the room, as though he was trying to peer through molasses. 'I need to find my wife . . .' His bleary gaze finally returned to the blonde's ear. He suddenly looked sombre, haunted. 'Let me tell you I love my wife. Have you met her? She's the best . . . the best person, and I don't deserve her. I will *never deserve her . . .*'

The videographer got bored and panned to someone else.

'He was drunk,' I said to Charlotte, flatly, feeling uncomfortably exposed. 'He's under a lot of pressure. That's how he relieves his stress sometimes.'

If she was thinking, *Do you have any idea what he was talking about?*, she had the good grace not to ask. As it was, I couldn't have enlightened her.

I pull my mind away from that disturbing memory now. 'I booked us at that place, Thai Heaven, for tomorrow night,' I say. 'Got the reservation for just after six so Daniel can go out with his mates later. Then maybe Zara can watch a movie and we can get a bit of time on our own.' I feel we need to talk about what happens when his one-year contract in London is up. Where do we go from there?

He shrugs. 'Great. We'll go to heaven and then we'll come home to hell.'

I tut. 'What's that supposed to mean?' Does he know I'm angling for a conversation he clearly doesn't want to have? It was his idea to take a job down south. I didn't see how a temporary position was really going to help us and would have preferred he just take a lower-paid job up here. But, as usual, when it comes to the sore subject of his employment, Eric does it his way.

He sees off the last of his beer, and sets the bottle down with a certain, overly scripted, 'That was nice. Sometimes all you need is one to hit the spot.' Then he does a double take at my face. 'What's up, Doc? I was joking. Lost your sense of humour?'

On Saturday morning my own screaming wakes me up. Always the same dream. Oddly, always Zara. Never Daniel. We are in hospital. I am holding her in the pale pink shawl my mother knitted for her. Eric is at the foot of the bed. But then a woman comes in and I know she's going to take her. *Noooo!* I scream and look to Eric for help, but he won't meet my eyes. My apocalyptic terror fails to penetrate him. It's like he is suddenly deaf, or . . . *in on it.* I have that horrible asphyxiating sensation of knowing I can't trust him.

A hand pats my leg under the duvet. 'Em,' he grunts. 'Chill out, man.' He has picked up that expression from Zara. I can't say I'm fond of it.

For a moment I recoil from his touch. *You bastard!* But then I realise he's not a bastard, is he? It was a bad dream. My chest is drenched. I sit up, feeling like I've done several rounds in the boxing ring, then pull my nightdress off and try to recalibrate reality.

My mother said it must keep happening because we nearly lost a baby. Daniel was born at twenty-six weeks. The doctors said even if he survived, eighty per cent of children born that prematurely will have some form of developmental or physical disability. It was the most agonising time we've ever lived through. Daniel ended up being in the lucky twenty. If we had lost him, I don't know how we would have survived it. *We can get through anything if we can get through this*, Eric said at the time, and I believed him. I felt like we were banded together because of what we'd gone through, and I trusted that feeling implicitly. But still, I must have a muscle memory for all that pain, which manifests itself in weird dreams.

When I come downstairs they are in the back garden tinkering with the bike. I listen to them ribbing each other, their easy banter. I stand there for a moment, taking in the rolling countryside and shifting shades of green on the other side of the garden wall. Then I go over to Daniel. 'Happy birthday, darling!' And I make him stand there while I perform sixteen tugs of his magnificent hair, a family rite of passage. 'Mum! Will you give over!' He chortles and tries to hide behind his hands.

'Can you tug me too?' Eric gives me a saucy wink. I have noticed lately that he's prone to a bit of innuendo, as though talking about being randy makes up for not actually being randy.

'Ha ha,' I say mirthlessly.

I go back inside and lay bacon in a pan and make myself a cafetière of coffee. I am still a little dull from the dream. I have noticed that grief for my mother has me one step removed from even the most routine of rituals. It's like being partially deaf. Life's noise is going on out there, but there is a buffer between it and my ability to be properly attuned to it.

I can hear Eric telling Daniel that we'll just buy him a new bike for his birthday, and Daniel's protests. My son is a frugal soul, with his own money and everybody else's. I wonder why Eric's voice makes me buck slightly. I can't quite decipher why I feel a bit of distance between us – what it is that he has really done. I just know that every time he goes away, he returns a little more of a stranger to me. I don't know whether this is an inevitable consequence of the distance, or whether it started long before he left, a bit like a silent cancer that metastasised with the stress of his lengthy unemployment. All I can really say is I sense something has changed between us lately. And like before when it happened, all those years ago – that awful time that still makes me shudder – I can't quite pinpoint what's behind it, any more than I could then.

They come into the kitchen. Daniel always walks like he has a song in his head. 'I'll drive you,' Eric tells him. He's got tennis practice followed by fitness at noon.

'So we can have the man-to-man talk?' Daniel grabs an apple from the bowl.

Eric pings his finger off the back of his son's head. 'I think you've taught me everything I need to know already.'

'Why does everybody in this house have to be so bloody loud?' Zara clonks down the stairs, and appears before us, plucking her flannel PJs out of her bum. Recently she has taken to swearing. 'Bloody' is her word of the moment.

Eric whistles. 'Here comes America's Next Top Model. All that, plus style *and* an electrifying personality.'

She collapses over the breakfast bar – anyone would think she'd had two hours' sleep instead of ten.

Daydreamer. Time-waster. Unmotivated. I've heard it all from her teachers. Or, the best one: *She hasn't found out who she is.* I mean, what fourteen-year-old knows who she is? I didn't really know who I was until I turned forty. But sometimes I sense she's become borderline depressed – especially since she fell out with Gracie, her best friend who dumped her for no apparent reason. And in my grief I have been too wrapped up in my own headspace to deal with hers – a fact I feel guilty about. Especially as I sense a dissonance between us. I'm sure it's because she thinks I have somehow failed to view her humongous teenage life crisis as on par with my own. Eric thinks that I'm looking for something that's not there. But Eric would probably say I do a lot of that in general.

'I thought we'd all go to the farmers' market when Daniel gets back,' I tell him as I flip the bacon. 'We could pick out a nice roast for tomorrow.'

'Why don't we just eat out? Make it easier?'

'But we're out tonight, remember? For his birthday.'

Eric looks up from the newspaper he just opened and gives me a blank stare. 'Huh?'

'I told you . . . We go to heaven then we come home to hell?'

'Ah . . .' he says, like I'm talking Swahili.

'Anyway, don't you get enough of restaurants in London?'

'I thought it'd save you from having to cook.'

'But I want to cook for my family.'

Family outings and dinners have become rare things. I miss them. I miss our cohesion. The way we would just plod around comfortably together, in our pack, sit and talk about anything or sometimes just a lot of silly nothings. No one else apparently gives a damn about this, of course. I am the only one who seems to want to be able to stop a ball mid-air.

'All right, Nigella Lawson. Have it your way.' He gives me a wink, then walks over to the hall cupboard and takes out his jacket.

When they leave, I think, *I must remember to pick up the cake. Don't let me forget the cake.* Damn it, I know I'm probably going to end up forgetting the cake.

At the farmers' market, we comb the various stalls. A girl is playing 'Winter' from Vivaldi's *Four Seasons* on a harp. Then Eric and Daniel go off to buy the bike.

I fondly watch them trek back to the car, Eric mussing the top of Daniel's head, Daniel ducking. Zara wanders over to a stall that sells knitted cat toys. I go and select a nice piece of free-range pork belly.

Later, when I'm treating myself to a bunch of fresh flowers, Zara nudges my arm. 'Guess what? I think I just saw that girl!'

I frown. 'What girl?'

'You know. The one who came to the door collecting for that charity a couple of weeks back?' She seems very animated all of a sudden.

'Really?' I remember the sad-eyed mother. 'Where?' I look around. I don't know why, but I can't say I feel like encountering either of those two again.

She indicates the vintage clothing stall with a flick of her head. 'Over there. But don't make it obvious you're looking!'

'Hmm . . . I don't see anyone.'

'Oh?' She stares over there too, and deflates. 'That's so weird. She was there literally two seconds ago. I swear. She was just watching me and watching me. It was a bit creepy.'

'Oh well . . .' *No great loss.*

We leave the market and start ambling up the hill. We are halfway home when . . . 'Damn! We have to go back.'

'Why?'

'I forgot the cake.'

'What?' She gawks at me like I'm colossally incompetent. 'I'm not going back! I'm going home!'

'You're coming.' I tug her jacket sleeve. 'You didn't bring a door key. Ha ha.'

'God!' She trots after me, grunting. 'Why does he have to have a birthday anyway? Didn't he have one last year?'

In the shop, a stressed-out Eastern European girl presents us with the cake creation. I'd been worried they'd mess up the tennis racket decoration. I'd supplied a good photograph for them to copy. But, oh no, they've done a stellar job. *Happy Birthday Denial*, the icing reads.

Zara laughs so hard she nearly cracks a rib.

FOUR

Otis doesn't seem to realise I haven't got all morning. It's spitting rain. We've actually been out way longer than I intended because he was off chasing squirrels and I didn't have the heart to spoil his fun.

As we're drawing closer, I see that the front door is open at the new guy's house. A man is standing in the doorway. He's actually half in and half out, so I am staring at an almost-precise bisection of him. Half a slim face. Mousy grey hair, plentiful and slightly messy on top. Half a slender torso in a navy sports jacket. A hint of white collar, a single white cuff. It's a rather disarming way to view someone, and I find myself trying to extrapolate the whole from the half. He's talking to someone back inside whom I can't see.

Just when we've almost sneaked past, he steps out on to the path and Otis starts barking, which makes him look over. *Gosh, yes*, I think. *He's attractive*. Charlotte didn't hugely exaggerate.

When he sees me, it's as though someone has just pressed pause; he makes a slightly prolonged study of me, then smiles and cocks his head. 'Should I be afraid of him?' He walks towards us, crouches down to the dog's level and strokes his head. Otis has a fit of happy hysterics.

'Very. He might lick you to death. You've been warned.' I look at the hand tickling behind the dog's ears; the clean, squarely cut fingernails.

He gazes up at me from his crouched position, which, oddly, makes me a little self-conscious. 'You're Emily.'

'Is it that obvious?'

A hint of a smile in the blue-green eyes. 'The photo in Charlotte and Garth's kitchen, from the Coldplay concert? I was at her little gathering on Saturday.'

'Ah! Right!' I vaguely recall her saying she was planning on inviting him; she gave me the saucy nudge-nudge, wink-wink.

'Plus Charlotte told me all about you.'

'Hopefully not everything.'

He stands up properly now and extends a hand. 'Steve Holden.' His handshake is warm and firm. 'And this is?'

'Otis.'

He doesn't immediately release me. I always think there's something about a person holding your gaze while they hold your hand that feels slightly more intimate than you are quite prepared for.

'Great name. Friendly old guy, isn't he?'

'He's only seven.' We both look down at him. 'He's just got one of those faces, you know . . . of an old soul.'

'I like that,' he says, after a moment's pause.

'You're an A&E doctor, I understand.' I can hear Charlotte gushing, *All that and he saves lives for a living!* He has quite a pronounced nose, and an open, good-humoured face. And a chin with a dimple in the centre.

'And I believe you're Daniel's mum.'

'And I have a fourteen-year-old daughter too. Zara.'

'Ah . . . Zara. Nice name . . .' He clicks open the back door of his car.

'I follow your son's progress in the newspapers. He's quite the local celebrity, isn't he?' He throws his sports jacket on to the leather seat. He's lean and athletic; quite the opposite of Eric. Possibly around my own age or a little older.

'Yes. We're very proud of him. And you have a son, don't you?'

'Henry. He's eight.' His driver's-side door lingers open. There's a scattering of rain spots on his shirt and on the car seat but he doesn't seem to be in any hurry to get going. 'I just employed a new nanny. I'm not sure how she's going to work out . . .' He nods back inside. 'Henry has had some challenges recently.'

'Oh, gosh, yes.' I wonder if my feigned surprise is working. Charlotte said his little boy was having a hard time getting over the loss of his mum. 'I suppose that can't be easy.'

He shrugs, and I think I see a flicker of self-consciousness cross his face. 'We all just deal with what we're given, don't we? Our first thought is always their best interests, isn't it?'

I nod. 'True . . . Well . . .' I gesture to the rain. 'It was nice to finally say hello.'

I make a move to leave and he says, 'Henry loves watching sport. Maybe one day he can meet Daniel.'

'Of course,' I say. 'That would be nice.'

I turn and gently tug Otis in the direction of home. As I walk up the street, I think, *Hmm . . . how should I angle it for Charlotte? 'We met. We looked at one another. And then we just fell into his bed!'* I am busy smiling to myself when his car rolls alongside me. He winds his window down. 'Fine wellingtons, by the way,' he says, with a straight face.

I'd forgotten I'm wearing Zara's hot-pink Hunter boots.

I do believe he's mocking me.

FIVE

I have just poured coffee and logged on to my work email, and I read a very strange message from a student who has registered for my class this term. I'm staring at it in disbelief when Eric pops up on FaceTime.

'Taking a little break. Been in work since six.' He looks a little rough.

'You all right?'

'Miss my family.'

'You only saw us a few days ago,' Daniel pipes up from the dining table, where he's eating his fruit and yogurt.

'I know,' he says. 'It feels like ages already.'

I smile.

It's the first time since he moved down there that he's said he misses us. I almost don't know what to say. I've told him to continue looking for a job up here. Just because he couldn't find one before doesn't mean there won't be one now. But clearly that must qualify as too much multitasking.

I hear Zara shaking cornflakes into a bowl. 'You don't have time for that!' I tell her. 'Just take a cereal bar and a banana and eat them on the bus.'

She tuts. 'Take a chill pill. Gah! . . . I can't eat breakfast any more. This is child abuse. Anyway, why's *he* just sitting there?' She stares at her brother.

Daniel is usually already at school. His teachers let him come in an hour early to catch up on his assignments.

'Because I fly to Spain this afternoon,' he tells her. 'Training at the Soto Academy all week.' He punches the air. 'Yes!'

'Some people have all the luck.'

'Look, while I have you here,' I say to Eric, 'what do you make of this?' I go into my email and send him the message from the student. Then I watch him perform all the appropriately theatrical mannerisms as he reads.

Dear Professor Mrs Rossi

I am joining U soon in yr course but have family wedding and some holiday, so I have 2 miss the 1st class and some others. RN I await booking ticket 2 India until U tell me U will send course outline + lecture notes so I can do in own time. For mid term I would like 2 sit exam at a later date that's gd for me. Appreciate yr help!!!! Thanx LMK ☺ ☺

Prajval Dhaliwal

'That's a nineteen-year-old university student?'

Almost every term there is someone I sense might be trouble. After all these years of teaching, you learn to spot the signs. Their unusual requests, unrealistic expectations, eagerness to vent on social media – the odd vindictive posting on RateMyProfessors.

com. Predictably, you do one tiny thing that affronts their millennial entitlement and they've got it in for you forever.

'You know, if you sign up for a course, it's your obligation to attend, not mine to accommodate you never being in class!' I say, mini-outraged. 'And who writes to a professor in textese?'

'Give him a bollocking but don't ask him to spell it. Or it might be a she. Or an it.' Then he says, darkly, 'Or a *they*.'

'Don't be inappropriate,' I say to Eric and drum my fingers on the table. I don't feel like replying to the message now.

Zara tuts. 'You guys are so politically uncorrect.'

'Incorrect,' I tell her.

'And proud!' Eric says, and winks at me.

After dropping Daniel off at Leeds airport, I have a quick coffee with my dad and then spend the next few hours doing a few things Eric would normally take care of – renewing our house insurance, shopping for a new lawnmower, and visiting the car dealership, where something a little odd happens. There was a warning on the dash that our back tyres were low in pressure this morning. But Eric just spent nearly a thousand quid on new ones. When I tell the mechanic this, he says the tyres can't have recently been replaced because they're actually over seventy per cent worn.

'What?' I say, puzzled. 'Are you absolutely sure?'

'Back ones are the worst. If you don't want to at least replace these ones now, you definitely might want to think about doing it before winter.'

I can't help but think they're trying to scam me because I'm a woman. I contemplate texting Eric to say, *You did tell me you'd replaced the tyres, didn't you? I didn't just invent it?*, but I don't really want to disturb him when he's at work. So, in my best no-messing tone, I tell the guy to just fill the back ones up with air for now and I'll make an appointment for next week.

By the time I rush to my hair appointment, I'm still a bit mystified about the whole tyre thing. The hair-washer manages to make me forget about it, though, as I succumb to the lovely feeling of a head massage.

I didn't touch up my grey roots much when Eric was unemployed. Especially after he thrust our Visa bill under my nose and reminded me I was spending eighty pounds every six weeks – ever since Zara was born he's been in charge of our finances, supposedly to give me one less thing to do. In reality the bill was more than that, because I was getting them to charge me separately for the cut and colour so I could pay for one in cash, just so he wouldn't go on about it to me. I felt so guilty about it, like I was committing grand-scale fraud. Eventually I couldn't live with this silly little deception, so I settled for doing a very bad job of colouring it myself: L'Oréal's Havana Brown. But now that we have two pay cheques again, it's the one little indulgence I afford myself.

When I get back home, it's the laughter that hits me as I walk in our door. Crowing. Crass.

They don't hear me. They are too into each other and whatever they're looking at on the iPad. The girl is raking a hand through a curtain of board-straight, lifeless black hair.

It's the cheap rings I recognise first.

Suddenly they both glance up. 'Oh, hiya, Mum,' Zara says.

I'm sure I must look like I've seen a ghost. I stare at the girl, waiting for some sort of acknowledgement or explanation, but it's like I'm not there. They quickly go back to the iPad, letting out splutters of goofy laughter.

'Bethany? Right?' I remember the mother: *Bethany loves dogs.*

It strikes me how they look so comfortable together, like they've been friends since primary school. When I get no response

I take the grocery bags over to the counter and dump them with a fraction more force than usual. For a second I think I hear Bethany say, 'Fuck!' under her breath. What? In response to me making a noise? But I could have misheard. I try to have a sidelong peek at what they're looking at. The blue banner of Facebook. I can't see much more.

'Have you done your homework?' I ask Zara. No reply, so I say, 'So you won't be wanting dinner then?' The rule is she has to do homework before we eat or it's a nightmare getting her to tackle it later.

'I'll do it after!' she snarls, in that tone that says I'm a tiresome nag.

Bethany gives a disrespectful snort and bends to play with Juniper. I stare at the top of her head, the parting where her true reddish-brown colour bleeds through the gothic dye. I don't like this girl.

'Oh, by the way, your lovely boiler man has been,' Zara says.

This sets off another fit of giggles. Bethany slaps a hand on her thigh, making the strangest, mannish cawing noise I've ever heard. It's way too over the top. A string of saliva hangs from her lips and she wipes at it with her sleeve. The behaviour doesn't fit at all with the doll-like little face. It occurs to me that she probably had the raw materials of being a fine young lady but somebody ruined it for her along the way. Like that weird mother of hers.

'I know,' I say. 'We have heat again.' Besides, his yellow invoice is on the sideboard. Normally I like to be home if strange men are coming to the house. But three days without hot water, and two inches of grey roots, were enough to turn me into an irresponsible parent just this once.

'I think the baboon stole my Converse.'

Bethany snorts again. 'The pink-arsed baboon!'

I throw Zara a dirty look. 'Why are you acting like this?'

'He did! He stole them! They were right there when he came in!' She points to the corner. I don't like this version of Zara, this method acting. This is not how she behaves.

Bethany says something I don't catch. They fall around laughing again, their heads drawing together like magnets. I watch them like they're a foreign film.

'You'll have put them somewhere. Probably in your mess of a bedroom. Anyway, I'm hungry,' I say to Zara, meaning, *The party's over*. 'Perhaps Bethany needs to leave now, so you can do your homework then we can sit down to dinner.'

Bethany finally looks right at me. There is something so jaded about her. Eyes that have seen a thousand sadnesses, as my mother used to say. We stare at one another, tautly and for too long. Suddenly the air has a slight malignancy to it, and for a moment I wonder where this is going to go.

'I still can't believe he stole my Converse!' Zara says, but the joke has run out of steam.

Then Bethany shuffles off the stool and says, 'Duh. OK. I'm going.' She slides her arms into an oversized cardigan. Her white regulation shirt stretches over her bony chest, hugging tiny breasts, and I don't know if it's a deliberate attempt to be sexy or if she has outgrown it and can't afford a new one. She cinches the black belt around her sylphlike waist and bends again to say goodbye to Juniper, who is playing with a tassel on her bag. Even her movements have a certain effortless grace to them. For a second I feel a little sorry for her.

'How's your mum?' I ask. She's just a kid. It's a new school term. Zara will befriend her for two minutes and then the novelty will wear off for Bethany, is my guess.

She freezes like a deer in headlights, blushes violently. 'She's . . . er . . . she's the same.'

I wait for her to add more but can tell she doesn't know where to take normal conversation with a grown-up. Our eyes meet, briefly, with less hostility this time. She suddenly looks kittenish, bashful. I realise I'm slightly intrigued by her. The stance, combined with the air of dashed hopes served up in her flat stare, makes me think of her as a dancer who failed her audition for the Northern Ballet.

'Maybe you should be nice and walk Bethany to the gate,' I say to my daughter. Any other of her friends, and I'd have offered them dinner.

As soon as they are chattering at the front door, I log on to Facebook on my phone. There, uploaded to Zara's timeline, is a close-up of the plumber in our kitchen. He's bending over. All you can see is his big pinkish backside – ah, *the baboon* – and a couple of inches of bum crack peeking from his jeans. Zara's status reads: *SLURP!!!!*

Zara would never have written that of her own volition.

'So what was that all about?' I ask her when she comes back in. 'I thought you didn't know her?'

'I didn't.'

I plonk my hand on my hip. 'That's not an answer.' *How long is she going to keep up the new smart-arse act?* I wonder.

She rolls her eyes. 'She was at the gate this morning as I was going in, with her mum. She looked really weirded out. Her mum saw me and said we should go in together because she doesn't know anybody yet.'

Did she, indeed? 'So she's new?'

'They just moved here.'

'Where from?'

'Don't know. Harrogate? Is this going to be twenty questions, because if it is I've got homework to do?'

There is a certain rangy quality about my daughter that unsettles me. I have seen what Zara is like when she decides she's going to be friends with someone. Her shameless hot pursuit, even in the face of rejection. Even as a young child, she would home in on the misfit or underdog. There were no play dates. No dance classes. No Girl Guides or birthday parties. She wasn't shy, as people wrongly assumed; I would get so sick of hearing that. She could hold her own, and state her case when it was important to her. Groups of girls just did nothing for her. In some ways, I'm like that too: one close friend over a dozen acquaintances. But I never placed friends on a pedestal from which I'd idolise them, blindly. This is where we differ.

'She's not really your type, is she?'

She glares at me. 'My *what*? Because she doesn't live in a big house like we do? I thought you're always going on about how you're not supposed to judge people because they've got less than you?'

'I'm not judging her,' I say, but of course I am. 'I'm just commenting that I don't know what you would have in common.'

With that one remark I am a gargantuan disappointment to her. Zara has never had a friend I haven't approved of. Gracie was a slightly nerdy but disarmingly quick-witted girl from Vietnam who didn't care if none of the other girls thought she was cool or pretty. And before that, lovely Hannah was a fixture at our house. Then her father accepted a job in America, and suddenly Hannah was gone. Zara tried keeping in touch by email but she never wrote back. I tried to tell her that is how some people are – they just get busy with their new lives; it's not personal. But for Zara, it is.

Because of her build – tall and stocky like Eric – she might give people the impression she's tougher than she is. But deep down she is the most sensitive soul I know. I am trying my best to give her a thicker skin, but sometimes it's like trying to open a lock with a toothpick.

'You'd better take that photo down from Facebook,' I say. How many times have I told her that everything you do on social media is a direct reflection of you, so you have to be careful about the image you project? I thought she understood.

'It was just a bit of fun!' She blushes hotly, but something about her seems recast.

'It's not becoming.'

'You're always on my case!' She looks like she might cry. The weight of my underplayed disapproval hurts more than if I'd just lectured her for ten minutes. God, she is extra-sensitive lately! Deeper pain. Deeper disappointment. Bigger dramas. Hormones, of course, and insecurity: everybody is dumping her and leaving.

'Just take the picture down,' I say, a little wounded. I'm not always on her case. But somebody has to parent her. 'And watch yourself with that girl. I don't think she should be coming over after school. You've got homework to do.'

'She's only come once, hasn't she! It's not like it's happened bloody fifty million times!' She sits down at the table, picks up a pen, sighs her end-of-the-world sigh.

She's right. Two minutes ago I was worrying that she was going to become a depressed recluse. Now I'm clipping her wings after I've encouraged her to find them.

'You don't have to overreact to everything,' I tell her, quietly, when the steam seems to have gone out of her.

'God!' she says, then she snatches the iPad and storms off towards the stairs.

It's times like these that I think we would have been better off travelling the world than having kids. I watch her chunky legs disappear around the corner. I often thought that maybe one of the reasons she didn't stick at ballet and figure-skating was because she wasn't cute or graceful like the other girls. Part of me hoped that might save her from teen sex, diseases, underage pregnancy . . . I had some fanciful idea that I would be able to hang on to my not-quite-ugly-duckling-but-not-quite-swan, then cast her into the path of someone suitable who would see her for the secretly kind and loyal person that she is. But really, I just want her to sail smartly through the cruel teenage years and come out liking herself on the other side. What more could a mother really ask?

I can still smell that girl's awful perfume. It clings like the ineffable stink of trouble.

SIX

ERIC

He steps out of the Holiday Inn and heads towards Curzon Street. With all his working away from home, the one thing he has never got used to is eating alone.

While he's not really a lover of London, he quite likes Shepherd Market with its Jack the Clipper barber shop and tumbling-down pubs. He walks into one of his regulars and is happy to see there's virtually nobody sitting at the bar. He orders a beer. If he ever recognises him, the barman never lets on, so Eric doesn't attempt to make conversation with him any more. The first thing he does is check his messages. Sometimes he thinks all he does is spend his life sitting in meetings and doing paperwork, and only when he's put a dent in all that can he get on with being a structural engineer and the design work that he actually enjoys. Design drew him to the career in the first place, made him think that one day he would literally leave his mark on the world. So much for that shit.

He is aware of a woman sitting at the bar, not five feet away. He glances out of the corner of his eye. His first thought is *prostitute*.

Ten new emails but none that can't wait. Good. It's been a long day; he can barely remember when it began. He's a bit bothered about what one of the assistants told him. Apparently they're thinking of putting him up in a flat in St John's Wood, because it's less costly to the company than four-star hotels. When he was signing his two-year contract, they agreed he'd spend seventy-five per cent of his time down here and work from home for the rest. But it hasn't quite panned out that way, what with them needing him to be more and more on site. A flat sounds too permanent. Em'll have a bird when he tells her. So he'll probably avoid mentioning it for as long as he can get away with it.

He quickly downs his beer and orders another. When he's at home he has to make it look like he's sticking to one drink – always a beer – so he doesn't get the lecture. At least until she's gone to bed, then he'll creep around the kitchen like an intruder in his own home, hold his breath until he's managed to lift the booze cabinet door half an inch as he opens it, to avoid it squeaking, feel a surge of triumph as his hand makes contact with the whisky bottle. But when he's in London, he has the glorious freedom to do as he pleases. It reminds him of what a mate once told him. He said he only ever cheated when he was on the road, but then again, he was on the road a lot. Eric hadn't exactly thought that was a very nice thing to admit, but it was funny. He doesn't get blotto any more, though. Well, rarely. Ish.

He orders a burger and fries. With working hard and doing so much eating out, he's packed on a couple of kilos. Fat runs in the family. He'd had some smart idea he'd start each day with a run through Green Park, and from time to time he has actually been delusional enough to set his alarm – but, really, when the buzzer goes off he's just too knackered. He's about to check stock prices online when a text pops up.

Where did you buy the new tyres from? Dealer??? Was in there this morning. Low pressure message.

He stares at this for a minute. He remembers an earlier conversation. Em looking puzzled: 'Why is it that I've gone to the bank machine two days running, and it keeps saying I've reached my daily limit?'

'Had to get new tyres,' he told her, after some quick thinking. 'Thousand quid.'

Yes, he types back, now. Dealer. Maybe one was defective?

He sees the little dots, letting him know she's typing. Mechanic said they were more than 70% worn. How can they be worn if they're brand new???

He stares across the room, tries to pluck something out of the ether. Glitch in their computer system?

Hmmm . . . she replies.

He waits, but luckily that seems to be the end of it.

He hears the woman next to him order a vodka soda. It's a smoker's voice. Once or twice he's felt her looking over. He turns his back to her, to send the message that he's not interested.

Ping! Another text. Fuck. She's like a dog with a bone.

Bit concerned. Z got new friend! Don't like this girl!

He sighs, but at least she's not still going on about the tyres. He's not big on texting for chitchat purposes. Oh? he types back.

Common girl! Barely knows her, now they're practically joined at the hip!

He suddenly remembers something he has to do tomorrow, so he just replies saying, Uh oh . . . Then he quickly types into his reminders: Review Raskin report. Discrep? Post collapse analysis!!! Meet w Ken.

Ping! Em again. Sorry to bother you!

What's he done now? These days he always manages to piss her off without even trying. What's he supposed to say about Zara having a new friend? Em never likes any of Zara's friends anyway; it's hardly breaking news. Plus he'll be seeing her Friday night. He's sure it can keep until then.

He decides he won't encourage her by replying. When she's in one of her moods there's no winning. He's damned if he does and damned if he doesn't. There were times when her never-ending disappointment in him made him want to rise to the challenge of winning her over again, but then he felt she took advantage. She knows he's a pleaser. In the past he'd have done anything to ingratiate himself, and when he looks back, maybe that's what has kept them married. Somebody has to play the underdog, don't they? But tonight he's got more on his mind than running up Em's backside. Things aren't going well with the High Line project. And with all their debt he can't afford to lose his job again, and Em of all people should know that. He's expected to be here and hold it all together, earn the fat pay cheque, then be back there and gear down for all the small dramas that Em thinks are world crises. Sometimes it feels like too much.

But his conscience kicks in. He can't *not* reply. As his religious mother often says, *Blessed are the peacekeepers.*

Sorry, he replies. Insanely long day. His food arrives.

'That looks delicious,' the woman says.

She's skinny, hard, and not at all good-looking. He wonders why, if you were going to use a prostitute, you'd pick an old one. Do they charge less? 'Yeah,' he says, to be polite. 'It does.' Then he pointedly goes back to his food.

While he eats, his mind spools through all the stuff he's got to do before he can fly home. He wonders if there'll be any more parties this weekend that Em's going to forbid him from going to, on the pretence of it being for his own good. Suddenly he remembers something else he should probably do tomorrow, and he makes a note of this in his phone too. His food goes down and he doesn't even taste it.

He still can't believe Em's pissed off with him. Though, to be fair, he knows he hasn't really been there for her since her mother died, because he's been so busy. Em tends to just get on with things, stiff upper lip, and maybe he's allowed that to be his excuse for not really making much of an effort. He feels bad about that, though. You only lose your mother once and he hasn't been the world's most devoted husband when she's needed him.

He wags a finger at his glass to let the barman know he'll have one more beer. Em would disapprove – but, oh well, she's not here.

He's just about to shut his phone down when another text pops up. He's sure it's her again, ready to launch another cruise missile at him, but . . .

He stares at the name for a moment or two, blinks.

Shit. The bottom of his stomach practically falls out. Not this again. He thought he'd made this go away. For a moment he shuts his eyes, telling himself he's not going to read it. But, as ever, curiosity gets the better of him.

Think carefully how you're going to play this, Eric. My advice. Think very carefully.

He reads it twice, three times. His heart starts beating fiercely. While he's trying to decide what to do, there's another ping. Another message.

Are you ready for the consequences?

Heat rushes over his face, anger bubbling up like hot lava. That sense of being trapped, all his options closing in on him. Fuck it. He sucks in a deep breath, powers down his phone and puts it in his pocket.

'Long day?' the prostitute says.

He wakes up and he's not sure what happened. His head is a dead weight. He is so damned thirsty and his tongue is practically glued to the roof of his mouth. For a moment he's not sure where he is, then he realises. He tries to think back. He remembers being in the bar. Walking back . . . He remembers there was a casino, with a baby-blue Rolls-Royce Phantom outside.

The texts.

Of course! The texts.

His world comes crashing in on him again. He stares vacantly across the room to the TV, his brain trying to work its way around this sticky little problem, but all he ever does is go round in endless circles on it. There's a small collection of empty Johnnie Walker bottles lined up like soldiers on top of the cabinet. His eyes home in on them. He has a go at counting them but his vision is off, and, in any case, he hopes he's miscalculated. Next, his eyes bounce off the clock. Shit! Why didn't his alarm go off? He stumbles out of bed and finds his phone. His day planner tells him it's Thursday. He checks his meetings. One at 8 a.m. It's 7.20 now. *Ah, man!* He pads naked to the bathroom, vowing that this can't ever happen again. Never again! He's got to get a grip on his drinking. He hasn't time to shower and his mouth feels like a sewer, so he twists his neck until his head is under the tap, getting a drink and a wash at the same time. He quickly brushes his teeth, pulls on a shirt and socks, his suit that's sprawled over a chair. He grabs his briefcase and barrels out of the door. The lift is right there. He shoves his arm in to stop the door closing.

There's only a young woman inside, in business attire, and she looks him up and down. Instinctively he sucks in his stomach, but then he lets it out – something about you can't have pride and a belting hangover. The door purrs closed. His head is still fuzzy and he's dog-tired, with a queasy gut. The woman clears her throat, as though to fill the stiff silence. Normally he'd say something, to be pleasant, but with the words of those texts sitting heavy in his head he can't drag it out of himself.

Have you ever been tempted by anyone while you were away? Em once asked him, so matter-of-factly, as though whatever his answer was, she would just be glad to have her curiosity on the topic satisfied.

He felt so offended. Em might drive him nuts at times, but he's never *not* fancied her or *not* wanted to be with her, though the feeling might not be reciprocated. Besides, despite whatever hard times they might be going through, he's never really considered shagging anyone else a solution. His answer was the only answer he could give. *Truthfully? I never have.*

When the lift arrives at the ground floor, he lets the woman step out ahead of him. He's aware of pale legs and navy-blue court shoes and of her saying, 'Have a great day.' American, obviously. No one else seems to think you can have a great day when you're going to work.

He follows her into the lobby. He's thoroughly queasy now and has broken out into an ungodly sweat. He wonders if he should try to find a toilet. It could come either end. To try to will it away, he reaches into his pocket for his phone and types Em a text.

Morning. You ok? Sorry I was a bit distracted last night. Wanted to ring you but phone ended up dying.

He suddenly turns shaky, tries to swallow down an excess of gummy saliva. *Ugh!* Fortunately he makes it to the gents, but he's barely through the door before he pukes his insides up all over his shoes and the newly polished floor.

SEVEN

Charlotte and I finally have a chance to meet in the village for a cup of tea in her lunch break.

'I never told you what happened at the party!' she says, her first benign reference to it since we had 'words' a couple of weeks ago.

'Do tell.' I love Charlotte's slightly inane stories, so long as neither Eric nor I are in them, of course.

'Well, three o'clock in the morning, everyone's gone home except Ann and Patrick. I said they could stay in our spare room given they were both hammered.' She wipes a big blob of cream off the end of her nose. 'It was a bit annoying because we hadn't changed the bed since we had my cousin over, so I had to scramble for clean sheets which I totally didn't feel like doing . . . But then of all the things! What do you think they did?'

'Decided to go home anyway?'

'No, darling! I wish!' She bounces up and down.

I frown.

'They had sex! In our *house*! Like we're some sort of dirty motel! They actually dared to shag!'

I press fingers over my mouth to suppress my smile.

'What's funny? How would you feel if you gave someone a bed for the night and they had it off? We share a common wall. Our bed was practically vibrating! I was getting motion sick!'

I wrinkle my nose. 'Ugh. I suppose it is a bit weird.' I am always powerfully aware of the sanctity of someone's home. I could never feel so comfortable in someone else's place to want to bonk Eric.

'I sent Garth in to do the sheets. I said, "They're your friends. You can clean up after them!"'

'Good heavens,' I say. 'That does add a whole new dimension to knowing your friends well . . .' My phone pings. Zara.

Going 2 B's tonite after school.

'Hang on,' I say to Charlotte, while I reply: Will her mother be home?

She sends me a thumbs up.

I could put my foot down. But she seems so much chirpier these days.

ONE hr! Plus homework done before dinner.

Only got Geog quiz!

ONE hr!

K, she replies, and inserts an emoji of a screaming face.

I tell Charlotte about Bethany Brown, and the baboon thing. I hadn't really intended to. I know I shouldn't have bothered when I'm mid-story and she's already looking askance.

'You need to break this little cosy little arrangement up. The last thing you want is Zara getting in with a bad apple.'

'We don't know she's that.' Whenever I hear 'you need', I find myself wanting to disagree for the sake of disagreeing, just to show I can. 'She's just a kid who doesn't have our kids' privileges.'

'Well, the second Zara's in with the wrong crowd, you know where that's going to lead. You've got to nip it in the bud. What happened to all her other friends?'

I frown. 'Well, firstly, the girl's new to the school and doesn't know anyone – she's not part of any crowd. And as for Zara's other friends – well, you know one of them moved away.'

'But what about that girl whose mother had three husbands?'

'Katy, yes.' I smile. 'She's still around. Zara's just not all that close to her any more. You know what they're like at this age.'

'Well, the second I sniff any of my lads hanging out with undesirables, that will be the end of it. That's why we pay for private schools. You need to keep that sort of thing at bay. And it usually begins with being tough with them, even if that makes you unpopular.'

I am just about to say, *There are plenty of undesirables at private schools – just rich ones. And, actually, I don't need a lesson in parenting,* when – 'Oh no! Speak of the devil . . .'

'What?' Charlotte shoots her head around to where I'm looking.

Bethany's mother is tugging down a golfer-sized red umbrella. The wind's beneath it and she has to fight with the thing, like a severe-faced Mary Poppins. Despite us being seated at the back of the busy café, she looks right at us through the window just before she enters – almost as though she knew we were here all along.

'Just pretend we're talking,' I say in a rushed whisper, telling Charlotte who the woman is.

'Well, we are.' My friend's eyes are in full twinkle mode now. 'About her daughter.' Charlotte loves a bit of drama. So long as it's not her drama, of course.

I watch Bethany's mother placing her order at the counter. The way she flicks a cavalier hand at the scones. I wonder if she ever smiles. She is wearing a knee-length trench coat and tall black boots and has her fair hair tied back in a stubby ponytail today. I am surprised how readily I recognise her given I am not great at remembering faces. Zara says Bethany calls her mum 'Janet'. Zara gets a kick out of this; I just think it's disrespectful and bizarre. Just as she's finished paying, the couple at the table next to ours stand up to leave, freeing up a place. Damn. I try not to look in her direction as she makes her way over.

'Bethany's becoming good pals with Zara,' she says, apropos of nothing, as though we were in the middle of a conversation. She sets the tray on the table, sits down and slides her coat off her shoulders, letting it drape around her hips like a blanket.

'Oh?' I hope my tone accomplishes friendly but distant. She still looks pale and tired. It wasn't just my porch light.

'She thinks Zara's the bomb.' She removes the lid from the teapot and inserts a spoon.

I watch her over-stirring as though she has a grievance against the pot. She isn't wearing any make-up except for some brown liner that accentuates her slightly heavy lids and the downturn of her eyes.

'Our daughters go to the same school,' she informs Charlotte, tiredly, as though she and I are members of a team that doesn't include my friend. 'They've become very close.'

'Zara has a lot of friends already,' I say, trying not to sound too pointed. 'And she has so much going on after school. So many extracurricular commitments!' Charlotte will probably be thinking, *Huh? Zara? Since when?*

'Bethany could use a good influence.' She sends a knife cleanly through her cheese scone. 'Zara seems like a nice girl.'

Thanks for the vote of confidence!

'And you have a son too.' Finally she glances at me. 'Bethany's very keen to meet him.'

I want to say, *Yeah, over my dead body!* I can just see it. Girls like her would get a kick out of going after their friend's brother, just for the conquest.

'Emily has two model children,' Charlotte says. 'And a wonderful husband too. She's the envy of many.'

'One child for me. And I can promise you that's been enough. And no husband, wonderful or otherwise.'

'Oh dear! Single mum?' Charlotte chirps sympathetically.

'It's not always easy.'

There is something so lacklustre about her entire demeanour that she drags you down just looking at her.

'No. I can imagine.' Charlotte glances at me in a way that says, *We're never going to get rid of her now.*

'Actually, it's something you can't imagine,' she replies, talking to her scone. 'Not until you've done it. People always think they can imagine things they've never been through, but they can't.'

'Right,' Charlotte says. She gives me another sly look that says, *I stand corrected!*

I find myself angling my shoulders toward my friend now, hoping Janet might get the message.

'I don't mean to keep you from your conversation,' she says, clearly on to me.

'Enjoy your tea,' I tell her, pleasantly. 'Your scone looks delicious.'

Where were we? I can hardly tell Charlotte what I was going to say – about how I'm not feeling close to Eric at the moment. How I sometimes feel like my marriage is a ball that's rolling downhill from me; I have lost my ability to pass and advance up the field. Or about how annoyed I was last night when I texted him about our daughter's new friend and he brushed me off, then this morning pretended his phone had died. So instead I say a banal 'Are you planning any more holidays?'

Charlotte gives me the knowing look, then tells me all the countries she plans to visit if she ever gets the time.

Then Bethany's mother pulls on her coat. I look over, waiting for her to catch my eye and say goodbye. But she gets up without uttering a word and walks towards the door.

'Weird!' Charlotte whispers as I watch Janet Brown go, my intuition echoing that very sentiment.

EIGHT

I spot him the moment I emerge from around the tree. Otis lets out an ungodly squeal. As we approach one another I am laughing. 'They meet! Finally! This is a big day in dog world!'

'This is Jasper,' he says. We both go to pet his chocolate Labrador and our fingers make contact.

'He's so calm! What a quiet boy!' No sooner are the words out of me than the dogs take off across the green like a couple of stampeding horses. 'Well, looks like they've really hit it off!'

'I'm hoping for the same for us,' he says, smiling broadly, and I laugh.

We follow the scampering dogs. 'Do you usually walk mornings?' I ask, surprised I haven't run into him out here by now. He's wearing a Barbour jacket with jeans, his brownish-grey hair sticking up in a few tufts, and if I hadn't known he was a doctor I might have guessed gentleman farmer, or member of the landed aristocracy.

'No. It depends on my shifts. Life never has any set routines, and that's both a blessing and a curse.' He stops, places his hands in his pockets and turns to face me. The fog is rolling in hard from the moors, quickly whiting out everything around us but his steady, pale blue-green gaze.

'That must be challenging. I've often wondered why doctors, who have one of the most stressful professions imaginable, have to work such exhaustingly long shifts.'

'Well, I've done it my entire career. I'm used to it now. But you're right . . . it's not ideal on the body or the social life.' I wonder if 'social life' means dating. I assume he knows I'm aware his wife died, that Charlotte would have told me. In the white stillness I can hear Otis and Jasper play-growling. 'What about you?' he asks. 'Do you work outside the home? Or are you a full-time mother?'

I chuckle a little. 'How very tactful of you.'

'Tactful?' He sends me a curious look. 'Hmm . . . Not been accused of that before.'

'Most people just say, "Do you not work?" You know, as though raising kids isn't a full-time job, implying you're somehow underperforming.'

'Ah.' Then he says, 'Really?' and looks shocked – or pretends to.

'Actually, I lecture PR and Communications part-time at Leeds University. I used to work in PR for a big firm in Leeds when I was first married, but I travelled tons; it didn't work so well once I became a mother. So I decided to go out on my own.'

'An entrepreneur.'

'Hardly . . . It was only doing some consulting. It was fine in some ways, but difficult with a new baby because Daniel wasn't well for a little while after he was born. Clients always demand one hundred per cent of you and they're not very forgiving.'

'Like how no one grasps that doctors aren't always on call.'

'Ah . . . you mean always wanting a medical opinion? "Doctor, it hurts when I laugh." So the doctor says, "Don't laugh"?'

He smiles. 'That. And drugs.'

I gasp. 'Oh dear! That must get annoying.'

'Not really,' he says. 'Well, no, really. It can be. Sometimes you just feel like saying to people, "Fuck off."' He doesn't look like the type to swear, or to want to tell people to fuck off, so it makes me laugh. 'Anyway, back to what you were saying . . . You gave it up?'

'After Zara came along. I decided to concentrate on being a mother for a while. But it didn't last long, unfortunately. My husband lost his job rather suddenly,' I say, tactfully. I don't really want to remind myself of Eric's mysterious layoff, and the big lie he told. 'Zara was only five months old. I had to quickly find work.'

'Oh.' He looks at me curiously. 'That must have been hard.'

'It was supposed to be an account executive position at an advertising firm, but I was mostly just answering phones and doing admin.' I remember feeling it was such a comedown but I had no choice; I needed to support my family. 'I'd gone to Durham just like my husband. I'd got a First in English, had a demanding career I loved. But I couldn't do that and be a mother . . .'

Yet Eric was the one who fell into a self-pitying slump. I clearly remember how he'd snap at me if I asked what he'd done with his day. He didn't seem to care that I was managing on very little sleep, then coming home, exhausted, to a sink full of dishes, a restless two-year-old and a baby with a face covered in caked-on food . . .

'It's hard, as a mother, to strike a balance,' I say, though I doubt this man's life is much of one either. 'You tell yourself it'll just be until they're a little bit older, and more independent, but then they become teenagers and you're suddenly in a whole other stretch of uncharted territory.' It occurs to me that I'm sounding very down on my life.

'Did you ever regret having kids?' he surprises me by asking.

I laugh a little. 'We seem to have got ourselves into some deep conversation, haven't we?'

'Is there any other kind?' He meets my eyes again, with that challenging expression of his. I like how he seems genuinely interested. Perhaps it comes with being a doctor.

'No. I suppose not . . .' I inhale the fresh air that has the lovely ability to almost smell verdant and green. 'To answer you, no, I don't regret having them. I mean, if I'm being perfectly honest, when I found out I was preggers with Daniel, I sort of went, "Ugh!" I was enjoying life, being newly married, my job . . . And yet, when he was born there was this huge cosmic shift inside . . .'

I remember blaming myself for his premature condition – if I had wanted him more, perhaps his little collection of cells would have decided from the outset that it was going to thrive.

'The birth of my son redrafted the world and reordered all that's relative, and then of course my daughter too . . . When you become a mother, no one else can even come close to making you feel how their little life makes you feel, so much so that you reposition everyone else you love. You love them all a slightly distant second.' I am hot with emotion and tug at my scarf.

He is studying me intently. 'Beautifully put,' he says. And then he adds, 'Wow.'

'How did we get on to this?' I suddenly feel very self-conscious.

'I don't know but I'm glad we did. And not to worry, the revelation of your inner psyche is safe with me.'

This makes me smile. 'Maybe it's because you're a doctor. People feel they can reveal themselves to you.'

'Yuck. I wish they wouldn't.'

I laugh. 'Sorry!'

'No, I don't mean you . . .'

We smile again. He has a way of looking a little down his nose when he smiles, a little teasing, a little superior. I like it.

'Your son looks like a great kid,' he says.

It always seems as though the scope of Daniel's achievement somehow negates poor Zara's unremarkable existence. 'He is. As is Zara. Though I worry way more about her.' Bethany Brown's face appears in my mind. 'I see changes in her lately that are just sort of coming at me out of the blue, and, well, you can feel out of your depth at times.' I frown. 'Good heavens. You're probably thinking I'm a real negative Nellie!'

'Not at all! I admire your openness. Not that there's anything wrong with negative Nellies, of course. They make the world a more realistic place.'

I peer at the time on my phone. 'Oh, shoot! I really should go! This was only supposed to be a quick walk. I've got to go into uni for a meeting at ten.' I holler at Otis. 'Now I'm never going to get him to come!'

'It's all my fault,' my new neighbour says, sounding a little amused. 'I unfairly encouraged the baring of your soul.'

'It really is!' As I catch myself in the pleasurable rip current of our banter, I feel a little red flag being erected in me. The mist has broken in the distance and I can see frolicking flashes of brown and beige. Then Steve gives one sharp whistle that pierces the silence. Jasper bounds towards him, with Otis dutifully following.

'Thanks,' I chuckle. 'Nothing like being reminded you've got the least obedient dog in the neighbourhood.' I put Otis's lead on as soon as I can reach him.

'Well, given I walk mornings more often now, I might see you again, do you think?' He cocks me a look that isn't loaded in any way, and yet I find my face heating up.

'For the next scintillating instalment of my life story? I bet you can't wait.'

'I really can't,' he says, playfully. Then he looks at me for half a second longer than is fully comfortable.

As I walk home I find myself thinking back over our conversation and realise I suddenly feel so very alive.

Then I berate myself.

Very alive?

Good grief. Get a grip!

NINE

I can't get Tom's reprimand off my mind! A student sent me an email that it seems I 'couldn't be bothered' to reply to, and the student complained!

I did actually forget about replying to the damned student, though I wasn't going to tell Tom that or he'd probably think I do it all the time. So I told a fib and said my outbox showed it as sent. But now I realise I'd better deal with it before I forget all over again. I log on to my computer, still feeling more than a little sore about being told off like a naughty two-year-old.

Dear Prajval Dhaliwal,

I'm sorry you didn't receive my email. Class attendance is not negotiable. It is every student's responsibility to be present, take notes, fulfil assignment obligations and sit the scheduled exam. Any absence can only be for a medical reason or emergency and requires a doctor's note or other appropriate proof. There are no exceptions made for holidays.

On another point, I strongly suggest you refrain from using textese in formal communication, and use spell check before you press send. It makes a very poor impression. Given this is a Communications course, if this email is any indication of your writing ability, you may wish to consider withdrawing.

Sincerely,
Emily Rossi

I debate whether or not to delete that last paragraph. But then I think it's important he knows he needs to smarten himself up so I decide to leave it in, and press send.

'What about this one?' I hold up a dove-grey jumper with a vertical cream stripe. The shops at Trinity Leeds are packed for a Tuesday evening.

'Bethany says grey is for old ladies!'

'This, then?'

'Pink?'

She picks up some cheap black sequinned thing with only one sleeve. *Couldn't afford one with two, love?* Sometimes I hear my mother's voice so clearly it's bizarre to me that she isn't behind me, that I won't turn and see her saucy smile. 'Bethany says I need to stop dressing like I'm you.'

That name. I'm becoming allergic to it. 'Food, then. I assume we can eat without Bethany's approval?' I can't believe they've only been hanging out for a short few weeks and it's like they've practically married one another.

'Not noodles, though. Bethany says carbs are giving me bad skin and it's why I'm a dough ball.'

'She called you a dough ball?'

'Well, I am.'

'And what do you think? Or do you not have opinions of your own any more?' I recognise it a mile off: the beginnings of Zara sticking to someone like a barnacle.

She shrugs. 'I'll never be as thin as her. It's not fair.'

'That's like saying I'll never have hair like Kate Middleton. You're entirely different builds. Maybe Bethany can live off lettuce but that's probably why she has bad breath.'

'You think her breath's bad?' My daughter looks at me like I've just divulged an outlandish secret.

'Starved-person's breath. The smoking probably doesn't help.'

'Everybody who smokes doesn't have bad breath!'

'Do you smoke?'

'No!' she responds, as though I've asked her something highly offensive. 'I tried it once and I hate it. Yuck!' We trot off toward the noodle counter and she orders broccoli with bean sprouts.

'You can't just eat that!'

'My belly. My business.'

'Good luck with that attitude.'

We will see how long this lasts. I order my regular pad thai with chicken, and the prawns as a side for her, for when she changes her mind.

'Bethany's boyfriend clearly doesn't think she's got bad breath,' Zara says as we sit down and start eating. 'Because he could probably have anybody but he wants her.'

'I didn't know she has a boyfriend. What's his name?'

'Craig Rathbone,' she replies, after a lengthy hesitation.

I can tell she's enjoying this business of feeding me titbits of stuff she knows I want to know, like I am a baby bird. If I want to keep them coming, the key is to show minimal interest. I poke around at my chicken for a moment or two, then finally say, 'Why can he have anybody, then?'

'Because he's really fit. And he's got a posh car. And he's rolling in money.' She has come alive again; her cheeks are slightly flushed.

'Car? How old is he?'

'Obviously old enough to drive.'

I know she wants me to take the bait here, but I'm not going to. 'What does he do to have all this money?' I ask loosely, after I finish chewing, like I couldn't care less.

She lolls her tongue out for a second. 'How would I know? He's not exactly talkative.'

I focus on my pad thai as though it's far more interesting than Bethany or her boyfriend, yet I am secretly steaming. Damn! Charlotte was right. I should have nipped the Bethany friendship in the bud. Why did I let myself believe it was harmless?

'He's always got lots of people around him though. Coming and going. Friends, or people. But he's never very nice to them.'

'Oh? In what way?'

Her ears are beet red now. 'He's very grunty. *Huh? Yuh! Uh?* You know . . . I don't think he can string a sentence together.'

'Have you met any of his friends?'

'Not really,' she says, after a hesitation, then she adds, 'Oh, I met one! He's OK. He always says hello to me.'

She looks down at her food and blushes. My pulse beats wildly in my head. Suddenly the concept of an older boy who hangs out with Bethany's nefarious boyfriend saying hello to Zara and my daughter being gullible enough to think he's just being nice, razes a small path of terror through me.

'Where was this?'

'Nowhere,' she says, guilelessly. 'Just around. If we're out and they drive past.'

'You don't want to get too chummy with friends of Bethany's boyfriend. You know nothing about them.' I can't really see Zara being a magnet for edgy types of boys. She's no Bethany. Though I've noticed that lately she's washing her hair every day so it no longer looks lank, and is painting her fingernails black on weekends.

She tuts. 'I'm not friends with anybody! I just said hello!'

'But like I said. They're older. You have to be careful. And I don't want you going off with them anywhere. You should never, ever be anywhere but a public place. You know that, don't you?'

'I'm not an idiot.'

'Does she speak much about her dad?' I ask, after a beat.

'He's a wanker.'

'That's not clever.' I stare at the top of her mousey-brown head, the fine silky hair and the pale pink parting. 'Don't try to become her, Zara. She's nothing to aspire to, I promise.'

'It's just what she calls him! I'm just repeating it! God, I can't even speak these days!'

Her deep brown eyes well up with tears. We are on a precipice. If I tell her to go this way, she's going to want to go the other. She had a stubborn streak in her when she was younger, as did Daniel. It was never fully fledged enough to be rebellion. But whereas Daniel channelled his in a positive direction, I always sensed Zara could be a little flame-throwing with hers.

'Does she see her dad?' I try to keep the conversation productive.

'Dunno. I don't think so. Her mum and him were together at one point. I think they were married and everything, but then he took off when she was born. I think he had another woman or something.'

I ask her if she wants these prawns but she says, 'I would rather die than eat bottom-feeders.'

I set about eating one or two – I might as well, given I've paid for them.

'She asks about Dad all the time. And about you.'

'Oh? What sorts of things?'

'About why he works away. If I like him. If I like you. If I get on with Daniel. She says it's because she doesn't understand what it's like to be in a family. Because there's only ever been her and Janet. She says it's so unfair that we were born exactly the same, and yet I get the perfect family and she's got it so crap, because she hates her mum, and her dad's a tosser who never wanted to be in her life.'

I didn't realise they'd had deep conversations.

'Well, that's very sad. But it's life, honey. There's always someone who appears to have it better than you. And somebody who's got it worse.'

My phone chimes to say I've got a text. Charlotte. *Our neighbour said he really enjoyed bumping into you. You dark horse!!! I think he fancies you! Bitch!*

I smile, inwardly. Then – silly – but I delete it.

We eat in silence. I can't shake my unease about Bethany having an older boyfriend. I just wish this girl would disappear. But I suddenly get an idea. 'Why don't you invite Bethany and her mum to dinner this Friday?'

At first she seems stunned. 'What makes you think they'd want to come to ours?' She says it as though they are the Ladies Grantham and we chop their firewood.

I think of her mother's easy familiarity in the café. I wonder if she knows about Bethany having an older boyfriend with money and a car. 'You could ask.' *Keep your friends close . . .* I try to go on eating nonchalantly.

'OK,' she says, after a long contemplation. 'Maybe I will.'

We don't talk any more. I abandon the prawns and we walk back through the shopping centre. There is a buoyancy to the silence, though, since I've signalled I might be embracing her new friend.

When we get to the car she says, 'Can we stop and buy a pasty on the way? I'm bloody famished.'

TEN

On Wednesday evening when Zara is at her granddad's and Daniel is at the gym, I pop over to Charlotte's for a glass of wine while Garth has the boys out at karate. I remember when the pair of them first moved in. They seemed so much more grown-up than us, even though we're virtually the same age. Right off the bat, Charlotte complained, in high-handed fashion, that one of our trees was blocking the light in her kitchen and she suggested we thin it out without further ado. We did, and she popped a note through our door to thank us, but I tried to avoid her after that. Then one day she was lugging some bags of groceries up her path as I was passing with Otis, who was a tiny puppy back then. She stood and chatted about a spate of break-ins in the area, and by the time we'd finished talking, neither of us had noticed that Otis had nibbled almost entirely through a bunch of kale that was sticking out of one of her bags. All that was left was the stalks. She had such a laugh. I hadn't really pegged her as being someone with an infectious sense of humour. The following day I bought her a new bunch and she invited me in for a cup of tea. We've been great friends ever since.

I like visiting Charlotte. Her house is chaotic – exactly the opposite of everything she projects – but it's homely. She doesn't care if her cushions are threadbare, or if the toilet bowl could use a go-around with the brush. She once told me she'd employed a barrage of cleaners over the years but had scared them all off. *I don't have any standards,* she said, *unless I'm paying for them! Then I have ones no one can meet!* And then she'd ripped out one of her glorious laughs.

'Everything's getting under my skin lately.' I tell her, among other things, about my reprimand that is still irking me.

'Darling, you need to ask our doctor for a little medication.' She gives me her dirty smile.

I felt that coming.

'Seriously, though? What's wrong? You haven't seemed yourself for ages and I don't think it's all to do with your mother or getting a telling off at work.'

Charlotte always attempts to get to the heart of your problems and never blows you off just to get back to talking about herself.

'I don't know,' I tell her. 'Not sure what's at the bottom of it. But I definitely don't think Eric and I are trying to make the best of him having to be in London. It's almost like we're becoming estranged, and we're both somehow OK with it.'

'Why don't you go down to London once in a while for the weekend?'

I suddenly turn sad. 'Because he's never asked me to. He's got that lovely big hotel room all to himself. You'd think he'd have wanted to share it with me occasionally. Maybe he thinks it would put too much pressure on us to do the whole dirty-weekend thing . . .'

I feel her scrutinise me. I am not given to intimate revelations about my marriage; some things are best kept private. 'You don't think he's sharing it with somebody else?'

I frown. 'No,' I say, after a second or two. 'Not at all. That's not Eric.'

'No. I don't think it is either, to be honest.' I can see her brain working overtime. 'Why don't you suggest going down? It's not like the idea has to come from him!'

'You're right, but I'd like him to show some initiative . . .'

She pats the back of my hand. 'It's fine, darling. You've reached that point we all reach in marriage. Where neither of us can fancy the other no matter how hard we try. It's normal.'

I smile, despite the awfulness of it. 'I'm sure you're still attracted to Garth.'

Or Girth, as Eric jokingly calls him. I once told him, *You'd better stop that or you'll say it to his face one day!*

'Of course I'm not!' she says, like she's protesting that she never steals or goes out without her underwear on. 'We've been married forever! Then again, I'm not sure I even was in the beginning! I think we might have just been very good friends who had reached that age where it felt easier to just be with one another, rather than set about searching for someone else.'

I think of when I first met Eric. I was very attracted. He was big and protective and gentle and kind. And he was sharp as a whip – the most intelligent person I'd ever known, but he also had the least ego of anyone I knew, which I loved about him. Then I witnessed him get shambolically shitfaced at a party, and I thought, *Is this something I need be worried about?* But like I always tend to do, I gave him the benefit of the doubt, looked to his good qualities, which were plentiful. Everybody gets hammered at uni and acts stupid at least once, don't they?

'Well, Garth certainly looks like he's into you,' I say. It saddens me to think of those early days and how they feel so very distant.

'I wouldn't bet on it. I think I might be the wrong sex.'

'What?'

'Well,' she says darkly. 'We've been watching *The Slap* on Netflix, after you recommended it . . . You know that scene where the teenage boy starts going to the swimming pool so he can spy on Hector in his bathing trunks? Then he takes a photo and Hector catches him doing it?'

I grin.

'Well, the kids were in bed. Something about that show sort of gets me going . . . I leaned over, and when I grabbed him, he was hard.' She performs that jaw-drop thing she does, because Charlotte's mannerisms are always endearingly over the top. 'He's clearly having gay fantasies.'

I nearly choke on my wine. 'Don't be insane!'

'What other explanation is there, darling? How would you feel if you grabbed Eric when he was watching a bit of boy-on-boy and he had a hard-on?'

'I'd naturally assume he was thinking of me.'

'No you wouldn't!'

It feels odd talking about Garth like this, in his own house. 'Well, you can't punish somebody for their thoughts.'

'Can't you? I asked him how he would feel if some teenage boy was taking photos of him in his trunks at the public baths . . . He said he'd probably be flattered.'

'Well, I'd say that's the sort of comment a man would make who didn't feel threatened by the idea at all. So you've nothing to worry about.'

'Well, you know me . . . I put it to another test. I rented *Call Me by Your Name.*'

'Oh no!' We read the novel about gay first love in the book club she persuaded me to join. Until I later decided I love reading but I prefer it when I'm the one who chooses the book.

'He only saw the first two minutes and then he took off upstairs saying he had some work to do!'

No sooner does she say that than we hear barking outside her window. She gets up and walks over, waves for me to follow. 'Oh! Now look at this!'

Dr Steve is in his garden throwing a ball for the dog. He is wearing a short-sleeved polo shirt, revealing his fit arms.

'I doubt *he's* having gay fantasies,' she says, sadly.

'You never know. Maybe we'd both be surprised.'

We smirk.

'I know you think I'm being ridiculous . . .' she says as she goes back to the couch and gets settled again. 'But what my husband should have said was, "I'd have grabbed his camera off him and shoved it up his bottom!"'

'Well, maybe not his bottom,' I say.

Fortunately she folds with laughter.

When I get home, the conversation is still ripe in my mind. Mainly as an experiment, to see how he'll react, and probably because I've had half a bottle of wine, I send Eric a text.

> What do you think about me coming down there, not this weekend but next? Dad can stay with the kids.

I can see it's read but he isn't exactly rushing to reply. Then I see he's typing.

Maybe.

I wait to see if any more is coming but it looks like there isn't.

> Maybe we talk about it when you come home Friday? ☺

> Not coming this Friday, comes the quick reply.

I blink. What?'

> Way too busy. Best I stay here this time. Knuckle down.

I stare at his words, trying to decide how to react to them.

When were you going to tell me? I ask.

There's a lengthy pause, then:

Telling you now.

His smart-aleck attitude infuriates me. I try to ring him but he must have quickly powered down his phone.

ELEVEN

'What d'you mean you're not coming home?' It has irked me all day and I'm surprised I've managed to contain myself until this evening.

'You know, Emily, my day was terrific, how was yours?' he says, sarcastically.

I sit on the end of Zara's bed, forgetting what I even came in here for.

After my stony silence, he says, 'Look please can we not go on about it? It's not like I want to work the weekend, you know. I've just got way too much on so it's best I stay down here and crack on with it.'

My pulse flickers in my neck. 'But I wasn't going on about it. I just asked one question.'

I hear his humongous sigh. 'Look, for God's sake, we don't have to make a federal case of everything, do we? I'm swamped, Emily. I'm struggling to stay afloat. I've got to put work first, without all this pressure . . . Maybe next weekend I'll take the Friday off so we'll get a long one. And I'll come home, or you can come down. Will that make you happy?'

It's not about making me happy, I feel like screaming. I'd have thought it would make him happy too. For the briefest of moments,

I think of Charlotte's comment. *You don't think he's sharing it with somebody else?*

Is this really what it is? An affair? I try to imagine it. Perhaps I'm mad, or ridiculously naïve, but I just can't see it.

When I can't muster up any words, he says, a little less strident, 'You don't want me to lose my job, do you? Or *do* you?' The subtle reminder of what we both know life was like during his various spells of unemployment. Eric seemed to become a different person after that very first long layoff after Zara was born. He took umbrage easily, always seemed to be one match away from an inferno. At one point he actually left a position at a small tech start-up because the CEO said *Fuck you!* to him. He later said it wasn't the fact that he'd sworn; what had rattled his chain was that he was ten years Eric's junior. He was jealous!

No, I think. *If I have to live through walking on eggshells and watching you lolling around the house, cracking open a beer at 1 p.m., I won't be able to go on.*

'You sound tired,' I say. I don't feel like getting into an argument.

'You'd be tired if you were me!' He is still a little defensive. 'On top of everything that's going on, there's some sort of generator issue in the hotel so I had to move rooms at bastard o'clock in the morning because of the noise.'

'Bastard o'clock?' I find myself smiling.

'You'd not think it was so amusing if it had been you . . .' Then he adds, 'Look, if you're in a funny mood shall we just ring off and talk tomorrow?'

'No,' I tell him. 'I'm not in a funny mood and I don't want to ring off, thank you. I haven't talked to you in three days.' My eyes latch on to a carrier bag sticking out from under Zara's dressing table. I get up, go over and tug it out. Normally he phones every night. Although I can't say I've massively missed talking to him.

When he can be so snappy, what's to miss? I peer in the bag and see some clothes from Primark with their labels on. Zara never said she'd gone shopping . . . I must remember to ask her about them.

'Look, I've not had the best day either,' I say. Although when does he ever much care about my day? 'I was called into another meeting with Tom this morning. About this student. He wants me to apologise to him.'

'What?'

'The student reacted badly to my remark about his communication skills.'

'But they were non-existent.'

'But Tom thinks it might become bigger if we don't pacify him. Anyway, he didn't say I absolutely had to apologise. He said I might want to *consider* it.'

'Isn't that the same thing?'

'Is it? I don't think so.'

'Well, doesn't it undercut your authority a bit?'

'Yes!'

'So what're you going to do?'

'I might just tell the lad to come have a word with me in office hours.'

'Well, be sure you've got somebody with you.'

'Why?'

'Then it won't be *he said, she said.*'

'I'm sure that's not necessary . . .' I yawn. His tiredness must be catching. I hear the familiar sharp chinkle of a seal breaking on a screw-top lid, the short glug – one, two, three, four – of liquid being poured into a glass. And I know he's pouring a whisky from the minibar – I even know the size of the pour – as sure as if I had X-ray vision. I thought he only drank beer these days?

'Did you eat tonight?' I ask, and I feel like adding, *Pour a whisky?* I have told myself that so long as he keeps to one or two drinks, then that's OK. He mostly has, except for parties. But of course I have no idea what he does in London.

'Nah. Had a late client lunch. Just grabbed a Pret sandwich tonight and had it in the room. A ham and cheese. And the pea and ham soup. It's been a ham kind of evening.'

'I can't believe you're not coming home tomorrow,' I say, unthreateningly, warmed a little by his attempt to be amusing. There are moments, in my indifference towards him, when I remember the easy-going, mellow Eric he used to be. Before life stopped swimming along nicely, and alcohol became a fixer for him.

'I know. But I'm not . . . Let's not get on this again, eh?'

'I know,' I say. 'We're not getting on anything . . . Sometimes I worry about us.' There. I've been angling to say it for ages. There is never a right moment. I am tired of always feeling there has to be.

'Don't. Everything's fine . . . Look, gonna hit the sack early. Call you in the morning?'

'OK.' Of course. Eric doesn't want to talk about it, so we're not going to talk about it.

He adds, 'Love ya.'

As I'm working my way around saying it back, I find I needn't have bothered. He's already hung up.

TWELVE

She brings Tesco Rioja and a bouquet of lilies. She steps inside our house like she's entering the state rooms at Buckingham Palace. Otis greets her like they're old friends. Bethany shyly offers me a knitted brown mouse for Juniper. 'I wanted to bring a gift for Otis too,' she says. 'Maybe they can share it for now?' I'm pleasantly surprised by her thoughtfulness, and thank her.

'This is quite lovely,' Janet says, of our house, though it sounds more like distaste than a compliment.

I take the flowers from her. 'Thanks. They're gorgeous.' I have never liked lilies since that horrible episode in our kitchen many years ago. I offer her a glass of the red I've just opened. The girls are giddy and gallop off upstairs.

'Why are you making lamb?' Zara asked me earlier. 'Bethany doesn't eat anything that has a heartbeat.'

'It doesn't have one,' I said. 'It's dead.'

'I thought we were trying to make a good impression on them!' Were we? I hadn't realised.

'I think I've seen this before.' Janet is staring at the photo of Daniel and Andy Murray on the fridge door. 'You were all in the newspaper a while back, weren't you?'

'Yes,' I say. I walk to the sideboard and show her the framed picture. 'In February. They did a nice feature on us because Daniel had just won the Winter Cup. They included that one of him, too, with Andy . . .'

'It's a nice one of your husband, isn't it?' she says, taking the frame from me. 'What's his name? I feel like I should know it by now . . .' She casts me an incurious look. The very one I've seen Bethany give.

'Eric.' I go back to the bench and carefully lay the crust on the apple pie.

'Ah, yes. Eric. The absentee father.' She says it tiredly, as though everybody has one of those in their life.

'I hope you like lamb,' I say.

She puts down the photo and then continues her blatant examination of our stuff, wandering over to the cabinet where all of Daniel's trophies are displayed. She has dressed nicely, in a black pencil skirt and a cream blouse with tulip sleeves. She is very thin up top but has a generous bottom and good legs. 'Look at all these,' she says, sounding underwhelmed. 'It must be such a gift to get such a great start in life.'

'Well, he works very hard. He definitely hasn't been gifted anything.'

She turns and faces me again. 'I hear you're a lecturer at the uni.'

'Yup. PR and Communications.'

'Must be lucrative.'

'I'm only part-time. One course a term. Sometimes two.'

'Sounds quite cushy.'

I think of my reprimand from Tom. 'Do you work as well?' I ask her. She is bending to stroke the kitten. I can see down her top. The ridge of bones down the centre of her chest. The highly padded, flesh-toned bra.

'Yes. Harvey Nichols accounting department. In Leeds.'

'Ah. That's why you dress nicely.' I shove the pie in the oven and turn up the gas.

'I said I work there, not shop there. I'm a single mother with zero financial support from Bethany's father. Harvey Nichols doesn't know that people like me exist.' She pointedly looks my clothes over, and I can't help but wish I'd worn my H&M jeans instead of the pricey Hudson ones I treated myself to when I swiftly lost ten pounds after my mother died.

'It can't be easy,' I say.

'As I was saying to Charlotte, until you've been a single mother, you really have no idea. Bethany was a nightmare from the day she drew her first breath. But I've got no choice, have I? No part-time options for me.'

I stop and look at her now as she stares out at the garden, thinking how blithely she just referred to my friend by name as though we were a cosy little trio of pals. 'So no help at all from Bethany's father, then?'

She does a disdainful grunt. 'You know what men are like. They tend to think that supporting their kids is your right but their option.'

'But surely he has to pay child support?'

'You're never going to get blood out of a stone. Or out of a man when he wants to be a bastard.' She stares at our wedding picture on the sideboard for a moment or two, then looks me straight in the eyes. 'You know, I'm a good person. I don't want to cause him harm. He's got his problems and I did once love him . . . A part of me has only ever wanted him to wake up and realise his responsibilities.' She looks off, solemnly, into the distance. 'I always say to Bethany, "Treat people how they treat you. And if people want to walk away from you, you have to let them walk." But then on the other hand, if they owe you something, they should pay up, shouldn't they? If they don't, then you need to hunt them down the rabbit hole.'

'How true,' I say, suddenly thinking, *God, you wouldn't want to get on her wrong side, would you?* Despite her words, she doesn't seem malicious, though; more like actively dejected.

'I don't know why it never works out for me . . . All I ever wanted was a kind, reliable man. Like you have. But they always treat me like I'm just a nothing, with no feelings, like I'm not a real person . . .'

'You must have some nice friends in the store,' I say. Anything to be a bit more upbeat.

'It's mostly men in accounting. *Married* men. And – oh! – keep me away from the randy wedded letch . . . I mean, if single ones are the misery they always are, why would I want one that has a wife in tow? And the sales associates are really just a pack of hens. You think they're your friend one minute, and then one day you see the judgement in their eyes. And you think, *Hmm . . . I wonder what terrible crime I've supposedly committed now?*

I let out a tight sigh.

'Oh, they think they're better than you, because they own their own homes and have solid marriages, and model children. They think it's because they made good choices and you made shitty ones, but it's not as simple as that, is it? Sometimes people just land on their feet, whatever they do.' She is back to looking around our house again, appraising our stuff like it's up for auction.

I pull the casserole out of the oven and contemplate putting my head in there instead. 'Where did you live before here?' I ask her.

'Preston for years. Then, when Bethany was ten, I decided to move back nearer to my parents.' She absently fingers the fringe on a green velvet cushion. 'Bethany had to change schools a few times. People were never very appreciative of what she had to offer. They only looked for the bad, as people will do.'

'Where do your parents live, then?'

'In heaven.' She looks at me bluntly.

I'm confused. 'You mean they passed away recently?'

'No. But even if they'd still been alive they were never very much use to anybody. They liked their caravan holidays and Sunday rambles in the country. That's about all they were good for, really, trucking around the great outdoors with a packed sandwich and a flask of coffee.'

'So how did you land on this place?' I ask, thinking, *Pity you did!*

'Oh, it's nice here. Though we don't live right in the village like you do of course. We can't afford it.'

'Dinner's nearly ready.' I add another pat of butter to the mashed potato.

'Your husband must love that you cook.' Suddenly, she has walked over to me and is standing so close I can feel the heat of her breath on my neck.

'I've really only got a handful of dishes.' When I glance over my shoulder, we are almost nose to nose.

'He had a lot of anger issues,' she says. There is something oddly withering in the way she looks at me. 'He hated that I'd got pregnant. I suppose birth control was meant to be my responsibility, even though he was the one with the penis.'

I notice that she speaks of him with the sort of repulsion you'd feel towards someone who had just recently dealt you some damage or disappointment. He absconded years ago, according to Zara, but Janet's antipathy is fresh. Her grudge is alive and kicking. It's very strange.

'He never wanted a child with me. Not with anybody, actually. Not that they ever do! That wasn't part of his grand life plan. So he just managed to convince himself that Bethany wasn't there. The business of pushing me around was how he got to take control of the situation when I told him I wasn't going to go gracefully.'

I slide out of her range, rub my hands on my apron, feeling a stricture in my throat. 'I'm sorry.' I say. 'How awful . . .' I hadn't realised she was married to a monster. But it fits now. The battered-women's charity collecting.

'If ever there was a girl who would have benefited from a father, it's Bethany.'

'But only from the right father, no doubt. Sounds like your ex wouldn't have been it.'

She just looks at me, somewhat flatly. 'You have no idea what it's like to do your very best for a man only to find they've got such little respect for you. Or maybe you have. How would I know? I know nothing about your life.'

'We should probably sit down at the table now,' I say. Suddenly, I think, *Woman, if I have to listen to this for another two hours I'll slit my wrists!*

The girls' giggling upstairs breaks the strain slightly. Bethany's mannish guffaw. 'I'm happy they've got each other,' Janet says. 'Bethany so badly needs a good role model. Someone to keep her on track.'

I am not too fond of this responsibility she is conferring on my daughter. 'You mentioned her having to move schools. Was there some sort of trouble?'

She drains her glass. 'I believe I need a refill.' She heads to the open bottle and helps herself to a big one. When she drinks she has a habit of flicking her tongue out like a snake. Once I've noticed her doing it a couple of times, I find myself looking for her to do it again.

'I didn't realise that Bethany has a boyfriend,' I say casually, when it's clear my question is going to go unanswered.

'It's old news.'

'What's he like? He's older, I believe?'

'Well, Bethany's old for her years, isn't she? Anyhow, sometimes older is wiser.'

Did she really just say that? *She's a kid!* I haul the dish of lamb over to the table, then go to the bottom of the stairs and shout for the girls, aware that Janet's eyes follow me. The air suddenly reeks of judgement. The girls join us reluctantly. We begin eating in a silence that becomes more strained by its length.

Then, crazily out of the blue, Bethany shrieks, 'This mashed potato is frickin' fabulous!'

Zara all but chokes on her food.

'Don't say "frickin'",' Janet chides her.

'Frickin'!' Bethany leans across the table, glaring at her mother, her tiny, pert bum lifting from the chair.

Zara's laugh grows in intensity like machine-gun fire.

'Stop it.' I give Zara the warning eye. Are they on something?

'Oh yes, you're funny,' Janet says. 'Hilarious! Both of you. Really clever, girls. Really clever. You'll both go far in life.'

She looks tired. Tired of Bethany. Tired of life. With the inclusion of Zara in her disdain, a toxic overfamiliarity starts to germinate in the air.

I'm convinced Bethany's high. Can't Janet see it? Was she like that when she came in? I was too flustered to properly pay attention. But Janet just looks at me as though we are partners in having two class-act disasters for daughters. 'Where is Daniel tonight, by the way?' she asks levelly, after a moment. 'I was hoping to meet him.'

'He's actually in Spain again, for the week.' I bristle at how easily she calls the people in my life by their names. 'I took him to the airport this morning. He gets to train in one intensive block, at the Soto Academy. His teachers have been very good. They pretty much let him organise his lessons and assignments around tennis, so long as he makes it all work.'

'Must be expensive.' She severs a lamb chop. She has perfect table manners, dainty hands that neatly cover the ends of her knife and fork. Unlike her daughter, who saws her lamb with her hand clenched around the knife, angling toward her chest. Though I notice that Bethany, who won't eat anything that used to have a heartbeat, is having no trouble tucking into her three lamb chops. She is barely sparing the bones.

'He works hard. We try to be supportive. Plus, there are grants.' I can't possibly tell her that grants don't even begin to cover the expenses associated with Daniel's sport.

'But look how much money he'll earn if he's like Andy Murray.'

'Well, that's a long way down the road. He's only just turned sixteen.'

'Oh. My. God . . . Andy Murray is *such* a wanker! Tennis is *such* a lame sport.' Bethany mimics hitting a ball in the air. 'Poing! Poing! Any retard can do that.'

'Don't use that word. If you talk like that any more, we're going home,' Janet says, devoid of any authority. No wonder Bethany walks all over her.

'Can I have some wine, please?' Bethany asks me, suddenly all Miss Manners. She's a metronome: one way then the other.

'What did I just say?' Janet says.

'Errrr! What did *I* just say?' she growls, in that mannish tone again. '*I* just said, "Please may I have some wine, Mrs Rossi." Pretty please. Just a little bit.'

'No,' Janet says. 'Stop being an annoying prat.'

Prat? A pain sears between my eyes.

'Why can't I have a little bit? What's wrong with a little bit?'

'Because you're too young, that's why,' Janet says.

'You're too old, but you don't let that stop you.'

I suddenly feel really sorry for Janet. Imagine if Zara were like this and I didn't have Eric? It must be dreadful.

'A-hem!' Bethany pretends to clear her throat. 'So how come I'm too young today, when you usually let me drink whatever I want? God, you are the most boring hypocrite.'

Zara catches my eye. Bethany has gone too far.

'If you don't mind if she has some wine, I don't,' I say quite matter-of-factly. I act bored. I will not let her win. This business of a child commandeering the table reminds me of when Eric has had a few too many, during one of his unemployment spells, and we've had to sit there and listen to his asinine prattle. He didn't care if he showed himself up in front of his in-laws. We'd all be sitting there thinking, *For God's sake shut up!* But no one was going to be the one to tell him.

'You're cool,' Bethany says to me, and I don't know if it's sarcasm.

'In France kids your age drink wine with dinner all the time. It's hardly a big deal.'

'Who gives two shits about France?' Her mood sharply changes. Another side of Bethany, uncovered in tonight's social experiment. 'I don't even want any, anyway. It's just calories, isn't it? And the last thing I want is an arse the size of my mother's.'

Zara and I hold eyes. *This will be it*, I think. After tonight, there will be no more Bethany Brown in our lives. So, in that case, this excruciating evening will have been worth it.

Normally, I like to leave a sociable gap between dinner and dessert. Today, I'm thinking, *Maybe I can say, 'Family emergency! Everybody out!'* As I cut into the pie I wonder if I can gash my hand. A trip to the hospital would end this evening. The way I feel right now I'd almost gladly give up a limb. I glance at Janet checking her mobile. Whiney Janet. Badly-done-to Janet. *I don't know why it never works out for me . . .* Then I berate myself. *Don't be unkind. Remember, she hasn't had your life.*

'Good grief.' I stretch my arms over my head. 'Long day!' Janet goes on sitting there like she's taken root. I get up more sharply than I intended, start gathering plates.

'I don't know about you but since I turned forty I'm just so tired all the time,' cheerful Janet says. I catch sight of my fed-up face in the window.

'Since I turned forty I have anal leakage and have to glue my false teeth in . . .' Bethany goofs around like someone speaking with no teeth. My God, I would smack her so hard they'd be hauling me off in handcuffs.

I am just sighing the mother of all sighs when Otis struggles up from his spot by the table and trots to the door. I can see the glow of car lights through the window. With a little luck, it'll be someone telling us there's a burst gas pipe and we all have to evacuate the area.

But then the door flings open. And to my amazement there's Eric. 'Surprise,' he says, staring at me and smiling. And then he says, 'Family matters more than work.'

But suddenly he seems to notice we have guests. The smile slides right off his face. I forgot to mention I'd invited Zara's new friend and her mother – as he wasn't coming home it didn't seem to matter. Bethany glances him up and down, in an insolent, vaguely sexual way that makes my skin crawl.

Then Janet says, 'Hello, Eric.'

By her easy familiarity, anyone would think she'd known him half her life.

THIRTEEN

ERIC

December 2003

Eric clicks out of his CAD software. He checks his email one last time, then clicks out of there too. A geotech report is sitting in front of him, but he might take it home and review it over Christmas. It's the skiving-off season, when 3 p.m. is the new 5 p.m. He can't leave just yet, though. Not until somebody else does. He rings his mother to see how things are on the home front.

'I don't have to stay for the dinner and drinks. Honest,' he says.

'No, don't be silly! You go, love. Enjoy yourself. You deserve to let your hair down. We can hold the fort here.'

'How's Em?'

'Sleeping right now. She's been a bit quiet today.'

'Should I talk to her?'

'Best let her rest, love.'

He feels a twinge of guilt at the thought of going to the party when he should probably be going home to try to cheer up his wife and relieve his parents of the child-minding. He knows his mum drives Em around the bend. Em waits all day for him to come home so she can sound off about them. Sometimes it's funny, other times it rubs him the wrong way; she could show a bit of gratitude occasionally.

'Daniel's not driving you barmy?' he asks.

'Aw! He's a little angel.'

His mother always puts a positive spin on things. He can hear his dad clowning around in the background with his son. 'Take a taxi home, though, if you're going to be drinking,' she says.

'They're putting them on anyway,' he fibs.

'Well, go and enjoy yourself, love. It's Christmas.'

Now he's been let off the hook, he thinks he just might.

He wades through all the party dresses, the sunbed tans and lacquered hair. Westlife are singing 'I Have a Dream'. Daftly, that song always makes him choke back tears. A group of lasses are hamming it up in their drunken, off-key voices. It makes him feel nostalgic for his youth. For when he was a slightly podgy, cripplingly shy teenager trying to catch the eye of the ugliest girl in the room just in the hope of getting some action. Even then he only got lucky about ten per cent of the time. A red balloon floats down, landing in front of his face. A girl touches it away like she's serving a volleyball, and it pops back up into the air. She smiles at him, that mix of sweet and suggestive. If he could relive his teenage years, all he'd wish for himself would be that he could have a little bit of self-worth. He was bright, tall and good at sports. He had parents who always showed him affection and showered him with praise. He doesn't know why that still translated to him having such a low opinion of himself. Fortunately all that changed when he went to uni. Durham changed his life, because that's where he met Em and realised an attractive, intelligent girl liked him for exactly what, and who, he was, and sod anybody else who didn't.

His office booked out the function room in the back, the one with the partially enclosed outdoor patio. He's only been here once, for a meal, ages ago. It's a bit out of town for him, not that he goes out a lot. Once he got married he let some of his friends fall by the wayside because Em became the only friend he really wanted to be with; he didn't care to waste nights in the pub when he could be spending them with her. He makes his way over, past the towering Christmas tree and the dancing party dresses on the floor, pushes his hair off his forehead. Slade are now singing 'Merry Xmas Everybody'. The season suddenly kicks in and he swells with festive spirit.

They've got heat lamps on when he steps on to the patio. It's boiling. He quickly zooms in on the bar and makes his way over there. It's been quite the week. On top of work dramas, his mum and his mother-in-law haven't been seeing eye to eye on childcare for Daniel, each trying to out-grandmother the other. And because Em's not supposed to have any stress, his mother has taken that too far and is ringing him every ten minutes for the smallest things: she can't turn the oven on; she doesn't know if the two fellas at the door offering to shovel snow for ten quid is too much money, or if Em usually washes towels on the normal or the short cycle.

He orders a beer right away. Since all the worry over Daniel, and the worry about the new baby going the same route, his drinking has ramped up a notch. It's not that he thinks he's got a problem, but he also knows he doesn't want it to become one. But it does take some pressure off at the end of the day to sit and have two or three beers. He gets sucked into conversation with Polly from accounting, and another girl, Anita, he thinks she's called. Funny how the women all want to know about Em. The men will be like, 'How's the wife?' Yup. Off that topic as fast as possible.

But the women love the gory details. It always prompts the sort of conversation that makes him squirm a bit.

'Ah! It must be really getting her down, poor thing!' Polly says.

'I know someone else who had an incompetent cervix,' Anita chimes in.

Eric always wishes they could have found another word for it. He thinks that probably added to Em's blues – the fact that her body was failing at some huge womanly life purpose.

'Three months' bed rest!' sighs Polly. 'I'd be fit to kill somebody!'

It had been a similar thing with Daniel. Though they've passed the twenty-six week mark this time around, and his fears about a repeat aren't as bad as Em's still are.

Polly gives his bicep an affectionate squeeze. 'Tell Anita what you did for Emily the last time.' At first he doesn't know what she's talking about and he gives her his best blank expression. 'You know, how you arranged the bedroom etc?'

'Ah, yeah . . .' He can't remember what bullshit he'd told them exactly. Fortunately he doesn't have to because Polly is all over it.

'He moved her bed so she'd have a view of the garden,' she says, like she's proud of him. 'He wheeled in a telly and a DVD player, and a small sound system with a stack of her favourite CDs. He even got her a few subscriptions to magazines, put a little table with all her snacks on it.'

The women go, 'Aw!' He feels himself blush, and smiles innocently. The first beer goes down fast. Then the second. He contemplates a whisky chaser. He knows he shouldn't, but it is Christmas, and the company is paying for it.

He sees her across the room.

For a second he isn't sure if it's the same person. She was pregnant the last time he laid eyes on her. But the minute he sees her she nods at him – so it must be her.

Ron from drafting sidles up to him. 'No missus tonight then, eh?' Eric gives him the short version. Ron winces. 'I am really glad I wasn't born a woman.'

She's still watching him. Every time he looks over. It's a bit of a predatory stare, really. He tells himself not to look again, but then of course he does, just to see if she's still doing it.

'Ron, do you know who she is by any chance?' He nods subtly in her direction. He's curious more than anything. Not because if he were single she'd be his type. Something about the wide forehead, the sad eyes, the complete lack of any smile. He likes warm, approachable-looking women, not sad sacks.

'Ah. Er, no. Can't say I've seen her before. Maybe she's new . . .' The company has two hundred employees; it's not exactly surprising. 'She likes you though, doesn't she?' He gives Eric two digs of his elbow.

She continues to stare at him. He thinks she's a secretary, maybe, or a temp. Which gives the impression he thought about her, and he really hadn't. She was just another face. 'Yeah, I think she's a bit weird.'

'Must be, if she fancies you.'

Some time later he is trying to flag down the barman when he hears, 'Hello.' When he turns around he finds himself staring into those big, sad, pale blue eyes.

'Hello,' he says, non-committally. He's not fond of pushy women, or of feeling cornered.

'Long time no see,' she says. 'How's everything going?'

'All right, thanks.' He is struck by her overfamiliarity. It's not like he knows her. He is aware of how close she is standing to him, how if he moved his arm only a fraction, he would probably graze her breast. He is always careful around women. You have to be these days. No innuendo. Sometimes even joking around is walking on thin ice . . . not everybody takes things the same way, or knows you well enough to know your moral code. He backs up slightly.

'You had your baby, then,' he says, just for conversation.

'Yes,' she says, after a moment. 'I had my baby.'

'What you have? Let me guess. It was either a boy or a girl.'

She deadpans. 'I had a little girl.'

'Ah. Nice . . . What's her name?' He has a quick look around for an escape hatch.

'Bethany.'

'Bethany. That's a very nice name, isn't it?'

'It means "daughter of the king".'

Suddenly he pictures Elvis in that white suit shortly before he died. 'Ah . . . So then . . . a princess, in other words.'

'Not a royal king.' She rolls her eyes and utters 'Please!' under her breath.

'Ah! Right. That king!' A possible religious nutter. Bonus. 'Well, nice to see you back to work.' He goes to turn away.

'I had to take some extra time off after Bethany was born. For personal reasons. But I'm trying to return to normal. Someone has to pay the bills, don't they?'

He generally likes to avoid women who let you know they've got problems. They're usually looking for an invitation to talk about them. 'Good for you,' he says.

'You're looking well, though, I must say.' She pointedly glances him over. 'Looks like life is being good to you, Eric.'

Eh? He actually had no idea she knew his name.

'Yeah.' He feels a little stumped for what to say. 'I'm well, thanks.' He knows it's a bit sexist, but if he found her attractive he'd make more of an effort, show a bit more interest in the kid.

'Everyone seems to have brought a significant other.' She glances around, looking flat.

'My wife is unwell at the moment.' He tries to stress 'wife'.

'And I don't have one to bring. A husband, I mean. Not a wife
. . . Then again, after what I know about men, I'd have probably
been better off being a lesbian.'

He sweeps the room, desperate for his exit.

'Are you bored talking to me already?' she asks.

Yeah, he wants to say. *Be a nice lass. Sling your hook.* 'No.' He's
aware of a prickling under his collar. 'But I have to . . . Ah! Look!
There's Larry!'

Larry from materials is dressed in a Santa suit and is over by the
fairy-lit palm trees. Eric can't stand him, but right now he's practically in love with him. He walks over towards him. 'Nice pervert
costume!' Eric thumps him on the back. 'I wonder what you've got
on under there?'

'If you're lucky I'll show you later.' Larry looks down at Eric's
beer. 'First, though, I think I'm having one of those. Fancy another?'

Larry makes off to the bar, and Eric is about to do the same
when he realises she's followed him. 'Why is your wife unwell?'

He tries not to visibly sigh. 'She's pregnant, and not having an
easy time of it.'

'First child, like me?'

'No. We have a son, too.'

'You're lucky.'

When he meets her eyes again she is studying him in an odd
way, as though she's got some detail on him. 'I am,' he says. At this
minute, comparing this woman to his wife, he's never felt luckier
in his life. 'But I'd better be going.' He nods over to Larry, who is
returning with the drinks. 'See you later, then.' *Over my dead body!*

Her blue eyes hold his, with a chilling deliberateness. 'Oh, I
think you can depend on it.'

FOURTEEN

'Good morning!'

Steve happens to open his door right as I am passing. His face bursts with pleasure. 'Well, hello. I don't normally see you on weekends.' He saunters down his path and we fall into stride and walk towards the common together. I don't think he can have been up long; something about the slight softness of his features. He might have just rolled out of bed and thrown on his clothes. The rather unexpected intimacy of seeing him this way gladdens me for some strange reason.

'No. My husband is usually home so I'm normally making breakfast at this time . . . He works in London,' I add. I can't help but feel a little miffed that this is the second weekend he's told me he's not coming home, that he has too much work, even if he did make a surprise appearance last week. I wonder if it's because I mentioned coming down to stay with him again – if this is his way of putting me off.

It's a bright and beautiful day. Otis and Jasper are already off cavorting across the green. We stand and watch them.

'They've missed each other,' he says, and then he looks at me with a certain quiet curiosity. 'So your husband works away? I thought I hadn't seen him around much.'

I keep it fairly neutral and brief. 'Anyway, how's the nanny working out?'

'Ah . . . She's not, I'm afraid. The twins thought she was a little gruff with Henry. So I decided to let her go.'

'Twins?'

'My father-in-law has a twin brother. Richard never married so he enjoys helping out with Henry, which means I get a two-for-one deal.' He smiles. 'I've been trying to construct things so we're not so reliant on them, though. They're seventy-six.'

'So's my dad. Sadly he's not the world's most doting grandfather, otherwise that could have come in handy. Especially since we just recently lost my mother. I actually think it would have been good for him.'

'Sorry to hear that.' He sounds genuinely empathetic. 'Were you very close?'

'Yes,' I say. 'She was a very tell-it-like-it-is person, and while it used to drive me mad growing up, it's the thing I miss most about her . . . She was only seventy. Fine one minute, then she had a massive stroke.' This might be the first time I've spoken about her without getting too emotional. Time blunts the edges of even the sharpest sorrow. 'Have you been a widower for a long time?' I ask.

At first I'm not sure I've done the right thing, but then he says, 'Two years. Diane had ovarian cancer. She was gone in six months.'

'How utterly awful. I can't imagine what that must have been like.'

'No. But you never imagine so much of what happens in your life, do you?'

I am wondering what else to say when he says, 'You know, yesterday a young woman was brought in right as I was about to go off shift. A mother of two children. Her husband found her bleeding to death on the bathroom floor. She'd attempted to slit her wrists.'

I gasp.

'We managed to save her. Her husband had absolutely no idea she'd ever suffered from depression or wanted to end her life.'

'Good heavens.' I contemplate how well we can hide things, and how deep denial runs. I've often wondered if Eric has some undiagnosed depressive issue. I once mentioned it to him but he didn't exactly thank me for it. 'How does that affect you as a doctor?'

'Well, you have to keep a degree of distance or you'd never be able to do the job. But some things penetrate no matter what . . . I felt bad for her. But for him too. He'd just found out that the person he was living with was a stranger, wrestling with a darkness he had no idea about.'

I nod, aware that this topic has rather silenced me.

'Hey, we never had that date with Daniel and Henry,' he says.

'You're right! Well, perhaps if it's sunny tomorrow? He's been at a tournament in Scotland but he'll be home later . . . I could send him over and he could show Henry some moves in the garden?'

He smiles. 'Let's do it. Why don't you give me your phone number so I can text you.' He reaches into his pocket and pulls out his phone and presents me with it. 'Here. Type it in and I'll send you one now so you have mine.'

I take the phone from him and do as he says, aware of him watching my hands as I type.

'Henry will be very excited,' he says. 'I must go, though. Short walk for me today.' He calls the dogs over. Not that it works this time.

'Neither one of them has a grain of sense,' I say.

'No.' He meets my eyes in a way that I feel very briefly in the pit of my stomach. 'But they're mad about each other. That's all that counts.'

I am almost at our door on my way to meet Daniel off the train when Pamela Benning comes hurrying out of her gate.

'This was delivered to ours by mistake.'

She hands me what looks like a magazine wrapped in brown paper. There's a tear along the top, and I see the title: *Asian Babes*. I stare at it in horror. 'It's not mine.'

'No. It's addressed to your husband.'

I peer at the label and see Eric's name. I pull some of the paper back and see that the cover has a semi-naked young woman on it, wearing pink knickers and cupping her small breasts. 'Well, there's obviously been some mistake!'

'You don't have to explain your life to me.' Her face is saying, *Poor bitch in denial.* 'It's addressed to your husband, so by law I have to give it to him.'

I'm just about to say more but Zara comes out of our door and looks a little bemused. She knows our grumpy neighbour rarely gives us the time of day. 'I'm off to get the bus. Meeting Bethany in town. She wants to buy Otis a toy.'

I clutch the filthy magazine. 'Why don't you come with me and we'll go and get Daniel instead?'

She gives me that face that says, *Well, that's a barrel of thrills!*

'OK then.' Shopping for a dog toy can't hurt, I suppose. 'How long are you going to be?'

I suddenly remember the clothes stuffed under the dressing table. But I can hardly say anything about that here.

'Couple of hours.'

'Text me if you're going to be longer.'

She walks past me while Pamela still stands there with an air of judgement about her. 'Zara?'

'Yeah!' she almost sings. 'I heard you!'

I go back into the house and place the magazine on the table and stare at it, like it's alive. My mobile rings, startling me. It's Charlotte.

'I just saw you coming off the common with Steve!'

Despite myself, I smile. 'Say nothing. No one can know.'

She sighs. 'Just tell me, was it magical?'

'Yes,' I say, all fluttery. 'You didn't see us kiss, though, did you?' I gasp.

There's a loaded pause, then she says, 'What? Seriously?'

'No! Not seriously! Though I might have imagined it in my dreams.'

She laughs. 'My God, you really had me going.'

I tell her my morning went rapidly downhill from there.

'Good lord!' She sounds aghast. 'Who buys porn mags these days?' I'm thinking she means because surely that's the stuff of fifteen-year-old boys, when she says, 'We all just get it online!' Then she adds, 'Look, Eric's a tech-smart guy. If he wanted to stare at naked women he'd know which sites to visit and which firewalls to install so he'd not get caught.'

'Thanks,' I tell her, not sure this little bit of opinion-shopping has actually helped.

'You don't seriously think it was his?'

'I would have said no, but it is addressed to him. How else do you explain it?' I don't know what Charlotte and Garth's sex life entails but Eric and I have never watched porn, and in all these years I've never had any sense it's something that interests him, or that, if it did, young Asian girls barely older than his daughter would be his taste.

'Somebody's idea of a practical joke?'

Suddenly, in the back of my mind, I see Bethany Brown standing in our kitchen giving Eric the full-on jailbait look.

I bet I know whose.

FIFTEEN

'Too early?' he asks.

I find myself smiling into the phone. 'No. I was just about to make a second cup of coffee.'

'Henry's going to his granddad's in a couple of hours but he's dying to meet Daniel, if he's free. Want to come here and I'll make us coffee instead?'

'Daniel's just in the shower,' I tell him. 'We can be there in twenty minutes or so.'

I happen to catch my coquettish expression in the hall mirror. The flush to my cheeks. Then I think, *For God's sake. It's coffee. With a neighbour. With your son. As Zara would say, take a chill pill.*

His house is clean, but not particularly tidy. Items of clothing are strewn on the backs of chairs; large, well-worn running shoes kicked off on a door mat. A collection of eggshells by the oven. The smell of omelette in the air. There's '80s music playing rather loudly in the background, which he turns down after having to hunt around for the remote.

'It's such a pleasure to meet you, Daniel.' He pumps my son's hand.

'Likewise,' my son says. Daniel's hair is still wet from the shower and forms separated curls that frame his handsome face.

'And this is Henry?' Daniel looks over at the little boy sitting on the sofa playing with an elaborate train set.

'Hello, I'm Henry.' He waves, on cue. 'And I am eight.'

We all smile.

'How old are you?' he asks Daniel.

'I'm sixteen,' my son says. 'That's a very cool train set.'

He goes and sits down beside Henry on the sofa. I was so happy that Daniel didn't kick up a fuss when I asked him to come here. Nothing ever makes my son uncomfortable. I'm not proud I think this way, but in this regard he's a breath of fresh air compared to Zara.

'How are you liking living here?' I ask Steve, watching him grind coffee beans. It's odd seeing him in a domestic role. I always find it interesting how you seem to know so much more about a person when you've been invited inside their home.

'It's good. Quiet.' He glances over his shoulder, cocks me a playful look. 'Nice neighbours.'

'Do you run?' Daniel indicates the big Nike shoes by the door.

'Yes,' he says. 'Done a few triathlons. At the moment – in a couple of hours' time actually – I'm training for a coast-to-coast off-road cycle. Two hundred miles, twenty thousand feet of hills in four days.' He throws the eggshells into the compost bin and wipes up spilt yolks. He moves swiftly and methodically and in an instant the kitchen is organised again.

'Cool!' Daniel asks him about the ins and outs of the ride. I hadn't really pegged him as an exercise junkie, and yet why hadn't I? He looks the part, and he's clearly an overachiever. For some strange reason I think of my mother calling Eric 'the lethargic lump'. Not in the early days. But later, once he started spending too much time in his own head.

Where's the lethargic lump today, then?

Do you think the lethargic lump will want mince and onion pie?

I can't help but secretly smile, though it's far from funny.

As I listen to Steve and my son getting along famously, it occurs to me how similar they are. Steve could just be an older version of Daniel. Curiously, the idea warms me. I go over to the sofa and sit beside Henry.

'This train set looks like fun!' He seems so rapt, and I stare at his long fair eyelashes.

But then he meets my eye. 'Thank you,' he says. 'It is.'

I feel Steve is tuned in to my interaction with his son. 'Look at all of this . . .' I truly am in awe of all the fascinating component parts – woodland scenery, trees, bridges, a field of sheep, post office, church . . . 'It's a work of art.'

'I had one when I was a kid.' Steve comes and stands beside me so I have to look up at him. 'It took up most of my small bedroom and then it sat in boxes for years. Probably would have been quite the collector's item. I finally unearthed it and gave it to Henry but that didn't work out so well, did it, buddy?' He rubs his son's head. 'So now we have this one. What's this set called, Henry?'

Henry says, 'The Highland Rambler.'

'Yes.' Steve smiles at me. 'And we've got the Flying Scotsman over here . . .' He walks around the table and shows us. 'And next month we're getting . . . What are we getting now, Henry? Remind me again?'

'Eurostar!'

'That's right. Henry has made me promise to buy him the Eurostar and take him on a real one in the summer, so we can come home and build Paris in our living room.'

'I think that's a fine promise,' I tell him.

'This is really cool,' Daniel says. 'What's your favourite bit, Henry?'

Henry seems a little shy and stares with trance-like fascination at my son.

'Henry. What do you want to be when you grow up?' Steve prompts.

Henry says, 'Oh, that's easy! I want to be him!' He picks up a model of a tiny conductor wearing a green hat and a huge moustache, and waves it at us.

We laugh. 'We don't have to play tennis,' Daniel says. 'This is way more interesting than tennis could ever be.'

I smile at my son then catch Steve's eye.

'Coffee?' he says, and gives me a secretive wink.

'Do you know why a smutty porn magazine showing Asian teenagers would be delivered to our house with your name on it?' I ask Eric some time later when I phone him. It's the first real opportunity I've had to ask him about it, and I realise I won't rest until I do. I also realise I'm on some sort of heightened alert for his reaction.

'What?'

I tell him. He is silent for a moment or two. Then he says, 'So you think it's mine?' I can hear utter disbelief in his tone.

'Well . . . no.'

'You do,' he says. 'You bloody think it's mine!'

'I don't.' I realise, as I say it, that I actually mean it and part of me wishes I'd never mentioned it. 'It's very odd, though, don't you think?' I am not sure my initial theory about it being Bethany was correct. Kids these days don't even know what a post office is, let alone how to send a package to somebody.

'Well, yeah,' he says after a beat. 'Not sure why anybody would get something like that delivered to their own home. Only a nutter . . . Maybe there's some sad, single paedo with the same name as me, and the addresses got mixed up . . . So what have you done with it?'

'Put it in the bin.'

He huffs. 'Get it back out and put it in Pamela Benning's.'

I can't help but smile. 'That's not a bad idea. Maybe I should.'

SIXTEEN

Mr Haddiscombe peers at me over the top of his glasses. 'The reason I've asked you to come in on a Friday afternoon is that Zara has been missing a lot of school.' He pulls out the register records and shows me. 'In some cases she has registered for second period but has failed to show up to any of her classes. Along with Bethany Brown.'

My heart is pounding, the pulse throbbing in my head.

'And something else. Zara's history teacher said her behaviour has deteriorated. He suspected that she might have been drinking, or she was high.'

It's as though I've been pelted with falling rocks. I think of Bethany's strange behaviour that night in our house. 'But Zara doesn't drink or do drugs.'

'If I had a pound for every parent who has said that to me I'd have a villa on the Costa Brava.'

Hmm. He's an officious little prat but as I flounder for a comeback, he says, 'She is in biology right now, and she's to report to me at the beginning and end of every class, but I need to warn you . . . Look, Mrs Rossi, Zara is a capable enough girl. She lacks drive and isn't the best team player, but her marks are decent and her homework is generally handed in on time. It's possible Zara could still have a very promising future with a little bit of guidance from you – and, perhaps, new friends.'

Guidance from you . . .

All I can see is Bethany Brown's face and how hard I'd like to smack it. 'If this has been going on for some time, why wasn't I advised before now that she has missed classes?'

He clears his throat. He is unable to look me in the eye, it seems. 'We did phone you. And we sent you a letter.' He digs among some papers, finds something, then recites dates.

'I'm confused. There must be some mistake.' The only time my phone is ever off is when I'm in a meeting or teaching. 'I didn't receive any letters or phone calls.' I think hard to make sure I'm right. But I know I am.

'We know you changed your number recently. We noted it in our system.' He peers at the paper and recites a phone number.

'But that isn't my number,' I tell him.

He takes off his glasses and meets my eyes at last. 'I'm confused.'

'Phone it.' I pull my phone from my bag and place it on his desk.

'Well . . . This is really not necessary.'

'I'd say it is.' My heart is beating quickly, the beginnings of what feels like an anxiety attack. I think of all the parent–teacher nights of old. It was always me. Eric was never there. I have never needed an ally but now I do, where is he? After a moment, Mr Haddiscombe dials, places the call on speakerphone. We hear ringing, but my phone stays quiet. Then a young voice. 'I'm not here today. Or possibly tomorrow. Or possibly ever! Leave a message.' Then there's a fit of giggling.

His cheeks have flushed. He puts his glasses back on. 'Well, this is most dismaying.'

'I think we need to talk about Bethany Brown,' I say calmly. He goes to speak but I stop him in his tracks. 'I'm not leaving here until you tell me everything you know. What went on in other schools? What did she do?'

He strums his fingers on top of the register. 'I'm not really at liberty to get into details. But I'm going to be frank with you. There have been some issues, you're right.' He seems to hesitate at my unflinching gaze, then adds, 'This is to go no further.'

I wait. My heart is leaping out of my chest again.

'Bethany Brown had a best friend in her last school. Apparently they were inseparable. At first. Then there was an incident.'

'Incident?' Something between a tingle and a shiver fans out from the top of my spine.

'Bethany Brown set fire to the girl's hair.'

I am aware of rapid, involuntary blinking. A coil of panic unwinds in my gullet and I can't swallow it down.

'The girl was very shaken up, as you would imagine, but fortunately not seriously hurt.' Then he adds, 'But I'm afraid it wasn't through lack of Bethany Brown's trying.'

SEVENTEEN

'We just go to the park and places!' Zara cowers into a wing of the armchair.

'The bloody park!' Eric paces like a caged animal. I could smell whisky on him when I picked him up at the airport. 'What do you do in the park when you're supposed to be at school?'

'Stuff! What do you think?'

'Don't talk back at me, madam! I'll ask you again. What do you do with Bethany Brown when you should be attending school?'

Grudgingly, she says, 'We walk. Go to the beach. The shops.'

I suddenly remember. 'I found a Primark bag full of clothes under your dressing table. Where did you get the money to buy two new tops and a skirt?'

'Granddad,' she says, after a delay.

My father never gives money to one without the other. Daniel always tells me because he hates taking it. 'So where are the receipts for all these purchases, then?'

She stares at me, as though her mind is trying out the right response. 'I lost them. What does it matter anyway? And why are you snooping around in my room?'

'Well, you'd better find them.'

She looks at me like I am vermin but I stare her down. I don't know who she is right now. All these horrifying concepts are coming at me like snowflakes in a blizzard. Truant. Drunk. Shoplifter. Drug addict. And others. Ones I can't even think about. Once I start, it's like a maelstrom of my worst fears. 'If you don't find them I'm going to accompany you back to the store and you're going to apologise to the manager for stealing and just hope he won't press charges.' I try to speak levelly. I have always had authority with her, even though I've never really had cause to test how far it might go.

'I didn't steal them!' she shouts. 'Why would I steal clothes? I'm not a thief!'

'Well, then, you should be able to prove to me that you bought them, then it'll be fine.'

She bounces up out of the chair, strides across the floor toward the stairs.

'Where are you bloody going?' Eric says.

'I'm sick of being ganged up on!'

'Sit back down,' he bellows at the top of his voice. 'We're not finished.' She freezes. Her ears turn beet red. I can't think of a time I've ever seen him this angry with one of the kids. There is a moment where she looks at me, cowed, then she tuts and sits back down.

'One of the teachers said you were high,' I say, firmly but calmly.

I'm expecting her to deny it but she says, 'So?'

'So what had you taken?'

'It was just weed.'

'Weed?' Eric growls. 'Who gave you weed?'

'It's no big deal. It's easy to get.'

'Bethany did,' I say. Does he even need to ask?

'It was only once. I don't even like it. It stinks.'

She said that about cigarettes. What else is she trying, only to later claim she doesn't like it?

'I thought they were supposed to be hard up?' Eric looks at me in amazement. 'Where does Bethany Brown get the money to buy weed?' He is pacing again. He is a tornado, and this is how I know. Eric rarely staggers around. The alcohol works its menace in surreptitious ways. He hasn't just had one or two on the plane. While I was upstairs trying to persuade Zara to come down so we could talk to her, he must have been at the whisky. My God. I truly thought we were past this.

Zara doesn't answer his question. She is shielding Bethany because this is what Zara does. Zara loves loners, underdogs and the disenfranchised; she has a bizarre way of martyring herself for them and will defend them to the end.

'And while we're on the topic of you doing stupid things,' I say, 'do you have any idea what a dangerous game you're playing by giving the school Bethany's phone number and pretending it's mine? What were you thinking? What if something happened to you? If there was an emergency and they couldn't reach me?'

'I felt bad about that,' she mumbles, blushing, and stares at the floor.

'So what else are you going to do just because she pushes you into it?' I stare at her lowered eyes and see two bubbles of tears. 'Look,' I say, after a moment, because Eric isn't exactly adding anything very constructive. 'We're not happy you've used weed or that you've bunked off school. That can literally never, ever, happen again, do you understand? And if I ever see anything that makes me suspect you've been stealing, I promise I will march you back to the shop. But that's not what concerns us the most.' She avoids my eyes in that I'm-not-listening-but-I'm-listening posture. 'I met with your head teacher today and we found out something about

Bethany. It's extremely disturbing and it means you're to have no more to do with her ever again.'

She rolls her eyes. 'The hair thing.' She says it as though she's heard it a million times before. 'It was an accident. They were only messing about. But *they* made it seem like she'd done it on purpose.'

'Who is "they"?' Eric asks.

'Her haters.'

Eric and I look at one another. Then he says, 'Of course she's going to tell you it was an accident! She's not stupid. But she's lying. She tried to hurt her best friend! And you know why? Because she's messed up and one day she's probably going to end up in prison – or worse, dead. So it's over. Your mother's right. You are to have nothing to do with her ever again.'

As Zara stares back at him, hatred rages in her eyes. He rubs his brow. Sweat has pooled in the lines of his forehead. Whisky always makes Eric perspire. His skin is a washed-out grey under his florid cheeks.

'That girl's been shifted from school to school her entire life. Everywhere she goes she razes the earth behind her.'

'You don't know anything about her!' Zara screams. 'She's my friend! She's the only person who gets me!'

I suddenly think, *I never told him about all the schools and the moving around. At least, I don't think so.* Or maybe I did. I suppose I must have. Zara's eyes are burning into her dad's – the teenage outrage at everything that it means to be an adult.

'I won't have a debate about this.' Eric stands over her, wagging his index finger near her cheek. 'You're not being asked. You will stop seeing her. Immediately. If we have to monitor you twenty-four hours a day, we'll do it. If we have to chain you to your room, we'll bloody do that too. I can promise you everything about this very nice cosy life of yours is going to change if we begin to even suspect you've been near that girl after today.'

'I hate you!' she says, and starts to sob. 'I hate living in this family! Nobody cares about me. It's all about you and Mum and money and Daniel. You don't even live here any more! So what right have you got telling me who I can be friends with? I hate my life! I'm not stopping seeing her! You can't make me.'

I can see him faltering now, a part of his psyche holding back, recognising the limitations of his will and his words. Zara is no longer a toddler. She can't be picked up, held still, carried off, plonked down, refocused and rearranged to our design any more. She is a fully fledged human being who is finding that every day the gap between herself and us is widening and in that space lies the sheer power of her own impunity. Zara's greatest ability to defy us lies not in answering back, but in knowing she no longer even needs to.

'Stay away from that girl. I'm warning you,' he shouts, wanting to be as big as his voice. But he is winded, weak. His face is purple. A flashback to years ago. It circles me, hovering, not quite landing.

'Fuck you,' she screams.

We are all momentarily stunned. Even Zara seems shocked by the force of her own revolution.

It happens so fast. Eric takes a step towards her. I practically feel the draught of his hand coming down. I grab his arm, but only manage to snatch at his sleeve. My nails are ripped back on themselves as he wrenches out of my half-grasp. The short, sharp pain. 'No!' I shout. For a mad second I think he's going to turn and hit me instead.

Then Daniel appears at the top of the stairs. 'Stop this!' he yells, his voice cutting like a scythe. Daniel never, ever loses his cool. Eric's hand freezes with the shock, the blow fortunately not landing. He seems to realise what he was about to do and his face turns ashen.

I look at my son – my calm, even-tempered son, who has never raised his voice like this in our house. Ever. I am guessing the very act of it is brand new to him. *You pig*, I think, of Eric. *You've driven him to this!*

'I'm going out,' Daniel says, when he can compose himself. His expression is full of bewilderment and raw betrayal.

'Son?' Eric calls after him, but he ends up speaking to Daniel's back as he strides out of the door.

When I look at Zara she is staring at the ground, bone-still except for a slight tremble.

'I've spoken with Mr Haddiscombe, and the school's officer.' I try to say it as calmly as I can. 'I will be getting daily reports from your teachers, and if there is as much as a hint that you are bunking off lessons, your dad's right, everything about your life and your freedom is going to change. We have to be able to trust you, Zara. You live in this house and you will live by our rules until the day you're old enough to leave this house. And if we say no Bethany Brown ever again, then this is for your own good because we love you, and whether or not you see our side doesn't matter; you will do what we say.'

She holds my eyes and then looks away. I am aware of Eric's adrenaline abating as I take charge. 'We hope this is the only conversation we have to have about it. But if you push against us, Zara, we'll have no choice. We'll have to take your phone away, your iPad, your freedom to go wherever you want, your pocket money . . . We'll do that until we can trust you again. We're either going the easy way or the hard way. You decide.'

I meet Eric's eyes but he swiftly drops his gaze to the ground.

EIGHTEEN

ERIC

January 2004

'Why do I always sense you're avoiding me?'

He has just refreshed his coffee from the pot in the staff canteen. He didn't even hear her creep up behind him.

Since the party, he's been seeing her everywhere he goes. On a morning she'll be sitting in Costa, gawking at him as he walks past her with his latte. She'll be in the lift as he's going down for lunch. One day she said, 'If you're on your own, maybe we can have our lunch together?'

'It's not going to happen,' he told her.

Now he's trying very hard not to take his lunch bang on noon. Even though having to think about it is a pain in the arse too. Today he just sent his secretary out to get him a sandwich because it felt like less bother.

He puts the coffee pot back on the warming stand. 'You've got a big problem,' he says, and makes a point of walking past her without looking at her.

In his office he shuts the door, then just sits there, inert, in his chair. He can't focus on the Gallings report, or the shop drawings he was supposed to have got back to the client about today. He has a meeting with the architect in an hour. He's not properly prepared for it. There are a million other things he has to get done before he goes home, too, but that exchange in the staff canteen has completely derailed him.

Harassment. The word just floods up in his mind. He's never really thought of a woman doing the harassing before – the man being victim. He wonders if there even is such a thing. His fingers fly over the keyboard.

Harassment

Workplace

Opposite sex

Stalking

Fatal attraction

There are so many hits it's overwhelming. Bullying and harassment, workplace violence, recognition and resolution, Alex Forrest and that famous film . . . He can't sit here and read it all so he clicks on one about how to arm yourself if you suspect you're a victim of uninvited attention, then he feels daft. Why's he doing this? Give her a week and she'll get the message. He sighs, raps a pen on the end of the desk. Rings Em.

When he hears her voice, a strange feeling comes over him. Loneliness? Not really. More like an emptiness or a craving for something you can't pinpoint. Better coffee? Booze? A cuddle? An orgasm? The past, maybe. Yeah. It's like a pang of nostalgia that's so intense it's physical. Just that moment of wanting your life back. The way it used to be. Before babies. Sometimes even before Em. Before life got so complicated.

She sounds like she might have been asleep. 'What's up?' she asks.

Em is always happy to hear from him. That brief pleasure he gets from this somehow saves him from his worst self.

'What's the matter?' she says, maybe because he doesn't answer immediately.

'Dunno.' He realises he's feeling a little bit emotional. 'Thought I'd say hello. Just wanted to hear your voice.'

'Hmmm . . . Are you sure you're all right?'

'Yeah.' He pinches the bridge of his nose, squeezes his eyes shut for a second or two.

'Well, what do you want me to talk about? I'm not feeling very imaginative. I was actually trying to take a nap.'

'Ah . . . I woke you. Sorry.' He feels a bit rejected, clams up, like he used to do when he was a kid and he felt sorry for himself and shamefaced for reasons he didn't even know.

'No. You didn't. I was trying but it wasn't coming.'

He hangs on to the melody of her voice. He could just tell her. He's never kept anything from her before. *Look, something a bit peculiar is going on. There's this woman at work . . .* No, that will only worry her, and the doctor said she's not supposed to have any stress. Besides, it sounds like he's only telling part of the story.

'You weren't yourself last night either,' she says. 'Something's wrong.'

Em is eerily perceptive. 'I'm fine. Just a lot on my mind. That's all.'

He thinks back to last night. To him lying on top of their bed. Em stroking him off. Or, trying to. Not because paying attention to his penis gave her any pleasure per se, but because she wanted to do it for him, because she's giving like that. He thinks of how detached he felt from her hand. How he had to really concentrate on one of his most outlandish fantasies, and even that barely produced a result.

'Just wish I could come home, that's all.'

'Can you?' She perks up. 'That'd be nice!'

Back when Daniel was a baby, he'd often take the afternoon off, bring work home. He just wanted to be around them. He was so grateful Daniel was alive, and Em was happy again. She was minding the baby and running her own business. They'd work together at opposite ends of the dining table, take breaks together, sometimes naps. Sometimes sex. It almost feels like a different life.

'Nah. Sadly, I've got a meeting on the tunnel project this afternoon. Got to finish some stuff or it'll be on my mind all weekend.'

'Oh God. That'll be a joy. Eric, with things on his mind.'

'Ha. Yes.' Suddenly he feels a tiny bit brighter again. 'You could try pandering to me sometimes, you know. It makes a man feel good.' She'd pelt him with the phone if they were in the same room. Blacking his eye is more like Em's idea of pandering.

She performs a drawn-out yawn. 'God, who would have thought lying around all day could be so tiring!'

'Yeah. Bet it's terrible.'

'It is! You might mock but you'd be surprised!'

When he doesn't answer she says, 'Why do men always have to make your suffering sound like it's nothing?'

'Because it's your suffering, obviously. It would be different if it were mine, wouldn't it?'

'Bugger off.'

'Actually, I'd better. If I'm to make my meeting.'

He hangs up, feeling loads better than he did five minutes ago. If he's being honest with himself, maybe he doesn't handle stress as well as others. He thinks it's because he's terrified of losing everything he's striven for. Part of him thinks that he doesn't deserve success and that the rug is going to be pulled out from under him; he's just waiting for it. His mother once said you can't fight fate. It stuck with him: this idea that no matter what you do, you will end up fucked if it was your destiny to get fucked anyway. He has always fought against it, but he has his moments where part of him feels he's fighting a losing battle.

He pulls out his file on the tunnel project, orienting his mind to the task at hand. He's busy making notes when he hears an email arrive.

He stares at the name, and at *Sorry* in the 'Re' line.

For real? He clicks on the message.

> I wasn't in a good mood in the canteen. Didn't mean to accuse you of avoiding me. Going through some grim stuff at home – my loser ex, and Bethany-related. Don't really want to get into it. I know you don't know me very well, but I'm a good person. I just want us to be friends.

Friends? He stretches his mouth wide open until his jaw cracks loudly. His first instinct is to delete it. But then he thinks of that article – maybe he shouldn't. He creates a new folder, ponders what to name it, then writes, *Evidence.*

He drags her email into it. He hopes that's the only evidence he'll ever have to put into it. Only – why has he got this horrible feeling that it's not going to be?

NINETEEN

The student is waiting at my office door. He glances pointedly at his watch, even though I am not late.

He is a tall, well-built young man, in a wool jumper that displays a V of dark chest hair, and a brown houndstooth blazer that gives him an older, country-squire air. He doesn't sit down despite my invitation. Immediately I'm not all that comfortable and wish I'd taken Eric's advice about having someone else present.

'The reason I find this so frustrating is that I have a wedding and I have to get my ticket to India very soon,' he says, right off the bat. 'And I can't do that until you tell me you will help me. Do you see why this is so critical?'

'Prajval . . .' I say gently. 'I really would prefer it if you would sit down, please.'

After a beat or two, he sits. 'It's the wedding of a close family member and I will miss the first exam. I want to do it later, and there are other classes, too, that I'll miss because I want to spend some time with my family in India after the wedding. All I want is the notes for those classes – if you could send them to me.' He holds up his hands, mimicking surrender. 'I don't know why you're making this so difficult for me.'

I sit back now, cross my hands in front of me, try not to feel intimidated by the flare of anger that has suddenly appeared in his eyes and the way his voice has become so easily raised. After a moment or two, I say, 'I am definitely willing to help a student in special circumstances. But, as I'm sure you will be able to understand, I can't accommodate everyone's holiday and travel plans or it would be impossible for me to run a class.' I try to be nice. I can see he's worked up and it gives me no satisfaction to rattle him further. 'If the class interferes with your schedule to this degree, then, much as I don't want to discourage you from your studies, you may have to consider withdrawing—'

He jumps to his feet. 'You don't want me in your class, that's obvious. This is very annoying. I don't know why it's such a big deal for you to just give me what I ask!' Some spit flies from his mouth and lands on my hand.

My heart suddenly starts to shuttle. He's an angry young man who will become an angry husband and angry father. And instead of cowering, I find my spine straightening. I will not be intimidated by a kid. 'Sit down,' I tell him, in my firmest voice, though the effort almost demolishes me.

He continues to stand there, towering over me. 'You think I'm a stupid Paki,' he says, a little less strident. 'But I was educated in Britain just like you!'

I flinch at the word 'Paki', but hold his eyes, forcing my gaze to be steady. In a calm and quiet tone I say, 'I refuse to continue this conversation until you sit back down. And I am certainly not even going to contemplate helping you if you don't calm yourself and lower your voice.'

Reluctantly, he sits again.

I realise I'm clutching a handful of my skirt. I try to take a discreet, steadying breath. Then I say, 'I can promise you this has nothing to do with where you were born or educated. I would be

117

saying this to any student who sent me an email like that. You were writing to a professor of a Communications programme. There's no excuse for textese, lazy writing, and for not at least using spellcheck. It's extremely unprofessional and doesn't reflect well on you at all. If you apply for a job writing like that, I can virtually promise you that you will never get one.' I don't really owe him any good advice, but he clearly needs some.

He is a mite calmer suddenly. Then he starts to repeat the bit about the cousin's wedding.

I hold up a hand. 'You don't need to tell me this again.' Part of me wants to deny him his requests, just to show him that you can't go through life thinking you can bully people into getting what you want. But I can't be that cruel. So instead I say, 'What I will do – this one time – is allow you to write your exam at a later date. But I'm going to need you to give me the dates of your travel in an email by tomorrow. Then I'll let you know when you can sit the exam.'

'And what about my holiday?'

'There will be no excuse for other absences unless they're medical, and I'll need a doctor's note; I'll expect your attendance along with everyone else. And I must warn you that if you fail to produce an assignment or appear for an exam, your mark will be zero.'

He doesn't move so I start shuffling papers. 'I think we're done here, don't you?'

At first I'm not sure he's heard me, but then, reluctantly, he stands. 'You've made this really difficult for me,' he says, and hovers over me for a moment, sounding wounded but less vitriolic.

I tell him, 'You're welcome.'

He has no idea what I mean.

As he opens the door, I add, 'Don't forget, I need that email by tomorrow.'

'You will have it,' he replies curtly, like an early-nineteenth-century lord of the manor with his long johns in a knot.

When he leaves, I let out a long breath. I don't have to put a hand up my shirt to know my back is drenched in sweat.

TWENTY

My father is hanging out with Zara tonight, as it's our anniversary. I'm not big on these occasions. They can feel a little phoney to me. I'm a believer that marriage, *life*, should contain an element of anniversary every day. Not in the platitudinous sense. Just a quiet daily appreciation for all that you have, personally and jointly. If it's felt, it should be shown – more often than once a year. And if it's not felt, well, then who are we trying to kid? But Eric wanted me to book a table in one of the trendier establishments that just opened in what used to be the old post office building, and it felt like a decent idea. Expensive, intricate, Instagram-worthy tapas. I still think he's trying to make up for the episode with Zara – to get back in my favour, because he's been a little sheepish and contrite around me and the kids of late. He's probably getting tired of having to keep up that behaviour, says the cynic in me.

I watch the toing and froing of plates as I sip on a rather lovely Rioja and Eric makes one beer last an eternity – like he'll always do when he's trying to prove to me that he can. We are sharing a starter of ten-year-old *jamón* and some salt cod *croquetas* that taste almost as good as the ones we ate in Barcelona a few years back, which he has just reminded me of, and we reminisce in the way that only perfect holidays can make you want to.

'This is nice,' Eric says, suddenly looking like he's given up the business of trying to relax and he now just actually is. He sits back in his chair and appraises me. 'Do you remember when we used to do this once a week?'

I do. We did date nights before people started calling them that.

'We've gone to the other extreme, haven't we?' I say matter-of-factly. But sadness momentarily breaks in, because I sometimes forget this other side of him – the quiet, easy-going, devoted Eric. At times it's almost unfathomable to me that I ever witnessed it. When I doubt everything I know.

He pushes the last of the croquetas into his mouth. 'You know when you mentioned coming down for the weekend . . .'

'You don't want the pressure.'

He shakes his head. 'No, that's not it at all. It's not that I don't want to be with you. I do. Very much. But I want to be with you at home. Not in London.'

He casts his eyes over the table, at our empty plates, as though trying to see his way around an obstacle. 'What I'm trying to say is that when I'm there I'm just getting on with things, you know? Getting through it. My home is where you and the kids are . . . It's not London. The city, the hotel, it's just where I have to be when I can't be home with you.'

His sincerity takes me aback. 'Well, yes,' I say. 'But given you've got to be there – at least for now – surely we could have made the most of it?'

'Yeah,' he says. 'Just . . . I don't really want to start to like it or get used to it . . .'

I gaze at his earnest face, the closely cropped auburn hair, his auburn eyebrows like overly straight brush marks above small, honey-coloured eyes. And I sense we've reached a tipping point; our pleasant evening is about to go downhill. 'But it's not like you've gone off to war,' I say, because it needs to be out there. 'I'm sure us making the best of a bad situation would have been healthier for our marriage than what we're doing now.' I realise I've just spoken in the past tense, as though we are a fait accompli and I've somehow yielded to it. The waiter tops up my wine glass from the half-empty carafe. I didn't really want to order it. No sense in making his struggle harder for him. But he insisted. I watch the surface shimmer as it plays with the light.

'Healthier for our marriage.' He hangs on to it, like I've committed some sort of infraction that has harmed him more than he expected to be harmed. 'Well, you might say I'm not off at war or in prison or anything like that, but in a way . . . when I'm down there it's like I deserve to be there, you know, on my own, miles away from my family. Like I'm doing penance.'

'Penance? For what?'

He doesn't answer. When did he get so deep and complicated? When did he cease to love life? Eric was always on the serious side but he knew how to let go and live on the edge a little. I miss that person. That sense of being swept up in his arms and carried buoyantly through every storm, with him somehow changing the weather as we went along, and making the sun shine again.

'I know you don't get it,' he says. 'But it's how I think. How I feel. I can't properly explain it . . . I'm down there because I didn't make it work up here. I messed up and I failed. I don't want to turn it into a party.'

He stares at me properly now, like he wants me to see he's being fully transparent. And I have this sudden, confused urge to either shake him or put my arms around him. Sometimes I wonder why I've stayed if I can't understand him – and, also, why do I go on trying to? In this moment, time and place have fallen away and all I am is athirst for a better understanding of what we've become or are becoming. But then the door opens and, to my surprise, Steve enters. He's with a stylish younger woman in a burgundy raincoat, her dark hair short and swingy. An ungodly flush washes over me.

I hear Eric saying, 'Can you possibly understand where I'm coming from?' And I should answer, but I'm aware that my attention has drifted from Eric towards Steve. It must be pointed because Eric follows my eyes, turning around. I glance away before Steve has the chance to notice me, conscious that my cheeks are burning. It's like I've committed all of the seven deadly sins in twenty seconds.

'No one failed.' I hear myself refuting what he said earlier, though the response feels sluggish and overdue. I'm aware this conversation is like a sort of life raft for us, if only I can hang on, so I try to focus. 'Life's not a test and nobody's measuring you . . . We didn't have the best luck, did we? You can't beat yourself up about your choices forever.'

'Can't I?' He looks desperately disillusioned and back in his own headspace again, and I find myself feeling a tad impatient with him. It all just smacks of the same self-pity.

'Let it go,' I tell him, my eyes longing to wander over to the door again.

'Easy for you to say,' he says. 'I can't let it go, as it happens.'

Some more of our tapas arrives. I've forgotten what we even ordered. The waiter is carrying a few plates, and almost frisbees one down, then repeats his nifty move at a couple of other tables. Food is the great leveller, I think. Eric will latch on to it and that will be the end of all conversation. And I'm right. And I'm grateful for it. As he goes to tuck in, my eyes follow Steve and his female companion who are being led to a table. If he saw me while he stood there waiting, he isn't letting on. As they walk, I notice his hand hovers near her lower back, like he isn't accustomed to touching her but perhaps he'd like to. Thankfully, he chooses the seat facing the wall so his back is to me, and because his head is in the way, I'm not exactly afforded a bird's-eye view of her either. I tell myself to stop looking and bring my eyes back to Eric's face, longing for it to be the only one I want to see.

But I can't help having that same feeling I've had before. That I don't really know who he is any more.

TWENTY-ONE

ERIC

January 2004

'I didn't know you got a different mobile.' His new secretary is on him before he's got his coat off. Her office smells of the Greggs cheese pasty she seems to always eat for lunch.

He frowns. 'What do you mean?'

'Your wife forgot where she put your new number.' She pushes her glasses up her nose and peers at him over the top of her computer.

He registers what she's just said, his disbelief robbing him of a voice.

She glances at the wall clock. 'She rang about half an hour ago. I told her I wasn't aware you had a new one. I said this is the only one I've got for you . . .' She reads out his number.

'You gave out my number to someone over the phone?'

A blush floods her face. 'To your wife!' She looks at him like he's bizarre. 'Er . . . OK . . . sorry.'

His heart hammers. 'OK. It's fine. No harm done.' He tries to relax his face, to let his tongue unstick from the roof of his mouth.

'But for the record, in future if my wife rings, just pass her on to me. And don't ever give out my number to anybody, whatever their reason for asking. My mobile is private.'

'I couldn't pass her on to you. You weren't here,' she throws after him as he walks into his office. 'And I thought it was supposed to be a company phone, anyway . . .'

He shuts his door, goes over to his chair, sinks into it, adrenaline rattling through him. He stares ahead blankly, trying to rally his thoughts. The back of his neck is suddenly dripping sweat. Before his brain even commands his hand, he reaches into his top drawer and, from right at the very back, unearths the small, monogrammed hip flask his best man gave him on his wedding day. He stares at his initials, *ER*. He has never done this before at work. Never been remotely tempted to drink on the job. He doesn't even know what possessed him to fill it up and leave it sitting there, barely at arm's length. To prove he didn't need it? Well, OK, he's lost that one.

'We need to have a conversation,' she says.

For fuck's sake! He's in the queue at the noodle place. He tells John to order for him, digs in his pocket to give him ten quid, and steps outside.

'You ring my secretary posing as my wife? To get my number? Are you out of your flippin' mind?' Because even a small hit of booze on an empty stomach manages to mess with his self-control. But his voice is swallowed by the sound of traffic in the rain, and the scream of ambulance sirens.

It didn't blow over in a week. It's been three now. He has contemplated going to HR, but what's he really going to say? There's been one email from her, not the string he anticipated. She's always there, wherever he goes, but who's to say it's anything other than coincidence? Once he makes a thing of it, it's out there for people to do with what they will, isn't it? And he knows what people's minds are like. There'll be somebody somewhere who'll think he must have slept with her, and then word will get around and it'll catch on like wildfire. This is the very stuff he's spent his career avoiding!

'I won't be ignored, Eric. You can't lead me to think we have something between us, then just disappear.'

He frowns. Is he hearing this right? 'Have something between us? What are you on about?'

He feels the press of panic in his chest, a tightening in his left shoulder. His skin under his shirt collar prickles, as though his flesh is suddenly rebelling at the feel of his clothes.

'What I'm saying is, don't pretend that nothing happened.'

'Happened?' His voice cracks with tension. 'What happened? Tell me . . . I barely know you!' She's not right in the head. He read about this. Some kind of delusional disorder. People can't tell what's real from what's imagined. They have unshakable beliefs in things that are simply not true. He paces in a tight circle, staring at the shiny, wet ground and his brown pointy shoes, reminding himself he has the upper hand here. The truth – no matter what her story, or what she thinks – is the truth. 'Look,' he says, trying to steady himself and not to think about walking into the nearest pub and getting plastered. 'I don't know what's going on in your life . . . Whatever it is – your daughter, your ex – I'm sorry you've got your troubles. But you've got to leave me alone. There is nothing between us. There never has been. We've barely ever had a proper conversation, and I'm married, remember?'

He glances inside the restaurant. John is paying. He'll be out any minute. He runs a hand through his hair, raking his fingernails into his scalp.

There's a dead pause and then she says, 'Ah. *Now* you remember you're married. Interesting.'

His heart races wildly. His teeth grit until his jaw nearly locks. 'What's that supposed to mean?' When she doesn't reply he says, 'Eh? Seriously? What do you mean by that?' He damn well wants his answer. He pictures gripping her by the neck and throttling her until he gets it.

Silence. Not so smart-mouthed now!

'You show up everywhere I go. You dream things up that never happened. You talk to me as if we've known each other our whole lives . . . It's fucking lunatic behaviour . . .' He's breathless and tries to get a grip again. People are looking at him as they pass. A part of him thinks, *Try not to overreact, or she wins.* 'Look, you can't call this number any more. If you do you'll give me no choice but to report you.' He pauses to hopefully let this sink in. 'I don't want to go that route. I know you've got a baby and you don't have a husband and probably the very last thing you need is to lose your job—'

She cuts him off. 'Oh, thank you. How kind you are. Thank you for thinking of Bethany . . . Oh my goodness, this is so funny.'

An impotent rage assails him. It's like a powerful electric shock. 'You have to back the fuck off!' He's walking, unsure where he's going, distantly remembering he can't go far because John will be out any minute with his noodles. So he turns around and walks back. 'Do you hear me? I don't know where you get your ideas about things from, but it's got to stop, or it's you who is going to come off badly. Do you understand? You'll be the loser in all this, I can promise.'

'Are you threatening me, Eric?' She says it flatly, so unflinching.

'Chicken udon.' John is presenting him with a white carrier bag.

He turns away slightly, lowers his voice. 'Look, you've heard me. OK? I'm warning you . . .

I have to go now.'

He snaps his phone shut and stuffs it in his pocket, sniffs up a big draw of air. His heart is practically jumping onto the road. John is still holding out his food. When he can rally himself to act, he snatches the bag from him, says thanks, ignoring John's curious look. They start walking back in the direction of the office. With each step he tells himself it's going to be fine. He reminds himself that he hasn't done anything wrong. She's got nothing on him, so why's he all worried? She's a lunatic but he doubts she's going to do anything that'll put her job at risk, not when she has a kid. He calms himself down a little bit.

'Anything I can help with?' John asks when the silence must be deafening.

Eric casts his gaze across the river. He sees it all so clearly: his life falling apart.

'I wish,' he says.

TWENTY-TWO

Zara pulls the car door shut and slumps down in the seat. 'Drive!'

'And good afternoon to you.'

Her face is bright red. She refuses to look at me. Across the road from the school gates, standing out among a sea of burgundy blazers, is Bethany Brown and this boyfriend of hers – obviously. He's definitely older, and exactly the type I imagined, if not a bit worse. The ridiculously roided arms. The shaven head. A huge tattoo snaking up his neck. Almost sexy in a horrible, *I can't believe my mind ran to that* way. They are kissing. A performance kiss. For our benefit, I believe.

'God! Can you just go!' Zara sounds so desperate.

Bethany stops the kissing pantomime and looks over at me. The familiar mocking stare, smugly slanted. I look away and concentrate on pulling out of my parking spot. Once we are back on the main road Zara comes up for air.

'Are you all right?' I ask her.

No answer.

I have been checking her phone since our big talk and I found one text to Bethany saying that they have to 'lay low for a bit' because she's 'in some trouble with my parents'. When I confronted her on the ambiguity of her message, she blew up and said, *What else am I supposed to say to her? I can't just tell her I'm not allowed to ever speak to her again! What's it going to make me look like?*

She has a point. She wants to save face. I get it. Eric doesn't. But Eric has never been a teenage girl. And once again I regret telling him everything. Sometimes I feel the less he knows, the better; less grief. I have tried to explain that Zara has always been the dumped, never the dumper. She doesn't know how to cut somebody loose. We have to give her the tools to handle it her own way. Eric just expects me to throw a bucket of water on Bethany, hoping she'll melt into a brown puddle like the Wicked Witch of the West.

'If you don't want to talk, that's fine,' I say.

'I don't want to talk,' she says, which is more than she'd say if she really didn't, but I don't have the energy to push it.

On Wednesday I am at the doctor's to get the results of some blood tests. He's just talking about low B12 levels when my phone rings and I see it's the school, and I step outside. Haddiscombe tells me that Zara didn't come in today, and neither did Bethany Brown.

I hang up then and scramble to ring her mobile but it's switched off. I try Janet Brown's number, but she isn't answering and there's no voicemail. Why wouldn't she have bloody voicemail? I ring Eric but can't get hold of him either. I'm just thinking what to do when I receive a text. Strangely, it's from Katy's mother, Sian.

Grant just saw Zara + Bethany Brown at park gate. Older boys! Something going on . . .

I hurry out of there, past the receptionist, out of the front door, replying, Which gate? Main road one?

Once I get to my car I stand there and text Zara. Where are you?! Phone me ASAP!

I log on to Facebook, try to log on to Zara's page but it jumps straight to a silhouetted head. *To see posts on Zara's timeline, send them a friend request.*

She has deleted me! I search for Bethany Brown. Of course she has an open profile. Her latest post is a selfie from the waist up, made *just now*. She is wearing a low-cut, skin-tight tank top underneath her parka, and a push-up bra, her tiny breasts spilling out of it. He is kissing her, showing off his biceps in a grey wife-beater. A tattoo of a seahorse curls up from his collarbone to his cut-glass jaw.

I stare at their tongues merged together. At the way his hand with its tattooed knuckles cups the side of her left breast, his thumb crooked down the top of her bra. She looks stoned.

The comments under the picture are mostly from boys. One says something so graphic about her body that I feel myself visibly whiten. To my horror I see that Zara is one of three people who have liked this particularly vile comment.

I lean up against the car door with my brain ricocheting, hand trembling. A new photo pops up. Another scantily clad girl. She is sitting on the park bench, sandwiched between two younger boys – younger than twenties, anyway. One of them is slouched on to her, possibly passed out. The other has his hand up her short, clingy black skirt – far up. The girl is stoned, too, or drunk. The head hanging to the side, smudged plum lipstick. The slack posture of a rag doll. Eyes squinting, ringed with too much black mascara. There is a one-litre bottle of vodka in the loose grip of her right hand, ready to drop out at any minute. Bizarrely, it takes me a moment to realise.

It's Zara.

TWENTY-THREE

Daniel misses practice and helps me look for her, as do Charlotte and Garth. I phone the head office to see if they can get hold of Eric but the message says they closed ten minutes ago. We drive to the park – to both gates. By one, we find a pile of empty booze bottles and a used condom. I can't stop staring at it over my shoulder. 'Come on,' Charlotte says, tugging me away. 'That's not helping!' But all I can do is re-enact that photograph in my mind: visualising, without censure, what they might have done to her or be doing to her right this second.

We walk the outskirts of the park. I am aware of the ritual stamp of my feet, and of an out-of-body quality – and Charlotte saying, in a voice that barely reaches me from the far side of my panic, 'I don't see any sign of them. Maybe we should go this way. They wouldn't go down there. Let's try up by the town hall . . .' I allow her to direct me, feeling like a horse out of the gate and utterly disabled at the same time.

'Zara,' I shout. Charlotte shouts. Garth. Daniel. We are a chorus of desperation. I ring her incessantly. I ring Eric. Again and again. Where *is* he? Charlotte suggests she and Garth keep searching the park, while Daniel and I go for another drive around.

At one point I pull over and try to reach Janet again. Her co-worker at Harvey Nics says today is her day off. I thought she said she worked full-time? Or did I just forget? There is no depth of field any more.

We drive by all the spots where the sort of teens you never want your child to be hang out: the small green at the back of the bus depot, the car park for the old cinema, the grounds of the disused former town hall. I say to Daniel that I might drive through town one more time but he suggests we go home. 'She's probably back by now,' he says. How could I ever tell him that she's probably in no fit state to make her way home?

She isn't back.

I punch the boyfriend's name into Google. Craig Rathbone.

His mugshot comes up. A police photo. An article: Drunken Thug Spared Jail After Breaking Man's Jaw. It says he was handed a suspended sentence for the incident that occurred outside of a Leeds bar in the early hours of 1 January 2011. It says his age. Eighteen then. That makes him twenty-five now. I wonder if Janet knows he's a decade older than her daughter! There's another article in the *Yorkshire Evening Post*, this one saying police confiscated cocaine and the financial proceeds of crime from his home. No indication of where he lives now. Nothing recent, just a few references to him being a boxing promoter.

I send the links to the two articles to Janet. Then I can't sit still, so I tell Daniel I'm going to go for another drive around. Next, I am in the car. I pick a direction, seeing only that condom and the boy with his hand up my daughter's skirt.

I revisit the park entrances, both north and south gates. Soon, it'll be dark, which is going to make her absence all the more pronounced. I ring Eric again. *Please, please, pick up.* Nothing. I feel like hurling the phone. When has he ever really been there when I've needed him? Why do I stay with this man?

I walk past one or two walkers out with dogs and ask them if they've seen a couple of teenage girls with older boys. People are kind when you express concern over your pets or your children. But I see it in their faces: the pity, the *You must be a bit of a shitty parent.*

They're right, I think. Looking back, all I can see is what I did for Daniel. The endless focus on his success, his needs and priorities, at the expense of Zara's. I've put us here. I got one child right, because he was the easy child and I didn't have to do a thing to make him that way. But the one who needed my guidance, who was vulnerable? All those years searching and never finding? Reaching and never landing? I failed her. I failed her abysmally and perhaps irrevocably.

Back at the same spot, their litter is still there. I can almost smell their primal sweat, feel the embers of their drug-fuelled fire.

On my way back home in the car, my phone rings. Janet.

'My God, where have you been?' I pull over, abruptly. Rage rises up in me with a force I didn't know it could possess.

'And hello to you too, Emily.' That same eerily reactionless voice. I feel like screaming, *What is fucking wrong with you?*

I tell her what I know in as much detail as I can. At one point I think she's gone off the line, or her phone has died. But then she says, 'Welcome to the world of parenting, Emily.'

'What?' My heart hammers. 'What did you just say?'

'You don't have to get so wound up. It's pointless being a mother hen. They're fine. Bethany always comes home.' She sounds like she just dragged on a cigarette. I didn't know she smoked.

'You don't even know where they are!' I shriek. 'How can you say they're fine? They're children! They're hanging around with boys who are ten years older – men! – and you seem fine with it. Why? Because "sometimes older is wiser"?' I parrot what she said in my kitchen. I realise I have to calm down, or I will pass the point where I am even able to.

She groans. 'Oh, how terrible for poor Emily. To be the parent of perfect Daniel, budding tennis superstar, and painfully shy Zara: Little Miss Browbeaten. Oh, what a burden. Zara has finally found her soul sister, but they can't be together, because Zara can't choose her own friends. Because Emily decides that Bethany is a bad influence.'

'A soul sister?'

Another puff. She *is* smoking! I wonder what else I don't know about her.

'Have you ever thought that by trying to keep them apart, you've driven Zara to this?'

Her words propel me out of the car. I pace in tight circles. Sweat is coursing down my back. I tug at the neck of my jumper because it's choking me, hear the taut rip of cotton.

'You shouldn't go through life assuming you're better than everybody else, Emily,' she says. 'I was really hoping that Zara would be a good influence on Bethany. But have you ever thought that maybe Zara isn't capable of being a good influence on anybody? That you're just deluded?'

It's possible I am delusional. Right now, if she were standing here, I would be mad enough to wring her neck.

'Look,' I find myself saying in a calm voice somehow, considering how choked on my own incompetence I am. 'Hear this clearly. If Bethany and her motley mates don't stay away from Zara – and I mean *away* – my next phone call will be to the police. I'll tell them I walked in on her threatening my daughter with a knife.' I haven't the first idea where I'm getting this from but it flows out of me with so much conviction that I don't doubt a single word of it. 'I'm pretty sure they'll believe me, aren't you? I mean, it'll hardly be the first time she's tried to harm a friend. If they ask Zara to corroborate it, I'll say she's too afraid to admit it for fear of what Bethany will do. After all, like you say, I'm deluded . . .'

Silence for a moment. Another puff on the cigarette. Then, 'A threat from Emily. That's meaningful.'

I click off, almost dropping my phone like it's on fire.

Back in the car, I slam my door, aware I'm a barrel of adrenaline and yet my brain is pumping harder than my hormones.

There is something about this. Something I'm not getting. I've had this feeling before in the past. This sense that something is awry.

A tap on my window makes me nearly jump out of my skin. It takes me a moment to process the face through the glass.

'Steve,' I say, and lower my window.

'I thought it was you.' He stands there, almost oblivious to the rain beating off him. 'What's going on?' His brows knit with concern.

I tell him in a scrambled fashion. It's hard to get it all out in one coherent piece. My voice is shaking. I feel bad he's standing there getting drenched.

'Look,' he says. 'You're in no state to be driving. Why don't you come with me? We can go back home and, if she's still not there, then I think we should call the police.'

We. It's just a humble pronoun yet I can't begin to explain how fortified it makes me feel. *We* is all I have ever wanted to feel with Eric. This profound sense of sharing, of being in this life, warts and all, together. And for reasons I can't explain, I haven't felt it in so long that I'm starting to doubt that I ever did.

The irony of the fact that I am not alone, that I have some bloke down the street who has more than enough life of his own to deal with, could almost dismantle me with disbelief, but I'm too busy thinking—

'Police?'

'A girl going off with older boys? In today's climate I can guarantee you reporting it is the right thing.'

Today's climate . . . I hadn't really thought of any climate. Why hadn't I?

'I'm not meaning to alarm you, Emily. Look . . . I'm just saying . . . Come on.' He opens my car door and I have no choice but to get out. We cross the street and I climb into his car. It's warm and smells of new leather. He closes my door for me, walks to the other side and gets in. I have an incredible feeling of safety, that everything's about to be all right. It will be a small thing to him, but my debt to him right now is more than I could ever articulate.

He briefly reaches a hand across and squeezes mine.

We drive back to our street in silence. And yet it's not awkward. It's full. Full of my thoughts and, who knows, perhaps his. I haven't ever speculated what those might be. Right as we're nearing our turn, Daniel texts.

'She's home!' I say to Steve, nearly expiring with relief. 'Daniel says she's tired and she's gone to bed.'

'So she's fine, then?' It's half statement, half question.

'He seems to think she is.' I can't help but feel we've had a narrow escape. 'Thanks,' I tell him, when he pulls up at my door. We could have been close to home or far away, but nonetheless, in some ways we've arrived too quickly. 'You were very kind.'

There is a captivating second or two where he holds my eyes in the semi-light. And then he says, 'It's not kindness.'

His words slow the train of my thoughts that should all lead to Zara. I should get out, hurry to her, and yet a part of me is dreading it; I just want one or two beats of pause. I'd much rather go on sitting here, absorbing what he just said and the way he said it, to make sure I won't later decide it wasn't real.

'I'll text you in a bit. Make sure everything's OK.' His voice is hushed, intimate.

'You don't have to.'

'I would like to.'

Our eyes meet again. 'OK,' I say quietly.

TWENTY-FOUR

She is lying on her stomach on top of the duvet, her face pressed into the pillow. Her eyes are closed, make-up badly smudged, her cheek damp to my touch. The tight black skirt – *Bethany's?* – scarcely covers her bottom. The room reeks of alcohol. I stare at the plump tops of her legs, the thighs melded together, the rashy, dehydrated skin. She looks like a passed-out prostitute.

'Zara.' I gently prod between her shoulder blades. It strikes me that I should be furious but I am so grateful for her – in any state. I'm just so ridiculously happy she's alive.

'Tired,' she mumbles. It crosses my mind that I have no idea what she has taken. No sooner am I about to panic again than my phone rings and it's Steve.

'How is she?'

I tell him I'm not too sure, then I fire questions at him. Should I make her walk? Stand her under a cold shower? What if she chokes on her vomit? What if . . .

'You need to take a deep breath, Emily. Take a long breath in – eight counts. Hold it for a few seconds, then let it out, just as slowly. Can you do that for me?'

I try. When I'm a mite calmer he says, 'I'd come up but Henry is having a tantrum.' I can hear the kid in the background. 'I'm going to ask you a few questions. OK? Has she vomited?' I tell him no. He asks, 'Is her breathing irregular? Do you know how to check her pulse?' I do, but he reminds me anyway. He asks me other questions. I answer, checking her over as he tells me to do. The way he seems to know and to take charge makes me feel so relieved. It strikes me how new this is for me; I am rarely on the receiving end of reassurance. And I'm struck by this huge, discordant void in myself, too. The gaping hole that my husband should fill, that right this minute is being filled by someone else.

'I think she's probably fine,' he says. 'Let her sleep. But if you have any doubts whatsoever then ring for an ambulance first, then call me back. OK?'

'I'm sorry,' I say, once my breathing somehow relaxes and the painful, pressing-out sensation in my diaphragm dissipates. 'I remember you saying that because you're a doctor people are always trying to involve you in their medical problems. I didn't want one of them to be me.'

'But they're not you,' he says. And the comment, like the one in the car, is left to lie there, unsettling the earth around me, rousing all these doubts from sleep.

Henry squeals loudly again. 'I should let you go,' I say.

'I'm here. Remember. If anything changes, just call me.' He reassures me again that she probably just needs to sleep it off.

'I can't tell you how grateful I am.' I am suddenly aware of how much he means to me, which takes me quite by surprise. The dilemma that could bring me rushes up, fresh and bright. A brand-new shoot of promise followed by all the associated impossibilities.

Zara stirs, attempts to sit up, pushing off from the bed like a first-timer at yoga. Her eyes are puffy, bloodshot. She looks my way but can't focus. 'What can I do?' I ask, softly.

'Thirsty,' she croaks.

'Do you know where you are?' I stroke the back of her head, pressing my fingers into the familiar shape of it, remembering how I used to do this when she was a little girl. The warm, downy-smooth hair. The pronounced curve before it slopes to the neck.

'In my room,' she says in that *Isn't it bloody obvious?* tone.

'Are you OK? Has anybody hurt you?'

'Huh?' Those terribly red wells for eyes.

'Did you take drugs?'

She shakes her head.

'What, then?'

'Just vodka. I am so thirsty.'

I go into the bathroom, fill a glass, feeling an element of relief – oddly pleased that it's alcohol, not drugs. As though one is definitely the lesser of two evils, simply by being the vice I'm more familiar with. She sits up a little, gulps the water down. When she's done, I get her some more. 'Do you want something to eat?' I stand over her in helpless desperation. 'Maybe you should get something in your stomach?'

'No,' she says, her voice croaking. 'I'm just so tired.' She rubs her eyes with the knuckles of her index fingers. 'I just want to sleep.'

We might have fast-forwarded five years, skittered over her entire adolescence. I am staring at someone I'm having a hard time recognising. My little girl has become worldly – but not in a good way – almost overnight. 'I'll let you sleep, then,' I say. She rolls back on to her stomach again. I stand there like a sprinter ready to push off at the burst of the gun, horrified she might roll on to her back and vomit. Suddenly there's just all this jeopardy between us.

Daniel taps on the door. 'Can I do anything?' He gazes at Zara cautiously, looking bemused and slightly betrayed. Daniel had ideas about who his sister was, too. We're all just reeling from so much new information.

'No,' I tell him. 'You've been a great help. I'm going to sleep in here. Go back to bed.'

He doesn't move. 'She's fine,' I say. 'We both are.'

'If you're sure . . .' He nods, then he carefully closes the door again.

I lower myself on to her beanbag in the corner by the window, so I can still watch her, but it's not very comfortable. I shift around until I can find a tolerable position for my back. In the darkness of the room, I peer at my phone and see I've a couple of missed calls from Charlotte. Nothing from Eric. I text her and tell her all is well and thank her and Garth for their kindness and help.

She writes back immediately. Want me to come over?

No. But thanks.

Call any time if U need.

Xx thanks.

The screen goes dark again, and I go back to watching Zara sleep. It reminds me of keeping watch over my mother. The way I sat there in a chair in the hospital, eyes never moving from her, seized by my own inadequacy, by the tangibility of her slipping away from me. I could not have conceived of sleeping. I wasn't going to miss a beat of her because keeping her in my sight was the only leverage I had left.

The blue screen lights up again.

Steve.

All ok?

Once again, the fact that Eric has disappeared into the ether and there is another man enquiring after our daughter is surreal to me. I text back, Think so. Sleeping.

And you?

Just tired.

There is a pause before I see he's writing again. It seems he's writing a lot. I find my eyes unable to move from the three little dots, in a state of held breath.

Try to rest.

I wait to see if he's going to say more, but it seems that's it. I wonder what he was writing that he changed his mind about. To try to bring some peace to my turbulent mind, I think of the interior of his house. Try to imagine him, perhaps feet up on that coffee table where Henry's train set was, watching TV, or sitting on the end of his bed, about to switch off his light. Will his last thought be of me tonight, like mine will no doubt be of him? How did it even happen that it could be?

I shuffle around a bit more, trying to get comfortable again, but have to give up on this beanbag. Instead I settle myself on to the end of Zara's bed, drawing my legs up and fashioning myself around her feet. I doze, off and on, between flashing back to events of the day. I don't leave the room until I am confident nothing's going to happen to her.

At least not this night.

TWENTY-FIVE

Eric is bemused.

'Are you still there?' I say.

'Yes.'

'Where were you?'

He is silent for too long. I have the strangest sense he's working his way around a lie. Then he says, 'I know you're not going to believe it . . . I left my phone in the toilets at Paddington station. I don't know how. I wasn't thinking straight – obviously.'

'But you weren't in your room. I rang so many times.'

'Because I went back, didn't I? I couldn't think where the hell I could have left it. And then it dawned on me.'

'And it was there?' It must have been. Given I'm ringing him on it. Unless he's lying.

'Got handed in. Believe it or not.'

I frown. I'm a little stumped for what to say. 'You didn't see all my messages?'

I hear the end-of-his-tether sigh. 'What's this? The third degree? It was low on charge. Was dead by the time I found it.'

I don't believe him.

He knows I don't. A suspenseful silence sits between us.

'You're never going to let me forget it, are you?' he says, after a time.

I don't even have to say, *Forget what?*

'One time, Emily. One error of judgement.'

Yes. When, five months after Zara was born, you got up for work, got dressed, went out that door, and you kept doing that for a whole month when you knew you'd been laid off and there wasn't a job to go to.

'I wasn't even thinking about that,' I say, unconvincingly. At the time he told me he spent the whole day driving aimlessly around the Yorkshire Dales. *I just didn't know how to tell you, so I tried to pretend it wasn't happening.*

'Yeah, right,' he says now, and tuts in either disgust or disbelief. 'One mistake. One time I wasn't honest and you're out to disprove every word that comes out of my damned mouth!'

It's such an unfair accusation. 'I have never thrown that back in your face,' I remind him. We had one steaming argument about it but then it was never mentioned again. I felt worried for him. I honestly thought he might have had a nervous breakdown. We coped the way we tend to cope with everything: silently, muting our true feelings for the greater good of our family. Which is something I sense we're still doing now.

I am waiting for him to argue back but instead he says, 'You're right. You haven't.'

'We can't go on like this,' I say, sadness pressing down on me. 'I needed you last night more than I've ever needed you and you weren't even reachable by phone! What if one of our kids had died?' I realise I don't know what I'm really saying. If I mean him living down there can't go on, or our marriage in general. What I do know is that if something doesn't change, we won't survive me finding another man more of a comfort than the man I married.

'That's why I have an idea,' he says, swiftly changing his tone. 'In fact, I've been giving this a lot of thought . . . Maybe we should consider moving down here.'

'What?' I laugh, after a second or two, because he can't be serious. 'You mean to London? How would we ever afford that?'

'We could get a terrace in East Croydon. It would be smaller, and we'd have a slightly bigger mortgage, but it's well located. A train from East Croydon station takes less than fifteen minutes into central London.' Then he adds, 'You like London. You're always telling me you want to come down.'

My God. It reminds me of years ago when he announced, out of the blue, that he wanted to move to Australia!

'Zara would like Croydon. There's a huge shopping centre – two actually. It's very up and coming. A good area for us to invest in. It means if we decide to retire back up Yorkshire way, we'll probably be able to buy a house outright and have a nice stash of savings to live off.'

'Are you serious?' I am still convinced he can't be.

'Yes. Of course. It makes perfect sense. It's less than half an hour on the tram to Wimbledon, which is going to be great for Daniel—'

'Eric?' I say in disbelief. 'Have you gone mad?'

'No.' He seems surprised. 'Not at all. I don't know why I didn't think of it sooner. You and I both know my fate is not back in Leeds. And Zara can easily find a good school. You could even find a teaching position if you wanted, or go back to your old career – there must be bags of opportunity for that down here. It would be a complete change for us, and the bonus is we'd get away from her.'

I am stunned how well he's thought it out. How he's been taking trains and timing journeys! 'So we're moving to the opposite end of the country to put distance between us and a teenager?'

'Well . . .'

'Do you think there won't be bad influences in London? People just like Bethany Brown? Maybe we could move to the moon and the outcome will be the same. Maybe it's to do with who Zara is as a person now, not geography.'

'You don't believe that.'

'I don't know, Eric. I'm not sure what to think any more. I'm seeing a different development in her every day.' And I want to say, *This is what you're missing because you're not here to see it.* 'But what I do know is we have a life here. We like our life here! We are Yorkshire people. We don't belong in Croydon. This is our home. Or, it's certainly mine.'

'So you're not even prepared to give it some thought?'

'No.'

He sighs. 'You're impossible, you know that?'

This makes me fume. 'For God's sake, did you really think I was just going to say, "Great! Let's move to Croydon!"'

Surely I have a right to have an opinion on whether we relocate to the opposite end of the country! Yet I honestly don't know if he believes I do. But then in the back of my mind I think, *Am I being too close-minded? Does he have a point? People* do *up sticks and move.*

'No! Of course not,' he says. 'But I'm presenting you with a bloody solution and you just dismiss it right off the bat! I don't think that's very helpful, either.'

I hold the phone away from my ear again. Maybe he's right, but I don't fully trust his judgement any more.

After a moment or two, he says, 'Well, one thing I do know is I can't go on like this, Em. Something has to give. I can't cope with all of this for much longer.'

He can't cope? *He* can't go on? He's borrowing my words.

'This is all too much for me . . . Way too much . . . Oh God . . .'

He sighs hard. I recognise this. This is Eric dying to sink a drink. Eric not being able to do anything with his agitation until his hand is on that whisky bottle. Because when you have lived so long with a drinker, you are as in tune to their need for alcohol as they are.

'I'm the one who's dealing with it, Eric. I'm the one that's here. Remember?' Old resentments surface but I try to say it calmly, to be the antidote to Eric's particular poison, like I've been our entire marriage.

'Because I'm the one who's busy paying the bills! The house! The cars! Daniel's tennis! Me! Not you.'

The same old argument. He actually believes it. The pulse pounds in my temples. In the past I'd have chosen not to antagonise him but right now I remind him of how much I am paid, and how I am not paid to run the home and raise his damned children – I get to do that for free. 'And when you had a grand total of four years' unemployment when our kids were growing up, I was the one working full-time and paying for everything. Remember?' This is another thing that I have never thrown back in his face. Until now.

We are over, I think. *Stay in bloody London. I am so sick of you. I'm done.*

I am shaking. I have to blow out a steadying breath. Once in a while I look back over the landscape of our marriage as if I were a bird and I see it so clearly, those fleeting episodes of perceived injustice where I find myself with the inalienable capacity to hate.

After a lengthy pause, he says, 'I'm sorry. You're right. I've failed you. It's me who has landed us in this . . . This is all my fault . . .' He sounds like he's so frustrated he's going to cry. 'The truth is . . . if only you knew . . . I'm sorry for so many things, I wouldn't even know where to start . . .'

Once again I am betwixt and between. How does he always manage to make me feel like the bad guy? It's true that he was only trying to find a solution. Normally he denies there's even a problem.

'Eric . . .' A question hovers there, unable to land. I am sonar in a black ocean.

'What?' he says.

I try to say it carefully. 'Are you being honest with me?'

There's a hesitation where I think he's going to say, *Here we go again!* but he says, 'What about?'

I almost don't know how to answer. There is something in his tone. 'About . . . anything.'

There's a very long pause. Then he says, 'Of course,' and he sounds like he is shattering under the strain of us. And for a moment I'm not even sure if *he* believes himself, let alone if I do.

TWENTY-SIX

Zara and I have a talk. I ask her where she got the money to buy alcohol and drugs or whatever it was she might have taken, because I don't believe half of what she says.

She has never been a girl to break down in front of me easily. Tears are her private shame. Sometimes, when she has stormed to her room and slammed the door, I have stood on the other side, and her silent heartbreak is a heat that travels from her chest to my stomach. I no longer know where I leave off and she begins; which emotions are mine, and which are only mine because they are first hers. Her hurt feelings stay with me for days. Her brokenness colonises my dreams.

She stares into her porridge and I know she won't look up because she doesn't want me to see.

'I'm going to need an answer. We can sit here all day.'

'Bethany's boyfriend,' she finally says. 'He just gives it to us for free.'

I can't get the notion of her making these independent and somewhat mutinous choices to feel real. Zara's free will has always been within the comfort zone of ours. Her choices have been the ones we've wanted them to be – or, at least, ones we could accept.

I go to the cupboard to get her an aspirin. The recognition of my inability to protect her, from yesterday, from everything that comes with her stepping outside this door today – my powerlessness to observe the world around her with X-ray vision and shepherd her to safety when she can't even recognise that she needs it – scares me stiff.

After she swallows the pill I say, 'You know I'm going to have to go to the police, don't you? An adult can't be giving alcohol and drugs to a minor.'

'Police? You can't! He didn't give us drugs! I told you! I didn't take them!'

'So he *did* offer you them, then?'

She shakes her head but it's not convincing. 'Please,' she whines. 'You have to promise.'

'Like how you promised me, Zara?'

She holds my eyes now, a hint of treachery and venom in her gaze. 'This is different. I'll do anything but you can't go to the police or he's going to know I grassed on him.' Tears roll down her face now. She doesn't even bother to wipe them away.

'You're frightened of him. Has he hurt you? Does he hurt Bethany?' I will kill him. I don't care if I get life in jail.

She shakes her head.

'So why are you afraid of him?' After a moment or two I say, 'Did you have sex with that other boy? You need to be honest.' Is it the one she said was nice to her? The filthy animal who had his hand up her skirt?

'No,' she says, looking genuinely outraged. 'Of course not!'

'But the photograph? And there was a condom left in the park.'

'It wasn't mine!' She blushes fiercely.

'You do realise I can take you to a doctor and they'll examine you and they'll know if you are lying.' I have no idea if it's true. It sounds true.

I see the sudden flicker of scepticism. Zara is doubting every truth I've ever told her and is positioning me as the enemy. 'I won't go to any doctor.'

'But you will. If I decide you're not being honest with me. You'll go, believe me.'

She looks away in disgust. Now is not the time to push it or test it, either way, on my part or hers. I think we both recognise that.

'Look . . . I'm trying to help you here.' I lean in, longing to reach a place of understanding in her. 'You think I'm the bad guy, but I can guarantee that in years to come you'll realise I was probably the only person who was wholeheartedly on your side. Well, me and your dad. And Daniel.' Eventually, she meets my eyes again. I can tell she's pulled in by her need to believe me; she is still a child after all, and I am still her mother. We are both recognising how easily that tie can come undone, how quickly it can all come asunder.

'Whatever you tell me will be safe with me. But you must be honest. If you've had sex, I need to know.'

She sighs. 'For the fiftieth time, I haven't had sex with anybody! OK?'

'But she's pressuring you to. Or you want to. To be grown-up. Like her.'

She doesn't answer. And that's how I know.

'Well, let me tell you, if you get pregnant, you're keeping the baby. Maybe some other mother would bail their daughter out, but if you're going to make adult choices, then you have to live with the consequences of being an adult.'

'Who says I'd get pregnant?'

'I'm just saying you need to know what will happen if you do. Same as STIs. They can't all be cured with an antibiotic, you know. Get herpes, and you've got it for life.' I know this is all taught in school. She's not as naïve as I was at her age. But I also know

153

that there is a point where education goes out the window when confronted with peer pressure. 'If you get a disease it'll haunt you forever. You'll have to tell every boy who wants to get close to you. Then you'll meet someone you really like and he'll probably just walk away. No one wants to be with a teenage slut. And that's what they'll assume you are.' My scare tactics carry echoes of my disciplinarian father. They might not sit with my principles but they're the only weapon I've got. 'I'm not saying this to frighten you. I'm telling you because you need to see the big picture that comes with your actions.'

'I didn't have sex with anyone! How many more times? They wanted to, but I wouldn't.'

'Who did?' The blood storms in my veins, along with murderous rage. She stares hard into her barely touched porridge. 'I'll find out. Do you realise they can go to prison? It's rape in the eyes of the law.'

'It's not rape if you consent!' She says it as though I missed that class at school.

'If you're under sixteen, the court says you are not old enough to decide for yourself, so it's statutory rape. Because you're still a child.'

'So what!' she fires back. 'If I want to, I will. You're not going to make every one of my decisions for me. You and him.'

I try not to let the way she says 'him' assail me. It's as though she's speaking of my on-again, off-again boyfriend rather than her own father. 'Look, I realise you'll do what you want to do, despite what I say. But know that once you have a reputation like Bethany's, there's no undoing it. You can't get your dignity back once it's gone, Zara. And you know what? Once you're seen as trash in other people's eyes, you'll eventually see yourself that way too.'

She suddenly places her hands over her ears. The chair scrapes along the wood and she hurries to the corner of the room. I watch her throw herself down on to the floor, draw her knees up and clutch them. Then she rocks and cries, rocks and cries. The tears are silent but unstoppable. I have never seen her do this before. I cannot pull my eyes away.

You were too hard on her.

You weren't hard enough.

'Zara,' I say gently, but she doesn't seem to hear me. I am no longer Zara's anchor, her safe haven, and this is perhaps the greatest loss I've known.

You should have made her feel more loved. If you'd made her feel she mattered as much as Daniel, she wouldn't have needed affirmation from anyone else.

The sight of her sitting there, rocking, breaks my heart in two.

She will remember this, I think. *Long after she has forgotten what the whole thing was even about. She'll hold it against you. You made her go and rock in the corner.*

TWENTY-SEVEN

ERIC

January 2004

His are the only footsteps in the parking garage. He's almost at his car when he sees her. She is leaning up against the wall, right next to his 'Reserved' sign. Ever so casual. Like it's perfectly normal to hijack somebody's parking spot.

'I have nothing to say to you!' he says. He clicks his doors open and tosses his trench coat into the back seat.

'I have to say, I think we communicate better in bed.'

His hand is reaching for the driver's-side door and freezes there. 'Bed?' This is surreal. 'When did we ever go to bed? What Neverland do you live in, eh?'

She moves towards him. He is vaguely aware of a tight grey dress, brown cowboy boots and bare legs, the cloying smell of cheap perfume. 'I'm sorry,' she says. 'I'm not trying to make you feel uncomfortable. I know that you insist on having some sort of negative impression of me . . . I just, well, I hoped I could ask for your help right now, that's all.'

'Help?' He sighs. This morning he received an email from a headhunter in Australia. He could tell it was one of those impersonal, sales-y ones, but for a few minutes he fantasised about packing his bags.

'My car wouldn't start this morning. I'm not feeling well. It's been a very bad day for me for a number of reasons. I don't feel my legs will carry me to the bus. I just want to get home. To my little girl.'

He watches as she cups her mouth with her hands for a moment or two and gasps quietly. He hasn't really seen her look vulnerable before.

'Please,' she says when she can speak again. 'I just hoped, as a friend, or even just a kind person, that you might give me a ride. I would not ask if I wasn't desperate.'

He sighs again. His instinct is to say, *Tough tits!* But he thinks of the kid. If this were Em just wanting to get home to her baby, he'd want somebody to take pity on her. That thought leaves him suspended between being a nice guy and a bastard.

'I promise I have no agenda,' she says. 'You can take me at face value. I just really need someone to do me a good turn right now.'

He doesn't want anyone to see them standing here looking like they're having a big heart-to-heart. 'Get in,' he tells her. He climbs in the driver's side then she opens the passenger-side door. Once she is in, she pulls a hankie from her coat pocket and dabs at her eyes. She is shivering, so he automatically flicks on the heater. As he pulls out on to the road, he realises he just made a left turn without really looking to see what was coming.

They ride for a while in silence. He catches himself drumming his fingers on the wheel, nervously, and makes himself stop. Normally he'd put music on, but that might send the wrong signal. Her body is angled toward him. The silence is eating him alive.

When he is done grinding his teeth, he says, calmly, 'What's all this about, Janet, eh? I'm genuinely hoping you'll just tell me. If I can help, then I will. But I'd just really like to know where all this is coming from.' He tries not to sound combative. Maybe he can get on her good side and make all this go away.

'I don't know.' She lets out a shaky breath. 'Have you any idea what it's like to have literally no one you can talk to? No one to share what you're going through with, Eric? I told you, all I ever wanted was a friend. One person who won't judge me.'

'That wasn't quite what I meant,' he says. 'I was meaning why won't you leave me alone?'

When she looks at him, her eyes are burning with disappointment and disapproval. 'Leave you alone?' She says it as though the concept is astonishing to her. 'You know, Eric, this is not a good time for me to be having this conversation. Not right now. It's not a good day for me at all. I am trying – trying to keep it all together – but it's very hard for me today.'

'Look, whatever you're going through . . . can't Bethany's father help? I mean, she obviously has one. Or your parents, maybe? You're a nice person; I can't believe you haven't got any friends.'

'It's best you don't pass comment on things you know nothing about.'

Even though it's utter madness, he actually does wish he could help her in some way. Mainly so she'd be grateful and leave him alone, of course, but there is some small part of him that genuinely feels sorry for her. 'Can I ask you something?' he says. 'And don't take this the wrong way. I don't mean it hurtfully. But are there times when, well, when you're not feeling like yourself? You know, when you don't think you're all that well upstairs?' He taps his temple, thinking back to his brief research into personality disorders. 'When you feel you're not in control . . . that maybe you've lost it?'

She throws him a look of disgust. 'Oh, I'm well. But I'm not so sure about you, Eric. Perhaps we should put your head under the microscope before we get to mine.'

She looks out of the window again. He's desperate to sink a drink. He's been doing a lot of that lately. Just one becomes just one more. Every time he goes too far he wakes up the next day and thinks, *I feel like shit. Em's pissed off. I'm burning through money, getting a gut . . .* But then he rationalises there really aren't any serious consequences. He only feels shit for a day. Em gets over it. He earns it, so he can spend it. Em doesn't care how he looks. His liver? Well, OK, there's that. But they say your liver rejuvenates if you lay off the booze for three consecutive days, and even if it gets shot to pot, it can still bounce back if you abstain completely for an entire year. He's never been a daily drinker. He can easily go for three days. Just not at the moment. He isn't happy about it, though. He tells himself he'll have one or two, but not get bladdered. It's just that when he gets to that point again, he loses sight of why it matters.

'I know we got off to a rocky start, Eric, and that you probably don't much like me . . .' she says, apropos of nothing. 'But, unlikely as it might seem to you, I bear you no ill will. I will always remember that when I first started working here, you were the only one who was nice to me. Nobody else gave me the time of day. Because I didn't fit their mould, you see. I was too intelligent for the secretaries so they were all intimidated by me, and yet I wasn't decked out with qualifications so the engineers didn't take me seriously – even though I'm brighter than ninety per cent of them anyway.'

'But I didn't give you the time of day,' he says. 'That's the whole point. Before the Christmas party we'd barely said two words.'

She meets his eyes. 'But you made up for that, didn't you.'

He stares at her for a moment or two, hijacked by her bullshit. 'How do you make that out?' He cautions himself to stop looking at her and focus on the road.

'You know, Eric, you act a certain way and you look a certain way, and despite what you say about your wife . . . my guess is you don't have a very happy life at home. I'm good at reading people and I feel I've got a very good diagnosis of you. You're a very disillusioned man at heart.'

Adrenaline suddenly fires in him. He accelerates accidentally when he should be slowing down and has to brake hard. She lurches forward, clutching the seat.

'Please don't ever bring my wife into the conversation.' He grits his teeth so much his jaw burns.

'Oh!' she says wearily. 'So that's all it takes, is it? For Eric to get ugly? Me to mention the little wife?'

His hands are clenching the wheel so hard that he doesn't think he can straighten his fingers. His shirt is sticking to his back, and his foot tingles on the pedal. Part of him would like to floor it, crash. Her head going through the window, not his. Though he knows that might not be the easiest thing to orchestrate.

His phone rings from the console between them. He glances at it. Shit. Em. His chest tightens. How can he answer it? Up ahead, traffic is getting heavier.

Before he can think straight, Janet has reached for it. She peers at the display. 'Oh, speak of the devil.' For a second he thinks she's going to answer it, but instead she holds it out to him.

He snatches it off her and puts it back where it was. Why did he let her in his car? He's his own worst enemy.

Before he can react, she picks up the phone again and presses 'Call Back'. It rings. Then, on speakerphone, Em says, 'Hiya . . . How's things? Are you driving? Where are you?'

He bites the inside of his mouth. 'Yeah. Fine. I'm in the car.'

Janet starts rustling around in her bag. Deliberately. He's worried Em's going to hear.

'We've nothing in for dinner. Thought I'd break the bad news early.'

'I can pick something up,' he says, after a distracted pause.

'I was hoping you'd say that. What do you fancy? Other than me?'

Janet rolls her eyes, and mumbles, 'Oh my God.'

'I'll think of something,' he says, glaring at her. 'Look, traffic's insane. I'd best go.'

'"What do you fancy? Other than me?"' Janet mimics when he hangs up. 'That's desperate. She sounds awful!'

He cranks the wheel. The car comes to an abrupt stop with a screech of tyres. The driver behind him blares on the horn then swings out to avoid his tail end. The bloke mouths, *Fuck you!* Not one of his better driving moments.

'Get out.' He stares straight ahead, aware of the steepness of his breathing. His heart is hammering. That constricted feeling in his windpipe.

She crosses her arms and turns her head away to look out of the window. 'I'm not going anywhere. You promised to take me home. And you know what, Eric, if you're this uptight, maybe you should come in and have a drink. We all know how that loosens you up.'

'You're unhinged.' He is sweating profusely. Then he adds, 'And, actually, for your information, I don't drink. Only at parties.'

'You need to continue driving,' she says, like a mother telling off her little boy.

'We're not going anywhere. You're getting out, and on Monday morning I'm reporting you to HR and I'm probably getting the police on you as well. I'm finished with being nice.'

She shifts in the seat so she can look at him more easily. 'OK, if we need to have the talk, then let's have it. Let me tell you what you *can* and *can't* do. You can't just use me, take what you want from me because in that moment you don't give a damn about your little boy and your Snow White wife – then ignore me, throw me away like I'm a fish-and-chips wrapper. Treat me like I'm not actually a real person with feelings, like that episode didn't matter.'

'What fucking episode?' His head nearly hits the roof. 'This is insane! And . . . *use* you! I didn't use you! What did I ever take from you? I never did anything to you!'

'You can tell yourself lies and try to believe them,' she continues calmly, after he's done. 'But we both know the truth. You're a selfish predator who takes advantage of women in the workplace. Single mothers who make very easy prey for you. You homed in on me from day one.'

He stares at her for a moment through his rising panic. Then he bullets out of the vehicle, charges around to the other side, hauls open her door. 'Out.'

She makes no attempt to move. That mean little mouth of hers is set in a tight circle like a cat's anus. He can hear the steady tick-tick of his indicator and another of his heart. 'I said, O. U. T. Or I'm going to drag you out.'

She slowly turns her head and meets his eyes. 'I'm really terrified.'

He has never seen a person be able to mock, antagonise, belittle, to the degree that she manages it – with barely any inflection. She knows he's not going to do anything. He hates himself for being so transparent and weak.

You bitch, he thinks. *I'll kill you!* For a second he believes he can, if it means protecting Em and his kids and everything he values, everything he's worked for – from a nutter.

But the way she is looking at him, she seems to see through him, right to his powerless centre. He feels himself cracking up. 'What do I have to do, Janet, to get you to see that there's nothing between us?' He stands there with curled, limp arms. '*Nothing*. Do you hear me? There never was. Nothing happened. Whatever you think happened, you've invented because you're a person with a lot of personal problems, and the truth is you're most likely mentally ill.'

She has shifted her face away from him but she turns slightly now. 'Why would you be so deliberately hurtful? I mean, what if I really was mentally ill? How would that make me feel?'

He is crushed. He's out of resources. She's won. Insanely, a part of him feels like crying.

'I would give this up, Eric, I really would.' She meets his eyes now. 'If it weren't for the fact that I don't really think it's what you want. You can't deny there was something between us from day one. I still remember how you looked at me that first day we met. In the hallway by the canteen. Do you remember? You don't look at somebody like that if you're not interested in them. You and I both know that.'

'Eh? What hallway? What look?' He genuinely has no idea what she's talking about. It's so stupid he doesn't even have a come-back any more.

'Marriages don't have to continue if they're not working. People meet other people all the time . . . It's nothing to be ashamed about. You'd hardly be original if you got divorced.'

Her sad eyes hang on to his, and for a moment he can actually see insanity in them. A certain glassy shine. A vacancy. Then her expression suddenly turns wistful. 'You know, I'd see you around and I'd just keep thinking, *Why can't I be married to someone like this? Why can't this man have been my little Bethany's dad – somebody normal and together and kind – instead of the loathsome waste-of-good-skin who actually is? I mean . . . why?*

The rain is falling heavily, cold spikes driving down on his head. He can both feel it and yet feels deadened to it at the same time. A profound despair gnaws at him. She's got to him. He doesn't know which way he can possibly turn.

'Cat got Eric's tongue?'

'I'm sorry,' he says, and he doesn't even know why he's saying it. He feels the tears come because he's just so frustrated. 'I'm really and truly sorry. If I have in any way led you on – and clearly I must have – it was my fault entirely, and I apologise deeply for it. It was not my intention . . .' He tries to get a hold of himself, despite the tears rolling down his cheeks and the sense of it all falling apart. 'You're a nice person and I respect you. I would never want you to suffer any mental anguish because of me, or anything I've unintentionally done . . .'

She looks away, as though she can't stand to see him. 'I just find myself being curious to know what Em would think of the fact that you came on to a woman while she was pregnant. It's not exactly a compliment to her, is it?'

He stares at her, aware of a rolling sensation in his head, a huge wave of despair washing over his brain. But his survival instinct makes him want to swim for his life. He points an index finger about half an inch away from her cheek. 'What did I say about mentioning my wife?' His hand trembles.

'Who? Wussy Em?'

He suddenly reaches down and grabs her bag, hurls it. It lands where the tarmac ends, just short of toppling off into the ditch. It makes a cracking sound as it hits the ground, then something rolls out. A cuddly toy. A pink rabbit with cream ears and piercing dark buttons for eyes. It's wearing a white knitted coat and booties.

'Bethany's bunny,' she says.

The toy lies there, face up, caught in the beam of his headlights. Before he can say anything she is already out of the car and hurrying to get it.

So trusting.

It happens so fast. He shuts her door then skedaddles around to the driver's side. He dives in, and shifts into gear, right as she's bending down to pick up Bethany's bunny.

'Goodbye, nutter!' he hollers, delirious with triumph.

Lucky for him there's a break in the traffic.

TWENTY-EIGHT

'I need to get some money off you.' Zara is scavenging a pile of raw carrots when I come in.

'For?'

She cracks one with her teeth. Otis is waiting for her to throw him the stalky bit. 'Stuff. Clothes. Tampons. Train fare.'

'Train fare?'

'If I want to go into Leeds. Shopping.'

'We can go shopping for whatever you need any time you want.'

'I want to go by myself!'

'With Bethany, you mean?'

'No!' she says, unconvincingly. 'With anybody!' Then, when I ignore that, 'I need my own money! I have a right to pocket money! I'm not being kept prisoner!'

I look her straight in the eye. 'Actually, you don't have a right to pocket money. And you're not being kept prisoner, but I have to know you're not sneaking off to go and see that girl.'

'This won't work,' she shouts. 'You can't do this to me!'

It takes a gargantuan effort but I walk out of the room.

Our paper delivery man never normally knocks at my door. When I open up, hit with a massive gust of wind, he hands me my rolled-up copy of the evening news.

'Some people will be up in arms about it, but, if you ask me, I think you did right.' His shoulders are square and rigid, the posture of someone who has something to get off his chest. 'We need to take our country back. These people can't come here and take all the power. We were here first.' He gives one sharp nod, then turns and walks back down our path.

I have absolutely no idea what he's talking about. But not for long. I go inside, opening the paper out as I walk. Good God! There, on the front page, is my mugshot. My work security-pass photo. Blown up and hideous. And the headline:

University Lecturer in Racial Discrimination Allegation

'What?' I say loudly, even though there's no one to hear.

A first-year student in the PR and Communications degree programme at Leeds University is alleging discrimination against professor Emily Rossi, mother of junior tennis champion and local celebrity Daniel Rossi. Mr Prajval Dhaliwal, 19, originally from Goa, India, alleges that, on several occasions, Rossi suggested that he withdraw from her course because his English failed to live up to that of a British-born and -educated student. Dhaliwal also alleges that because of Rossi's failure to return his email requesting special permission to travel to India for a family emergency and the alleged verbal abuse he was subject to during a face-to-face meeting with the professor during her office hours, Dhaliwal suffered emotional distress which exacerbated his atrial fibrillation: a condition he was diagnosed with four years ago. Rossi was not answering her phone at the university, and so far the university has not been available for comment.

A letter follows in the post the next morning.

Dear Professor Rossi,

Pursuant to Leeds University's policy, this letter serves as notice of your suspension, effective immediately.

It is with great regret that we are forced to send this. When Prajval Dhaliwal made his initial complaint against you, I advised you to send him a written apology, promptly. It was my belief that this highly distressed student would be pacified by this, and that, with your peremptory actions, no further damage to the student, or to Leeds University, would be done. It is a great misfortune that you chose to ignore my instruction. As a result, the integrity of the university has been compromised and we have no choice but to suspend you, with pay, for thirty days, or until this matter has been investigated further, and pending the outcome of a disciplinary hearing. We will notify you of forthcoming proceedings once an independent investigating officer has been assigned to your case. In the meantime, you are to have no contact of any form with colleagues or students of Leeds University. We trust that you will cooperate.

Yours sincerely,
Tom Green

Cc: Greg Ashington, Dean of Business School;
Olaf Jonsson, Chancellor

My phone rings and rings and it's Charlotte. When I don't pick up, she texts and says she saw the paper, we need to talk; she has lots of advice for me. But I feel I need to get my own thoughts straight on all this, before I listen to anyone else's.

TWENTY-NINE

'Aren't you going out tonight?' I ask Daniel. He lost a big tournament two days ago. He's been quiet ever since.

We are eating the chicken curry that Zara and I made from scratch. Eric has managed to wangle working from home for a few days, supposedly to make me feel better. But he has been virtually mute these past couple of hours, and even now he is sitting here supposedly having dinner with us, but with his laptop open. I am surprised I could even rally myself to cook, but lately all I can do to keep my sanity is stay busy and prevent my mind from going down dark *what if?* paths. Keeping Zara busy in the process is a bonus.

Daniel shakes his head. 'No.'

'That's a bit unusual. John and Ryan not around?'

He shrugs. 'I'm not sure. I think they've got family stuff.'

It's not like Daniel to be so tight-lipped, so I sense it's not just about losing the match. I set my fork down on my plate. 'Are they saying things? About me?' I stare at the top of his head, waiting for him to look up.

'No,' he says. 'No one's said anything.'

He sounds a little impatient and still won't look at me. So I think, *Of course, he's lying low because he's embarrassed in case they do.*

'It's not true,' I say. 'Nothing in that article carries even a note of truth. I never implied anything about his English not being as good as someone British-born and -educated. It was his attitude and sense of entitlement, and his use of textese that were the problem.' The words of that article are haunting me. I just keep playing them over and over, burning with injustice. Why would he say all that about me when it wasn't true? How can they suspend me when I have an impeccable ten-year record and have never once received a complaint of any nature from a student? Eric thinks it's all because the student didn't get out of me quite what he wanted, and this was his way of putting the boot in.

'I know,' Daniel says. 'I just don't feel like going out tonight. If that's OK?' His tone says he's fed up of this now.

I open my mouth again to speak, but Eric looks up. 'Em, let it drop.'

He's right. I try to focus on loading pieces of chicken on to my fork, and to forget about it. I actually thought I was rather accommodating with the student, that I handled the meeting well. I think of him towering over me in anger, reminding me a little of Eric. My sense of wanting to put my foot down at one more big guy who thinks he can raise his voice at me and intimidate me just because I'm a woman . . . But was I, in fact, harder on him than I needed to be because I was pushing back in all the ways I feel I can't push back at Eric? I wish I had some sort of recording so I could re-examine my behaviour, or get an objective opinion on it.

We sit in silence, like there's an elephant in the room, until Zara says, 'Can I go out with Katy tomorrow night?'

It's been two weeks since the episode in the park; Zara has mostly toed the line. I am daring to believe that perhaps her fixation with Bethany Brown is over. Which is good, because I don't think I could cope with it now, on top of this work accusation.

'Since when did you start talking to Katy again?' Eric asks.

'What do you mean, "since when"?' Zara frowns. 'We never stopped.'

'What do you plan on doing?' I am just so relieved to hear Katy's name instead of Bethany's.

'Maybe see a film. Her mum said she'd take us and pick us up.' She names one I haven't heard of. And I find myself having to decide whether or not I can trust her again.

'You'll text me when you're in her car?' I say.

'Chill out. Don't I always?'

While Eric says, 'How much money do you want?' I push my plate away then text Sian just to make sure Zara isn't lying about them getting a ride. Then I google the movie to make sure she's being honest about that too.

'Want or need?' she says to her dad.

'I'll give you a tenner, so long as you bring me home a bag of Revels.'

Whenever I used to take her to the cinema when she was little, she always insisted on bringing her dad home a bag of Revels – his favourite. Sometimes I'd think she only ever wanted to go and see the film so she could bring him home a present.

'If you want the Revels, I'll need fifteen. Inflation.'

He titters. 'Your mother taught you well.'

Yes, Sian replies. 6:45 show. Will be at entrance to collect at 10.

I'm pleased she didn't lie. 'I'm fine for you to go,' I say, still a little apprehensive.

THIRTY

'Go,' Eric tells me. 'Daniel and I will be fine without you.'

'I don't know,' I say, twirling strands of my hair.

'You need to stop dwelling on it. A night out will do you good. It'll be interesting to get Charlotte's advice. Plus we need to get rid of you so we can watch *The Walking Dead*.' He nudges Daniel, who is tinkering on his phone.

'Er, yeah,' Daniel says, after a delay. 'Mega.'

I go upstairs, not sure why I'm dragging my heels. The bed is littered with outfits. I try to settle on a wrap-around frock but somehow it looks too dressy. Damn. When I get this frustrated over clothes it usually means I don't want to go.

'I should text her I'm going to be late,' I say, when Eric comes upstairs to see what I'm doing. I don't know why my instincts are telling me this is a bad idea.

'She'll have worked that one out for herself in a few minutes.'

I'm on the verge of saying, *To hell with it*, when he says, 'Put the tight black jeans and the flouncy blue blouse on. You look great in it.'

'How do you know? You haven't seen me in it!' I pick up what I tried on earlier.

He grins. 'I'm anticipating.'

He drops me off at Les Follies Bistrot. I am twenty-five minutes late. It's not like Charlotte to not answer her phone.

I see her at the bar. It looks like she's already downed half a carafe of wine. She is squeezed in among the businessmen and dating couples eating steaks and *moules-frites*, with her back to the door. Her coat is saving my seat.

I bypass the hostess. Charlotte has her hair pinned up chignon-style – her night-out hair, as she calls it – and a dress exposing pale shoulders with the familiar peach-like birthmark on the left one. She's talking on her phone. So that's why she wasn't picking up. Knowing how she is when she gets talking, she probably hasn't even realised I'm so late. We can hope. I cut through the crowd. It's warm, and the atmosphere is heavily laced with voices trying to make themselves heard above the music. Charlotte is naturally loud even at the best of times. But even she has to shout in here.

I am just about to tap her shoulder and surprise her, when I hear her saying, 'Yes, well, I'm on a mission to cheer her up tonight. She's having a right rough time of it lately, poor thing. She's been suspended from her job and that daughter of hers is turning into a proper little tramp!'

The music fades into the background. The serving staff moves around me in slow motion. My head careens, a sensation that carries right down to my stomach. I stare at the single loose coil of hair at the nape of her neck. Still she rattles on. On to something else now. The comment is said and is behind her, lost in her litany. I take a step back, two, bump up against someone, mouth an apology, then flee.

As the door closes behind me I register the falling away of noise and the snap of cold air. But her words cling to me like witches' fingers. I can't shake off the ugliness of them. I stand there, regrouping, trying to breathe, rebounding from the betrayal, my heart sinking, my brain just wanting to make it all go away.

Proper little tramp.

There's a loud noise. It sounds like a train in the distance but there are no trains; I realise it's my heartbeat in my ears, banging through the tunnel of my thoughts. I start to walk, not really sure where I'm going or what my plan is. I absolutely don't feel like going home. I get a text and panic, thinking it must be her, but when I dare to look I see it's only Sian.

Girls r at movie. All good . . .

I type back a brief thanks.

Proper little tramp.

I am slightly nauseous. A combination of hunger and horror. The damp cuts through the fine wool of my jacket. Up ahead there's a pub, people clustered outside drinking under the lamplight, their breath clouds in the cold night air. I see them through a haze of sadness. *Walk on. Eyes down.* My longing is for invisibility. To be beyond all this, at some point in the future, when none of this will matter any more. And then I hear a voice.

'Emily.'

I am almost past the huddle of males before I properly register that someone is speaking to me. A hand lands on my arm. A sturdy grip.

He is holding a pint, poised to smile, but then he must see my face.

Steve.

'Are you all right?' he asks.

Charlotte's words rattle around in my head. But then they stop for a second and all I can think is, *Gosh, Steve, you are always – conveniently – there.*

'No,' I say. 'Not exactly.'

As decisive as ever, he passes his barely touched drink to one of the other men. 'Come on,' he says, and after a few words to his friends, he ushers me off down the street. I notice we are hurrying, as though we are suddenly joined in an unlikely kindred purpose. Next, he is guiding me through a door. Into another pub. The beery warmth hits me as we enter, and I feel better already – like going to Narnia through the magic wardrobe.

'Drink,' he says. It's not a question. 'What would you like?'

'To disappear?'

'But failing that.'

'Whatever you're having.'

I can hear the gentle concern of his voice and want to gravitate to it like a moth to a light. I am aware of his hand on the small of my back and I am reminded of the night I saw him on his date with that girl. How quietly envious I was of her.

He goes to the bar and I find a seat in the corner. But no sooner do I have my coat off than my phone rings and it's Charlotte. *Proper little tramp.* Blood rushes to my head. I can hear the ringing of her laughter in my ears, see that loose coil of hair. I switch my phone off.

'Thanks,' I say, when he returns with two glasses of red wine.

'Go on then.' He sits down, our knees brushing briefly under the table. 'Give it to me from the top.'

For a moment I can't bear the idea of repeating it. I'd rather just concentrate on the unlikeliness of us finding ourselves sitting here together – the crazy upshot of this awful night. But then I give him an account of my evening so far, without naming names. Not the bit about her saying I've just been suspended. I'm going to rely on my hope that he doesn't have time to read the local newspaper.

He doesn't respond at first, though I've come to notice this is part of his charm. Steve listens to you intensely, and then it's as though he carries on listening long after you've stopped talking.

Finally, he says, 'I'm sorry. That must have felt terrible . . . It's odd to actually hear yourself being talked about, when it's not intended.' Then he tells me of the time he picked up the phone at work only to get crossed lines with a nurse telling another nurse what a shitty doctor he was. 'I might have thought she was just feeling sore about something I must have said or done – but she went into such grim detail. And while I didn't agree with her, it was still hurtful to hear.' Then he adds, 'Of course, she wasn't my neighbour and close friend.'

'How did you know?' I ask.

He shrugs. 'When you were mimicking her. I know you were doing it unconsciously, but I could hear the very rounded, strident vowels.'

Despite the awfulness of it, I smile. 'You should have been a detective, not a doctor.'

'I'm sure that rotten nurse would probably agree with you.'

'And I should probably have been anything but a wife and a mother, as I'm clearly so very bad at both.'

'Don't say that,' he says. 'Don't let one person's stupid comment make you question anything about yourself.'

'No,' I say. 'You're right. I won't . . .' I tell him how it's just so sad. She's known Zara for years. 'What's crap, too, is that I've always valued her judgement . . .' I take a drink of the wine, knowing I'm probably going to polish it off quickly if I'm not careful. 'Those solid years of our friendship are stacking up in one corner, ready to go head-to-head with this new version of Charlotte that I've never seen before. I mean, I've seen it. Just not directed at me. And it's truly the last thing I was prepared for.'

'Consider the source.' He leans his forearms on the small table, so the gap between us closes a little. 'She's never been a mother to a teenager. She's got it all to come.'

'I can hope,' I say uncharitably, and he grins. 'So where is Henry tonight?' I ask, feeling we've said enough about Charlotte for now.

'At his granddad's.'

I look at his hand resting on the table by his phone. 'Does Henry like to stay with him?'

'No. But sometimes I need a night off. You think that by being there at every opportunity you're being a better parent but you're really just being a burned-out one.'

'How true.'

'I only send him there once a fortnight. He sleeps in the room his mother grew up in. Even her teddy is still there. Mr Chubby Bear.' A half-formed thought fleetingly clouds his expression. 'If he really doesn't want to go, I don't make him, of course. But I can usually talk him round.'

'We seem to spend a lot of our time talking about kids, don't we?' I say. 'We should make a point of talking about the things that don't keep us awake at night, rather than the things that do.'

'Great idea,' he says.

I smile. 'But what does that leave?'

He finally takes a sip of his wine. 'The nice thing is, it's wide open.'

As we walk back up the high street I feel pleasantly buzzed and a tiny bit better. But then we have to pass the restaurant. 'Ugh!' I clutch his arm.

'I doubt she's still going to be waiting for you.' He sends me a wry glance.

'No. But I feel so sad! It was my favourite place to dine out! It's ruined for me now!'

'OK.' He stops and turns to face me. 'You've got to go back in. Right now.'

'What?'

'It's the only way. Or you'll never go in there again. I promise you.' Before I can say or do another thing he takes hold of my hand – only for enough time to direct me to the door. 'Come on. I'm sure you've got room for one more drink.'

In the toilets I turn my phone back on. I've several missed calls from Charlotte and three from Eric. 'Where the bloody hell are you?' he barks when I ring him back. 'Charlotte's been phoning incessantly! She's wondering where on earth you are. As am I!' I can tell he's been drinking just by his tone and the molasses-like quality of his words.

'Is Zara home?' I ask.

'No. The movie's not out until ten.'

Oh yes. I remember now. I look at my watch. Another hour. I quickly text Katy's mum. Still on course to pick the girls up?

While I wait for her reply I tell him what happened with Charlotte, tell him I've just been walking around, trying to get to grips with it. Oddly, perhaps with verbalising it twice, it no longer feels like the end of my world – just the almost-end.

'Oh.' His annoyance subsides. 'So you mean you just walked out and left her there without her knowing you'd heard her?'

'What would you have recommended? Me to open my bag and take out my hatchet?'

He blows out a sigh. 'Well, you have to ring her back.'

'Why?'

There's a pause. 'Because you can't just leave her hanging.' Then he adds, 'What if she rings here again? What am I going to say?'

Sian texts back. No prob. All sorted.

'Don't answer,' I tell him. 'Or tell her I'm having an emergency hernia repaired. It's up to you.'

'So it's my job now?'

Oh, poor you!

'Anyway,' he says a little less belligerently when I don't reply, 'where are you? I can hear music.'

Someone tries the toilet door. 'I'm in a restaurant. I needed to eat.' I don't lie well. Plus, lying makes this something it isn't. So I add, 'I bumped into our neighbour. You know, Steve, the doctor? So I'm probably going to have a quick bite to eat and I'll be home soon.'

There's a pause and then he says, 'You're having dinner? With the fucking doctor?'

I can tell where this is going. Right now I am so grateful I'm here and not at home – for the small advantage it gives me. 'It was hardly by design,' I say.

'What's going on here with this guy, anyway? Daniel was just saying he invited you and him down to his house . . .'

'To meet his eight-year-old son who is having a hard time after his mother died.'

There's a pause, then, 'I think you should get yourself home. Right now.'

He sounds like my father. So I say what I would never have dared say to my dad. 'I'm staying here. And I'm going to have something to eat. With our neighbour. Because I'm hungry.'

There's another pause where I'm expecting him to blow his lid, but then he says a bewildered 'Em . . . You're not behaving like yourself.'

I feel like saying, *Finally!* My heart is hammering, a tiny part of me wanting to relent. He's probably right; I should probably get myself home. But it's overruled by my newfound sense of power. 'Look, I have to go. I'm in the toilet. There's a queue.'

'What? Look . . . where the hell are you? I'm coming to get you. You can tell bloody Steven to go and make a play for somebody else's wife.'

I am bolstered by the fact that he can't come to get me because he doesn't know where I am. Nonetheless, I say, quite calmly, 'I am not a child. And neither are you, so stop behaving like one. He's our neighbour. He'll bring me home when we're done eating.' I walk out of the toilet and ignore the dirty look from the young girl waiting in line.

'You'll be lucky if I let you in,' he says.

You'll be lucky if I come back, I think.

When I get back to the bar, Steve shifts so I can squeeze into my seat. I see he has ordered me another wine, and what looks like sparkling water for himself. When my eyes land on it he says, 'I'm driving.' I smile and he asks, 'Are you hungry?'

I nod. 'I don't have long but I could probably sink a plate of chips.'

THIRTY-ONE

'I'll just get out here,' I say, as his car noses on to our street. I doubt Eric will be pacing in front of the window, ready to punch Steve on the nose, but still, I resent the thought I might be being spied on because I am not trusted.

Steve sends me a glance – part curious, part charmed. 'Sure.'

When he parks the car, there is a viscosity in the air between us. Or perhaps it's my imagination. I feel, bizarrely, a little like my younger self being dropped off from a first date. Though my suitors were never this magnetic, or driving such lovely cars. For a beat or two we just go on sitting there, neither of us saying a word, the silence oddly galvanising, even if it's only in my mind. For some reason I can't quite instruct my hand to open the door. I am sure that my reluctance to go inside my own house is palpable. He'd have to be dead not to feel it. It occurs to me that there are so many ways of knowing someone, and sometimes your greatest insight comes from the things they don't say. Soon the interior lights go out and we find ourselves in darkness. After a time he looks across at me and I'm aware of the gentle warmth of his gaze on my profile. And I let myself go with this uncommon and rather lovely feeling of someone looking at me as though they too might be remembering how this sort of thing used to go. When I turn to face him, he smiles – part sad, part something I can't quite define, but I'd love to be able to.

'I seem to spend half my life thanking you,' I say. It's the strangest thing, but my troubles feel like they've floated a world away, and everything seems a fraction more manageable.

He glances at my hands clasped in my lap and suddenly I'm aware my fingers are locked tightly with the suspense of it all. 'It's not at all necessary,' he says. His gaze scans my face, and I'm reminded of that first day we met at his gate, how he looked at me as though he was marking the encounter out in some way. 'I'm sorry the circumstances were as they were, but I'm glad you look happier now than you did a couple of hours ago,' he says.

He shifts slightly in his seat to better see me, an intoxicating invasion of my personal space that perhaps occurs only in my overactive imagination. All the same, it makes me say a rather pathetic, 'I should probably do the wise thing and get myself safely indoors now.'

He continues to sit there long after I've closed the car door, and I have a profound sense of his eyes not leaving me. It's only when I've walked up my path that his car quietly rolls past me and I've half a chance of breathing normally again.

I am just putting my key in the door when my phone rings. It's Sian.

No sooner do I pick up than she says, 'I am so sorry, Em . . . When Katy came out she was on her own! She said Bethany Brown and her boyfriend drove up and Zara went off with them – like it was all planned.'

'Oh, good God, no!' My heart sinks to the ground. All my instincts were telling me this was going to happen, even if I forgot about them for a while. 'When?'

She tells me it was about ten minutes ago.

When I go indoors, Eric is sitting in the armchair watching TV. 'Ah . . .' he says, looking vaguely in my direction. 'She returneth.'

His gaze slides back to the TV.

'Where's Daniel?' I ask, my heart beating hard.

'Upstairs.' He says it in a childish, petulant tone. 'Got sick of being with me.'

I stare at his boozy profile and fill with disgust. It's astonishing how much he loses his looks when he's intoxicated. His face is suddenly robbed of its youthful structure. The small, kind eyes are like marbles sinking into the shapeless form of a Cabbage Patch doll.

'Zara didn't get in the car with Katy's mum. She's gone off with Bethany Brown.'

He turns and looks at me again, but his eyes are off in la-la land. 'Gone where?'

'I don't know.' I can smell whisky a mile off.

Daniel's room door opens, then he comes down the stairs. 'What's wrong?'

'I'm phoning the police,' I say to Eric. I wake my phone up but just stare at numbers, my passcode completely escaping me in my panic.

'Don't be ridiculous.' Eric gets off his backside now, staggers to the dining table and picks up his phone. 'Let's just call her. She can't be far.' I watch him dialling, looking befuddled, rocking slightly on his feet.

I am fully expecting that this won't work but then I hear her say '*Hello?*'

'Where the hell are you?' Eric barks. 'We've heard you've gone off with Bethany Brown!' He places a hand at the back of his head, rubs it to self-soothe. When Eric is wasted, his responses are all inner-directed. His anger isn't really about Zara. It's about having his love-in with the whisky bottle curtailed.

Daniel gives me a knowing look that's filled with disgust and disappointment.

'What do you mean "chill out"?' Eric says. 'You were supposed to be coming home with Katy! In her mum's car!' There's a pause while we register how ineffectual he's being, then he says, quite pathetically, 'I am keeping my hair on! And no, you're not just staying out for one more hour!'

I snatch the phone off him. 'I'm coming to get you. If you don't tell me where you are I'm calling the police and giving them Bethany Brown's home address.'

'We're not there,' she says defiantly.

'Well, then where are you?'

I'm certain she's not going to tell me but then she says, rather defeatist, 'Her boyfriend's. We're at Craig's, OK.' She tells me where that is. There is something in her tone that suggests to me that her evening hasn't turned out as she planned. I can hear music in the background. Laughter. Bethany's mannish guffaw. Bethany sounds stoned.

'I'm coming to get you right now and I want you to leave that house right this minute and start walking.'

'All right!' she says, surprisingly without any argument. 'I will.'

'I'll go,' Eric says, like the big man. He pads, flat-footedly, to the hall table to find his keys, but then doesn't seem to know what he's really doing.

'You can't.' I all but spit the words out. 'You're inebriated.'

'You are, Dad,' Daniel says. 'Look at you, you're swaying all over the place. You can't drive like that.' Then he says to me, 'I'll come with you, Mum.'

I would never normally have mentioned Eric's drinking in front of one of the kids. But it's hardly something Eric has managed to keep secret.

A few minutes later, Daniel is sitting in the passenger seat, and I can tell he's trying to contain his emotion, while he tries to plug Craig Rathbone's address into my satnav.

∞

His street is a row of Edwardian terraces on the outskirts of the village. I spot Zara long before I need satnav to tell me we have arrived at his door. She is walking towards our car, quickly, with her head down, like someone not wanting to be seen by anyone but us. When I pull to a stop she opens the back door and dives into the seat.

I stare at her in the rear-view mirror, needing her to look at me. 'Zara?'

'Can we just go?' Her voice wobbles with pent-up emotion.

'Have you been taking drugs?'

'No,' she says. 'They all did but I haven't had anything.' She meets my eyes now and she doesn't look high or drunk, or anything except fed up and tired. I throw the car into gear.

'Mum?' Daniel says. 'Why don't you just turn around?'

But I am not turning around.

'Come on, Mum.' Zara sounds worried. 'What are you doing? I just want to get out of here.'

I drive at a crawl down his street. It's obvious which house is his, by the music. *Boom, boom, boom.* Our car practically vibrates. I stop right in front of the decrepit gate, park the car. I am out before I've even thought about what I'm doing, down that path, banging on a navy-blue door. Distantly I hear a panicked chorus: 'Mum!'

It's impossible that anyone is going to hear my knocking over the music. I push at the door but, oddly, it's locked. I have some insane urge to kick it in but realise only I will come off badly in that scenario. There's a bright light on in the front room. I can see slivers of it around the badly hung bed sheet that serves as a curtain. It's a dump, a squat. *Bethany's boyfriend has money . . .* I think of Zara's words. It's only then that my eye goes to a collection of old, muddy bricks – like someone might have taken down a low wall and abandoned the rubble. As I pick one up I hear both Zara and Daniel yell at me again. When I turn, they are out of the car. Daniel is hurrying towards me. I only have to look at their faces for my hand to still.

'Come on!' he says. 'This is nuts. Get back in the car.' I have never seen my son look so out of his depth before, or so terrified.

Zara is almost crying. 'Please can we just go? Please can we just go?'

'Mum?' Daniel says, more urgently, standing about three feet away from me. 'Put the brick down!'

So I put the brick back on the pile. My heart is jumping out of me, but I try to focus on doing what I have to do. On being a responsible parent in front of my children, not a thug. On returning to the car and getting my kids home safely.

THIRTY-TWO

There are few things more bizarre to witness than Eric after the night before.

Instead of skulking around all sorry for himself, like the rest of us when we have a hangover, Eric becomes puffed-up and posturing. I watch him pad around the bedroom, purposefully putting away sports shirts that he's just pulled out of the drawer – a pointless occupation considering all he had to do was pick one. His face is patchy purple, his eyelids thick like a lizard's. I have often wondered if the armour he appears to be wearing is his defence against any inclination I might have of hauling him over the coals. His way of saying, *Back off before you even go there!* He won't want to talk about why he was almost passed out on the sofa when we got home last night, instead of being sick with worry over his daughter's safety. He'll want that to go away. Today is a new day.

I watch him and feel neither love nor loathing. I am in that no man's land of pity. The reality is, I don't want to have the conversation either.

'I'm walking the dog,' he says snappily. I don't think he's met my eyes once so far.

'Take the long way,' I tell him.

It's only when he's gone that reality seems to settle in around me and I find myself mentally feeling for a place to land. I have no reason to hurtle out of bed. I have no job. No departmental meetings to attend. The words of the newspaper article still sting. While I don't really buy this business of my contributing to the worsening of his atrial fibrillation, I'd be horrified to think that I had. Had I really been that hard on him? I just keep coming back to this same question. So much has happened that I can't fully remember. But in light of what I almost did last night, I wonder how well I know myself any more.

Which brings me to Charlotte. I don't really want to do this but I pluck my phone off the night table and see if I've any messages. Seven. And three missed calls. I take myself down to the kitchen. Zara isn't up yet and Daniel would have been up early to go to practice. I pop an English muffin into the toaster and set about making a cafetière of coffee. When our landline rings and I see it's her, I stare at it like it's an alien life form.

She doesn't leave a message, so after pushing the muffin into my mouth I reach for my mobile and type:

I heard what you said about Zara. I don't want to talk to you.

It feels a bit pathetic, considering she's right next door. If only I could muster up a little of the courage I had last night . . .

Next she is standing on my doorstep looking ghastly pale. Before I can react, her face folds and the tears pour. 'I am so sorry!'

Oddly enough, a surge of emotion hits me like a tidal wave and it takes everything I've got not to break down too.

'How?' she says, when she can speak again. Her green eyes are bloodshot. She wipes her nose with the back of her hand.

I tell her how. With recounting it, any desire to cry disappears. As I watch her cup her astonished mouth, I feel nothing but antipathy.

'I am so sorry,' she says again, after a spell of me staring her witheringly into the ground. 'Would it be any consolation at all, and could you possibly believe me, when I say that it wasn't at all what I meant? I honestly don't even know why I said it.'

She reaches out a hand, but I instinctively put mine behind my back. I should be able to say, *No, that wouldn't be believable at all, but I'm glad I now know how you think.* But it's all bottlenecking and contorting. 'I don't want to talk about it,' I manage to say. I can't look at her.

'We have to.' She is firm now. 'If we don't, we'll never get past it.'

It reminds me of what Steve said about how I had to go back to the restaurant, or I'd never go in there again.

'I can't lose you as a friend,' she says.

We stare at one another now. 'Perhaps you should have thought of that before you called my daughter a slag.'

'Em . . .' She looks sorrowful but a little steely now, as though she has reached the end of her humble rope. 'All I can say is please know I feel so utterly horrible. You have to at least believe that.' She stares at me with a face full of hope.

I do somewhat believe it. But I still say, 'I've got to go.'

THIRTY-THREE

When Eric comes back from walking the dog, I have my coat on. 'I'm going to meet my dad for a cup of tea.'

'Knock yourself out,' he says, but he sounds contrite. Then I pass him and head out of the door.

As it turns out, I don't phone my dad and, instead, just drive around for an hour, with no real sense of where I'm going, trying to see a way through all this. When I return home, Eric is sitting with his back to the door in the chair that faces on to the garden. He is eerily still. Otis and the kitten come to greet me, but I can't take my eyes off my husband. And then he turns around.

'Janet Brown just rang the house. Bethany overdosed last night. She's in the hospital.'

We process this the way you would any bad news about a kid. Shock. An element of disbelief, even though in theory we probably should not be surprised. Cold pity on my part. A question. If I had hurled that brick through the window, is it possible that this wouldn't have happened?

'Do you want to go in and see her?' I ask Zara some time later, noting how she has become like an empty shell since we broke the news.

Eric looks up from his MacBook. 'What? Are you off your rocker? Why would you ask her that?'

'It's OK,' Zara tuts at him. 'You don't have to speak about me like I'm not here. I don't want to anyway.'

'I just thought that maybe if she sees her she'll have more of a grasp of consequences,' I tell him afterwards, when Zara has gone upstairs.

'That's not what'll happen. She'll want to protect her like she's a broken bird. Is that what you want?' He glares at me. 'Because for an intelligent person, sometimes I don't understand how you operate, I really don't.'

Speaking of not knowing how somebody operates.

'I've been thinking,' Eric says a couple of days later. We've heard that Bethany has been sent home. All seems to be well. He is hanging up his shirts as I put away piles of laundry. 'Maybe we should offer to pay towards Bethany getting some treatment.'

For a second I assume it's a slip of the tongue, and he really means Zara.

'Rehab.' He looks me in the eyes, bluntly. 'I know it sounds a bit mad. But it's what Zara wants.' When he sees my face he says, 'Look, we had a talk earlier, me and the kids . . . She wants to help her. And you know what? Maybe it's not a bad idea to let her.'

I abandon putting away the laundry and drop on to the end of the bed. 'All three of you?' I frown, feeling a little ganged up on. 'Why didn't you tell me?'

'I'm telling you now, aren't I?'

I stare at him in amazement. 'You're kidding, right? This is some sort of bizarre joke?'

'No,' he says. 'Look, they were friends. Zara doesn't want to see her meet some sticky end, which you know is going to happen if she doesn't get some help.' He stops trying to squeeze shirts into the small wardrobe and looks at me. 'We brought her up to be a caring person, with a big heart, and the fact that she is one – well, you should be pleased actually.'

I gawp at him. 'Pleased? That our family wants to contribute to Bethany Brown's rehab? The very girl who's doing her best to destroy our daughter's life?'

He plonks his hand on his hip. 'Look, Bethany is fucked up because she's a drug addict, you and I both know that, and she's a drug addict because she's fucked up. But at least if she cleaned up, maybe that would solve one part of the problem. Maybe she'd no longer feel the need to drag somebody down to that level, if she wasn't on that level herself any more.' While my mouth hangs open he adds, 'Zara said she'd gladly forgo some Christmas presents if she could add something to the kitty instead. Daniel said he would, too.'

I briefly put my face in my hands. 'This is unreal.'

When I look at him, he is standing stock-still in the middle of the floor, as though he's judging me for not responding the way he wants.

Out of curiosity, I say, 'How much is this treatment?'

'About two grand,' he says, without missing a beat.

'What?' I nearly shriek.

'We looked into it.' Then, before I can say anything, he adds, 'Briefly! It's not like we've made it our life's cause.'

I can't believe I'm hearing this. In fact, no, I must have mis-heard. '*How* much?'

'I know it sounds like a lot. But it is what it is. These things don't come cheap.'

Something is rolling away from me. I have the urge to chase after it, and follow where it leads. But before I can work out what it is, he says, 'If, in lieu of some Christmas presents, we let her donate a couple of hundred pounds – and Daniel too – or even a hundred each, it would be something, wouldn't it? A contribution. Zara's chance to do some real good for a friend in need, with Daniel showing he supports her decision.'

'But who's going to put in the other one thousand eight hundred?'

He goes to speak but nothing comes out. He rubs at the back of his head. 'Well, I don't know. Maybe we could put a bit. Maybe Janet's got family. Or . . . Bethany's dad.'

I don't feel like getting into how I pretty much know they'll not get a penny out of Bethany's dad. 'Eric,' I say quietly. 'I've just been suspended from my job. You're on a one-year contract that's already more than half over. We've got a big mortgage. Bills for Daniel. He wants to compete in Japan in February—'

'Since when?'

'Since forever!' I gawp at him in disbelief. Does he pay attention to nothing? 'We're not funding Bethany Brown's drug recovery. Not even the cost of the bus fare. That's the end of it.'

'Fine,' he mutters. Then he adds something strange. 'On your conscience. Not mine.'

THIRTY-FOUR

ERIC

February 2004

'I know you've got a million cousins in your family that you've never met, but any idea who Aunt J is?'

Em is sitting on the couch surrounded by wrapping paper, cards, a sea of pink. She holds up a cuddly toy, waves it at him.

He's just pouring coffee. He's been out for a run – running is the only way he can fight the urge to just sit and drink his brains out.

'I haven't got an Aunt J.' He stares at the little bunny. It's only then that realisation hits him. It's identical to the one that fell out of Janet's bag.

'*For baby Zara. Welcome into the world. A blessing from heaven. A miracle on earth.* She sounds a bit religious. Any churchgoers in your family?'

He walks over to the fridge mainly so she won't see his face. It could be a coincidence. Just because it's a pink bunny wearing a white knitted coat . . .

'Eric?'

He struggles to snap out of it and act normal. 'You know how people are with babies . . . everybody's an aunt. It's probably just a friend of my mum's or a neighbour.'

'Well, whoever it is, she's certainly generous. Look what she sent Daniel!'

He turns around, feeling his head spin in the process. Leaning up against the back of the sofa is a child's bike. Green with blue stripes. 'You're shitting me,' he says.

Em snickers, probably because that's not really something he ever says. 'Shame she didn't include a gift for me!' She studies him when he fails to be amused. 'Surely you've got some idea who might have sent it.'

Part of him thinks, Phew! It can't have been her. She's a single mother. How could she afford to do all this? He feels overwhelming relief.

'We'll have to ask your mum. Maybe she can solve the mystery. You'd think she'd have left an address or something.'

He stoops to scratch his ankle under his sock, his brain running all over the place. As much as he knows it couldn't possibly be her, he knows it *was* her. He scratches until he draws blood. He has a strange sensation that he could topple forward, as though something is messing with his centre of gravity. When he stands up again he sees stars, feels slightly nauseous.

'I'll have to send a card or find some way to thank her – when we find out who she is!'

In his mind's eye, he sees Janet's face.

He knows exactly how he's going to thank her.

THIRTY-FIVE

Because of the mood that has fallen over the house, I decide to book us a week in Greece over the half-term break. We haven't had a holiday together in more than three years, plus, as a bonus, I won't have to be endlessly worrying that Zara has all this free time on her hands to plot hanging out with Bethany. I am just on my way into town to buy us some sunscreen and supplies when I get a text from Charlotte.

Please tell me we haven't fallen out. I can't bear it.

My cold heart cracks and a trickle of compassion enters in. What am I supposed to say? *Of course we haven't! Tea this week?* Before I can overthink it, I text her: I need a break.

I hear the ping of her response as I'm putting on my coat. Please let's have a proper conversation! Tonight? Mine? Wine?

Then I see she's still typing. You're my very best friend. I can't lose you! I'll do anything to put it right!

Being the pleaser that I am, my first inclination is always to make peace. Yet I find myself in a state of utter paralysis, the two sides of me – the friend and the mother – at odds with each other. The forgiving of one is such a betrayal of the other.

I respond, I said I need a break.

I put my phone down but then it pings again. Meet for lunch tomorrow? Pub out of town?

Unbelievable! I hurriedly type back, What part of I need a break do you not understand?

And why would she be suggesting out of town?

A new text pops up. Did I miss something here?

Oh dear! Now I make a point of looking at the name and my heart races with the recognition of my mistake. Steve. I stare at what he's written. Lunch. Pub out of town. Hmm . . . I have never really imagined Steve and me rendezvousing anywhere but on the common, where it feels respectable and above board – where it would almost be unneighbourly *not* to walk with him.

Sorry, I write. That message wasn't meant for you.

Phew! he replies. And then after a pause, So what's your answer?

His steadiness and his neutrality draw me in like a moth to a flame. Yet I picture us sitting tautly at the end of our street in his car. Two people pulled together, yet their better judgement getting in the way – a hurdle they simply can't cross.

Pub out of town. There is nothing even vaguely neutral about it.

Not sure, I type back, already regretting being a bit of a wet blanket.

Moments later. You mean if you want to . . . ?

I feel myself heat up with being put on the spot. The desire to type *I want to* is suddenly so strong, and yet how would I react if Eric were sneaking out of town for lunch with some woman? Even with our current half-marriage I would feel so betrayed. But then I think, *It's just lunch. He's almost a friend. How do I know that Eric hasn't gone for a sly lunch with some woman in London? Or worse?*

I am egged on by my own nagging sense that sometimes I'm living a lie.

OK, I reply.

THIRTY-SIX

He is sitting at a corner table when I walk in the door. My eyes land first on the back of his neck, the kink of curl, the forwards tilt of his head. He's looking at his phone. The sight of him there, with an aura of patience around him, combined with the knowledge that he's waiting for me, is all it takes for the bottom to drop out of my stomach. I briefly contemplate doing a runner. I could text him and say something came up. But right then, as though by grand design, he glances over his shoulder and sees me, one foot in and one foot out of this bizarre and not entirely scripted thing that we are doing. I've been holding the door open and have probably let in a draught of cold air.

'Hi.' He stands.

'Hello,' I croak. He takes one step towards me but then I realise he's going to help me off with my coat, not kiss me, which I'd first thought. I accept his gentlemanly gesture then cock him an eyebrow. 'Pub out of town?' It comes out slightly more flirty than I actually intended.

He colours, looks a little caught out. 'I just thought that if I said one *in* town you'd automatically say no. And then that would be the basis for you to say an even firmer no if I went and proposed somewhere else.'

I sit down on the aged velvet bench. 'So you didn't think it through much, then?'

He smiles an ice-breaking – heartbreaking – smile. 'I think on that note I'll get us some drinks.'

When he comes back from the bar with two glasses of wine, I realise that he's paid again, so I decide I'll buy the food. 'So what made you want to be a doctor, Steve?' I feel the need to keep the conversation wholesome after the false start. He does the slightly mocking, slightly disdainful looking-down-the-nose thing that I like. 'I've never asked you this before,' I say, and offer up a shrug.

He rests his elbows on the small table and looks at me. 'Well, when I was sixteen I had viral meningitis. I was in hospital for two months. I watched a team of doctors essentially save my life and I just thought, *Right, that's what I'm going to do one day.*'

'Wow,' I say. 'That must have been terrifying.'

He cocks his head, like he's remembering. 'I don't recall being terrified – more . . . curious. Like I was watching it all from afar.'

For some reason this leads to me telling him about Daniel nearly dying, and my strange dreams and then – not sure how I get here – about my suspension. 'Didn't you see it in the newspaper?' I realise I've just needed to get it out there.

'No.' He shakes his head. 'I don't get much time to read the local rag, though I probably should. Do you think it'll all go away?'

'I'm not sure,' I say. 'I hope. I might speak to a lawyer and discuss defamation. Implying I'm a verbally abusive racist is utterly horrifying to me. So I feel I've got to defend myself somehow. But there's so much going on, and Zara has to be my main priority . . .' I sigh, then sip my wine. 'I can't believe how life used to be so much more straightforward. Then my mother died, my husband took a job in London, my daughter went off the rails, and I'm suspended and wind up in the newspaper!' I shake my head. 'What next, I wonder?'

'It doesn't bear thinking about,' he says. Then adds, 'But as for your husband working in London, I'm assuming you've got a good marriage, that it can stand the separation . . .'

If my face shows my surprise at how seamlessly he's segued into that, he doesn't react.

'You know, I saw you in Cielo a few weeks ago. I assume that was your husband. I've only seen the top of his head in the garden before.'

'You saw us?' I don't ask him why he didn't come over, possibly for the same reason he doesn't ask why I didn't let on I'd seen him. 'So you've concluded I've a great marriage because we were eating together in a restaurant?' It's an avenue I hadn't expected to walk down. Something about it feels like it's going to land me in quicksand.

He cocks me a look. 'Why, am I wrong?'

I stare at him, then smile. 'Speaking of that restaurant . . . Do you do a lot of dating? I'm assuming that's what she was.'

'Nice move. And no, no I don't, actually.'

'A nurse?'

'Pharmaceutical rep.'

There's an awkward pause. He rotates the base of his wine glass. 'She's a very nice person, but I don't really see the point in wasting someone's time. Or my own. She's young. Thirty-three. I think my personality needs someone more on my own level.'

'This is a first! A man in his forties turning his nose up at someone a decade younger, who is pretty, and very keen on him.'

'Well, I'm not really turning my nose up. And I have no idea if she's massively keen on me, though she did ask me out . . . And I didn't really know how to say no.'

I grin. 'That might be the corniest line I've heard in years.'

He laughs. 'What I mean is, clearly I'm a fossil because I've never had a woman ask me on a date before. But also . . . part of me thought I should push myself. Put a toe in the water. But the bottom line is I'm not sure a woman thirteen years my junior could really take me on, with everything . . . I think relationships work best when you've both suffered a few hard knocks, rather than just one of you.'

'Sorry,' I say. 'I wasn't trying to be personal.'

He looks at me rather tenderly. 'No. You weren't . . . I suppose I'm awkward around the whole topic because after I met Diane I never really imagined I'd have to date again. It's taking some getting used to . . . It would be different, probably, if I didn't have Henry. I'd be more gung-ho, no doubt. But it's hard with a child who still misses his mother. I'm not sure how he's going to take to a strange woman. Not that she'd be a stranger, of course, if I was involved with her . . .'

I picture his home, his easy pottering around his kitchen. A woman being at the centre of those Saturday mornings. Some lucky nurse, or doctor, or someone he meets on one of his sporting ventures . . . And I have a profoundly blindsiding sense of lost opportunities. 'Well, I'm a big believer in timing,' I say, my spirits taking a nosedive. 'When you're ready, you'll know.'

He looks at me in a way that I can't read. I believe I've turned him a little retrospective, just like I feel.

'We didn't have the best marriage,' he says.

The barriers fall away: the awkwardness, my guilt. 'Oh?'

'Before she got sick she was having an affair. She told me she was leaving me for a thirty-two-year-old adventure-travel-company owner who she met on a business trip to London. And then she got her diagnosis . . . and she stayed.'

'Good grief!' I search his face.

'I didn't see it coming. I thought our marriage was fine – strong, actually. We had a good life. I honestly didn't sense any restlessness.'

'Do you think she would have stayed if she hadn't got bad news about her health?'

'No,' he says. 'Absolutely not.'

'Hmm . . .' I try to wrap my head around that one. 'So how did you feel about that?'

'Well, I didn't feel very good! I think once she got the diagnosis, all she really needed, for the remainder of her life, was to feel safe.'

Yes. I can imagine how the lure of an affair would suddenly go out the window if you heard you were dying. I look at his hand lying inertly on the table, the neatly cut nails, the small scar along the side of his index finger.

'The positive – if you can find one – is that Henry never got to find out that his mother was prepared to leave him and go off bear hunting in Canada or whatever, with a man ten years younger.'

'She was going to leave Henry?'

'Well, she could hardly take him with her.'

'Oh my.' *How awful!* I think of how nothing, and no one, would ever come between me and my kids. I would risk life and limb. I would kill for them.

'That day when I met you on the common and you were saying how having children made you reposition everybody you loved – that you loved them all a distant second? Well, I just wish Diane had felt that way.'

I am blown away that he remembered my very words. To hide my shock, I glance over at the bar, at a crop of menus, and say, 'Shall we order some proper food this time?'

'Why did you ask me to come here?' We are walking to our respective cars. I find that I need an answer, a way to understand what *this* is.

His pace slows. I no longer hear the scrunch of gravel under our feet. 'I wanted to see you again. I wanted to . . . do this again . . . Is that wrong of me?'

He faces me. I stare into his eyes, seeing only the weights and measures of eighteen years of marriage, Eric inserting himself into this picture, intruding, incapacitating me, throwing cold water on it. 'I sense it's probably more wrong of me.'

There is a low burr of an understanding between us: we are both responsible parents; he used to be a husband, and I am still a wife. There is an attraction – something neither of us anticipated. It's becoming a point of departure.

'Some things aren't wrong,' he says. 'They're just not what we expected.'

I look at our feet. How did we get here? I honestly don't know. There have been moments in the past where I've recognised that, with one word this way or that, I have the power to actually change my life in a profound and maybe positive way, but I always end up making the safe choice, the one that leaves me feeling flat and unchallenged. I wonder what it would feel like to venture out of that safe space. It's a grim, glorious tease.

We resume walking in silence. Then he says, 'The truth is, I wanted to ask you a question and maybe now is the right time for me to just come out and say it.'

Something about his demeanour tells me he's not about to say he's going away for a few days and will I keep an eye on his house.

Our cars are coincidentally parked right alongside each other. He stops at his, turns to face me again. 'Suppose I got us a room somewhere – not anywhere too local, obviously – and I gave you a time and a day, would you meet me there?'

I am hit by a stupefying rush of disbelief. 'What?'

It makes him smile a little, awkwardly. 'I had a feeling that might be your reaction.'

A breeze wafts my hair but it can't cool the infrared quality of his gaze that somehow whips up the blood in my veins. 'Steve . . .' A laugh almost bursts out of me to hide my wild surprise. Surely he isn't serious? I am hot suddenly, and pluck at the hem of my jumper, hoping to let in a little air.

He continues to stare at me intently in a way that makes me stop breathing, then he takes a step towards me, as though we are already committing the very thing he's proposing, his eyes sweeping my face.

'I was really just thinking that if you know in your heart you're unhappy, you should maybe take some steps to changing that, that's all.' Then he quickly adds, 'Sorry. That came out more bluntly than I intended. I'm not very good at this.'

I play this back. Am I unhappy? Hearing this assessment of me is so strange. Is it really that obvious to anyone who cares to look?

'Sorry . . .' I say. 'I'm just stunned. I had no idea—'

'I felt like this? I think I felt something from that very first day.'

'Wow.' I put my hand to my chest. My heart is doing that unnerving thing where it performs a few leaping beats, before seeming to stop altogether – like I've suddenly experienced a massive high, then died.

He briefly gazes up at a blue sky. 'I never set out to have feelings for a married woman. Why would I? I've probably subconsciously avoided this kind of thing for my entire life. Plus I had a wife who had an affair, and, from the other side, I know what that's like, and I don't relish inflicting that fallout on anyone . . . even someone I don't know. I'm just saying that I have an overwhelming need to just be able to kiss you, and for it not to feel like the eyes of an entire neighbourhood are on us.'

His eyes, his suspense, are weighing on me. I realise I'm being called upon to say something, to speak the truth – but he isn't calling me; *I* am somehow calling me. 'I know,' I say eventually, feeling utterly overcome with a slew of emotion. Rather daftly, I start digging in my bag for my keys. And that's the closest I can come to admitting that the feeling might be mutual.

There's a very long silence in which we both seem to be weighing what's just been said. I stare at the keys in my hand, and they blur until I can no longer even make out their shape. I have never been unfaithful to Eric, mainly because I never imagined any lover could be worth the complications adultery would bring to my family – to *me*. Besides, despite our issues, I have always trusted Eric and I believe he's trusted me. How can I be the one to shatter that?

'Think about it,' he says chirpily. 'I wasn't expecting you to just say yes.'

I look up at his face and for a moment we are held there, and then he breaks the tension with a smile.

'All right,' I say, wondering how I'm now going to think about anything else.

THIRTY-SEVEN

Our rental, on the island of Paros, is a sugar-cube house on the edge of the sea; we can open our back door and literally jump right in, which Daniel and Zara get a kick out of. I watch him attempting to teach her the proper way to butterfly-stroke, the tentative reappearance of past alliances. We are all clearly trying so very hard to get our old selves back. By day, when Eric isn't working on his laptop, we rent bikes and strike out to all corners of the island. At night, we either buy fish for a nice dinner at home – whole bream, which Eric cleans outside, leaving the bones and entrails for the multitude of cats to feast on – or dine out at one of the few tavernas in town or by the sea.

In one such taverna, while Daniel and Zara have gone off in pursuit of gyros, Eric sips a beer and gazes across the water. 'I wonder if they need any British engineers in Greece.' He cocks me a partly serious glance.

'You'd never stand the summers. Not with your freckles and red hair.'

'There's such a thing as sunscreen, you know. Factor three hundred.'

We smile.

'Maybe we'll retire here,' he says.

I contemplate this, try to somehow fate-stamp it, but the future beyond this week still feels so very uncertain to me. I still catch myself having these guilty but somewhat unavoidable moments where I'm sitting across from Eric but it's Steve I'm seeing in his place.

'Yes,' I say.

It's been a lovely few days. Perhaps the change of environment has made it easy to forget that home life is real life, but we really do all seem more relaxed. From our window I watch Eric and Daniel help the neighbour, Costas, stain his two fishing boats. Eric seems so content working away with his son and an elderly man who can barely speak English. And I want to believe in the veneer of things, that our marriage can be painted afresh like that boat.

One day when Eric and Daniel go out with Costas, I walk with Zara all the way from Naoussa to the next town along the beach. 'What happens if they sack you?' she asks, quite out of the blue. Perhaps because we are due to go home in two days' time, reality is circling and attempting to land for all of us.

'They won't.'

'But if they did? Would we have to sell the house?'

'Why do you say that?'

'I heard Dad talking about us moving.'

I stop walking and look at her. 'To who?'

'Dunno. But he was really annoyed. But then he's annoyed a lot, isn't he.' She pulls a thin smile.

'Well, we're not moving, and I am not going to be sacked.' I glance at her out of the corner of my eye again. Then something occurs to me. 'Why? Do you want us to move?'

'I don't think so,' she replies after seeming to think about it. I can tell she's not finished with this when she says, 'You know that night? When you came to Craig's house?' She blushes because it's a night we're both probably keen to forget. 'I got into a fight with

Bethany. She said if I walked out that door she'd lock it then I'd be dead to her.'

'Why?' I ask, remembering that the door was locked when I tried it.

'Craig cheated on her. And then he was sitting there in his house, with his friends in this shifty circle, just ignoring her. And she was just sitting there, pathetic, waiting for him to give her some attention . . . I told her she could do so much better than him! But she said I had to shut up about him or else.'

Or else. I seethe. I reach out and remove a strand of her hair that's sticking to her lip-gloss. 'You're a very good person, Zara. You should be proud of yourself for trying to talk sense into her.'

'She didn't listen to me, though! She thinks that because he's well off she couldn't do better than that. She really blew up. Sometimes she blows up for nearly no reason.'

'Doesn't that get tiresome?'

She nods. 'But she's my friend.'

'People can grow out of friends, you know. Even at my age. Especially when their dramas start bleeding over into your life. Sometimes you need to distance yourself a little. Sometimes, it's even fine to let them go altogether.' My mind goes to Charlotte. But instead of anger, I am hollow with loss.

'I know. But I wanted to help her. She's really got nobody. Her mum's hardly around now because she's got some boyfriend.'

'You tried. She can't appreciate what you say because she has no self-esteem. She can't see the value in herself. And, sadly, she's the kind of girl who probably never will.'

I know that, despite the good the holiday may have done us, Zara is still not over what happened to her friend. I am just trying to decipher where all of this is going, when she says, 'When she realised I really was leaving, she said she'd kill herself.'

I stop walking. 'Ah! So that's what this is about! You think she overdosed on purpose and you're to blame?'

She looks at her feet and the tears drop.

I take her gently by the shoulders. 'Zara, what happened to Bethany is not your fault. And whatever she does in the future can never be your fault either. She's trying to manipulate you, and that's nasty behaviour. She makes her own decisions, as do you. Do you understand what I'm saying?'

She stares beyond me, out to sea, sniffles. 'I just want to help her!'

'Then be a role model for her. Exercise your own mind, make your own choices. Show you have boundaries. And I can promise you she'll look up to you and respect that. Maybe she'll even want to be that way too. Don't come down to her level. She's friends with you because she sees something in you that she admires.'

'Do you think so?' she asks, glancing up at me.

I highly doubt it, but I say, 'I know so . . . But I think you need to give her a little space. She's been through a lot and she might need to think a few things through on her own.'

'I know,' she says. 'You're right.' We meet eyes again. She gives me a pallid smile. I have noticed, particularly on this holiday, how grown-up Zara looks suddenly. With the loss of her puppy fat since Bethany came into her life, and the slimming out of her face, her eyes look bigger and more lustrous, her lips fuller and slightly pouty with their cute dimples either side. But her conversation reminds me of all the ways she's still just a child. 'I'm so sick of the people she hangs around with,' she says. 'They're, like, way too old for her, for starters, and they're not even *nice*.'

Thank God. Thank God. Every disappointment she expresses about Bethany is music to my ears.

'I'm proud of you.' I put my arm across her shoulders and pull her in for a hug. 'You should never be around any person who makes you feel uncomfortable. If your instincts are telling you to walk away, you have to walk.'

'I know,' she says.

We plod on in silence now, my arm still around her, our hips gently bouncing together. Like this, it's so hard for me to think of her as that girl in the short skirt who was sitting drunk on a park bench with a bottle of vodka in her hand.

'If I'm not friends with her any more can I maybe start getting my pocket money back?' she asks.

I grin. 'Yes. But I've heard your promises in the past. I have to be convinced you're not just going to say one thing to me now and then go and do the other.'

'I'm not,' she says. 'I promise.' Then she adds, 'I'm never ending up like her.'

'Look!' I cry. There are half a dozen kittens frolicking on a fishing net that hangs over the side of a brightly painted blue boat. 'They must smell the fish!'

She chuckles briefly. 'I miss Juniper! I hope she's OK!'

'I'm looking forward to going home,' I tell her. For the briefest of seconds my stomach fizzes like a can of pop at the thought of seeing Steve again and having to give him an answer to his question.

'It was good we came here,' I say to Eric on our last night. The kids have sent us out for dinner. I tell him about how I'm feeling the Zara–Bethany friendship has turned a corner.

He tops up my glass with the last of the wine and fills his own with water. 'Yeah. You were right, as usual.' We gaze across a dark ocean then he looks back to me, somewhat sad and mellow. 'I know I sometimes doubt your approach to a lot of things, but I am all actions and you are all words, and sometimes it's words that win.'

Then he adds, 'And with the conversation I had with her mother, I don't think Bethany Brown will be bothering Zara again.'

I must look very puzzled. 'What conversation?'

'When she rang to tell us that she'd overdosed. I laid the law down. I said they can't see one another ever again or there would be ugly consequences.'

'God . . .' I try to picture this. 'And she took that lying down?'

'Seems so. Some things just have to come from a man. I mean, if you try talking to her it'll end up in a big cat fight, won't it?'

I'm not sure I agree with that but my head is too busy scrambling for questions. I want details. What exactly did he say to Janet? But then he says, 'Lately I've had a lot of stuff going through my head. A lot of reflection and a lot of regrets. I've been a shit husband and dad, haven't I?'

I'm taken aback because Eric isn't given to self-analysis. 'You haven't been a shit anything,' I lie. I have often wondered why he's always had such abysmally low self-esteem when he has so much going for him. I'm not sure I've ever known Eric to actually sound proud of himself. 'You are who you are. You try to balance everything as best you can. We haven't had the easiest ride. Daniel adores you.'

I watch as the compliment tries to settle on him. But I can tell he's having a hard time owning it.

He stares out across the water again. 'I'd hate to think how many times you must have thought about leaving me.'

I don't answer and then he huffs an ironic laugh.

'You're better than me, you know. In so many ways – every way, in fact. And I'm lucky you've had the good grace not to remind me of that.'

We hold eyes. I don't really know what to say. I wasn't expecting this. It saddens me, because it's a pedestal I never sought to be placed on. Fortunately the waiter returns with our whole grilled fish and a plate of marinated aubergines. He asks if Eric would like some more wine and Eric says, 'No, I'm trying to give it up.' Then when he's gone he says, 'I'm going to do better,' and he leans across the table in earnest. '*Be* better. For you. For us. For everything that we have. I'm going to change. I'm going to try.'

Something my mother said years ago comes back to me. *He'll make a lot of promises and you'll believe them, until you won't.*

'I'm going to take a look at my drinking. I know it's got a bit out of hand. A lot out of hand . . . It doesn't bring out the best in me . . .' I watch him glance away and stare out across the water again, like he's holding back tears of self-loathing. Surprisingly this is the closest he has ever come to admitting he has a problem. Its unexpectedness breaks my stride, hits the guilt nerve, allows a crack of hope for us to illuminate the darkness of my doubts.

'You don't deserve it. How I've been . . . It's wrong. All wrong . . .' He looks back at me. 'I'm putting a stop to it. I'm going to get some help once and for all. Proper help. I've already looked into it.'

When I can't think of what to say fast enough, he reaches for my hand lying inertly on the table, cradles it in his own, stares at it as though it's so very precious. 'It's a lot to ask, but I'm going to ask you to believe in me. Because if you can't, I won't be able to do it. I know that about myself.'

His emotion and the conviction he's throwing into his words hits me in the solar plexus.

'Will you believe in me?' he asks. 'I'm not asking you to go through it with me, but I am asking you to give me one more chance. I honestly feel we're going to be fine if I can just take these steps, with your help.'

His optimism is even vaguely contagious. But it should be his own battle to fight, and I resent that he's making it part mine. I stare at his thumb stroking my knuckles.

'Will you do that for me?' he asks.

THIRTY-EIGHT

It's the shattered glass we see first as we come in the front door.

The young ginger-haired policeman finishes writing up his report and looks at us across our dining table. 'It was a tidy search. They didn't take the TV, or anything burglars normally make a beeline for. It seems whoever did this knew exactly where to find your clothes and jewellery.'

'I know who did it,' I say. 'It was Bethany Brown.' I'm convinced I can smell that perfume of hers; I thought so the moment I walked in. When Eric goes to protest, I say, 'Why would anyone break into our house and cut up my clothes? This was targeted at me. It was personal.'

'I'm sorry for this.' Eric somehow manages to undermine me. 'My wife is understandably very upset. We don't know it was my daughter's friend.'

'Who else would do this?' I wait for him to see sense. 'When has anything like this ever happened before she came into our lives?'

The policeman continues to study me like he's not sure how to take me. 'Mrs Rossi, if you have reason to believe—'

'She doesn't,' Eric cuts him off, then he says to me, 'Em, the kid was just in hospital fighting for her life. What are the chances she's going to be out doing something like this?'

'It's so sick!' Daniel is petting Otis, who we just picked up from my father's. Daniel was the one who went into our bathroom and found the unflushed toilet. Though my son is strong and stoic, I can tell he's trying not to cry. The perpetrators might be long gone, but the whole house is rank with the violation of their presence. It's hard not to picture them mooching through my things, ransacking my drawers; nothing feels mine any more. I'm suddenly aware that Zara is sitting balled up in the corner of the couch, and since all this happened has been rather quiet.

'Did you tell her we were going away?' I ask. 'I'm guessing you must have.' Juniper is making a fuss, and I remember we put her in the laundry room to stop her treading in the broken glass. I get up to let her out. 'It's all right. I'm not upset. But you have to tell me.'

She looks at the floor and turns red. The kitten comes running out in a flurry of meows. 'I sent her a text asking how she was. I said I'd phone her when we got back from holiday.' The tears come.

'Ah! What did you do that for?' Eric's tone is strident and the policeman shoots him a look. 'You said you had no interest in talking to her!'

'You guys were telling me to go visit her one minute! Now you're upset I texted her?' She looks so confused and betrayed.

'She's right,' I say. Now isn't the time to make her feel any worse than she does. Of course Zara was going to enquire how Bethany was. That's her nature.

She dives off the couch. 'I'm sick of everything always being my fault!' she says and strides upstairs. Two seconds later her bedroom door slams and we all look at one another through a bemused silence.

'What's the likelihood you're going to find who did this?' I ask the policeman, trying to get hold of the situation again.

Underneath his smattering of preposterously large freckles, he blushes. 'Hard to say. We'll run some checks. The fingerprints, blood sample . . .' Someone cut themselves when they were hacking my clothes up with a particularly crappy pair of our kitchen scissors. 'If the person who did this has been arrested before, they'll be on our database. We'll know who they are.'

I know who it is! I want to say. *I can save you the trouble! We don't need a damned DNA sample!* But Eric is giving me the warning look so I remain silent.

'If you have photographs of any of the jewellery, that would help too,' the policeman says.

In addition to probably hundreds of pounds' worth of destroyed clothes, by my latest estimation I have lost my great grandmother's wedding ring, my mother's beautiful rose-gold locket that I have treasured, the diamond tennis bracelet Eric's mum gave me on our wedding day – *something old*. Daniel's St Christopher pendant. There might be other things, but right now I can't think.

'I don't know that I've got any photos,' I tell him. 'Maybe one of the locket, somewhere.' I think I have one of my mother wearing it.

'You could draw us a description.' He slides a notepad and pen across the table. I stare at the blank page, draw an oval, then put the pen down.

'You don't have to do it right now,' he says. 'You can send it to us later.'

I get up and go to sit beside Daniel and the dog on the sofa while the policeman chats some more to Eric. Daniel just stares hard at the floor and refuses to look up. I can feel anger emanating off him. When the police have gone, we all fall into a state of stunned silence.

Eventually Daniel says he's going out. I don't ask him where, or when he'll be back; I can tell that, at this point, he doesn't actually have a destination. He just wants to be away from us. How quickly all the good of the holiday has been reversed. Eric wanders around sighing, then goes upstairs to put the tatters of my clothes into bags for the bin. When I can rally myself, I ring my father and tell him what's happened and ask that the kids stay at his tonight. I think it's best they're not here. At least until I can make this house feel like a home again.

∞

When it's finally just the two of us, Eric makes me a cup of tea. 'Here, you need a splash of this in it.' He goes to the cabinet and takes out the whisky bottle. 'Medicinal.'

I watch him pour a generous measure into my cup. I look away, probably green-lighting him to pour some into his own. I am not so concerned about his promises right now, or when they'll take effect. Or that I should have been firm and told him no, I won't give him a second chance like he asked for. Instead, I said nothing, leaving it hanging but with my tacit support. Truth is, he's already had far too many chances, only he hasn't noticed.

'You have to eat something,' he says, gently, setting down a plate of buttered toast.

'I'm fine.' I am still infuriated that he undermined me to the policeman, made me look like I was slightly off my head.

I sit for a while, then realise that if we are ever to go to bed, I have to face going upstairs again. Eric has already cleaned the bathroom but I go in there anyway and start scrubbing the toilet bowl where some filthy pig defecated and left it for us to find.

'There was obviously a boy with her,' I say.

'You can tell that from somebody's faeces?'

I'm not sure how he can find it in him to be smart with me at a time like this.

'It's clean,' he says, hovering over me, impotently. 'Look, you're not doing yourself any good. Come back downstairs and we'll order some food in. You've got to eat something or you're going to get sick.'

'How can you not be furious?' I look at him like he's not even human. 'What's wrong with you?'

'I am furious,' he says. 'But I don't see how acting out is going to help any.' He nods to the door, to our kids' rooms, even though they aren't there. 'We have to keep it together for them, don't we.'

I want to challenge him and yet it's the most sensible thing he's said in ages.

When he goes back downstairs, I stand in the doorway of our bedroom and stare at the two bin bags that contain my shredded clothes, unable to make this feel real. I can't smell her any more, which makes doubts set in. All I can smell is toilet bowl cleaner.

One last look in the drawers. Maybe they didn't get my mother's necklace. Maybe I just overlooked it. How would Bethany have even known where to find my precious jewellery? Only if she'd been in my bedroom before. Has Zara ever come in here with her? Has my daughter let her friend rootle through my things? The thought of Zara sanctioning this feels so disloyal that I have to push it out of my head. *What else did Bethany and a boy do in my room?* I wonder. Suddenly my rage and sense of injustice take flight. I yank one of the drawers open – maybe the necklace slipped down the back. But I don't know my own strength because it comes all the way out and goes crashing to the floor, an edge of it landing on the top of my foot. I shriek in agony.

'Jesus Christ!' Eric finds me sitting in a puddle of self-pity on the floor, pain tearing through me.

'I wish when she overdosed she hadn't been so lucky,' I tell him.

'Don't say that,' he says. 'She's somebody's kid.'

THIRTY-NINE

'I am so, so sorry. I just heard.'

Charlotte is standing at my front door holding a huge bouquet of white roses.

I look down at both our feet. Mine in my Ugg slippers and hers in burgundy, almond-toe boots, and feel the tears come.

'Please,' she says when I finally look up and she pushes the roses at me. 'It's a peace offering.'

I don't really want her flowers, but I haven't quite got the heart to continue this miserable business, so I take them from her. 'Thanks.'

'Can I come in so we can talk?'

'It's really not a good time.'

She inhales sharply, then lets out a little sigh. Ordinarily, Charlotte isn't the best at eating humble pie, so I am sure this is hard for her. I wait to see if she's going to get a little vexed with me for not budging but instead she says, 'I wanted you to know that I ordered a cleaning service. They're coming shortly, probably in about ten minutes. If you're not going to be home I can let them in.'

I must look a little puzzled.

'When I was in uni, my place was broken into. I was so disgusted. I couldn't bear touching anything they might have had their hands on . . . I know it won't undo what's done, but you'll get a spanking-clean house out of it at the very least.'

'You really shouldn't have done that,' I say inertly. 'It really isn't necessary, but thanks.' I look at our feet again.

'I'm trying to ingratiate my way back into your favour.'

I take a shaky breath. As ever, Charlotte is always disarmingly frank, but the note of lightness in her tone makes me rear up. 'You called her a proper little tramp.'

She throws up her arms. 'I was wasted! I hadn't eaten since a piece of toast at breakfast, then I got there too early and sank almost a carafe of wine!' She looks at me in utter despair. 'I don't know why I said it. I was talking to my sister . . . Not that that makes it more forgivable . . . I honestly don't know where it came from, it's not even how I think, and I'd do anything to take it back but I can't, can I?' She inhales sharply. 'Please, please know that this is eating me alive . . . Every day I wake up and I think of you and I just want us to be all right again! Will you please try to see your way to forgiving me? If for no other reason than we have to go on being neighbours – if we can't be friends.'

It's true. If she didn't live next door it might very well be different. She's not exactly going to be easy to avoid. 'I can try but I can't promise,' I say, attempting to open myself up to the idea. It occurs to me that for so long I've managed to forgive Eric for the things he said and did in drink. Why is this different? Is a friend easier to walk away from than a husband? Or is it because my expectations of my friend were higher than those of my husband?

'I really do appreciate the flowers and the cleaners, though . . .'

Fortunately we are spared from saying any more because a bright pink Shiny Shack van is pulling up at my door. Next, two chubby lassies wearing pink mob caps get out and purposefully start unloading their tools.

∽

My two-hour meeting with the investigating officer regarding my suspension is hard to read. I furnish him with my emails and as detailed an account of my in-person meeting with the student as I can remember, as well as my conversation on this matter with Tom. He asks me questions that are either relevant or seemingly completely out of context. Before the grilling comes to an end, he asks me how my personal life is, and whether I am generally happy. Naturally, I lie and tell him, 'Of course, everything is fine.'

As I am walking back to my car, I am so incensed that I realise I'm actually muttering out loud to myself. Am I generally happy? How dare he? But then my mobile rings and I see the young police officer's name.

They have a forensic hit. His name is Gary Mitchell, a twenty-two-year-old car mechanic from York with a previous conviction for burglary and supplying Class A drugs.

'But what about Bethany Brown? She was there too. Obviously.'

'I'm sorry,' he says, with the sound of a sigh in his tone. 'The only person we can confirm at the scene is Gary Mitchell. We don't have any evidence that there was a second person present, I'm afraid.'

'It's one of her boyfriend's cohorts,' I tell Eric, because I can't wait until I get home to give him the news.

'This has to stop,' he says. 'The police have just told you who it was.'

The rain beats hard on my windshield as I sit there in the parking space. My wipers are booming. As is my heart. 'Why would a boy cut up my clothes?'

'I don't know. But this is getting ridiculous. You've got to let this go.'

I stare at the wipers, carried off into a trance for a second or two by their momentum. 'But the smutty magazine . . . The break-in. You honestly think this is just random?'

'For God's sake! You're a dog with a bone! Can we leave it?' I can tell he's trying hard to stay civil. For the past ten days since getting back he has been trying very hard in all respects. If he's drinking, I haven't seen it or smelt it. But his efforts are wreaking their own form of havoc on his personality. Again I have this sense of him being one match away from an inferno.

'No,' I say. 'We can't leave it!'

Because it wasn't random. I know it wasn't.

But I am talking to dead air. He has hung up on me.

I purposely drive home the long way, and stop to pick up a few groceries. Even though it's raining and visibility is atrocious, I just don't feel like going back inside that house. When I reach our door, I sit in the car for ages just staring ahead at the cheerless expanse of trees shrouded in mist. Two houses down, there is a light on in Steve's front room, and I can't allow myself to picture what he might be doing in there. I close my eyes and let out a long, slow sigh. That not so very long ago he invited me to some hotel room feels like a flight of my imagination. An invitation issued by someone else, to someone else, that someone told me about. And yet right now I don't know why I was so torn.

When I walk in, it's the first thing I hear. The chink of bottles. A cabinet door squeaking closed. I am too quick for him. There is an instant where he sends me the shiftiest of glances, then he follows it with a taut smile. 'Just washed the glasses. Putting them away.' His speech is slow. His tongue is thick.

I'm going to change. I'm going to try.

He turns away from my cold, hard stare, busies himself folding a tea towel. I glare at his back, loathing filling me from the ground up. Sneaky, lying Eric. Alcoholics always think they're cleverer than you. *Remember, sneak-drinking is still drinking*, I once said, when I caught him tipping whisky down his neck in the laundry room. He was so furious I'd caught him, as though *I* was in the wrong. *When you're lying on the slab and your liver has blown, it won't matter that you lied about it.*

Fuck you! You self-righteous bitch! he hurled back. And then he made some frustrated grr-ing, wild-animal-like noise after me. Would he hit me? Would petulance turn to violence? Did I know him well enough to say it wouldn't?

I walk into the kitchen and set the shopping bags on the work-top. 'So we're back to this,' I say calmly, quietly.

'To what?' He stares at me hard, but I refuse to look at him. 'Eh? What are we back to?'

He moves in on me, getting so close that his boozy breath makes my hair waft. I reach up into the cupboard, setting cans of beans on the shelf, trying to act like I am not intimidated. But there is something about an angry man who is a full foot taller than you and a hundred pounds heavier, stepping towards you like this, getting so in your personal space . . . I am hauled back to Valentine's Day all those years ago. The room seems to lose oxygen.

'I said . . . what are we back to?' he repeats, his tone menacing. He continues to stand there, crowding in on me.

He won't change. I remember my mother's words when the kids were small. *Once an alcoholic, always an alcoholic.* I wasn't prepared to label him that even if I suspected it. I wouldn't be reduced to that level of judgement. It belonged to an old-school way of thinking.

I was a different generation. Educated. Binge drinking – drinking to relieve stress – wasn't really alcoholism, was it? It was the new norm. I would prove her wrong.

'I'm waiting for your answer,' he says.

My heart pounds. I want to be wrong. I always want to be wrong. I have spent a married lifetime telling myself I've been too hard on him, or I have exaggerated the problem, or failed to give him the benefit of the doubt . . . I have managed to blame *me* and completely absolve him. But I can't do it any more. I can no longer deny the problem before my eyes.

'You drunken waste of space,' I say. I try not to look at him but I'm hyper-aware of him, and of the thin sheet of ice we are standing on. In the back of my mind I think, preposterously, *Maybe if he hits me then I'll have enough justification to leave.*

There is a moment where time stands still. But then, instead of what I'm anticipating, he leans closer to my ear and laughs.

The laughter becomes hysterical, until he doubles up in a bizarre, wheezing cacophony of embarrassing mirth. My hands can't complete their task. I am sadder now than I've ever thought possible.

'I can't do this any more,' I say. I say it so quietly I wonder if the words actually came out of my mouth, or did I just think them?

'What?' The absurd laughing performance abruptly stops.

'I said I can't do this any more, Eric.' I turn, and steadily meet his eyes. 'You're a drunk. I want an end to my marriage.'

I have long ago accepted that alcoholism is a disease. I made a pledge to myself that I wouldn't act like I am any better than him – there but for the grace of God go I. I have tried hard to retain a degree of empathy. I can support him, but I don't have to stay for him. I think I am only just realising the difference now.

'What's that supposed to mean? A drunk?' When I look away, he says, 'Maybe I am a drunk . . . But given you're so clever, wouldn't you say I had a reason to drink, eh? With everything that's going on at the minute? Stuff you know about, and stuff you have no idea about, Emily. No idea. Because you don't live in the real world.'

'You disgust me,' I say.

'You disgust me too. Can't keep your eyes on your own fucking life and your own business, can you? Got to meddle in mine.'

Suddenly, that memory again: a broken vase of flowers on the floor.

I know every beat of this tune, every step of this dance. 'We are over,' I tell him. I am elated to finally say it, and to actually mean it. I have never realised how much I've needed to voice those words, until now. We hold gazes until he breaks away. My hands are balled into fists, my nails biting into my palms.

He is looking at me again, but he's not seeing me any more. His eyes are seeing a whisky bottle and he won't settle until it's drained. How many times has it been this way? People might say, *Oh, come on! You can't know that!* But I know how the alcoholic thinks. The only time Eric isn't thinking about booze is when he's asleep. I have been wilfully blind.

'I want a divorce.' Even saying the words, all I can think is, *I'll be free of you!*

'Divorce?' His tone is incredulous. 'You can't. I'm not going to let you.'

He drags out a chair from under the table and sits – not quite as full of himself now. I look at his back, the red, chicken-skin neck peeking out from his emerald-green polo shirt. The one he wore the day they came to take our family portrait. When I smelled the peppermint on his breath, and spotted the glass he'd hid behind the cookbooks.

'I'm not letting you divorce me,' he says again, this time folding in with sorrow and self-pity. I stare at his head tipped forward. I used to love him. Calm, kind, self-effacing, slightly unconfident

Eric. That first time I met him felt like coming home. What a bottomless tragedy. I cannot think about it or it's going to drag me under – or make me change my mind.

'You have no choice. I can't – I won't – go through this again. I won't survive it.'

'I'll get help.'

'You've already said that. I didn't believe it then, and I don't believe it now.'

'OK, then I won't!' he says petulantly. 'If you're going to have no faith in me then I might as well not bother!'

That day, after the episode with the flowers, I said to myself, *I'll stay until the kids are older. Maybe when they've gone to uni, if I feel like leaving at that point, if I get that suffocating certainty that leaving him is the only way I can live the rest of my life, then I'll do it.*

Everything is accelerated.

'I know I've done wrong.' He looks up. 'More wrong than you can know.'

'I don't care.' It's true. Liberating and true. I am aware of the seismic gap between us, all of a sudden. We are on two opposite sides of the earth that has literally shifted.

I hear the sharp intake through his nose. I realise he's crying yet it fails to penetrate and make me care.

'I'm sorry,' he is saying. 'It's all my fuck-up. I am so tired. So very tired.'

Drama and self-pity: the hallmarks of an alcoholic. When he used to say he was tired, so tired, before, I thought he meant he needed to sleep. I'd encourage him to go to bed, feel better; tomorrow is a new day. I didn't know he meant he was tired of the intolerable state of his own existence.

'It doesn't matter,' I say. 'It doesn't matter whose fault it is. No one's blaming anybody. It's not about that.'

'You're wrong. It does matter.' He swipes a tear off his cheek. 'It matters greatly. In fact, it's all that matters.' Otis trots over and shoves his nose into Eric's hands. I watch my husband pet his dog and the sight of it rips at my heart.

But my lack of desire to argue tells me how final this is. I sit down on the chair opposite. Far enough away. We are islands. It occurs to me that from this point on I will never have the right to monitor and disapprove of his drinking. Somewhere down the line, there is potential for me to feel good about all this, but right now, it's all too tangled in *Why could it not have been different? Why did alcohol have to ruin a great guy's life and my family's?*

We stay like this – him sitting in silent tears, me staring through him. Eventually, after a very long time, he says, 'So how do we do it? Am I supposed to move out? Are you intending to keep the house? I'm assuming you've thought it all through.'

'I don't know,' I say. His lack of fight makes me wonder: *Does he want this too? Is he relieved? Is he secretly aware that life with me, living with my expectations, has been more than he's been able to cope with?* 'I've thought nothing through,' I say.

I stare at his face. Now that we're here, I realise I never really believed this moment would come. There is a rawness about this reality that a part of me can't process.

'Well, this is your decision, so you'd better come up with some sort of plan.'

There is a web of thread veins either side of his nostrils that makes me wonder what shape his heart and liver must be in. And two angry boils on his cheeks. It's as though all the poisoning that his body has suffered has manifested itself on his face. I can't believe I ever found him attractive.

'I think it starts by you going back to London and not coming home for a while,' I say.

FORTY

Eric, February 2004

The flowers are the first things he sees when he walks in. A big bouquet of lilies in the middle of the table. His first thought is, *Em's got an admirer.*

'I thought you'd be home a bit earlier,' is the first thing she says.

He slips off his jacket, convinced he detects judgement in her tone. 'Had to finish a report.'

She's set the table nicely for two. The house smells of steak, and a chocolate flan sits on a wire rack by the window. He fills with guilt.

She kisses him, throws a hand to the flowers. 'They literally just arrived. I've barely had time to get them in the vase. They're beautiful! I was surprised, mind . . . But thank you.' She scoops some plastic wrapping and a purple bow off the bench, reads from a small card.

'Happy Valentine's Day.' She chuckles. 'Did you forget to tell them I have a name? I mean . . . I assume they're for me!'

As she stands there making a joke, the penny drops. It crashlands like a tonne of bricks. The blood storms in his veins. 'Of course they are.' He tries to smile his panic away. 'Glad you're happy with them.'

She studies him closely, her seeing-through-him stare. 'You OK? You seem a bit off?' Then he sees the sudden change in her. The smile fading. The falling away of her good mood. 'You've been drinking.'

'No,' he says quickly. 'I haven't.'

'Yes, you have. How much have you had?' She plonks a hand on her hip. His guilt, however, is mitigated slightly by this tendency she has to always think badly of him. It hits like a giant swipe across his face.

'You weren't late because of any report. You've been to the pub.' She doesn't sound angry. Not really. More dismayed. All the dashed hopes line up in her eyes.

'It was just one,' he says, hating that she reduces him to lying. Her face is asking, *When do you ever have just one?* He tries to ignore it, goes and gets a drink of water. It tastes funny because of the peppermints he's just sucked to disguise his breath. 'I was feeling stressed. Overwhelmed,' he says. It's true. Fury about the flowers beats in him. *Don't think about Janet right now.*

'Overwhelmed,' she repeats.

Zero sympathy. As though his stress is nothing. There are days when he can let this go, but right now he just thinks, *Fuck this!* He's conscious of the whisky bottle being about three feet away in the cabinet. It pulls at him with the gravitational force of a planet.

'So what are you so overwhelmed about, then?' she says, her tone a bit less judgemental now.

'Work.' He doesn't feel like talking. He doesn't really want to stand here and be made to feel like a two-year-old. He can smell the fucking flowers now. The stink is sticking to his face. He goes over to Daniel in his playpen and rubs his head. 'Hello, son.' Zara is sleeping in her Moses basket and he tickles the top of her downy head.

'That's what you always say. One word. "Work."' They meet eyes. The death stare of her disappointment. 'Why don't you try telling me about it instead of going to drink your brains out? It might help.'

'Because you'd bloody never listen!' His fuse just blows before he can do anything about it. 'Will you just get off my back?' The blood is pounding in his temples. That smell is suffocating him now. He glances at the vase. 'Look, can we just sit down and eat, please.' He can feel his shirt sticking to his underarms and to his back. He paces around, telling himself to calm down.

'What? Just like that? You come in, blow a gasket, and then we just sit and have our dinner?'

There's a challenging note in her tone, and yet he feels so bad because he knows part of her genuinely does just want to sit down and have her dinner, and he's ruined it again. He could appease her, and he normally would, but something in him . . . He just says, 'Ah, well then . . .' He strides to the booze cabinet, pulls out the whisky bottle, half fills the big glass he's just drunk his water from.

'Drink that and I'm leaving.' Her voice is firm. She is standing stock-still. The baby starts crying. His hand is shaking on the bottle. She looks like she's shaking in her slippers. With indignation. 'I mean it,' she says.

Daniel makes a noise and the baby fusses. He wipes the back of his wrist under his nose, sweat and mucus combining. 'Fuck you. I'll drink the whole bloody thing. I don't need your permission.'

'Drink it and we are leaving you,' she says again.

Her face is violent red when he looks at her again. Em might be small but she is a strong woman. A strong woman to his weak man. He can tell she has never been more serious in her life. 'Don't think I'm going to sit here and watch you turn into an alcoholic. Not in this house. Not with my children growing up in it.'

Her breath is short, quick with anger. She walks over to the baby now, picks her up, jiggles her. Zara is quickly pacified by her funny faces. He wonders how she can do it: how she can show two diametric emotions.

'It's my life,' he says.

'Yes. And you can do what you want with it. But not as part of this family.' She throws a hand to the door. 'Drink that whisky and it's over. You walk out of there.'

He looks at the glass, contemplates putting it down, but suddenly her threats and the sight of Janet Brown's face in his mind's eye just press a button . . . He picks up the vase and hurls it with megawatt force at the patio door. It breaks to a chorus of the children's screams. Flowers and water and glass, everywhere. He puts his hands over his ears. The noise lances through his head and keeps echoing. A chorus of terror. When he looks back, Em has her face buried in Zara's shoulder, and has lifted a terrified Daniel from his playpen and is holding him by the hand.

His heartbeat rages. Even he is stunned by his own behaviour. Suddenly, at the sight of the soggy, strewn flowers, the tension has somehow left him at an anti-climax and all he feels is a tidal wave of disgust and regret.

'Get out,' Em says.

He stands and shakes his head like a two-year-old. No . . . He doesn't want to get out. This is his family. His home. He wants to cry and beg her to forgive him. The only thing that stops him is his pride and the thought of her loathing. She is still watching him, clutching the kids, trying to pacify them. Disgust is written all over her face. He wants to say, *Can you just back off, can you just stop disapproving of me? Just for once?* But he knows he has no argument.

A part of him waits to see what happens next, what she'll do. But she does nothing. So, like it never happened, like he wasn't the cause of it, he sets about carefully sweeping up the mess, the swimming flowers, the broken shards. He finishes by running his hands over the wooden boards, carefully searching for slivers that his son might stand in.

Surprisingly, she doesn't tell him to leave again. She puts the baby down, lifts Daniel back into his playpen, and goes to turn off the oven. He sneaks a look at her out of the corner of his eye, feeling contrite, but she walks back over to the kids and starts playing with them, her voice fake-cheery. It's like he's not there at all.

He feels like a million spotlights are blazing on him, showing him up for his monstrous behaviour. *I'll change*, he thinks, shrinking and disappearing into his own shame. *This is never going to happen again.* A surge of hope comes over him at the thought of winning her around, getting past all this, being a better version of himself.

'Hey.' He goes over to Daniel. He can't bear to look at his kid's face in case he sees fear still in his eyes. Instead he fixes on Monkey Boy, Daniel's favourite toy from his grandma. 'Can Monkey Boy tell me what he and Daniel have been doing with themselves today?' He picks up the toy and uses it as a puppet, and his ventriloquism makes Daniel chuckle.

He tries to smile but has to squeeze his eyes shut to stop the tears from rolling out.

FORTY-ONE

I take Otis on to the common. It's cold but brightly sunny. The grass looks greener, the sea in the distance more Mediterranean than English Channel grey. I could almost be somewhere else. I try to own that feeling – that I actually am somewhere else – and just enjoy what that might look like. But I can't quite get there in my head. All I can think about is, *How are we going to tell the kids?*

On my way home, just as I'm passing Steve's house, his door opens. And there is a moment of déjà vu. It reminds me so much of our first meeting that it makes a part of me smile through my sadness. He is with Henry this time.

'Hello!' I say to his little boy. 'You're up bright and early.'

'Daddy is taking me swimming but I don't want to go because I've got a broken knee.'

I meet Steve's gaze now, and try to keep my eyes neighbourly neutral. I am sure he's aware how very long ago it is since he asked me that question. I'm sure he thinks I've been avoiding him. Or perhaps he's had second thoughts and regrets it now. 'Oh?' I try so very hard not to read his face.

'It's not really broken,' Steve says. 'More like scratched. From two weeks ago. It's pretty healed now.' He looks down at his son and beams lovingly. 'Henry fell while he was playing with Scott. Or, what I think really happened was, Scott pushed him.'

Scott, the biggest terror of Charlotte's triplets. 'That would be unheard of,' I say.

'If it happens again I may have to sit down with our neighbour. But as for now, Henry is taking it like a man. Right, buddy?' He scratches the top of Henry's head and the boy flinches.

'No,' he says.

'Good luck swimming with that broken knee,' I tell him, smiling. 'I think the water is actually going to be very good for it and you'll feel a whole lot better after.'

'OK,' he says. 'Thanks.'

Steve and I smile. Then I set off walking up our street, my heartbeat on a rampage. A minute or two later I get a text.

How's your thinking going?

I discover her missing on Monday morning.

Her bed hasn't even been slept in.

The two police officers sit in our kitchen at 10 a.m. Eric has done an about-turn and is on his way home again.

I try to give them as detailed an account of the last few days as possible. Everything seemed to be fine. She went to bed last night around ten, as is fairly normal. I didn't see her or hear her from that point on. They say she must have snuck out. I'm surprised because I'm a light sleeper; I would have thought I'd have absolutely heard something, or the dog would have, and then I would have heard the dog. I tell them I've rung Janet Brown's mobile four times and she hasn't picked up or returned my messages. But when I say this I don't see any real reaction on their faces.

'Can we take a look in her room?' the female officer asks. 'And it would be helpful if you could give us a recent photograph.'

I stand in the doorway of her bedroom while the female police officer looks at the magazines on Zara's bedside table, opens and closes drawers, asks me if she keeps a diary. When she opens her wardrobe, I say, 'I told you she hasn't taken any of her clothes . . .' That was the first thing I checked. The only items of clothing missing are her favourite pair of light blue jeans and her bottle-green hoodie.

She looks under Zara's bed, out of the window, gazes at the shed at the bottom of the garden. Then she says she'd like to take a look outside if that's OK. I must seem puzzled because she says, 'You'd be surprised how many parents think their kids have run away and the children are actually hiding somewhere on the property.'

I want to say, *She's not hiding in the garden! She's not six years old. And even when she was, she didn't go and hide in the shed!* But instead I follow her back downstairs. The two of them go outside. I watch them talking in the mist, then I go and sit impotently at the kitchen table, beside the half-drunk mug of tea that I made myself earlier, and wait for them to come back in. After a moment or two of semi-positive thoughts spiralling into bad thoughts, then into the riptide of panic, my phone rings. I practically jump on it when I see it's Janet Brown.

'No, I don't know where Zara is,' she says the instant I pick up. 'It's not something I would know given that Bethany wants nothing to do with her after Zara labelled her a burglar.'

I had no idea that Zara had talked to Bethany about that.

'Well, where's Bethany now?' Zara wouldn't just run off in the middle of the night to go and hang out with herself! The thought that they might have set her up, lured her into something, suddenly lands on me.

'She's at her boyfriend's. Not that it's really any business of yours,' she says.

The police come back in and I hang up on Janet. 'I think she's with Bethany Brown at Craig Rathbone's house.' I tell them of my concerns, my voice ratcheting with dread. The young policeman offers to make me another cup of tea.

I stare at it but can't even lift the cup. Life before this girl came along feels so very long ago. I ache, with every fibre in me, to crawl after it and claim it back. Once I've simmered down a little, they tell me they are going to be taking Zara's computer, her medications – all they can find is an out-of-date bottle of antibiotics that she was prescribed for a throat infection about a year ago – the photo I've given them, her hairbrush.

'Why do you need her hairbrush?' I ask. But I suppose I know.

The young male constable simply says, 'It's just procedure . . . As for Craig Rathbone, we'll run him through the police system. If needs be, your case will be referred to the Public Protection Unit and appropriate steps will be taken.'

He goes on to tell me that most kids do come home within twenty-four hours so I should try not to worry too much, but where older men and young girls are concerned, they definitely take matters seriously. I hear the words 'trafficking', 'sexual exploitation'. And I just think of every story I've read about men grooming, terrorising and abusing underage girls, forcing them into gang sex. Every documentary with a silhouette of an anonymous victim telling their story, and gradually the voice becomes Zara's.

He stops when he sees my expression, the blue of my fear. There is an unhealthy pause where my worst nightmares are all dropping into the space between us. Then he places a hand briefly on my shoulder.

'You might want to put a post on Facebook about her going missing and ask Zara's friends to do the same.' He tells me they will probably be able to triangulate her phone. I try to remember from every police show I've watched what that means. The female officer is still combing our house, inspecting piles of opened post, the magazines on the shelf under the coffee table, which makes me feel invaded all over again.

'I know this sounds daunting but it's just procedure,' he says. 'We do it so that no time is lost in cases where children are potentially in harm's way. Please don't panic or worry too much. The best thing you can do is be strong, keep calm and keep your phone on.' He reassures me again that he suspects Zara will be home in the next few hours.

When they leave, I try to remember all the things they said I have to do but I can barely think straight. The house feels so silent and empty, denuded of Zara's presence, stripped bare of her soul. All I can hear is the thundering noise in my head. The resounding accusation of how much I have let her down.

Bethany always comes home.

I have to remember what Janet once said.

But Zara isn't Bethany. Zara is still a child in ways that I don't think Bethany ever has been. If I had to guess, Bethany will probably ride out her rebellious years then emerge with chrysalis transformation on the other side. It's my daughter who will be collateral damage.

It suddenly occurs to me, what if she never comes home? If time stands still as of now? If I am forty-five, fifty-five, sixty-five, and still searching the streets of Leeds, Manchester, London, showing her photograph to homeless people, asking, *Have you seen her?* Always hoping that one day there'll be a knock at the door and she'll be standing there, and she'll say, *Hello, Mum.*

Adrenaline suddenly courses down my legs and I shoot out of the chair, out of the front door. Normally I would have gone fleeing to Charlotte's but there is only one person I want to see.

He opens the door just seconds after I knock, almost like he knows. I fall into his arms in the most literal and least romantic sense of the expression. My legs buckle, and he catches me, and he holds me, wraps his arms around me, and settles his warm chin on the top of my head. And I would burst into tears if I could, but I can't even manage that successfully. It's as though I must have cried them without even knowing, so now I am dry.

'What can I do?' he asks.

But he's already doing it.

It is an hour or so later when I walk back to my house. After he has given me tea, and talked me down from my crisis. I can't properly fathom that she would do such a mutinous thing as sneak out in the middle of the night, that she has told me endless lies, that there might be more to come. It causes a tremor in my body like the shifting of tectonic plates, but it's all forgivable if she just comes home.

I know she won't answer her phone. So I text her my very own plea to God that just keeps repeating in my head.

We love you, Zara. Absolutely nothing else in the world matters. Please just come home.

FORTY-TWO

Emily, March 2004

The ward feels like half a mile long. I wheel the pram around the corner. Eric occupies the bed nearest the window. I spot his big red head, the incongruous turquoise smock and I just think, *Thank God.* Despite the ugliness of Valentine's Day still lingering in my mind, I had no idea how unprepared I was to lose him until the possibility arose.

'What on earth . . . ?' I lean over and kiss him.

'Where's Daniel?'

'With my mum and dad.'

Zara starts to fuss. I lift her out of her pram, put her over my shoulder and stroke her tiny back. There are tubes running into his hand. He is hooked up to a machine that displays rows of undulating lines. I stare at them. I want to know what they mean. I have so many questions. 'I got such a shock when they rang! They made it sound like you were nearly dead.' I place a hand on top of his and he rubs my knuckles with his warm thumb.

'Sorry to disappoint.'

I try on a smile. 'You look like hell.'

'I suppose that's a bonus if you've been rushed to hospital,' he says. 'And, actually, I feel like hell. Or at least purgatory, maybe.'

I put the baby back down and perch on the bed beside him. 'So what happened? You passed out after chest pains . . . ? They were so vague.'

'Dunno really.' He turns his palm up to mine and we clasp fingers; his hand is sweaty. 'It was weird. I was in a meeting . . . I was just talking . . . just felt this sweeping pain across my chest and down one arm. My heart was going like the clappers. Then I was sweating. It was pouring out.'

'What have they said it is?'

'Haven't seen the doctor yet . . . The ambulance woman said it was doubtful that it was a heart attack. Ah . . .' He looks past me. 'This might be him now.'

Sure enough, I look up to see a middle-aged man in a white coat, wearing dark-rimmed glasses that have slid halfway down his nose. 'You must be Mrs Rossi,' he says, as though I am the patient, not Eric. Then he tells me he's Dr Platchard. 'And this is?' He leans over the pram.

'Zara,' I croak.

'So you, for one, are no stranger to hospitals.' He smiles down at the baby. Then he looks directly at Eric like he's a bit of an add-on. 'Well, the good news is, there's no bad news. It wasn't a heart attack. Your blood pressure is high, though. Do you have a family history of it?'

'No,' Eric says, looking at me. 'Not that I'm aware of.'

'One sixty-five over one hundred and ten. What are you doing to yourself? There's some sludge in your gall bladder and your liver enzymes are quite high.' He doesn't wait for any answer, but adds, 'How much do you drink, Eric? Some of this is in keeping with someone who drinks significantly above recommended daily levels. Do you drink heavily on a daily basis? Or maybe you're one of those bingers?'

Eric looks both stunned and scolded all at once. 'I drink sporadically,' he says, 'if that's the right word. When I'm stressed. But not really at other times.'

The doctor looks at me. 'Would you agree, Mrs Rossi?'

'He's been stressed quite a bit lately,' I say, trying to be tactful. I see no sense in lying to a doctor.

He looks back at Eric. 'Do you suffer from anxiety?'

Eric shrugs like he's mystified. 'No. I can't say I do.'

'When you had this episode at work, how did you feel, if you can recall?'

Some colour comes to Eric's cheeks now, almost as though he's embarrassed to be the centre of attention. 'Panicked. I genuinely thought I might be having a heart attack. I was thinking only of my family. My wife and little boy. My little baby . . .' He looks at me and his brows briefly flex, and in that instant everything we mean to him is written there for all to see. 'The thought of having to leave them . . .' For a moment I think he's going to break down, and I'm torn between wanting to feel he's allowed to and being a little embarrassed. He goes on looking at me as though there's more he wants to say, but I can't read what it is he's telling me.

The doctor looks at him over the top of his glasses. 'It's possible you have an anxiety disorder. You mention drinking when stressed . . . Are you under a lot of stress at the moment? Your wife seems to think you are.' He is speaking to Eric but he looks at me.

I tell him how our life hasn't been great lately, to fill Eric's sudden awkward wordlessness. How I was bedridden for the last three months of my pregnancy. How it's been hard.

'I think what you suffered was a panic attack,' the doctor says.

Eric looks doubtingly at me. 'But I thought only women get those?'

'It's definitely more common in women, but men do get them. I have one or two more test results to get back first, but I'm not anticipating finding anything. Then you can go home, take it easy, and if you don't find a healthier way of managing your stress you might want to ask your doctor to refer you to a psychiatrist who specialises in anxiety disorders. And you might want to familiarise yourself with what a normal, healthy intake of alcohol is for a man your age.'

Zara wakes up again and is fussing. I lift her out of her pram, jig her up and down. 'I might take her into the gardens for some fresh air,' I tell him when the doctor leaves. 'Maybe try to feed her . . .'

'Take your time,' Eric says. 'I'm fine. Go and get yourself some tea if you like. You look pale.'

I pop her back in her pram and rearrange her blanket. 'I'll be back shortly, then.' I give him a kiss. Part of me is thinking that maybe today will have been the wake-up call Eric has needed. Maybe now that it's a doctor – not just me – telling him he drinks too much, Eric will mend his ways. I am secretly a little pleased about this.

As I'm heading down the corridor, there is a woman walking toward me. I am struck by the authoritative clip to her heels, yet she looks tired, jaded, like something she wasn't expecting has just happened to her.

'All in a day's drama,' she says tiredly as she passes me, and I think, *How odd . . .*

FORTY-THREE

She smells terrible. I make her take a shower, but when she emerges, her hair is still lank and her face mottled. She still looks like she needs a good wash to me. She sits on the couch and refuses to meet my eyes or speak a word to me.

The young policeman sits opposite Eric and me with a cup of tea, and asks her some questions which she answers with nods and head shakes and eyes down. He asks if anyone hurt her and what happened before the police raided the house and Craig Rathbone and two of his mates blew out of the back door and across a fence. She says nothing really happened and I want to take heart from that but her countenance, her eyes, are changed somehow. She is empty. Hollow.

Something has happened. I know it has.

I sit down next to her, rest a hand on her forearm, stare at the long brown eyelashes, the smudge of black mascara under her bottom lids that's still there even after she has washed her face. The hands clasped together in her lap. The chipped black nail polish; raw, bare knees. The policeman explains the nature of the charges that could be brought against Craig Rathbone and his friends, explains why it's very important for Zara to tell the truth and to not be afraid; the police will protect her. He explains exactly what that means, looking from Zara, to me, to Eric.

'Can I ask you again then, Zara,' he says in a softer voice. 'Can you tell us what happened in the house?'

She glances at Eric and it's then that I realise. 'Can you give us a minute?' I say to him.

'What?' His face registers utter disbelief.

'Maybe you could take the dog out? Just for a few minutes?'

He looks at Zara, who is staring at the floor but her ears are beet red now. He sighs, calls for Otis. Moments later the front door slams a little too pointedly.

The policeman and I look at Zara.

'Who gave you the drugs, Zara?' he asks. 'You're not going to get into any trouble by telling me. I can promise. Was it Craig Rathbone?'

She moves her hand so I am no longer touching it, and grasps a handful of her T-shirt bottom. I can see the white of her knuckles. A damp spot on the fabric where the sweat from her hands has transferred.

'Did someone force you to have sex with them?' I ask her.

'No,' she says. 'I haven't had sex. I told you this at the beginning.'

But I do not believe her.

'Is there anything else you'd like to tell us?' The policeman is trying his best. 'If there isn't, we can leave it for today and talk when you've had a chance to get some sleep.'

She doesn't answer at first. But then she says, 'He said bad things happen to girls who talk, and to their families. He said if I make up lies about him he'll firebomb my house, he'll rape my mother and cut my dad's something off with a knife.'

'I appreciate that you've told me this,' the policeman says. He tells me that they will set up a special escort service for her getting to and from school for the next little while, and that our house will be placed under police watch – an officer on duty will pass by every so often to make sure all is well. I can't take it all in but then his phone rings and he says, 'I'm sorry, I have to get this . . .' He slides open our patio door and steps outside.

We sit there waiting. 'Your dad and I are not afraid of Craig Rathbone,' I tell her. 'He can't intimidate us. You don't have to feel you need to protect us.' She looks at me, somewhat lost. 'Please tell the policeman if there's something else you want to say . . . Please, please. You've done really well so far.'

She won't look at me. I stare at her unreadable face, at the way she stares at nothing. 'There's something else, isn't there?'

I know there is.

But before she can say anything, the policeman comes back in. There is a new purpose to him now. He pulls the chair out from under the dining table, sits on it so we are directly facing one another.

He rests his forearms on the table, clasps his hands. 'I believe you know a Prajval Dhaliwal.'

'Yes,' I say, after a second or two. 'He's one of my students. Or, he was.'

'Well, I'm afraid that Mr Dhaliwal was attacked yesterday evening. The assailant, a male, apparently said to him, "This is from Zara Rossi's mother."'

He must see my stunned face. 'Mrs Rossi, I know this is probably not the best timing' – he pulls out his notepad again – 'but unfortunately I'm going to have to ask you some questions.'

FORTY-FOUR

Sometimes I think I must have dreamt the sunlit picture of what was once our family.

Tomorrow is a new day. But not a good day. Zara won't speak. Zara won't look at me. Zara barely surfaces from her room. And I don't know if I am more relieved when she does, or when she goes back in it. Daniel comes in from school, goes straight to his room after he eats and puts his headphones on. I don't know if he's listening to music or just trying to block us all out.

In addition, I can't stop thinking about Prajval Dhaliwal again, worrying about the impact on our lives. Charlotte said she had some thoughts on the topic, from a legal perspective, but I can't bring myself to knock on her door to ask for her help. Aware that my worry only spirals when I'm not occupied, I ask my father to come and sit with Zara while I run out and cross a few things off my to-do list. On my way into town, I am already feeling better being out and about. But then I'm approaching the traffic lights up by the primary school. It's morning break and the kids are in the playground. Even with the car windows up I hear their childish squeals and laughter. I sit there and just let the familiar cadence wash over me. In no time I am besieged by memories, carried back by the whirlwind force of nostalgia. The brush of her tiny damp kiss on my cheek. Her skipping through those very double doors, the oversized pink and green satchel that her gran bought her, hoisted awkwardly on to a shoulder. The backwards wave. She always checked, just that once before she disappeared inside, to see that I was watching her, and I always was; that wave made everything OK in my world. I see it all like it was yesterday. Her smile. How incoherently happy it made me. It always amazed me how you could lock eyes, even from that distance, just two of you in a crowd, and it felt like there were only two of you in the entire world. *My daughter*, I would say to myself. *I have a girl.* I always secretly wanted a girl. Daniel never looked back the way she did.

I hear something now, over the screaming and the shrill laughter coming from the playground. A car horn. Maybe two. I realise I've been sitting here in a trance. I can't throw the car into gear even though the light has changed and I must. I try again but it's as though my left arm is paralysed. She is standing on those steps and she is smiling at me.

I am bolted to what once was. I cannot leave.

After the weekend, I drop Eric off at Leeds airport again with a slightly bigger suitcase. We decided that, with recent developments, we can't tell the kids just yet. So for now, Eric will come, we will act a part, Eric will go – it will all look and smell the same, only it will exist differently inside our heads, the two people who know that this marriage has been falling apart a long time before it fell.

He sits there when I pull in but he doesn't get out.

'I don't actually want to do this,' he says after a fraught, suspenseful silence. 'I've been thinking . . . we're making a mistake. I believe we still love each other and we owe it to ourselves and the kids to find a way forward from this.'

I gaze straight ahead of me, not able to bear looking at him. I don't love him. Though I'm not sure I know what love is any more; perhaps that's the problem. Love is what I felt before I felt dread.

How many times and ways do you say you are over until you actually are? When do these half pledges amount to something inerasable? Grafted on to your consciousness and your heart?

'There is no way forward,' I tell him. Of this I am quite certain, though in my darkest moments I may have wavered and I will waver again. He knows it. He knows me. 'I can't go back on it.'

We are civilised. He's not blowing his lid because he doesn't want me to say, *See . . . this is why*. I have watched him move around our house, aware of only a loose detachment in the face of all that is crumpling, and the latent pulse of my keenness to have him gone. Now that he is going, I only wish we could fast-forward.

'Can I phone you?' he asks. 'You know, later in the week, maybe? Once you've had a bit of time to maybe think about this?'

I shake my head. 'There's no point. I'm not going to change my mind.'

I feel nothing but profound relief knowing he's not my responsibility any more. How many times have I tried to distract him from drinking, protect him from things that might make him want to drink? The endless worry – what if he hurts himself, or tries to harm himself? My belief that preventing him from getting intoxicated was my action to be taken, my problem to solve. I am finally going to be free of it.

'There is literally nothing you could ever say or ever do that would make me want to give us another chance,' I say, because I need to hear myself say it.

'What are we going to do about Christmas?' he asks, seeming not to hear.

'We talked about that.' He will come home. We will act as a family. For the kids' sake. We will tell them after. 'Anyway, it's a long way off.'

'It's five weeks. And we didn't specifically talk about it.'

I look at him now. His face is ashen. He looks like he's lost weight. When he's drinking more, he eats less. Or he goes to bed in a self-pitying pout, throws his dinner in the bin. I want to care, for all the years I have known him. I want them to add up to me feeling some form of compassion, pity – something – but I feel nothing.

'I can't think about Christmas,' I say. It's only then that my phone rings as it sits on the console between us. There is a brief moment where it lights up and we both see *Dr Steven Holden*.

I am aware of Eric staring at it.

Then he says, 'Hang on . . . Are you having an affair? With *him?*

'No,' I say coldly, flatly, though it's not particularly convincing.

He stares hard at my profile until I turn and meet his eyes. Then I say it again. 'No.'

I can see him trying to read my face. 'You bloody are, aren't you? That's what this is all about. You're fucking the next-door neighbour!' He doesn't say it angrily. More in dismay. As though the blinders have suddenly come off.

'Get out,' I say quietly, flooding with guilt for something I haven't even done.

I stare straight ahead of me, his eyes boring into the side of my face. He no longer has the right to wait for explanations. I owe him nothing any more.

After a tortuous spell of silence I say, 'You're going to miss your flight.'

My heart is belting but I keep my composure. 'You're fucking the doctor. I can't believe it,' he says, more to himself than to me. I ignore this. Eventually he opens the car door. I watch him in my rear-view mirror as he walks around the back and snatches his suitcase from the boot. As I'm about to pull away, he taps on my window. Reluctantly I lower it.

'I don't care if you're fucking the doctor. I still love you.' He rests a hand on the roof, leans in, glances at my phone as though he's in some sort of strange competition with it. 'I'd forgive you.'

There are cars waiting for me to pull out of the drop-off spot. We both seem to register them at the same time. 'I have to go,' I say. His hand falls away.

As I drive on to the short road, I can see he's still standing there, staring after my car. I have to stop looking. Despite the albatross that falls off my back as I leave, I can't look in the mirror for my tears.

FORTY-FIVE

Because he accused me of fucking the doctor, I decide I really need to see Steve to explain a thing or two. So we meet at our out-of-town pub. As soon as I join him at his table he smiles in that very appealing, laidback way of his.

'I've missed you.' He stands, makes to kiss my cheek and I turn it towards him, warmed by the rather deliberate way he lingers there, momentarily, his face close to my own.

Once we've got our drinks I give him the story.

He listens well and I realise this is the thing I appreciate most about him. 'I'm sorry,' he says, eventually, when I suppose I've said all that needs saying on the topic of my marriage. 'I hope I haven't contributed to that.' There is a certain pained anxiousness on his face.

'No.' I try to choose my words carefully. 'But this is why I wanted to see you today . . . I'm not having doubts about my marriage ending, but I've been married to him for eighteen years and I owe it both to him and to myself – mainly myself – to be very straight in my mind about what I'm doing and why.'

'And you don't want this to complicate things.'

'I don't want it to cloud my judgement, and it's unfair to keep you hanging on in suspense.' Suddenly the world feels a little still and lonely, while I ponder the possibility of having just lost the one good thing I've never actually had.

We seem to undergo a little thought transference, because he leans across the small table, casually resting on his crossed arms. 'I'm not going anywhere, you know.'

The doubting side of me thinks, *No, you might not think so, but you'll meet someone else.* I'd say it's almost inevitable. Our timing is unfortunately against us.

'She left her husband and ran off with the neighbour,' I say in a put-on voice that's not my own, and offer up a thin, sad smile.

'Let them say it. Whoever they are. Who cares?'

I am caught out by his earnestness, trapped by its beautiful possibilities, elated and devastated all at once. 'I care. I can't be anyone but who I am.'

He gives me that smile again, the one that is slightly down his nose, part serious, part teasing. Lots reassuring. 'No. And nor should you. I love who you are.'

I cock my head, wondering if he means it the way it could be interpreted.

He watches me closely for a while, then adds, 'Plus, I can always move.'

We smile.

'Charlotte might be a little surprised if I tell her you're moving in,' I say.

The smile flashes broadly across his face. Then he says, 'Maybe we should do it just for that reason alone.'

Zara still isn't herself.

I go into her room expecting to find her getting ready for school but she's lying on top of her bed in her pyjamas with her back to the door.

'Zara?' For a second I panic but then she turns and looks at me. 'What's the matter?'

Since the police brought her home from Craig Rathbone's house, Zara has grown a wall around her and erected a sign that reads *Do not trespass*; and, like a foreigner in a strange country, I don't quite know how to navigate this new territory, how to venture in.

I sit down beside her, feeling the mattress give. The room smells of sleep and the peppermint oil I rubbed on the soles of her feet last night, because she was coming down with a cold and was coughing.

'Are you not feeling any better?' I lay a hand where her waist curves steeply into her hip since she lost weight. She flinches under my fingers, the electric current of her distaste.

'Can I make you some cinnamon toast? What about hot Ribena?'

'Leave me alone,' she says, and inches away from my touch.

I stare into the wall of her back, at the ever-so-slight scoliosis that you wouldn't notice unless you were looking for it. I detected it when she was about eight, when I used to tickle her back as she sat on the floor with her face resting on my knee.

'Zara. You've got to tell me what's wrong. Something is. I'm not blind. And if you're not going to, then I'm going to have to make an appointment for you to see someone. A doctor. Maybe it'll be easier to talk to them.'

She tugs at the end of the duvet, tries to pull it over her head, but gives up. 'Can you just leave me alone? You've got no idea! About anything!'

Distantly, beyond the dullness of my headache, is a fear that I'm struggling to keep at bay. And I realise this sort of sums up my life. I spend most of it thinking I should know things I can't know. 'Then if I've got no idea, enlighten me. Please.' My patience is fraying but I try to be as gentle as I possibly can.

'No,' she says. 'Just go.'

I wait a bit longer then give up. I go back downstairs, sit at the kitchen table. Some time later, perhaps five or ten minutes, I hear the post through the door. There is a letter from the uni. Oh God. With everything that is going on, caring about my job has slid so far down the priority scale. Though I have to care about it if I am splitting up with Eric – more so than ever. I literally cannot afford to lose it.

When I take a deep breath and manage to open it, it says I'm being invited to attend a disciplinary hearing where the investigating officer's recommendation will be presented, and the head of department will make a decision. I have the opportunity to make representations and am entitled to bring a supportive co-worker, or a trade union rep. They give me the date. There is more nonsense about what happens if my case goes to appeal, but I only skim it because Zara startles me by coming into the kitchen. 'I'm going out for some air.'

'I'll come with you.' I put the letter back in the envelope.

'No!' she snaps. 'I just want to be on my own, OK? You don't have to be so clingy. I'm not going anywhere.'

She is baked in misery. My heart hammers. I watch her pull on the hot-pink wellies at the front door, her Barbour jacket that matches mine. Then she disappears into the grey of the pouring rain, the door closing behind her. I walk to the window and, from around the curtain, keep an eye on her until she reaches the common, aware only of the powerful invisible cord of my motherly love stretching but refusing to snap no matter how I might secretly wish it could – even if it were just for five minutes, to give myself some sort of reprieve.

Even her walk is dejected. I go back into the kitchen, put on the kettle for some tea. I try to pay some bills online, noticing from the statement that I normally leave for Eric that he made a withdrawal of a thousand pounds less than a month ago. I try to think back. What did we buy? Unless it was something he bought for himself and just managed not to tell me about.

I become immersed in googling myself, just to see if anything about my suspension or Prajval's attack comes up, then I see that she's been gone an hour. Zara never walks this long. Not even on a sunny day, never mind in the rain. I throw my Barbour on and go, leaving the dog looking bereft.

It's teeming down. The common is completely deserted, not a soul out, and no sight of Zara. I dial her phone but she doesn't answer. If she's left through the main access, she might be walking home via the main road. That's probably it. I realise I'm so in tune with worst-case scenarios that I'm now actually inventing them without cause. I turn and walk back towards our house.

Steve's car is parked at his door; it wasn't there fifteen minutes ago. But I'm not going to run to him every time I feel blind panic. I pass Charlotte's without looking in the window, hoping she isn't just happening to be looking out.

'Zara?' I shout as I open the door.

The house is quiet. I don't bother dragging off my muddy boots and go straight upstairs to her room. She isn't there. But her phone is lying on top of the duvet. She never goes anywhere without it.

For some reason, once I've seen it, I can't pull my eyes away. Long before all this Bethany business began I had insisted I know her passcode at all times. For the longest time it was her birthday. Then she changed it to mine. I try both, with no success. Then

Eric's, then Daniel's. Then for some odd reason I punch in the month we got Juniper – August of this year. I am immediately in.

There are texts. Lots of them, from Bethany.

Bitch!

I H8 U!!!

Watch out U watch *o^t .

More. Most of it nonsensical. Zara hasn't replied to any of them.

Dirty Bitch. This last one catches my eye. And then I see there is a link. To a video.

I am just about to click on it when I hear the door slam. I click the screen off, throw the phone back on the bed, and zip out of the room.

'Where did you go?' I peer over the bannister. She hasn't had her hood up and her hair is saturated. She picks up the kitten, kisses the top of her head.

'I told you, I went for a walk.' She comes upstairs, still carrying Juniper. 'My feet are freezing. I'm going to take a shower.'

I continue to stand there until I hear the running water, the familiar click of the shower door opening and closing. My heartbeat is loud in my ears. I creep back into her room. Her phone is exactly where it was. I pull up the link and press play.

FORTY-SIX

Our front door squeals open. It sounds jarringly loud yet out of range, somehow, as though I've been smacked in the head and my hearing is dull. I can't remember if I left it unlocked deliberately; the last twenty-four hours are a blur.

A gust of cold air fills the room but gets quickly cancelled out by the heat from the gas fire. Despite the fact it's been on for hours I am still chilled to the bone. My hands are clasped in my lap, fingers neatly strangling themselves.

Eric sees me sitting there, as still as one of those statues in a Paris garden, and he stops in his tracks. I can feel the hollow of his pause, or his surprise, perhaps. 'Em . . . ?' There is a spike of worry in his tone that trails off into confusion. Otis is fussing around him but Eric doesn't respond, taken off guard by my stillness, I imagine.

I turn my head slightly, keeping my eyes fixed on the same spot on the floor. It's like being partially paralysed and testing your range. I feel that if I look him in the eye he'll know more than I am capable of putting into words.

'Where's Zara?' he asks. He comes to stand in front of me. I find myself staring at two scuffed black shoes.

I want to say, *What are you doing home? It's only Thursday*, but I can only answer his question. 'My dad's.' I clear my throat and add, 'She's fine. Really.' Then I say, 'Don't worry,' because it came out sounding like I wasn't committed to the answer.

His chest visibly collapses. He was expecting something else.

Our eyes meet. A good three seconds' worth of staring one another down. I imagine telling him what I did, step by step, exactly as it happened, but already there are details I don't clearly remember. I picture him backing up, nearly toppling over the coffee table, but of course it is me who is careening around. Just the idea of saying it makes my breath quicken.

'Are you all right?' There is something different about him. Like his spirit has somehow evacuated his body.

'No,' he says. He slowly shakes his head and stares wretchedly at the floor between us.

And it's only then that I realise he really, really isn't all right. 'What's wrong?'

He continues to stand there as though he's in a state of mild catatonia. His arms hang at his sides. His face is deadly pale. Then he says, 'I don't feel very well.'

He turns and makes off towards the downstairs toilet. I hear the door slide open with an urgency, the handle pinging against the wall. A seat being lifted. The haul of his insides, the violent burble of his throat. It strikes me that I've never heard Eric vomit before. Not even at the height of his drinking. Eric was never someone who puked.

My legs are jelly when I get up and follow him. Even the dog trots after me for a look-see. Eric is leaning over the toilet bowl, his head appearing to dangle off the cliff-face of his shoulders.

'What's wrong?' I ask him. 'Are you ill?'

He's not finished yet, clearly. Another haul-up. I am sure they'll hear him two streets away. I've never seen my six-feet-four-inch husband look so cut down to size. Eric puking his guts up is mildly fascinating. The dog tries to poke his head between Eric and the bowl, for a closer look at the contents of Eric's digestive system.

Eventually he snaps paper from the holder, dabs his mouth; strings of saliva cling to his chin. He tugs at them, wipes his hands on his trousers, flushes the loo. Then he slumps back against the wall like he needs it for support. He is red and sweating profusely.

When he is able to compose himself, he says, 'She's dead.' His brows knit together and his face mashes up, like he's about to cry.

My pulse beats in my ears. I watch him slowly slide down the wall, until his backside meets the floor. 'She's gone.' He is staring blankly ahead as though utterly felled by shock. Then he says, 'Bethany . . . She's gone , . .' His tone is vaguely bewildered.

'How?' I hear myself asking.

He tries to clear his throat. 'Apparently it was, er . . .' He is trembling. 'It was another overdose, they think. I'm not quite sure. It happened yesterday.'

I stare at him hard, but he doesn't look up at me from his place beside the toilet bowl. The air is thick with gloom and his puke. There is something so defenceless about him. But I can't give it much thought because I find myself telling him the one thing I was convinced I wasn't going to – until this second.

I say, 'I know.'

He looks up at me cautiously, as though he may have misheard. 'What do you mean, you know?'

I am aware of the moments ticking down, conscious of time moving in a way that I've never really been conscious of before. Almost like it's alive.

I watch his lips moving. The ashen face. The knit of his brows. His face is sceptical, dreading. He still looks like he's not fully here. 'I don't understand. I only found out this morning. Did Janet ring you? How can you know?'

I take a deep breath then let it out in a long count. Then I say, 'You'd better come and sit down, and you'd better prepare yourself.'

FORTY-SEVEN

I pick up my phone, find the link I copied and press play.

It's very short. But long enough, of course. I must have replayed it two dozen times; that's why I don't need to watch it again now. I know exactly what happens, frame by frame. With every burst of Bethany's sick laughter I could tell you what they're doing to my daughter. I close my eyes briefly and hold my breath when I hear Bethany saying that menacing, 'I swear I'm not telling you again . . .'

When I open them, Eric's face is puckering and folding, collapsing in on itself. I know exactly what he's looking at. Zara on her knees in front of a boy with his trousers down. Bethany is standing immediately behind her. She has hold of Zara by the hair. Someone off camera is laughing, stoned. The boy who has his trousers down says to Bethany, 'Look, can we just stop this?'

'Do it!' Bethany tells Zara. This time she yanks Zara's hair hard and my daughter yowls as her head snaps back.

'Jesus, no!' Eric squeezes his eyes shut.

The picture shakes, goes black. Through garbled sound, Zara screams, 'Noooo!'

The video comes back on, right as Bethany brings up her knee to the back of Zara's head. One swift, hard jab. A boy says, 'Oh

God. Ah . . . shit . . . Stop.' The video cuts out again. The last thing we hear is Bethany telling Zara, 'Shut the fuck up, you whore!'

Eric makes an animal-like sound, then he tips sideways in the armchair and pukes again on to the floor. There is nothing left to come up. I listen to his violent retching with a degree of coldness, look at the pale green patches of bile on the cream rug. When he is done he hangs there, his upper body limp over the chair arm. Like there is nothing left of him.

I find myself watching him like he's some sort of exhibit. His shoulders do small involuntary pulses. It's almost like he's crying internally; the action just hasn't worked its way up and out of him yet. Eventually he straightens up, forces himself through a couple of steadying breaths, wipes away tears, sniffs them back.

Then he finally says, 'You did something, didn't you? What did you do?'

FORTY-EIGHT

I fled from the car like a launched rocket, propelled down her path by raw adrenaline, the video sharp and throbbing before my eyes.

The door was open a crack, because when I banged my fist on it, it just gave way. Next I was standing in a small entrance hall, stairs to the left, coats piled on to a bannister. A mountain of shoes under a small table and mirror. 'Bethany!' I shouted into the silence. Somebody was in here. I could feel it. I didn't care if it was her bloody mother. She had it coming too.

There was a shifting darkness and draught. 'Bethany!' I said again, my voice rife with menace.

Nothing. I stood there, inert, aware of the slight breaking of my stride, a momentary faltering of my nerve. Among the pile of coats on the bannister was her long black cardigan, the one she wore that day in my kitchen when she reminded me of a jaded ballerina. Then suddenly I found myself re-noticing the shoes. Zara's pink and white Converse. Well-worn and filthy.

The boiler man stole them! I could hear their laughter. Bethany's mannish guffaw.

There was a noise. I strained to hear where it was coming from between gaps in my own thumping heart. Down a dark passageway was a kitchen. I could see a counter with a coffee maker and a stack of groceries on it, smell Heinz oxtail soup – a blast from my childhood. I could almost hear my mother saying, *What on earth are you doing, lass? Get out of here!* And something about how you can't take the law into your own hands.

Can't I?

'Anybody here?' I shouted, fiercely again, a lion ready to wage war on the beast that had hurt her cub. My back was slick with sweat but when I turned the corner into the kitchen it was only the soup spitting furiously on the stove, brownish blobs landing on the white Formica worktop. I switched off the gas and everything went quiet.

I stared at the open can. The bowl for one. The mucky tea towel. *Bethany's mum has a boyfriend,* Zara had said. *That's why she's hardly around now.* I felt a sudden presence behind me. Swivelled. Ah. Only a cat. A ginger tom, tail high, looking at me like he was telling me he wanted feeding.

I went back down the hallway, took the stairs two at a time. Up at the top, a tiny square landing. A small open window. 'Bethany?' I was unwavering in my conviction that I wasn't alone. She was in here somewhere. I looked around. Three doors. One of them was ajar. She was in there. The atmosphere was thick somehow. Like someone nervous, hiding, trying to be still.

You bitch, I thought. *Once I get hold of you, you'll be wishing all you felt was nerves!*

I walked over, almost on tiptoe, had some vision of her springing out – *Haaaa!* – maybe like they do in horror movies, with a knife in her hand. Then the mannish laugh. I pushed it away, tried to shove the door open but it resisted against the pile of the carpet.

At first I couldn't quite process what I saw. Legs. Pale feet overhanging the bed end, twitching slightly. Plum-painted toenails. A tarnished silver ring on the second from baby toe. She was lying very still on top of a dark green duvet. My eyes travelled the length of her bare legs to the frayed hem of a denim miniskirt. The palm of her right hand was upturned by her side, the fingers coiled unnaturally. Her black vest top had ridden up so I could see a silver belly ring with a tiny green stone in it, a pronounced ribcage. When I got to her face, her eyes were open, and as soon as they met mine her gaze slid off to a vague point in the distance. I followed where they led but there was nothing and no one behind me. When I looked back at her she gave a slow, communicative blink.

I opened my mouth to say something, but my jaw was stiff and resisting. The emotion of the past couple of hours had laid some sort of attack on my throat; I had no voice. I stared at a bubble of white spittle in the corner of her mouth. She was making a sound like a quiet snore. It seemed to wake me up suddenly, out of this catatonia I'd fallen into. I had to do something. 'My God,' I said. She was trying to say something. I stared at her mouth. Then I realised. Even though the words, and her ability to say them, didn't exist any more than my ability to move a muscle. She was somehow communicating, *Help me*.

FORTY-NINE

'I went there convinced I was going kill her,' I tell him. 'I'm not going to lie. There was not a single doubt in my mind I was going to make her pay for what she did.'

I can still see the spittle in the corner of her mouth, the glassiness in her stare, the shallow rise and fall of her breath. 'She was looking at me and mouthing, *Help me*, and all I could think was, *I can just turn and walk back down those stairs . . . It would be like I was never here.*'

He is looking at me like I am a stranger, or an alien, but I don't allow that to send me off course.

'I felt nothing.' I can see the bitten fingernails, the hand curled by her hip. 'No compassion. Not even loathing. I was just . . . destroyed by what I'd seen her do to Zara.'

He stands up after a few seconds' delay. 'I need to get a drink.' He says it unabashedly, as though there is relief in there being no secrets between us now. His will is stronger than his body, though; he veers off balance slightly, corrects himself with a certain stiff effort.

I hear the squeak of the cabinet door, the familiar chink of bottles – sounds that long ago turned my heart to ice. The clunk of heavy-bottomed crystal landing on the countertop. Liquid pouring.

Just like when he was pouring one in his hotel room, I can gauge exactly how much he's giving himself just by listening to it glug into the glass and doing my own silent count. By the time he returns to the chair, half of it is gone.

'What did you do?' His hand is shaking as it curls around the glass, sending drops of gold liquid on to the rug. 'Did you not try to help her? Tell me.' He gulps down the rest of it, stares at the empty glass like he's not sure where the contents went.

I clear the nerves from my throat.

Help me.

'I rang for an ambulance. I said there was a girl in distress . . . possible overdose. I gave them the address, and then I left.'

His colour that had pepped up, momentarily, with the hit of alcohol, drains from his cheeks. He looks like he might puke again and I think, *No wonder* – hard alcohol on a raw stomach. His capacity for self-abuse disgusts me.

'What do you mean, you left?' he asks. 'You didn't stay until the ambulance arrived?'

I shake my head. 'What use was I to her? I couldn't bear to touch her. Not after what she did . . .' I can't let my mind go to that video again. I have to keep pulling it away or I will cross over to a place I will never return from. I will be no good to Zara. 'I did what I had to do, and then I got out of there.'

I remember how I was shaking when I got back into the car. As though everything I'd bottled up over the past days and weeks had just suddenly burst out of me; I was exploding and imploding with wrong and right, and guilt and anger and sorrow, and a profound sense of how none of us would ever be the same again after this. No amount of willing, or blocking it out, could ever undo what's been done. 'I got back into the car and then I sat there thinking, *What am I doing? I should go back in.* But then I didn't. I started the car, and I left.'

He stares at me with a sort of slow comprehension that turns to frigid hollowness. The dog comes over to nudge his knee but he doesn't seem to feel him. I have the notion that if I moved out of the space where he's staring, his eyes wouldn't follow me. After a moment or two he looks down at the empty glass he's almost forgotten is in his hand. 'Whose . . . whose phone did you use to ring the ambulance?'

'Hers,' I say, wondering why it matters.

He nods. 'OK, well, at least that's good . . . If they saw the number or bothered to trace the call, they'd know you were there. They might have thought . . .'

'What?'

'That you walked away from the scene of . . . I don't know.' He lets out a weighted breath. 'I'm not sure, to be honest.'

We fall silent. Then he gets up. I know he's going to fill up his glass again, and I find myself anticipating that I'm going to care, but nothing comes. I follow him into the kitchen. But if that was what he intended, all he does is stand there with his back to me, gripping the counter with both hands. And then I see his shoulders shaking.

'It's all my fault,' he says. It comes out in a pained, high-pitched cry. 'Oh my God . . . What have I done? What have I done?'

I'm puzzled. 'I don't know,' I say to his back, feeling a shiver down my spine. Suddenly, though, my mind goes to that video from Charlotte's party, where he was saying to that young woman: *I've done things. I'm a bad person.* And I just thought he was being pitiful.

'What have you done?' I say. My brain tries to join the dots, but, as usual, I never can with Eric.

After an age, he turns. He looks like he badly wants to bawl again, or scream, and it's trapped in the vacuum of his body, with a seal he can't break.

'Tell me,' I say firmly. That video from the party is now blazing with eerie significance in my mind.

'I can't do this any more.' He looks at me candidly as though he's expecting I have half an idea of what he's talking about. I think he's alluding, bizarrely, to our marriage again, but then he says, 'I can't! I just can't do it.' He throws his head back and his face crinkles like a baby's. 'I've tried and I've tried . . . And I did it! I did it for so long . . .' He turns and clutches the counter again like he's going to fall over.

The world seems to swing on its axis. The entire arc of my life feels like it's about to be altered. It is dreamlike. Nothing feels real.

Eric is sobbing. It goes on and on. The force of his despair seems to have no beginning and no end.

'Eric . . .' I am powerless, locked out of my own ability to speak.

'You don't understand,' he says, when he can speak again. His voice is so quiet, as thin as my hopes. 'I was a good lad. A good lad . . . and I messed it all up.'

A chilling memory comes to me. Years ago I came home and he was talking to someone in his study. He was very emotional. I stood with my ear to the door. *You've made a lot of mistakes, lad. Why did you have to mess it all up? Eh? Why? Why?* I had no idea who he was talking to so I nudged the door open a crack. Bizarrely, he was alone. He was sitting on the ground with his back to me, clutching an old photo of his eighteen-year-old self. A small, passport-sized one he used to carry around in his wallet when I met him. I realised he was talking to the naïve, smiling person he used to be.

'If I don't understand then tell me,' I say, pushing that disturbing memory away. I have to reach a hand to the wall to steady myself.

He turns around again. His face is grey, a concavity of tiredness and wretchedness. 'I did this,' he says, more soberly now. 'This is my fault.'

It is there again. Something I can't grasp. A dissolving flake in a snowstorm, hard to make out because it was so loosely formed to begin with. A chill gathers at the top of my spine. My sense of self-preservation tells me to brace myself. 'What's your fault?'

'I'm so sorry,' he says. 'I think it's you who'd better sit down this time . . . I don't know how to tell you this, except to just say it . . .'

FIFTY

'Why are you doing this to me and my family?' He arrives at her table in the busy café and the words are out before he's even sat down.

She looks at him steadily. Always so calm.

'Sending bikes and stuffed toys and cards. Fucking Valentine's Day flowers!' He hauls the chair out, plonks himself down. The people beside them cock him a look.

'*Why are you doing this to me and my family?*' she mimics, then rolls her eyes and mutters, 'Oh please!'

'But they are my family, Janet!' Rage surges in him – the plick, plick of his pulse in his neck – the kind he normally only feels after a few drinks. His chest tightens again; he grinds his fist into his leg.

Before he can reply she says, 'If you must know, I sent the gifts because you were nice to me so I was being nice back . . . I didn't realise it was a crime.'

Her sense of her own logic both astounds him and paralyses him. 'And the endless phone calls to my house and the hanging up, day and night? Let me guess. That's because you've got a good heart, too?'

Em finally got the phone company to block private callers. He made up some excuse about pissing off a telemarketer, and this being their revenge.

'No. I did that because you're ignoring me. It's just so antisocial, and plain rude! I think you need to remember there are three people in this equation. She needs to know I exist. She doesn't get to live in a bubble. Maybe she feels secure for now, but, well, if you don't play fair with me then that's not going to last for long.'

It takes him a moment to realise she's just threatened him because he was so taken aback by the equation comment. 'What do you mean by that exactly?'

'You know, Eric . . . Do you know what I think? I think you're just being blind to the fact that you've got a lot more feelings for me than you care to admit.'

'Fucking what?'

The waiter sets down sandwiches for them that she must have ordered, and glances at them curiously. Eric stares at the prawns on top of the open face of the bread. His stomach gurgles and it ripples down to his bowels.

'When I think of what you've done – led me on, made love to me, then turned around and told me it was nothing and you love your wife and children – part of me believes I owe it to myself to destroy this man in any way I can. And I would. If I was that kind of vengeful person. But lucky for you I'm not, or the outcome could have been very different.'

He tries to let a breath out, but it's stuck. She is looking at him so witheringly. Again he pictures her dying. The road accident in which he survives. Her slumped across the dashboard eyes open, blood oozing from every orifice.

'Janet.' He leans across the table, says it low and slow, gritting his teeth and trying not to lunge and grab her by the neck. 'What you're saying is a pile of shit. Made love to you?' He laughs in disgust. 'I never made love to you and I never led you on. And do you know why I didn't? Because that would have required me to fancy you, and to regard you with respect. I was pissed senseless. You were there. I've never found you even vaguely attractive. See, that's what the booze does. It makes even dogs look appealing.' He holds her gaze, fired by a sense of power that comes from the fact that she is no longer intimidating him; finally it's the other way around. 'You came on to me, remember? You followed me downstairs into the men's and I fucked you the only way that you deserve. And you know what? Since that hideous encounter, I've felt revolted every time I have to look at you.' He remembers her being up against the wall, him pushing into her from behind, the sickly smell of scent at the back of her neck. 'You don't mean that to me!' He clicks his fingers. 'Nothing. Do you get that? NO-THING.'

Tears stream down her face, but she doesn't flinch. 'I didn't come on to you,' she says, after a second or two. 'How can you remember it that way? I didn't follow you into the toilets. That part was your idea.'

He looks at her with scepticism for a moment. 'Yeah! Right!' He's not going to let her derail him with her bullshit . . . 'You know what I'm going to do?' He starts to feel a slight surge of promise, like finding a life raft but realising there's still no guarantee you won't drown. 'I am going to come clean and tell my wife. I'm going to have you served with a restraining order. And I don't care if everybody at work finds out what happened. I've sought legal advice. You will lose your job. You will never be able to come near me or my family again, and if you do, you'll be put in prison and Bethany will end up in care. Do you understand what I'm telling you? It's your kid who will suffer. Is that what you want?'

They hold eyes. She doesn't even blink. He can see her process-ing how much of this is fact and how much an idle threat. Then she says, 'All right. Believe what you want to believe. But if you're going to tell Emily, then you had better tell her everything.'

'Oh, mark my words, I will,' he says. He is still buoyed with this new business of finally having the upper hand. It's not going to be easy, but he has every faith Em will believe him, and that there's a chance – a small one – that he won't have wrecked everything, that he might win back her trust in time. Either way, he's going to have to take the consequences because he can't live like this. 'What I'm going to tell her is that you came on to me and I turned you down and for some reason it's messed with your head because you were deranged to start off with, and you've got some daft idea there's something between us . . .' He looks her over from the waist up. 'Trust me, when she sees your ugly face she'll believe me.' He drags the corners of his eyes down and pulls a drooped mouth, not caring that it's the cruellest thing he's ever said or done to another human being.

The couple at the next table are staring at him like he's Jim Carrey. His back is streaming with sweat. The spotlights in the ceiling seem to be aimed at his face.

She just looks at him like he's one impersonation away from a mental health unit. Then she says, 'Oh, I have reason to think she'd believe me.' She unearths something from her bag. A manila envelope. Slaps it down on the table, slides it across.

'What's this?' he asks, a chink in his confidence.

She stares him in the face, like he's a pathetic kid. 'Open it and see.'

FIFTY-ONE

Eric, March 2004

He is staring at a blurry photograph. It takes him a minute to realise what it is because he's seen one before. Two actually. A crescent moon sitting in a dark sky. Two areas that look like . . .

A head and a body.

He hears a whooshing sound in his ears, feels like he felt that day right before he wound up in hospital. The words are out before he knows where they came from. 'It's not mine. I've had a vasectomy.'

She is looking at him as though to say, *Nice try!*

'Seriously. I'm telling you.' He perks up with the conviction of his own bullshit. 'It can't be mine. It's impossible . . .' When she still doesn't dignify this, he says, 'I can show you my medical records.'

She continues to watch him like he's both amusing and pathetic. Eventually he wipes a hand across his mouth. 'For God's sake . . . I mean . . . *Fuck!* The people at the next table look across at them. He grits his teeth. 'Weren't you on the pill?'

'No,' she says with an air of quiet disdain. 'I had no reason to be. I wasn't in a relationship and I don't go in for casual sex, much as you might find that hard to believe.'

He stares at her like she's an alien. 'It's not hard to believe, Janet. It's fucking impossible! You followed me into the men's toilet . . .' At least, he thinks . . . He distinctly remembers going to the one downstairs because the restaurant down there was closed and he knew there'd be no one in those loos. Admittedly, there are other bits of things he doesn't exactly remember . . . 'You were on me like a fly.' He is bolstered by his own version of events. 'You assaulted me. You were rabid for it.' He sneers. 'I don't know too many nice women who'd behave like that.'

'Yes.' She looks at him and nods her head, like he's the lowest form of life. 'I really had to rape you. I recall.'

He feels the irrevocable shift of his present and his future, the earth separating into two distinct parts. He sees Em, Daniel and Zara in a vortex, whirling away from him, and himself reaching for them to try to grab them back, but they are gone and he is left only with the look on Em's face imprinted on his retinas for the rest of his life.

It takes him a long time to get the next bit out, to wend his way around the words. But he manages it. 'You're obviously not going to keep it.' He used to be fervently against abortion, but that was back when unwanted pregnancy was other people's misfortune, not his own.

'I am,' she says. 'Firstly, because I want to. But even if I didn't, abortion is a sin and I would never do that.'

He imagines his lungs filling with water. That he's going to drown. He mops his brow with the napkin but the sweat won't stop pouring out of him. 'But you've already got a kid that doesn't have a dad! How do you plan on coping with another?'

'This one will have a dad,' she says. 'You.'

He blinks. 'Are you insane?' A concrete slab is being lowered on to his chest. He doesn't know if he can take his next breath before it crushes him. 'I'm not paying a penny towards some kid I don't even know is mine! I will never acknowledge it. Never.'

'*It* . . .' she says, nodding and judging him with that withering look again. 'Interesting, that on top of everything else, you'd let a baby die. Without so much as a backward glance, I bet. Have you ever stopped to think what a nasty piece of work you are, Eric?'

He looks away. He'd kill the baby and kill her if he could. And he would do it right now if he weren't sitting here with forty witnesses.

'I'll get a paternity test.' It's all he's got left.

'Do.'

He jabs his index finger at her, hating how she knows she can call his bluff. 'I'll prove you to be a slut and a fucking liar.' The people at the next table look over again. 'I'll prove I'm not the father.' For a moment, his righteous sense of being wronged is so potent.

She rolls her eyes. 'Do you ever get tired of your own bullshit, Eric? You've clearly got a problem. Some kind of personality disorder. You need to get some sort of help.'

He realises that's the very thing he once said to her.

He doesn't know where to go from here. He undoes the top button of his shirt. His hands feel fat and his wedding ring tight like it's strangling his finger. 'I can promise you, if you keep it, you're on your own. One hundred per cent. I will not let your bad decision ruin my life.'

'I wonder what Em will think of that. And your children, when they grow up and learn they have a half-sibling that you deprived them of. A child you decided to just opt out of providing for . . . of loving.'

His head swims. He can't take a full breath. When he goes to speak his cheekbones seem to bear downward, like they're about to slide off his jaw. 'So . . . so you're going to live the rest of your life blackmailing me with this? Is that it?' His voice is weak. Everything is swimming. By the stiffness of his face, he wonders if he's having a stroke. 'With the threat of coming out and telling them?'

'No. I told you, I don't seek to do you any harm. If you play fair, I'll play fair. But that's in your hands, isn't it.'

The cyclone of terror hits him, at the insane idea of a kid being born, growing up. *His* kid who he won't acknowledge. Living possibly just a town or two away. Em never knowing. Until one day when Janet Brown decides it's time.

He can barely hear her for his panic now. He wants to scream, *Somebody help me!* He looks around the room. Seconds tick by. *Think of a plan . . .* She sits there in no hurry, like she's waiting for his move on the chessboard. 'Look, Janet,' he finally manages to say, and to say it calmly, quietly. *Be nice.* 'If you tell me right now that the baby isn't mine, that you made all this up for whatever reason – because you're unwell, or I inadvertently made you feel used – then we can walk out of that door right now and we can both get on with our lives.' He needs to take a breath but keeps on, the strength draining from his lungs. 'I promise I won't hold it against you that you fabricated this terrible and potentially quite catastrophic lie about me. That you threatened everything I hold dear.' He tries not to lapse back into righteous indignation and instead keep it conciliatory. 'If you need some money – a loan – until you sort yourself out, well, I could probably manage to do that too, if that'll help things. But if you tell me one more time that I'm the father of your unborn child and that you're going to use that against me and my family, then I can promise you that, one way or another, you're not going to have this baby.'

'And what does that mean?' she asks him, as unfazed as ever.

He looks her hard in the eyes. 'You decide what it means.'

FIFTY-TWO

'You slept with Janet Brown?' It comes, goes, then snaps back to me.

Bethany's mother.

Bethany's mother!

'While I was pregnant with Zara?'

We have come back into the living room. I can't stand but nor can I move. I am pinned there in the wake of what he's just told me, in the truth that writes itself across his face.

'You had an affair with her and you got her pregnant?'

'It wasn't an affair,' he says. 'I told you. It was one time. She became obsessed. She was sick. Threats, emails . . . Stalking me everywhere. The presents, flowers . . .'

The Valentine's Day flowers that arrived with no name!

Something is spinning. The walls. I step back. Back, back, hit the sofa, feel the cushion give under my weight. My brows knit together, my lips move around questions that I can't articulate. I am weightless with his words, pieces of a puzzle falling as if from the sky, but I can't grasp them and place them where they need to be. A vague truth unfurling that has existed for me on some unattainable level. 'How?' I say redundantly. 'Why?' My voice cracks.

He stares at the floor ahead of him, like he's trying to re-see it. 'I told you I was off my face. She came on to me. I don't know why I did it . . .'

I picture her in our kitchen. *Hello, Eric.* Almost as though she knew him.

Because she did.

'But . . . you got her pregnant . . .' I'm confused. 'Where's the child now? She only has Bethany . . .'

He bluntly meets my gaze. 'Bethany Brown is my daughter.'

I frown. Clearly there is some mistake. Or I am unwell, or just not understanding this correctly. 'But . . .' The earth has tilted. 'I don't understand . . . I thought you just said that when you met her at the Christmas party she'd just had a baby . . . she was a single mum . . .'

'I thought she was,' he says, after a moment, a fraction more level in his emotional control. 'She'd had her baby, but it had died.' He looks briefly at the floor again. 'No one knew at work, apparently. She never told anyone. I didn't even know for the longest time . . . Not until she announced she was calling the baby – my baby – Bethany.'

He says '*my* baby' as though the idea is still foreign to him.

'What?' I almost laugh. My first instinct is not to believe him.

'Don't ask me why she gave her second child the same name. She's not right in the head, is she? How do we know why people like that do the things they do?'

I can't speak. Janet had a baby that died, then she had another one and called her by the same name? I try to get my head around it. It occurs to me, too, that I've always assumed Bethany was a little older than Zara, even though they were in the same year at school. A part of me thought maybe she'd had to repeat a year, considering her track record. But she is actually a little younger? Conceived while I was carrying Zara? Eric's daughter? Zara and Daniel's half-sister? I cover my nose and mouth with my hands.

I am aware of him slowly studying me, but from a place of remove. He is very calm now. There has been a turning of the tide. A secret finally told. He's relieved.

'I always thought that if you didn't find out, then the longer it went on, the longer it would go on . . . everything would somehow be OK. And it was. It almost was. I managed this for fourteen years.'

'Managed it?' He sounds almost proud.

'Well I did, didn't I? Kept it separate so it wouldn't interfere with our lives . . . I suppose, somewhere in the back of my mind, I always expected I'd have to tell you eventually. But then the longer it went on, it just really felt like *eventually* was never coming. Until it did, of course.' He hangs his head.

You were always weighted down, and I never knew why. That outrageous bout of drinking right after Zara was born. I never knew why. You were taken to hospital after some sort of panic attack, and I never really knew why . . .

This was why.

'But why now?' I scramble to hang on to the threads of this before my emotions take over. 'It makes no sense. Why would she suddenly come into our lives after all these years?' Fourteen years he kept it, like it was nothing more than a little white secret. 'It makes no sense. Why would she just turn up out of thin air?'

'Because I stopped child support,' he says quietly.

It takes me a moment to process. Then, 'Ah . . .' Of course. Unexplained withdrawals from the bank machine. Regular but not big enough to warrant suspicion. The car tyre fiasco! Eric generously deciding that he would take charge of managing our finances. One less thing for me to have to do, he said.

'I paid her unofficially,' he says, so very coldly. 'Out of my own money.'

'*Your* money?'

'What I mean is . . . I wasn't going to take anything from what you earned while I wasn't bringing anything in . . . I wanted it to come directly from my own pocket. I didn't want you having to pay for my mistake.'

His logic, and his sincere belief in his noble position on our joint finances, bowl me over. It's such a bizarre way of thinking that I can't even argue with it. I stare at him like he's got two heads. *How can you think in terms of my money and your money? We are married. We have a home and children.*

Then he says, 'She didn't just decide out of the blue to come out of the woodwork.' He hangs his head again. I have the vaguest sense this is actually hard for him. Then I think, *Of course it is!* A lifetime of lying and now he decides to be honest! The truth is entirely foreign to him. 'There was a bit more to it than that . . . Before I took the contract in London, when I'd been laid off for eighteen months, I told her I couldn't pay her until I started working again.' He looks frankly into my eyes. A liar finally being honest brings a certain heightened suspense to things. Yet rather than be floored by what he says, I'm just hanging on to see what he's going to tell me next.

'Go on,' I say.

'Well, then I started working in London and at first I didn't really know whether that was even going to work out, did I? . . . At best it was a two-year contract.'

'Two? It's one.'

I don't have to say, *Another lie?* Because I can tell by his face that it is.

'I was going to tell you . . . I thought it would be easier to accept in the beginning if I told you it was only one year.'

My jaw drops but I can't formulate a single word.

'The minute she found out I was in London she was on my back about it right away. I said, "Look, it doesn't work like that. You're just going to have to be a bit more patient until I pay off a few of my debts." And then . . . well, that's where I might have messed up.'

That's where? Might have?

He rubs his forehead as though he's trying to rub away a reality. 'I suppose I kind of snapped. I think deep down I was just so sick and tired of her always having me by the balls. All these years, I was really only getting away with it because she was *letting me* get away with it. It had gone on fourteen years! I suppose I just wanted to push back.'

He had a lot of anger issues, she said that evening in our kitchen. Would Eric have knocked her around? He's been near-violent with us, and we are the ones he purports to love.

'I told her, "You know what, Janet? I've changed my mind. Fuck it." I said, "We've got bills to pay – there's Daniel's tennis costing a fortune . . . I can't pay another penny towards Bethany. Besides, the kid's practically an adult. Let her go out and get a part-time job like every other kid."'

But not ours. I picture her in our house staring at our stuff, judging. Commenting on my nice life and part-time options . . . My God. That face. Her disdain. It all makes sense now.

'I finally stood up for myself. For us,' he says, almost proudly. 'I told her, "I've played fair for a very long time. But it's over. I've got Daniel and Zara to think about. From now on I've got to do right by my family."'

I find myself processing this from Janet's perspective and hearing myself quietly saying, 'I can't believe this.' I am just sitting here, shaking my head, saying, 'I can't believe this,' over and over again. Because I can't.

'She said she'd tell you. But I just thought, *Yeah, yeah! Threats. Typical Janet!* I thought, *If you'd been going to tell Emily about this you'd have done it a very long time ago.* I thought it was an empty threat.'

It's like I'm listening to a stranger's story. It's so fantastical to me that I seem to have been robbed of every response but incredulity. 'So that's why you were happy enough to be working down there. Because it suited you. Because you were away from here, from *her*.' It's like someone has just thrown a bucket of iced water over me. Him wanting to move to Australia! Wanting us to move to London! All the little things I thought were so strange at the time but I could never connect the dots. Because you can't know what you don't know.

I couldn't have known.

Couldn't I?

Shouldn't I?

How couldn't I? I am not a fool, so how could he have fooled me?

'Believe me,' he says, 'no matter how it might seem, I have never ever been free of her.'

I can't stop staring at him. I can't close the horrible floodgate of his lie. It's just pouring into the empty space, making me doubt every single word he's ever said to me since the day we met.

'It was that photo of us in the newspaper that did it.' He glances over to the sideboard where it sits proudly in its frame. 'The article said I'd recently had to accept a job in London to help pay for Daniel's tennis. Janet didn't know I'd started working again.'

Of course! 'You weren't planning on telling her.'

He shakes his head. 'Not right away.' He drops his chin to his chest. 'There we all were, this portrait of the perfect family . . .'

The article ran at the end of February. Eric had only moved to London a few short weeks before. I remember how jovial he was that day, clowning around for the journalist. Then I spotted the glass stashed behind the cookbooks. He wasn't the good fun fellow that he might have seemed on the surface. He was a liar hiding a secret that was getting more unmanageable than he knew how to deal with.

'My God,' I say. I can clearly picture me showing Janet the photo – *showing off* the photo. The perfect portrait of our family life, or so it looked; the family I wished we were. I am suddenly hit with the urge to boomerang back all that he's told me – to un-know it so it can't possibly be true. 'No, no, no, no, no,' I hear myself saying, thinking of a woman who has lost two children, and this foreigner I have been married to, who was responsible for one of them, sitting here opposite me. This alcoholic who has lived a lie, and consequently has made me live one too. This man who went through spells of darkness and intense drinking, and I never stopped to ask myself, *Why?* What was really at the root of it?

'Who are you?' I say. I cannot get my head around the fact that someone I thought I've known inside out is someone else. That I've given more than twenty years of my life to this fraud.

His eyes are filling with tears again. 'I know it's hard for you to believe but I didn't conspire to lead some kind of double life. It was one wrongdoing. One wrong choice, and all my other choices ran away from me.'

Eric is Bethany's father. I cannot comprehend it.

Then something else breaks in. 'You were her dad. Didn't you care about her? She was your flesh and blood.'

I think of Zara saying Bethany's mother and father were in love and married and then he took off and wanted nothing to do with her . . . I had pictured a chancer, a charmer, a fly-by-night. Not *my husband*.

He doesn't answer, just stares hard at his feet, colour rising in his face again. He looks like he's about to burst.

'How did you live with us, knowing you had a child out there, so close by? Another daughter? That our children had a half-sister and she lived just a few miles away? Didn't you want to see her? To be in her life?' I think, bizarrely, of him wanting to pay towards rehab for her – making it sound like it was Zara's idea. And of a thousand pounds mysteriously leaving our account recently. Did he give it to Janet? His half of the two grand?

Eric's ears are burning bright red. *This is shame*, I think. *You're mired in your own shame! That's why you can't answer.*

Then he finally does. 'I never asked for another child,' he says, still staring at his feet. 'I had no choice in the matter, did I?' His words are defensive but his tone is not. Even he can't uphold his own shitty behaviour. 'I didn't think of her as my daughter. I didn't want to see her . . . Have to feel guilty about her . . . Do you know what I'm saying? I was either going to be a father to her or I was going to be nothing at all . . . It was the best way. For everyone.'

I struggle not to be derailed by his almost-inhuman coldness. Eric has always been kind. He may not have been the most involved parent but I have never doubted his capacity to love. 'I just can't believe it . . . You must have had *some* feelings. Some guilt! You could have changed the course of her life, by being *in* her life.' *If you'd stepped up and been a father, maybe she might not be dead.*

He nods. He knows what I'm thinking. But he says nothing.

I stare at him, waiting, needing to get to the emotional pit of this. *I want to know how you did it!* I want to shake him, scream, *Tell me!* But still he stares at the floor.

'You stood in our kitchen that day and came face to face with her . . .' I remember him looking stunned. I just put it down to there being strangers in the house that he wasn't expecting.

'I know,' he says. He cannot raise his eyes and look at me.

I get up and go to the window, stare vacantly into the trees. I am trying to think – what if he had told me in the beginning?

Would I have left him? Would I have cared so much about him being in her life, as I seem to care now? Or would I have been complicit in shoving her under the rug like he has done? If I had known, could we have made it work? Could I have accepted her, and made the best of it? Would I have thought, *Eric has made his bed and now he has to lie in it? It's inconvenient but it's our new reality.*

I honestly don't know.

When I turn and look at him again he is still sitting there in that posture of quiet, contemplative regret. 'Say something,' I say.

He sniffs hard, like he's suppressing another meltdown. 'Well, as I'm being honest with you . . . you might as well know I didn't get laid off from Kellar's all those years ago,' he says. He clears his throat, steadies himself. 'I resigned. I couldn't stand seeing her every single day – pregnant with my child. Getting bigger . . .' He puts his head in his hands. 'She wasn't leaving. She made that clear . . . There's no way I could have stayed. My sanity. I thought I was doomed. It was all coming apart. I didn't really think far enough ahead to see that I was doomed anyway, wasn't I?'

He finally meets my eyes.

I always knew there was some sort of mystery around him leaving that job! But I thought his only lie was that he was going to work when he wasn't! I return my gaze to the trees, focusing hard on the familiar finger-like pattern of bare branches. So much is shifting, and rearranging. I lock on to their consistency, their static beauty, for balance.

'After you left that job nothing ever went right,' I say.

'Trust me, it wasn't going very right before then, I can promise.'

I turn and look at him again. 'So are we going to tell Daniel and Zara?'

FIFTY-THREE

The funeral is on a Friday.

There is no way I can bring myself to go, so Eric attends by himself. I don't even have to convince him it's the right thing to do.

While he's gone, and Daniel is at school, Zara comes downstairs. 'It was Bethany who sent that magazine to Dad. The porno.' She says it apropos of nothing. 'I feel bad I never told you before.'

'I know,' I say. 'I guessed.' And while I haven't thought about it for some time, I'm still relieved to know Eric isn't a paedo, on top of everything else.

'It was Craig's. She found it in his bathroom. I didn't want to say anything, but it doesn't matter now.'

'She broke in and stole my jewellery too . . . cut up my clothes.' I want her to confirm it.

'She said she didn't.'

I can't tell if it's the truth or if she's covering for her for some absurd reason. But I don't want to interrogate her. Instead, I tell her I saw the video.

What I will not tell her is that Bethany is her half-sister, that someone who is partly her flesh and blood did that. Eric and I decided that this is best, for our children. If Bethany were still alive, it might be different. But even then I am not convinced I would feel differently. Zara and Daniel must never know. Some secrets die with us. Eric's, sadly, didn't. This one must.

I tell her that while it cut out at a critical part, I have a feeling I know what she was forced to do, that she did nothing wrong, that she was a victim of assault by a bad person who had once masqueraded as a friend. I tell her that it's going to take some time for her to get over this, that there will be plenty of secrets between us in life, possibly bigger ones, but they will never get in the way of my love for her. By sharing them, no matter how ugly or embarrassing, we deal with them together, and then we put them in the past where they belong, where they can't do us any more harm. But, first, I tell her that we have some decisions to make.

Bethany Brown might not be here any longer, but the boy who was complicit in sexually assaulting my daughter is. I explain that the right thing to do is for us to show the video to the police, and for him to pay for what he did, so he won't do that again to other girls. But I say I know that's going to require her to be brave and strong, and for her to relive it to some degree in the process. I tell her I will leave it with her for her to think about. Whatever her decision is, I will respect it.

'He didn't really do anything,' she says, after a time. She has been lying with her head against my ribcage like she used to do when she was little. I can't see if her eyes are open or closed. 'He got scared and he ran out.'

I know that, despite what was done to her, Zara still can't believe that Bethany is gone. I don't delve to see if there is any sense of relief in it; she's entitled to her private feelings and thoughts.

'Really?'

She struggles to sit up now and looks right at me. 'I'm not just saying it. It was her making me. Not really him. But then he was like, "I'm gone."'

A tidal wave of relief rushes over me. I don't want to give her the third degree. It occurs to me she might be making this up to save herself some embarrassment, but no need to prolong it and make it harder than it already is.

'But next time, with another girl, he might not be so nervous,' I say. And I leave the comment to lie there.

When Eric comes home from the funeral it's the first time I truly see him as a man with his spirit broken. He stays in his study, out of the way of the kids. As soon as they've gone to bed he surfaces.

'It was open casket.' He sits opposite me on the sofa and cries.

'What did Janet say?' I ask him eventually – quietly – because my need to know outweighs any curiosity I might have about how he would have felt staring at his dead daughter. 'Did you ask her what I told you to ask her?'

He nods. 'You don't need to worry. She's just lost her daughter. Telling our kids who Bethany was is the last thing she's going to be thinking about.'

Her daughter. I stare hard at him, in a state of fresh disbelief. 'Maybe not now. But is she going to hold this over us forevermore until she decides to wreak further retribution at some point down the line? Like she did with you? Did you ask her that?'

'No,' he says. 'She's not going to. It's over.'

His judgement is hardly sound, but right now it's all I have to go on and a part of me can't think much beyond the immediate present. I get up from the chair and hand him his coat.

He has the nerve to look stunned. 'Where can I go at this hour?'

'I don't know. A hotel? Your parents'? Hell?'

He lingers there, like he's going to challenge me but realises he can't. A moment or two later he heads to the door. I watch him walk down our path, to his car. I think I will picture the dejected sight of him for the rest of my life.

~

For the next few days we plod on much as before, but then something shifts in me. I am unable to shake off the sight of Bethany's knee coming up to the back of Zara's head, Zara's yelp of agony, and then what I imagine happened next, that I still don't know if she's telling the truth about. On the pretext that I have a bug, I send Daniel and Zara to my father's, and then I capsize and allow myself to grieve the way only a mother is capable of. I don't move from my bed until I tell myself I must let the dog out or feed the cat. I don't shower. I barely eat. I sleep . . . endless sleeping. But when awake I am tormenting myself with questions. Was I culpable in some way – would Eric have told me if he'd felt he *could* tell me? What is wrong with me that I can even begin to blame myself for Eric's actions?

When I am at my most despairing, Charlotte arrives at my door, clutching a hotpot.

'I saw you staring out the window. You look dreadful.'

'Come in,' I tell her.

In the middle of all this, I've been thinking about forgiveness. I am sure that part of the reason I was so furious with her was because the words she uttered about my daughter had echoed my very own thoughts. Not only did they touch a nerve, they made me confront a harsh truth. Perhaps we will never be the friends we were. But I can't hang her for being honest. So I choose to try to move past this, in the spirit of none of us being perfect, in the hope that one day, if I ever say something that's not meant to be overheard, a friend will be prepared to wipe the slate clean for me.

So, much like old times, I make us a cup of tea then I bring her up to speed about Zara and Bethany – minus the part about Eric being Bethany's father. She listens well, and when I am done, she says, 'That girl being gone is probably the very best thing that could have happened.'

And then I mention my worries about my suspension and the upcoming hearing.

'I'll come with you,' she says. 'Not necessarily as your lawyer but as a friend. I'll give you some advice, and you can decide what you want to do with it.'

'Thanks,' I tell her. 'That's good of you. Maybe I'll take you up on it.'

Then I tell her about how I've left Eric.

'It's the drinking, isn't it?' she says, looking completely unfazed.

I am genuinely astonished. 'How did you know?' Then it occurs to me. 'The video your friend took?' Never in all our friendship have I implied Eric actually drinks like that on a regular basis.

'Darling, no! I didn't need any video . . . It's abundantly obvious to anyone with eyes.' She grabs the top of my hand. 'He's a piss tank. You only have to look at his face. It's written all over him.'

I am more than a little bemused. How long has she known? And how have I known for years – deep down, I always knew – and yet I have managed to deny it for so long? I have accepted alcoholism is a disease and it can't be got under control without professional help, yet I've somehow convinced myself that he was 'managing' it and doing an OK job of it.

'He's not a bad man,' she says. 'We've always found him very entertaining after he's had a few. But you can see it's there. Thin ice . . . Deep down he's not a happy drunk, is he? And they're the worst kind.'

If only she knew why.

The truth is I probably knew even before I married him. My mind flashes back more than twenty years, to him slumped on the floor at a house party, legs splayed like a rag doll's. His mates' guffaws. Me standing over him, paralysed. As his girlfriend, I should have been venturing in there to try to pull him together, but all I felt was tarnished by association. My intuition shrieking, *Get out before you get in too deep.* But somehow I listened to the other part of me that said, *He's a good guy in all other respects. You can't hang him for one slightly weird and embarrassing episode . . .*

'Why have you waited until now to leave him, is more my question,' Charlotte says, and she sips her tea.

I can tell she's not really looking for a response, but I find myself wanting to answer, mainly to confirm it for myself. 'I think it's because it wasn't all the time. There were many times when Eric was still that good-natured man I married . . . I think I just somehow accepted he drank, on some occasions more than on others, and when he did, if he had a few too many, his mood wasn't always the prettiest. But somehow I felt it was our problem to live with . . .'

'Your problem? But that's insane!'

'Maybe to you, but . . . you have to realise, none of his behaviour was *that* extreme. He didn't knock me around. Our kids weren't living in fear . . .' I think of his outburst on Valentine's Day with the flowers. But that really never happened again, until he recently almost struck Zara. 'In our day-to-day lives I didn't feel like we were victims of anything . . . It might be an odd way of looking at it, but it was just our normal.' I shrug, because her face is saying, *It's a very odd way of looking at it, indeed!*

'Plus, I did love him. I've known most of my adult life. We have children together. We'd gone through so much heartache when we thought we were losing Daniel . . . Eric might have been my husband but he was my family too. I felt a certain responsibility to him. A part of me worried about how he would survive if I left him. He's not strong . . . Plus, if he had cancer, I wouldn't just walk away, so why would I do that if his particular disease is alcoholism?'

'But what about your needs in all this?' she asks.

I huff an ironic laugh. 'Clearly I thought I wasn't entitled to them!' I say. But even as I say it, semi-seriously, I know that if I'm being honest with myself, part of me had wanted out for years. But just not badly enough to act on it – that was the crux of it.

'Eric has made some very poor choices,' I say, after a time, which rather feels like the understatement of the century. 'But I don't think he made them intending to cause harm. I just can't use that as my excuse to look past them any more.'

Speaking of looking past things . . . Later, when Charlotte leaves and I am alone again, I realise our conversation has fired something up in me. I *do* have needs. And in all other priorities except for my children, I have a right to put myself first in my own life.

One need right now is to keep a door open that might be slowly closing. I knew all along that I would only think about Steve when I felt I could think about him without wanting to lean on him or be rescued. Suddenly, the way I'm feeling this moment, that time might be sooner than I'd thought. So I text him a simple message.

Say I got us a room sometime in the not so distant future – perhaps a week or a month or two. Nowhere local. And I gave you a day and a time, would you meet me there?

He texts me a simple reply.

Yes.

FIFTY-FOUR

The disciplinary hearing rules in my favour. My tenure is being reinstated, and as of the first week of January I will resume my teaching position as before. While I could just let all this go and turn a new page, I find I still can't stop thinking about Prajval Dhaliwal – contrasting my memory of him standing over me in my office that day, hot-headed and irate, with an image of him flat out in a hospital bed, a victim of a cruel, deliberate attack. Rightly or wrongly, I can't help feeling somewhat responsible. So even though Charlotte advised against this, I dig up his email address then think very carefully about what I want to say.

Dear Prajval,

I was terribly shocked and saddened to hear that you had been the victim of a brutal attack. It is appalling to me that the person who did this implied they were doing it on my behalf – or that you might have thought that. I hope the perpetrator receives a severe penalty and that you are recovering well and in time will be able to put this behind you.

When I replied to your email at the time I never imagined that any of this would be the fallout. In hindsight, I can fully understand how my comment about your writing ability could be perceived as offensive. It was a poor choice of words, especially considering I am a professor of Communications. I am sorry for them. It was definitely not my intention to offend you.

A new term will begin shortly, and I highly encourage you to consider continuing your education and not to let any of this put you off. I am sorry that signing up for my course could not have been a better experience – for both of us – but I do wish you well in your future. If there is anything I can do to help, please do let me know.

Sincerely, Professor Emily Rossi

I don't expect he's going to reply. So when one comes in about thirty minutes later, part of me dreads opening it.

Dear Professor Emily,

Thanks for your email. I'm sorry about your suspension. I was angry and I overreacted, I guess. My broken arm is healing, but I will be in India for 6 weeks to see my family and the time away will do me good. See you next term.

Praj

Eric comes back for fleeting visits and we go to see a divorce lawyer that Charlotte recommended. And then we sit down with the kids. We tell them that their dad will continue to live in London, where he has a good job, and I want us to stay here, where I feel we belong. We agree that Eric will continue to come north for weekends, and during school holidays Zara and Daniel can go stay with him down there in the flat they've put him in, in St John's Wood, for as long as they want. We don't tell them that it was never a one-year contract, but two. I've no wish for my kids to think their dad a liar. We merely say it got extended.

I allow Eric in our house for as long as it takes for us to talk to the kids. Going forward, the deal is if he is here to see them, I won't be. As he opens our door to leave, the young policeman who came to the house when Zara disappeared, is walking up our path.

'Good timing.' He smiles. 'I was hoping I would catch both of you . . .' He asks if he can have a word and I tell him it's best we have it out here, away from the kids.

He tells us he thought we might like to know that they have arrested Craig Rathbone, that he supplied the ketamine that killed Bethany Brown. They believe he was in the house at the time, and may have fled the scene. They can also directly link him to the assault on my student. The person who committed it had a text from Rathbone saying they were free to break every bone in his body, and they believe it was racially motivated after the article appeared in the newspaper.

Eric glances at me for a second, then says, 'But back to Bethany . . . Can he get away with doing what he did to her? You know, not staying around to help a person in distress?'

The PC looks abashed. 'I can't really answer that. You'd have to speak to a lawyer. Is a drug dealer likely to stick around while someone he's supplied overdoses?' He shrugs. 'Generally speaking, a person doesn't owe a duty to rescue. In other words, if you're swimming in the sea and you're getting into difficulty, I'm not legally obliged to wade in there and help you. Especially if it puts my life at risk too.' He blushes a little, as though proud of his analogy. 'Anyway, I probably shouldn't be telling you all this, but the autopsy report showed that Bethany died as a direct result of alcohol and ketamine toxicity, and central nervous system depression. The levels of ketamine that she had in her blood weren't actually all that high . . . but the combination of the two is what did it, sadly. So there's really nothing anybody could have done for her. Not even him, if he'd been so inclined.'

While I'm relieved to hear this, I suddenly have an awful thought. 'Zara won't be required to give any sort of evidence . . . ?'

'No,' he says. 'We have enough on him. We're pretty sure he supplied the drugs and probably the alcohol and I'm sure he'll go down for that . . . Fortunately people like Craig Rathbone have more enemies than friends.'

Eric and I watch as the PC gets back into his car then pulls off. I breathe out a steadying breath. Finally this might all be coming to a close.

FIFTY-FIVE

ERIC

March 2019

He comes up from the Tube at Swiss Cottage. There are days when it all seems so far away, and days when it sits there so fresh in his brain and he can't see his way around ever dislodging it. Sometimes he will be doing the most routine of tasks and he will suddenly be hijacked by the potent and very vivid image of what he saw on that video. It just enters his head like a flash of lightning. And every time it happens, once it passes he sees no future for himself. He doesn't know what this means. But it's an ungodly feeling. He doesn't know how to claw himself out of the hole he dug, and at times he doesn't even want to. But he once made a promise to Em, and while he might not be the best handler of the truth, he is determined to keep it, even if his marriage is in the bin.

Three weeks ago he was called into his boss's office. John told him that his colleagues had complained he stunk of alcohol. The final humiliation. How could he explain that the drink helps to silence the nightmares of a dead girl, and a picture of Em pointing at him, asking him with withering contempt, *Is this your daughter?*

After a skinful of drink, his mind doesn't endlessly go back to the same memory of Janet Brown showing him that scan in the restaurant. Him hearing himself saying that bullshit about *I've had a vasectomy*, and *I'll get a paternity test*. Sometimes he doesn't understand himself. He is haunted by that panic of knowing he was walking ever deeper into a trap of his own making. It's like a cyclone going round and round in his head.

He's using the satnav on his iPhone to find the street. He knows that if he has to faff around trying to find the place he'll take this as a sign that he shouldn't be going. But for once in his life he's determined to be strong, not weak. To do something he can take pride in. Also there's a job in Australia that's all but got his name on it. Sydney. It's a long way from the kids, but given what it pays, he's calculated he could bring them over twice a year, maybe fly back himself for Christmas or Easter. And given Oz is the land of opportunity, more so than England is at the moment, maybe one day his kids will want to live there.

He finds the street and now he just has to find the community centre. He pictures it being like it is on the telly, and while he dreads it, there's something comforting in having a vague idea of what to expect. It's pretty obvious which building it is. Once he crosses the road, he stops for a second or two and just looks at the navy-blue painted wooden door. He could turn around and walk to the nearest pub and sink four whiskies, then finish off what's left of the bottle in the flat. It's an enticing proposition but he reminds himself his mission is to do one right out of a thousand wrongs, so he pushes the door open instead. It's heavy and resists him and he tries not to take that as a sign too. It's one of those old community centres like the one he used to take Zara to when she was little, when they were trying to encourage her to dance. The old memories come sweeping back. Zara, who tried everything and stuck at nothing. An old argument flung at him: he had no job and yet he still couldn't find time for his kids. It wasn't true. Not entirely.

He almost loses his nerve the minute he sees the filled seats. There isn't room for him. So that makes it easy, then. But instead of turning to go, he finds he's standing there helplessly, like it's his first day at school. They are seated in a semicircle. Off by the window is a refreshments table with coffee, water, snacks. Somebody takes their big coat off a chair and now there's a single empty seat. Somehow he manages to put one foot in front of the other until he's over there and sitting on it.

An older man with a full grey beard turns his head and says, 'Howdy. Welcome.' He angles himself a little to face Eric, and his belly pushes into Eric's arm. He introduces himself as David and says he's a doctor. Eric is a bit puzzled. 'You mean you're here as a doctor? To these people?'

David says, 'No,' and smiles. 'Though I have treated plenty of alcoholics in my practice.' He glances wistfully around the room. 'The thing with drinking is, the longer you stay away from it, the more you convince yourself that it no longer has a grip on you. Some of us, well, even after twenty years of sobriety, we want to test it, because we think we can. We decide we deserve that one glass of champagne at our daughter's wedding . . .' He looks off into the distance, and when he looks back at Eric there is no trace of humour on his face any more. 'I am here because I need to be here. Because you can't test it and win.'

Eric wants to ask how all this normally proceeds, but he quickly realises that he's about to find out. The chairperson, he supposes you must call him, is a beanpole in his thirties, dressed all in black, with longish hair and funky glasses. He looks like an advertising creative. Eric is fascinated. He wasn't sure what he'd expected. Dirty, smelly people staggering and stumbling into chairs? A bunch of predominantly lower-class old people? Instead he is looking at about a dozen men and women who look exactly like him.

The funky guy starts by saying, 'Hello, folks and newcomer. I'm Nevis and I'm an alcoholic.' To which everyone gives the stock response.

Eric is so busy thinking, *Shit, the newcomer is me*, that he checks out of what is being said next. He only tunes back in again when David nudges him. Nevis says that he'd like the newcomer to introduce himself by his first name only. All eyes are on him.

Eric swallows. If he's going to bolt, now's his moment. If he bolts, he knows he'll never come back. He sees Em. He hears his son saying, *Dad, you're an alcoholic and you need to get help*. He stands.

'Hello, everybody,' he says. He eyes sweep over the faces in the semicircle. He knows how to do this. He's given many presentations before in his job, and that's what this is, in a way.

'My name is Eric,' he says, and then he adds, 'and, I'm here because I suppose I'm an alcoholic too.'

'Good evening, Eric,' everyone says.

FIFTY-SIX

The room, number eight, is one I'd quite like to place a reserved sign on forever to ensure no one but us ever gets to use it. I have come to treasure these afternoons once a week, and by the way he looks at me now, I'd say I'm not alone in this.

'What do you feel like doing later?' he asks, his right hand playing with my hair as I lie with my ear where his heart is. A chaste May sun is streaming onto the bed.

'Later? Is there going to be a later?' I sit up a little and look at his dimple.

'I've taken the next four days off. Henry's with his granddad.'

Zara and Daniel are in London for the bank holiday. Today, Eric took them on the Eye. I smile. 'Well, fancy! Thanks for just telling me now.'

He laughs a little. 'To be honest I wasn't sure until a couple of hours ago that I wouldn't have to cover a shift, so I didn't want to get your hopes up. But they can be up now. It's all good.'

I think about it, resting my head on his chest again. I have not yet spent the night in Steve's house, nor he in mine. Even with the kids away, this is something I long to protect. Taking it public, even to Charlotte, might happen in time. But that will be in my time, not anyone else's. 'You know, I think I'd like to stay here. If they'll let us.'

'I already checked. They will.'

'Urgh. But I haven't any clean clothes.'

'I wasn't planning on you needing clothes.'

I grin. 'Oh. Well, that's good then.' It has been quite the novelty to feel like I am both dating and desired again, that this unexpected turn in my life is fresh and for enjoying. That I've somehow skipped the searching stage that would have been thrilling at twenty-four but utterly horrifying now.

But every time I think like this I remind myself not to get ahead of myself. I still have that sense that it's too easy, that Steve is too good of a gift. I keep waiting for someone to tell me he was never intended for me in the first place, and that I have to give him back.

'We can pop to the shops later,' he says. 'If you want to pick up a tooth-brush. On our way back from dinner.'

'You've thought of everything. Remind me to phone my dad so he can take care of the dog.'

In the months since I've officially called myself separated from Eric – made that distinction in my mind – Steve has been everything I could have asked for. He has been there for me to talk to. And sufficiently at a distance when I've needed that too – which has been more often than I might have imagined.

I don't know what we're really doing or where this is going – if it is going anywhere, or if it needs to – but what I do know is that I won't allow us to rush it. A bad marriage behind me isn't justification to run out and try to have what I should have had with Eric, with someone else. If Steve is in my future, I want it to take a very unforced course.

I turn a little emotional and sit up to be able to see his face. 'You know,' I say, because it needs to be said, 'you always make me feel a little better about myself when I'm not feeling very good. You're a patch of daylight when I'm floundering in the dark.'

He smiles. 'That's what friends are for.'

'Are you my friend?' I tease.

His eyes wander over my smiling face. 'I hope so. That, and many other things, I think.'

One day, if that day comes – and if it does, then this particular secret may be more easily told – I will tell Steve that Eric was Bethany's father. But I still need to find ways of seeing around that reality, having it clear in my own head before I expect it to be clear in anyone else's. Besides, it's an extra piece of baggage that doesn't really need to be unpacked. 'You could have so easily shied away from someone else's darkness when you've had so much of your own,' I say. I had never realised there was such a void in my life until he came along and filled it so spectacularly – so much so that now what he gives me is almost all I'm aware of, and that makes me want to do things and say things I need to hold back, for now.

'You mean everything to me,' he says. 'And I never thought I'd say those words to anyone again.' And in case I might doubt it, his face launches into another smile.

How long do we sit looking at one another like this, reaffirming that all this is enough? It feels like a slice of forever.

FIFTY-SEVEN

I am washing out the plastic draining board rack when I hear a text come in. Thinking it's probably Zara saying she has missed the bus home from school, I dry my hands quickly and go to find my phone.

When I see the name, a tingle rushes up my spine and gathers in the back of my neck, turning me queasy. I stare at the words, and for a moment can't take them in.

Please can we meet? she has written.

I arrive first. This is deliberate. I need time to prepare, to try to look a lot more relaxed than I feel. I order a cup of tea but when I go to pick it up my hand shakes so much I wish I hadn't overfilled it.

Breathe.

At two minutes to the hour, I see the red umbrella. It takes me back to that day with Charlotte. Everything about the moment. It's almost déjà vu. She walks past the window so at first all I see is a pair of flat brown sandals and some beige-coloured capri jeans. It's only when she gets to the door and puts down the brolly that I see she actually looks nothing like herself. There's about three inches of mousey-brown root growth in her hair where she's failed to keep up her blonde highlights. And she is ghastly thin, even though she was never overweight before. I wouldn't have known her.

I can't do this. The thought just sails through me on the crest of my panic. The nausea climbing from my stomach to the back of my throat. I swallow a couple of times, in an attempt to keep down the sandwich I wolfed an hour earlier.

Too late now. She sees me.

For a very long moment we simply hold one another's eyes. Only when she breaks away and goes to the counter to order something do I realise I'm holding my breath. A headache has started at the front of my head. I bring my teacup to my mouth, not caring that I spill a few drops down my black T-shirt, and take a steadying drink.

'How is Zara?' she asks before she has even sat down. Her first words. Even that reminds me of the time before. The apropos-of-nothing way she begins a conversation. As though we had just been chatting a few minutes ago.

I try not to react to how awful she looks, and can't help but look at her thin torso in a filmsy white T-shirt as she takes off her summer-weight navy jacket. This is what grief looks like on a mother. The weight loss has taken its worst toll on her face. She looks way older. There are hollows under her cheekbones and shadows under her sad blue eyes. Then I remember this is the second child she has lost. How unthinkably horrifying.

'She's well,' I say. My mind slides to the video that Janet knows nothing about. I could hardly have sent it to her once we knew Bethany had died.

She picks up a knife and cuts off a third of a chocolate toffee square and quickly pushes it in her mouth like it's a first priority. As she chews, her eyes drift to the window but she is staring without seeing. I wonder if she's on antidepressants. Her eyes have a certain glazed blankness. *Of course she will be*, I think.

'Sorry,' she says, after a moment, cutting off another section of the square. 'I missed breakfast and didn't have time for lunch. I just need some sugar.' She pushes the new piece into her mouth and gives a small moan of joyless satisfaction. I watch her chew, then when she's done she sits there motionless for a moment or two, as though she might have forgotten what she's doing here.

'How are you doing?' I ask, immediately realising it's the wrong question. It's six months since her daughter died. How do I expect she's doing?

For the briefest of seconds I think she looks annoyed, like she might repeat the very thought I've just had, but then she shrugs. 'Oh . . . well . . .' Everything about her, except her demolishing of the chocolate square, seems slowed down ten per cent, her response lagging far behind my question. 'I don't know, to be truthful.' She frowns. 'I suppose I'm still putting one foot in front of the other and trying to get through my day, because the alternative is . . . well . . .' She finishes by way of a headshake.

'I never said I'm sorry for the way my husband behaved,' I say, pleased I've said it. In the months that have followed I have thought a lot about this. About our side of the equation, but about hers too. I have tried very hard to put myself in her shoes.

'I'd rather not talk about it,' she says, firmly but vulnerably. 'If it's all the same to you, I just . . . it's my way of dealing with things. At the moment, anyhow.'

I nod. I wonder why I am here. It strikes me that I feel tremendous pity for her. I am horribly sorry for everything she has gone through. Perhaps if she hadn't been wearing her loss so conspicuously I might have convinced myself she wasn't suffering so significantly, and I could have gone on telling myself that people like Janet Brown don't grieve like normal folk, and because of what she did she doesn't deserve my pity – in fact, I should probably hate her. But I can't. I hadn't expected to stare at her and see, so profoundly, the absence of Bethany – in her eyes, in her demeanour, in her aura – and to hear it so hollowly in her voice. Her suffering is obvious to anyone with eyes.

I take another sip of my tea, which is cool now and developing a film.

'Why did you want to meet?' I ask. It seems pointless beating around the bush.

She takes time in answering; I can see she is choosing her words carefully. 'He told me at the funeral that you knew. That he'd told you everything. But I'd like to suspect Eric's version of *everything* is not the same as mine.' She sniffs, like she knows him oh so well.

'I'm not sure it matters at this point. It can hardly change anything.'

'No. But it matters greatly to me.'

My eyes scan her face. I am trapped with the unease of not knowing where this is going, and yet relieved that we are here at last. 'I know you had a baby and I know she died,' I say.

She nods. 'My waters broke at thirty-five weeks, but I didn't go into labour. I'd had a healthy pregnancy. There were no signs of infection – nothing that would indicate the baby or I were really at risk, but I was advised to have her induced.' She looks up at the ceiling briefly, and I wonder if this is going to be too much for her and yet I can tell she wants to say it.

'I was due to go in on 24 March, and the day before, I met with the doctor on a matter that was completely unrelated, but she examined me and said the baby's heart rate was very good. When I arrived at the hospital' – her voice begins to tremble – 'they hooked me up to the heart-rate monitor right away, and then there was a flurry of concerned faces. When I asked them what was wrong I was told that they couldn't find the heartbeat . . .' She frowns, clearly reliving it fresh as day. 'I knew there was one. I mean, I just heard it the day before . . . But they kept me waiting two hours for an ultrasound and I remember being confused about why any of this was needed.' She looks right at me and automatically places a hand on her stomach. 'I could feel the baby kicking. I knew she was fine, and maybe she had just been sleeping really softly . . . I tried to tell them this but they weren't really listening. They were talking around me as though I was not there. Then the doctor was standing over me saying, "There is no heartbeat. The baby is dead."'

She meets my eyes now, again, glazed and somewhat distant.

'Dead? I was . . . I was saying, "But she can't be dead. She was alive yesterday at four p.m. . . ."'

I place my fingers over my lips briefly. How I once feared a doctor saying those very words to me.

'I had to deliver her because I'd already gone into labour. All I really remember after that was that she was born, she was there, and I was thinking, *Why aren't you slapping her? Why aren't you getting her to cry? Every baby cries* . . . I very vaguely remember somebody saying something about me being in shock, and how it was all a lot to take in . . .'

I briefly close my eyes, trying not to see my own personal situation, all those years ago, reflected in hers.

'They give you a lot of options . . . they throw a lot of decisions at you, expecting you to make them. They say would you like to see her, hold her, bathe her, dress her . . . ? Of course I wanted to see her and hold her! I couldn't understand why they were asking . . . So I held her in a bloodstained blanket and gave her a pink rabbit. I remember being so fascinated by how still she was and calm! I placed a tiny hat on her head that I'd crocheted. And then they were saying it was best I gave her back to them. And none of them looked happy. I couldn't understand why nobody was happy for me and my baby . . .' Her brows pull together. 'I'm not sure what else happened but I remember arguing with them and saying, "Look" – I could see her breathing. She was alive because I could see the tiny rise and fall of her chest, and why couldn't they see it? I remember being in a taxi. I was going home. Alone. The driver was chatting away and asking me if I'd been visiting someone and I said no, I've just had a baby . . .'

'Janet, I—'

'If they'd just taken her without my ever seeing her, I know things would have been different. *I* would have been different. I'm not saying it wouldn't have been hard, but it would have been healthy.' She looks off into the distance and I think more is coming but she stays silent.

'Did you ever find out why she died?' My voice sounds tortured with emotion.

'The placenta had separated and caused a blood clot inside the amniotic sac, which cut off circulation to her. But it also kept me from bleeding to death. The doctor didn't know why it had happened. She said sometimes it's from trauma to the belly. But I hadn't had any trauma . . . The autopsy also revealed that she would have been one hundred per cent healthy had she lived. Had she been born one day earlier she would have been perfect.'

Our eyes meet again.

'I'm so very sorry,' I say. It's unthinkable. I don't know what else I can add.

She takes a drink of her tea. 'Why I'm telling you this . . . what I need you to know is, I went into hospital an expectant mother, and I left there as a mother – in my own mind. And for some reason, for a very long time, I couldn't accept reality.' She takes a deep breath, and I can tell the past and recent events are converging and this is very hard for her, and a small part of me thinks, *Damn, why did you have to tell me? Is this a sympathy trip? An exercise in clearing the conscience?* I almost want to block my ears, and yet now I've heard it I can't unhear it or unsee it, or stop comparing myself. I am lucky. My baby lived. Both my children live. And despite what has happened, they will still have good lives. I will see to it that it won't be any other way.

'When I met Eric I was not in a normal frame of mind. I don't know how else to describe it. I'm not the kind of woman who has sex with men at parties. I am not a *casual* person.' She makes air quotes around the word. 'Even when I was a teenager, I'd never done anything like that before . . .' She looks like she's reaching for some extra strength to keep going. 'I am not sure what he told you. But it's probably the same version of events that for the longest time he tried to tell me.'

I am not really following, but I want to. 'He said you came on to him and he was really drunk.'

'It wasn't quite like that. I remember it quite clearly.' She looks completely unsurprised. 'He was walking down the stairs to go to the men's. I was coming out of the ladies'. We stood and chatted. I could tell he was tanked . . . He said life was hard for him right now. You were in bed. You'd had problems with both pregnancies. Daniel had nearly died . . . He was very upset, terrified the same was going to happen to the new baby . . . He was distraught.'

That sounds a lot like a drunken Eric.

'He was going on about how you're so strong and he's weak and worthless and he's never had any guts . . .'

I close my eyes for a moment.

'I felt very sorry for him, actually. He was a nice man with his own set of problems, and I was in a very vulnerable place, and I hadn't really imagined there were other people out there feeling as low as I did . . . We came together and it was mutual. I can promise you I didn't initiate it. It didn't happen all because of me.'

She looks at her hands clasped together on top of the table. 'Afterwards, of course, he had no memory of any of that sorry conversation. Or if he did, it was selective. I honestly do think he managed to put a completely different spin on it in his mind – that he can lie to others, but lie just as convincingly to himself.'

I swallow hard. I remember how convinced he was that he was the one who took Zara to dance classes, gymnastics. When it was me. While he sulked and dwelled in his own headspace. Eric is good at believing his own fiction.

'If I hadn't been so messed up in my mind, I would never have gone into the toilets with him. I am better than that . . .' She draws a short breath, like she's suppressing the urge to break down. 'I don't know how we got there, why I didn't stop it . . . All I can really say is I don't know who I was at that time. That person wasn't really me.'

She takes another sip of tea while I am captured, held fast, in the wake of her words. After a time she says, 'I'm sorry. I'm sorry for what I did and for how I behaved. I wasn't myself.' She places her napkin on top of the table. It's a shredded, damp ball by now. 'I meant you no harm. That's why I asked you here. I didn't intend to ruin your life, or Zara's. I would never, ever, have done what I did if he'd played fair. I just wanted . . .' She sighs heavily, shakily, and it strikes me that she could be ill. And a part of me thinks, *How much more can one person take?* 'I just wanted it to penetrate – with him. He kept this denial up for so long . . . Then when he couldn't deny it any longer he just mentally disposed of my daughter. I wanted to just shout out and say, *What about Bethany? You owe her a responsibility!* I felt I had shouted that so many times, and I was never being heard . . . I didn't understand how he could care about two of his children and not his third.'

There it is. The crux of it. She lets the concept sit there for a moment, between us, displacing all that has been said before.

'Was he ever violent with you? Sorry . . . I need to know. You said that day in my kitchen that he pushed you around – Bethany's father.' I swallow a gummy thickness that will barely go down.

'No,' she says, after a short hesitation. 'I meant that figuratively, not literally . . . He wasn't violent. He was good at bullying and browbeating. I often thought it might turn to violence but it never did.'

I wipe my eyes, at least relieved about that. I don't know why I'm crying. Sitting here, woman to woman, I am so deeply ashamed of the crimes of my husband. I am hot. I want fresh air. I want to breathe deeply and tell myself, *All this ends today. There's a lot of life left. Start living it the way you want to live it, the way you should have been living it all along. For you, not for a man.* This is what my mother would have said.

Janet moves as though she's about to leave and catches the table with her knee. It wobbles, and my virtually untouched tea slops on to the cloth. Slowly and methodically, she pulls on her jacket as though she'd be incapable of going any faster.

'Why did you call your second baby Bethany?' I ask. I force myself to look her in the eyes. 'I'm sorry, I'm just curious.'

She becomes very still and I'm not sure she's going to answer. Then her big sad blue eyes turn red with tears. 'I always loved the name. It was what I was always going to call my daughter if I ever had one.' She smiles, thinly. 'It might be hard for you to understand but when I got pregnant a second time, it felt like fate, you know . . . I just felt that if I called my second baby Bethany then I would never, ever forget that my first daughter had existed. Because even though her life was short, it was still important; she was still loved. She had lived in my womb and had been perfectly healthy and she should have had a life . . .' A tear rolls down her cheek. 'I knew that every time I said my daughter's name, I would think of my firstborn, too. She would live on through her sister's life.'

She looks at me sadly, and I know we are done now. She stands and picks up her bag and umbrella. 'Goodbye, Emily,' she says, flatly.

And with that she turns, and I watch her walk the length of the café, to the door. I watch her step out on to the cobbled pavement, and put up her big umbrella. She doesn't go back the way she came, but walks to the edge of the kerb, stops, looks both ways quite purposefully, then crosses. On the other side of the road, a car is waiting. She gets into the passenger side, and I notice the bulky frame of a man in the driver's seat. I watch the car drive off until I can no longer see it. A nice car. *Bethany's mum has a boyfriend . . .*

Treat her well, I think. *Whoever you are . . . Be good to her. Don't be Eric.*

FIFTY-EIGHT

Daniel has got Zara and me training to walk the Herriot Way – fifty-two miles in four to five days – by the end of summer. Zara has regained a little of the weight she lost, but now our combined mission is just to be strong. This morning the three of us completed a ten-mile hike in the Dales, and called in for a hearty pub lunch that we polished off while laughing at the fact that it's Daniel, not either of us, who has managed to get a big blister.

On our way home we drive past the most beautiful of ivy-clad country hotels. 'I wonder what it costs to stay there,' Zara says longingly.

It suddenly occurs to me. 'I know one way we can find out.'

It's completely irresponsible. But as the weather hasn't been the best for June, the desk clerk says they're not too busy so he offers us a suite with two bedrooms for a huge discount.

When Zara sees the room she gasps. 'Oh my God! It's beautiful!'

It truly is. Larger than two of ours put together, with a bathroom that's almost the size of our kitchen – and the same for Daniel. There's a king-size bed decked out with an inviting array of oversized pillows and a dove-grey duvet, on to which Zara dives. 'What are you looking at?' she says to Daniel, who settles into an enormous dove-grey flock armchair with bronze feet and faffs around on his phone.

'No one,' he says, emphasising 'one'.

'Then why are you smiling like that?' She clambers off the bed and goes to grab his phone.

'Ooh! Daniel's got a girlfriend and he's got her as his screensaver!' She smirks and stuffs the phone under my nose so I can see a blown-up picture of a pretty brunette with a pixie cut.

'No I don't have a girlfriend!' he says, semi-outraged. Then adds, 'Yet,' and grins deviously at us.

I have often wished Daniel would show a little more interest in girls, if for no other reason than to get a little more healthy balance in his rather single-track life. After all, plenty show an interest in him. So this is a surprising, and not unwelcome, development. I can only hope that this won't be another chapter of our lives I'm little prepared for.

Even though we ate a big lunch we're hungry again when 5 p.m. rolls around – must be all that fresh air. So once I've rung my dad and asked him to pop over and sleep at ours to let Otis out, I order us a fine spread from room service. After we've cleaned our plates we watch a spot of TV then end up settling on a movie, the three of us lying on the bed in our fluffy white dressing gowns – Zara relishing taking photos of Daniel in his. She nods off before it finishes, and he gets bored and goes off into his room, and I struggle to keep my eyes open until the end. When I switch the TV off, everything is so quiet, as though the walls have an impossible degree of soundproofing, shutting out life and every negative thing that goes with it, and we are cocooned in our own silent and temporarily perfect world.

I sleep surprisingly soundly, ten hours straight. Zara sleeps on as I wake, and I listen to the soft surge of her breathing, resisting the urge to stroke the long brown hair that fans out on her pillow, in case I disturb her. After lying there for twenty minutes or so, I get up, pull on my clothes, check in on Daniel – who, no surprise, must have gone out for a run – then I sneak out of the room without as much as splashing my face or combing my hair. It's a sunny morning. I walk to the end of the road and buy a coffee in a take-out cup and three croissants from a local baker. Then I take it to a viewpoint overlooking heather-clad moorland and sit on a bench and eat my croissant, shaking buttery flakes off my light wool jumper.

As I stare across the vast, empty space I think back to last night, to soon after I shut off the TV. Into the silence I fell so swiftly, into that quicksand between wakefulness and sleep. My brain fluidly cycled between memories and deep emotions, hazy thoughts and vivid recollections – things that were neither properly fact nor fantasy, and yet, in the moment, they were a kind of both.

This is what I saw.

Me in that house, in that bedroom.

She can't speak.

Help me is all I can decipher. Her eyes, imploring me, yet quickly glazing over. I stare at her but am drawn to something in my peripheral vision. My eyes pull away, to an ornament; the kind you hang your necklaces on, like a tree. Four or five pieces of cheap silver-coloured costume jewellery. But also . . .

My mother's rose gold locket

The St Christopher that Eric's mother gave Daniel.

I can't peel my gaze away from the precious items that are mine. The items she stole.

I knew it!

She makes that small snoring sound again, as though she has drifted off to sleep. Beside the jewellery tree is an empty Absolut bottle with the top off, some other detritus: packets, a white powder like tiny shards of glass, pills, tissues – one dotted with blood.

She is struggling to move the air in and out of her lungs. Her eyes flutter again. Open for a millisecond, looking at me.

Call an ambulance, the voice in my head says. It's so instinctual. My hand goes to my mobile. A small spasm ripples in her neck. I watch it, and see it happen again, and then I find I can't take my eyes from it. When I look at my phone it's like a foreign object lying in a hand that is not mine. The palm, my fingers, I don't even recognise them and yet I have a vague sense of them being attached to me. I realise now; I was phoning for an ambulance. I am unsure why my fingers won't move.

Do something! the voice of my instincts and my conscience says again. But it's a quieter, much less insistent voice, and I can't recover the feeling in my hand.

Her eyes flutter open again, and we look at one another. The white spit and the bluish tinge to her lips. I am looking at her eyes, desperate eyes, but they transpose into violent eyes. The ones I saw seconds before her hand shoved Zara's head into the boy's groin. Bethany's lips move again, but all I can hear now is the sound of Zara's howling.

Her lips might be moving, but she isn't seeing me. I realise this now. Perhaps she never did. I am not there. Then it comes to me.

I am not here.

I still don't believe I intend to walk away. But then I am in the hallway and everything feels easier than it did thirty seconds ago; reason is yielding. Then I am at the top of the stairs. Then halfway down the stairs. The squeak of a board. Her syncopated breathing falling off behind me. My feet hit the bottom stair and I am not thinking. I am stepping over a coat that has fallen, over Zara's Converse. I am outside into fresh air. The cat is there looking at me.

Only the cat knows I was here.

The pungency of the oven, and the scalded soup, and the guilt, cling to me, then let go.

I get into my car. I shift gears, and then I am driving away, back down that street.

I was never here.

ACKNOWLEDGMENTS

This is now my sixth published novel, and I'm tremendously thankful that I remain published and that I have the support I need to make that happen on both personal and professional fronts.

At Lake Union, thanks so much to everyone who works to put my books in the hands of readers – Bekah Graham and the marketing team, the creatives who design my wonderful covers, and my terrific and supportive editor, Sammia Hamer. I'm lucky to have an editor who is passionate about what she does, brings great insight, and who champions my novels with such genuine enthusiasm. Huge thanks also to Arzu Tahsin, who helped make this novel the best it could be, and is a pleasure to work with, and to Gemma Wain whose copyediting skills saved the day.

Thanks to Lorella Belli, my terrific agent, and her team, as well as a few friends who assisted my research during the first draft of this book when it was a rather different story – Bill and Pauline Abram, and Nellie Williams.

My husband, Tony, and my mother have always believed I could do this, even through the toughest times when my doubts were running rampant. I can never thank them enough.

I've really enjoyed hearing from readers and developing friendships with some of you on social media. I truly am grateful for everyone who does their bit to help get the word out about my novels, and for those of you who have taken the time to leave a good review on Amazon, Bookbub, Goodreads, etc. If we don't know one another yet, then please do friend me on Facebook, and remember to follow my Author page on Amazon so you'll get to know when I have a new book out.

ABOUT THE AUTHOR

Photo credit: Tony Capuccinello 2018

Carol Mason was born and grew up in the north-east of England. As a teenager she was crowned Britain's National Smile Princess and subsequently became a model, diplomat-in-training, hotel receptionist and advertising copywriter. She currently lives in British Columbia, Canada, with her Canadian husband. To learn more about Carol and her novels, visit www.carolmasonbooks.com.

Made in the USA
Middletown, DE
07 May 2020